MW00380449

Sovereign Stone

Sovereign of the Seven Isles: Book Two

by

David A. Wells

SOVEREIGN STONE

Copyright © 2011 by David A. Wells

Edited by Carol L. Wells

This is a work of fiction. Characters, events and organizations in this novel are creations of the author's imagination.

www.SovereignOfTheSevenIsles.com

To Madeleine and Samantha

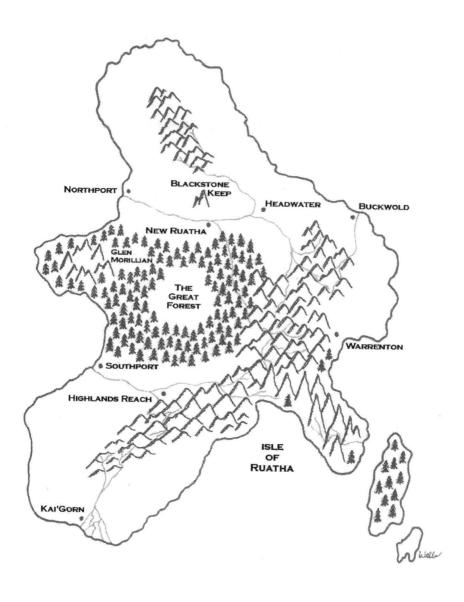

NORTHPORT

BLACKSTONE
KEEP

HEADWATER

BUCKWOLD

NEW RUATHA

GLEN
MORILLIAN

THE
GREAT
FOREST

WARRENTON

SOUTHPORT

HIGHLANDS REACH

ISLE
OF
RUATHA

KAI'GORN

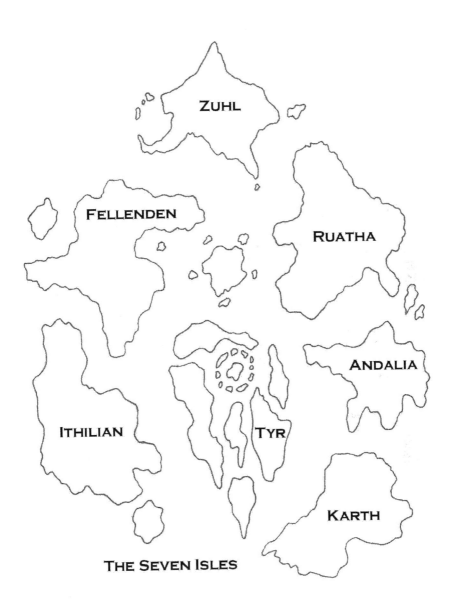

ZUHL

FELLENDEN

RUATHA

ANDALIA

ITHILIAN

TYR

KARTH

THE SEVEN ISLES

Sovereign Stone

CHAPTER 1

"Lord Alexander, come quick," the Ranger shouted.

Alexander stopped his sword form, raced to the low stone wall that separated the paddock from open sky, and looked across the chasm to the bridge platform on the other side.

A cloud of darkness was swirling in the center—thick, soot-filled smoke, only darker, whirling in a column fifty feet high and half as wide. It seemed to draw in the morning light and cast the area around it into shadow.

Abigail, Isabel, and Anatoly came up next to Alexander. They all tensed at the sight.

Anatoly barked an order to the nearest Ranger: "Find Erik and tell him to ready his men immediately!"

The Ranger nodded smartly and raced off toward the barracks.

Alexander couldn't see clearly what was happening—the bridge platform was over five hundred feet away. He heard Slyder cry out overhead as Isabel tipped her head back and closed her eyes. A moment later the cloud of swirling darkness suddenly condensed with a loud clap like thunder, then dissipated just as quickly.

What Alexander saw next sent a chill up his spine. Isabel gasped and opened her eyes with a look of shock and dismay.

The creature strode purposefully toward the archway leading to the bridge abutment, stopping only feet from the edge. It stood eight feet tall and had smooth, obsidian-black skin and chiseled muscles. It had no hair, no eyes, no mouth, no genitals. Its head was smooth and bald and had no ears.

In the place of eyes and mouth were small indentations; a nose was represented by a bump on the unfinished face. Its arms were overly long and its hands each had six fingers ending in three-inch, razor-sharp talons. Its feet were taloned as well, three in front and one in back like a raptor. It had the knees of a canine. Alexander had seen this creature before when he used his clairvoyance to watch Phane conquer Karth.

A smaller creature, only eighteen inches tall, had also emerged from the darkness, beating its batlike wings furiously.

"I have to get over there," Alexander said as he sat down and cleared his mind. With practice, he'd trained himself to find the place of calm emptiness quickly. Now he put his training to the test.

He sank into the quiet of his mind, rebuffing intrusive thoughts with greater ease than he'd been capable of even a week before. It wasn't long before he was floating on the firmament, drifting on an ocean of possibility, riding the wave of creation as it manifested in the present moment. He let his awareness settle for a moment before he coalesced above his meditating body.

With a flick of his mind, he directed his vision across the chasm amidst the enemy. The nightmare beast stood at the bridge abutment, frozen in place like a statue.

The smaller creature hovered at eye level in front of Jataan P'Tal. It spoke with a raspy, whiny voice that sounded less than human.

"Master commands that you retreat to Headwater immediately, where you will raise an army worthy of him." The horrible little creature wrung its clawed hands as it spoke. "The scourgling will keep the fugitive from leaving the ancient traitor's keep. You must leave now. An army comes."

"Very well," Jataan P'Tal said. "Does Prince Phane have any further instructions?" It was obvious to Alexander that General Commander P'Tal did not like this dark little creature.

His men were even less happy with the little monster and they were openly frightened by the scourgling, even though the netherworld beast had done nothing since taking up its post at the edge of the bridge abutment.

"These are his only commands," the little creature said, then touched its ring, and a cloud of swirling darkness quickly engulfed it. Jataan P'Tal took a step back. With another loud clap that sounded like thunder, the darkness dissipated and the little monster was gone.

"Strike camp," Jataan P'Tal commanded. "We move for Headwater."

The soldiers followed his orders quickly. Alexander could tell from their fearful glances and bits and pieces of their whispered conversation that they wanted to be as far away from the scourgling as they could get.

Alexander understood completely.

When he opened his eyes, his entire force of Rangers was fanned out along the stone wall with bows at the ready. His friends stood around him in a half-circle, looking across the chasm at the impossibly black netherworld beast that had taken over the siege of Blackstone Keep.

Within minutes the enemy soldiers were making their way off the bridge platform.

Alexander stood. Isabel took his arm and looked up at him with a hint of fear in her beautiful green eyes. "What is that thing?" she whispered.

"The little demon called it a scourgling."

Lucky took a sharp breath. "A scourgling is a hunter demon," he said, "also called a soul stalker. The stories of the Reishi War describe them as relentless, tireless, and extremely deadly, although not terribly smart. They're immune to most weapons and magic. Physical trauma simply has no effect on them."

"Phane had two of them with him in Karth," Alexander said. "Another creature brought this one here. A little demonic-looking thing about a foot and a half tall with leathery grey-black skin, hateful yellow eyes, and batlike wings. It told Commander P'Tal to fall back to Headwater and start building an army for Phane. It also said there's an army headed our way; hopefully, it's from New Ruatha."

"If we do have a friendly army coming, we need to warn them to approach with caution," said Lucky.

Isabel tipped her head back and closed her eyes, linking her mind with Slyder. "Looks like about five thousand soldiers coming up the road from New Ruatha, but they're still about a day out."

"Good, that gives us time to send warning, but I want to try something else first," Alexander said. He reached into the Keep Master's ring with his mind and brought the bridge into existence with a thought. It shimmered briefly, then materialized out of thin air, spanning the gap over the long fall to the spur below.

The scourgling didn't hesitate. The moment the bridge appeared, the creature started running toward Alexander. It revealed no excitement or ferocity or emotion of any kind, except for a single-minded determination to reach Alexander. It ran with frightening speed in great loping strides.

Everyone tensed when the netherworld beast started its charge. Anatoly spun his war axe up into his hands. Abigail slipped her bow off her shoulder, drew an arrow, nocked it, took careful aim and released, all in one graceful motion. The arrow flew true, striking hard in the center of the advancing monster's glistening black chest. The scourgling didn't seem to notice. The shaft shattered into splinters on impact without leaving a mark.

It quickly covered half the distance across the bridge and was still gaining speed. It was already running faster than any horse, probably faster than nether wolves. It was a terrifying sight, or would have been if Alexander didn't have the situation well in hand. Erik called out to his Rangers to make ready, but Alexander forestalled the command with a raised hand. He reached into the ring again with his mind and sent the bridge away. It shimmered and vanished like it had never even been a part of this world.

The scourgling fell without a sound, tumbling toward the rock face of Blackstone Keep in its long descent toward the spur a thousand feet below. Everyone ran to the low stone wall at the west end of the paddock and leaned over to watch as the creature hit the side of the cliff, bounced away, and continued to fall toward the spur that joined the central mountain of the Keep with the outcropping that formed the bridge platform. It hit the side of the spur a moment later and bounced off, tumbling down the sheer cliff face and plummeting to the plain below.

It came to a stop thousands of feet below and could only be seen as a black speck on the grey grassland. It was still for only a moment. Then the speck started moving.

Isabel opened her eyes and her face went pale. "The fall didn't even faze it. It hit so hard it left a hole in the ground then it bounded to its feet and started running toward the road like nothing happened. Alexander, how are we going to kill that thing?"

Alexander put his arm around her. "I suspect I'm going to have to see how sharp the Thinblade really is."

She looked up at him with her green eyes flashing, but it was Anatoly who spoke first.

"Are you sure that's wise? If your new sword won't cut the scourgling, then what?" Anatoly asked. Abigail and Isabel nodded in agreement.

"That could be a problem," Alexander said. "If the Thinblade won't kill it, then I doubt we have anything that will, at least not anything we know of yet. There might be something in the Keep that would do the job, but that's only speculation. Hopefully, there are a few wizards with the army coming our way. Maybe they'll know something about that thing that we don't."

"I can send them a warning with Slyder," Isabel offered.

Alexander nodded. "We will, but later this afternoon. I'd like to keep an eye on the scourgling and P'Tal's force for the time being. I want to see what the scourgling does when it encounters the soldiers from Headwater on its way back up to the bridge platform."

"Do you think it might attack them?" Jack asked.

"We can hope," Alexander said. "Mostly, I want to see how the soldiers react to it. When I was watching them a few minutes ago, they seemed afraid of the thing—not that I blame them. It might give us some insight into the level of allegiance the people of Headwater have for Phane. I suspect they don't really know who they've gotten into bed with. If the scourgling kills some of them, we may be able to use the story to our advantage in sowing seeds of discontent."

Jack smiled slowly but broadly. "I like the way you're starting to think. Stories are the most powerful magic of all because they sway the masses." Jack cocked his head like he was looking at Alexander in a new light. "You might have made an excellent bard, if it wasn't for all this business about being King." He smiled with a sparkle in his eye. "Well, no matter, I'll get started writing a song about the murderous indifference of Phane and his netherworld minions. No sense letting a bunch of soldiers tell it, they'll undoubtedly leave out the important parts."

Alexander chuckled. "Good. Isabel, if you could keep an eye on the scourgling, I need to go check on something else."

"Of course. I'll let you know what happens."

"I'll stay as well. I might get lucky and be able to witness the encounter firsthand. Could provide useful detail for my song," Jack said.

"What are you going to check on?" Abigail asked.

Alexander took a deep breath before he answered. "Phane. If he doesn't need the scourgling in Karth anymore, then he's probably on the move and I need to know where he plans on going next."

"Is that wise?" Lucky asked. "We don't know if he can harm you when you look in on him with your clairvoyance. Last time he wasn't aware of your capability, but now he may have taken precautions."

"I'll be careful, but I want to know what his next move will be. If he's coming to Ruatha, we need to know. I also want to take a look at the army that's headed our way and see who's leading it."

CHAPTER 2

It had been a week since Alexander found the Thinblade. Seven days spent searching Blackstone Keep and they hadn't even scratched the surface. The place was enormous. Under different circumstances, he would have been happy to spend months exploring the ancient fortress. It was full of mystery and possibility that ignited his imagination and gave physical form to many of his childhood fantasies.

Even the mundane was miraculous in Blackstone Keep. After several hours of meditation on the Keep Master's ring, he'd found that he could command the ceilings of any room to glow with soft illumination. It was a simple thing but very welcome in the pitch-black inner rooms of the Keep. After a bit of further investigation, he discovered that once awakened, the light in any given room could be turned on or off by touching a panel on the wall near the door.

After he and the Rangers had spent a few days exploring the quarters on one side of the paddock, they found a small part of the Keep meant for housing soldiers, and the Rangers moved from their camp under the stars. Alexander knew there were plenty of other quarters available but he didn't want to venture too far into the Keep just yet. There were other matters of greater importance than the comfort of their lodging, and the barracks would be more than adequate for the time being.

On the third day after their arrival at Blackstone Keep, Jataan P'Tal had shown up with a company of about a hundred soldiers from Headwater. Alexander was confident that they couldn't reach across the gaping chasm that served as the primary defense for the Keep, but he doubled the watch just in case.

It looked like the General Commander of the Reishi Protectorate was settling in for a siege, a fact that didn't present any immediate problem but troubled Alexander just the same. He was trapped. Fortunately, he was safe within the Keep, but in time he knew he would have to return to New Ruatha, and the small army camped on his doorstep was in the way.

At first he had worried about an adequate food supply, but then he discovered a larder that was even more magical than the lighting. The room was clearly a storeroom, but its storage bins were empty when he first discovered them. The thing that caught his attention was a waist-high pedestal just a few steps inside the door with the imprint of a hand in the center. It took an hour of focused and deliberate meditation on the Keep Master's ring to discover the purpose of the room. But even after he did, he was frustrated to learn that he couldn't make it work. It required a connection to the firmament that he couldn't seem to create except when he was in a state of deep meditation.

When he brought Lucky to the room, he was struck dumb with awe when the alchemist placed his hand on the pedestal and linked his mind to the firmament. The storage bins in the room quickly filled with dried rice, beans, salt pork, and jerky. The storeroom was a magical larder that could produce basic food staples, provided a wizard capable of making a reliable connection to the firmament was there to operate it.

He had discovered that the seven rings in the jeweled case he had found in the Bloodvault were similar to the Keep Master's ring. He wanted to give one to each of his friends but quickly found that a connection to the firmament was necessary to use the lesser rings as well, so only Lucky received one.

Lucky reported that the ring allowed him to see the Keep in his mind's eye as well as to control the bridge. Alexander was happy to hear that, since he would have to leave eventually and he wanted to make sure that his people would be able to protect the Keep and still come and go as necessary. The secondary rings solved that problem.

On the fifth day, he had discovered the beacon towers. Once he understood what they were, it was a simple matter to activate them. Tall towers topped with cones of stone rose from the four cardinal points of the massive Keep. With a flick of his mind, the cones began to glow with a bright white light, sending a clear signal that Blackstone Keep had a new master.

He had practiced with the Thinblade daily, testing its power and sharpness. He was awed by it. The Sword of Kings was beyond his wildest expectations. He could cut through a stone the size of a man's head with a simple flick of his wrist. No real force was required, only motion. The Thinblade was sharper than sharp, but much more. He discovered, quite by accident, that the blade would not cut him.

He'd been trying to wield his new sword like he would have wielded an ordinary blade and it made his movements clumsy. In a moment of terrifying carelessness, he misjudged the position of the Thinblade and would have, should have, cut off his hand just above the wrist, but the blade simply bounced off his arm. After a moment of stunned gratitude, he tried, much more carefully of course, to cut himself with the Thinblade and found that the thin edge would not make contact with his flesh.

Anything else was fair game though. He cut through stone, wood, or steel with ease. With a bit of practice, he found that he could wield the Thinblade with much greater quickness than he could wield a normal steel sword.

Every day he had meditated and sought to make contact with the firmament. His practice was paying off. It usually took several minutes of calm empty-mindedness before he found his awareness floating freely on the currents of the firmament. He tested his limits and was pleased to find that he could stay in the timeless ocean of possibility indefinitely while still maintaining a connection to his physical existence.

His connection to the firmament was different than that of other wizards. They had to be cautious of becoming lost in the limitless possibility and rapture of creation. Alexander didn't experience the firmament in that way, but he also couldn't make a connection as reliably or as quickly as other wizards. It was a source of frustration, but he'd made up his mind to focus on the capabilities he could rely on and make do with them.

While limited in scope, his magical vision was profound in the insight it gave him. He'd been able to see the aura of living things since he was a child. The colors that surrounded others gave him a window into their character, intent, and capacity for magic.

Much more recently, he'd discovered a limited form of clairvoyance that allowed him to see all around him even with his eyes closed. It was like seeing his immediate surroundings with his peripheral vision all at once. With a little focus, he could direct his all around sight to a single point nearby and see clearly, down to the smallest detail.

He could even see a few moments into the future, although he had no idea how to make it happen deliberately.

Perhaps the most powerful magic he had was long-range clairvoyance. It was his only magical capability that required a deliberate connection to the firmament, but it allowed him access to information in a way that few others could match.

***

Alexander returned to his quarters. It was a simple room cut into the interior of the mountain and had a small balcony on the west wall facing the bridge platform. He took a quick look down to the road below but saw no sign of the enemy soldiers or of the scourgling.

Sitting on his balcony, he started the process that led to the firmament. It was becoming more familiar and reliable.

He started with several deep breaths, relaxing his muscles one body part at a time. Once he was physically relaxed, he focused each breath on deepening his relaxation and allowing tension and anxiety to drain away.

When his body felt heavy and warm, it was time to begin quieting his mind. He allowed any thought that came to him to capture his attention and focus, but only for a moment. He acknowledged each stray thought before dismissing it. One by one, he let the thoughts come to him, and one by one, he let them go, until they came more slowly and then not at all.

When he found himself in a place without thought, where his mind was quiet yet alert and aware, he knew the firmament was close. Sometimes it took several minutes of holding his mind in a state of empty-mindedness before he would slip free of his physical form; other times it happened quickly.

This time he found himself floating in the limitless expanse of the firmament after only a few moments. He let himself drift, listening to the music of reality humming with impossible complexity in the background before he focused on his location.

With a sensation of impossible speed, his point of awareness formed just outside his balcony. He took in his surroundings, looked at his meditating body, then turned his attention toward the bridge platform. He focused on moving his awareness slowly rather than simply willing it to be in a different location.

Floating toward the smaller peak, he saw movement on the spur road. The enemy soldiers were crossing the spur just as the scourgling was coming up the road from below.

With a flick of his mind, Alexander moved his point of awareness to a place a few feet off the side of the spur road and twenty feet overhead.

The scourgling didn't even seem to notice the soldiers on the road as it charged with single-minded determination back up to the bridge platform. If the soldiers had been on foot, they might have been all right. But when their horses saw the beast running toward them, many of the terrified animals bolted. More than thirty of the panicked horses slipped off the sides of the spur, carrying their riders to their deaths on the plains far below.

Several of the remaining soldiers managed to survive by quickly dismounting and allowing their spooked horses to go over the edge without them. Still a few others were able to rein in their horses tightly enough that they couldn't bolt.

But the scourgling didn't attack.

It simply ran, headlong, through their ranks like they were little more than brush on the side of a trail.

Jack would have his story.

Alexander refocused his vision on a splotch of dust rising on the horizon. In a blink, his awareness was hovering over the leading edge of a force of five thousand soldiers, all wearing the crest of New Ruatha. The army moved slowly but steadily toward the giant black mountain that was Blackstone Keep.

More than anything else, the sight of Kelvin Gamaliel leading the army gave him hope. He'd worried about the Guild Mage many times since the battle with Jataan P'Tal at the palace in New Ruatha. The north wing had collapsed while both men were still inside. Alexander had held out hope that Kelvin had used some form of enchanted item to protect himself when he brought the entire building down with his magical war hammer.

He was gratified to see that his hope was well founded. The half a dozen wizards riding with the Guild Mage gave him even greater hope.

Alexander relaxed his focus, and his awareness melted back into the firmament. He was no longer in any single place. Instead, he rode the wave of reality through time, with every thought, feeling, and action taking place in the present moment thrumming in the background like a symphony of impossible variety. He took a moment to float there on the crest of the wave before bringing his real purpose into focus in his mind's eye.

His awareness coalesced high in the air above the ocean. Below was a ship sailing north on a strong breeze. Alexander cautiously descended toward the vessel. It looked to be manned by experienced sailors. Two things immediately caught his eye: the Reishi flag flapping in the wind atop the main mast and the soldiers of the Reishi Army Regency manning the catapults and ballistae on the fore and aft decks.

Alexander moved closer, looking cautiously for the Reishi Prince. When he didn't see him on deck, he moved his point of awareness next to the captain of the boat. The grizzled old man was holding the wheel of the ship and listening to another wind-worn sailor.

"Captain, I'm telling you this is a mistake. The Reishi Isle is cursed. Its waters are filled with unspeakable things," the sailor said.

"Be that as it may, I couldn't very well refuse Prince Phane. He's an arch mage and I fear him far more than I fear whatever's in the dark waters around the Reishi Isle. Besides, the Prince paid well and in advance."

"Indeed I did."

Alexander felt a thrill of fear at hearing the calm, confident voice. He moved his point of awareness back several feet off the side of the ship and saw Phane. The sailor who had questioned the wisdom of their destination went white.

The captain grunted. "Didn't hear you come up behind us with the wind in my ear. We'll make good time to the Reishi Isle if this keeps up. I trust your quarters are adequate?"

Phane smiled graciously. "Your stateroom is more than adequate, Captain. And I'm happy to hear we're making good time, but I didn't come up on deck to listen to your first mate whisper doubts in your ear."

Phane turned to look straight at Alexander. "I came to have a chat with my most resourceful enemy. Hello, Alexander. I see you've managed to elude Commander P'Tal. I must say I'm impressed, especially for one such as you."

Alexander shifted his position, and Phane's smile widened as he tracked the point of Alexander's awareness.

"Of course I can see you, Child. You're clumsy and unskilled in the use of your magic, although I must say you do have an impressive degree of power at your disposal. With the proper training and guidance, you could be most formidable.

"Alas, there are none alive today capable of providing you with the tutelage you need to fully realize your potential. Except me, of course." Phane smiled warmly.

The captain and first mate looked around, clearly wondering who Phane was talking to. He ignored them as they shared a worried look.

"You've impressed me with your resourcefulness," Phane continued. "Bow to my command, Alexander. Serve me and I will spare you and your family. You can rule Ruatha under my authority as the Reishi Sovereign."

Phane paused for a moment as though he expected an answer. Then he chuckled with genuine mirth. "Ah, you don't know how to answer me. How unfortunate. Looks like we'll be having a very one-sided conversation, but I don't mind if you don't. I'm not actually interested in anything you might have to say—with the exception of your oath of fealty to me, of course.

"In the spirit of good faith, I will freely give you the information you seek. I've conquered Karth and I'm consolidating my army there. The King of Andalia has agreed to my terms and allied with me. I control one of the larger islands of Tyr and I expect to bring the entire island chain under heel once I've completed construction of my navy. Furthermore, Commander P'Tal will raise an army at Headwater and conquer New Ruatha by summer's end.

"You have, no doubt, met my scourgling and are trapped within the walls of the old traitor's keep. So you see, Alexander, I am well on my way to victory. You should carefully consider my offer. I could use a strong king on Ruatha.

"Finally, and this is really the crown jewel if you will—I'm headed to the Reishi Isle to retrieve the Sovereign Stone. Once I have it, all will bow to me and your cause will be lost." He smiled with triumphant glee.

"Think hard on my offer, Alexander. I will not make it again. For now, I tire of you. Begone!" Phane waved his hand, and Alexander's awareness plunged back into the firmament and scattered to the edges of reality.

CHAPTER 3

He was lost in the firmament, disoriented. The cacophony of world events reverberated through him with an intensity like nothing he'd ever felt before. He struggled to maintain a hold on his identity, to remember that he was a unique individual and not just an echo rippling through the ocean of creation.

He fought to keep from losing himself in the endless sea of possibility. He felt like he was drowning and he started to lose track of time—even the concept of time began to slip out of his mental grasp. Fear slammed into him. What if it was already too late? What if he'd been lost in the firmament for too long and his body was wasting away?

It was the fear that saved him.

It reminded him of the safe place within his psyche, the place where the witness lived. He retreated into the refuge where emotion had no power, where detached reason was master. Piece by piece, he reassembled his identity, searching throughout the firmament for the scraps of his scattered consciousness until he was whole again. Then he found a thin thread of consciousness leading back to his physical body, and with an effort of will he followed the thread. His awareness returned to his body with such force that he fell over. For several long moments, he lay on the cold black stone of his balcony, breathing hard and trying to calm his pounding heart.

Trembling, he sat up and put his head in his hands. So many questions swirled around in his mind that he couldn't focus on one before another pushed its way in.

Things were moving much faster than even he had expected. In the last few days, he had managed to find the Thinblade and gain the loyalty of two out of nine Ruathan territories. Now he was facing a war with Headwater for control of the heart of Ruatha, a war that would likely be bloody and destructive whatever the outcome, leaving Ruatha weakened and vulnerable.

Phane had already conquered one island, secured an alliance with another, and controlled part of a third. Worst of all, he was close to retrieving the Sovereign Stone and with it the loyalty of the remaining islands, not to mention the secret of Wizard's Dust. The war hadn't even started and already Phane was nearing victory.

Alexander schooled his thoughts. Despair would not serve him; he needed reason and a plan.

***

When he returned to the paddock, it was midday and the Rangers were cooking lunch. Despite his anxiety, he felt the rumblings of hunger in his belly.

He found Abigail and Isabel talking quietly and watching the scourgling at the edge of the far abutment waiting for the bridge to become real again. Alexander wondered if the netherworld beast would fall for the disappearing bridge again or if it would simply hold its ground and prevent him from ever leaving Blackstone Keep.

Isabel and Abigail turned when he approached. As one, their brows furrowed with worry at the look on his face. He told himself that he had to learn to control his emotions better if he was going to be taken seriously as King, Thinblade or not.

"What's wrong?" his sister asked.

"Quite a bit actually, but nothing we can do anything about at the moment. How's our dark friend?" he asked, motioning toward the scourgling with his chin.

"It hasn't moved since it stopped a few feet short of the drop," Isabel said. "It did manage to kill several soldiers on its way back up here though. Unfortunately, everyone leading the little band of thugs managed to escape unscathed. I was really hoping it would knock Truss over the edge."

"I know how you feel. But at least it gave Jack some fodder for his story." Alexander looked over at the bard, who was sitting on a nearby rock and writing in his little notebook.

"That it did," Isabel said. "He grilled me for twenty minutes about every detail of the encounter."

"I should probably go talk to him about it. I managed to be watching at just the right moment and had a pretty good look. I might be able to add a few things that he could use."

"So you were able to use your clairvoyance again?" Abigail asked. "It seems like it's coming to you more easily."

Alexander nodded. "I feel pretty confident that I can make it happen when I need to, provided I have the time to meditate. I took a look at the army headed our way. It's from New Ruatha and Mage Gamaliel is with them."

"Really? That's wonderful. I was so worried for him when the palace collapsed." Isabel smiled with genuine happiness.

Alexander wanted to withhold the rest of his news just to enjoy her smile, but he needed counsel and they needed to know the truth of their situation.

Her smile faded at the grim look on his face. "What is it?"

"I saw Phane," Alexander said. "We have a lot to talk about and I'd like the rest to hear it, too. Let's discuss it over lunch."

"Is it really that bad?" Abigail asked, more from the look on his face than what he'd said.

He nodded as he took Isabel's hand. The three of them walked back to the cook fire with Jack in tow and were soon joined by Anatoly and Lucky. Alexander sent a Ranger to find Erik, who showed up moments later with Chase at his side.

They sat at a makeshift table cobbled together from the remnants of an old, broken stable door that had managed to withstand the ravages of time. Lunch was rice and beans with salt pork. It was simple fare but filling and hot. No one complained. Lucky even seemed to enjoy it.

Once everyone had eaten, Alexander recounted his experience with Phane. He held nothing back, not even the offer Phane made to spare his family if Alexander bowed to his authority. Everyone listened quietly until he was finished, then remained silent for several long moments.

It was Abigail who broke the silence. "Sounds to me like the easiest item to clear off the table is the ridiculous offer Phane made."

Alexander nodded without hesitation. "Agreed."

Chase looked surprised and dismayed. "But how can you reject such an offer out of hand? He's offering to spare you a war that could devastate all of Ruatha. Surely, that deserves some consideration, Lord Alexander."

"You speak out of turn, Chase," Erik said to his Second.

"No, it's all right," Alexander said. "He wouldn't be at the table if I didn't want to hear what he has to say."

Alexander turned to Chase. "Phane can't be trusted. His offer isn't genuine and would only lead to the enslavement of every life on Ruatha. But more than that, I value the integrity of my soul and I will not give my allegiance to a man who would bring something like that thing into the world of the living." Alexander pointed toward the scourgling standing stone-still across the chasm. He could see from Chase's colors that he wasn't convinced, but he didn't object.

Anatoly weighed in next. "Phane's swift victory in Karth and his alliance with Andalia are troubling, but at the moment there's nothing we can do about either island. As for his plans to conquer Ruatha by summer's end, I'm afraid the Prince will be disappointed. Headwater may be able to raise an army, but I doubt they'll be a match for the combined forces of New Ruatha and Glen Morillian's Rangers. With the strength of the Wizards Guild behind us, I'd wager that Ruatha will be united under your flag rather than his by midsummer."

"I tend to agree with you," Alexander said, "except for the fact that Phane can send more creatures from the netherworld to support his army. We need to unite the rest of the territories quickly and assemble our army as soon as possible."

"The force headed our way is a good start," Anatoly said, "but you're right, it's nowhere near the numbers we'll need."

"It's good to hear that Mage Gamaliel is with them," Lucky said. "I was worried for his survival. His counsel on these matters may prove invaluable, but the issues of armies and troop movements are of less concern to me than the other two parts of your story."

"I agree with Lucky," Jack said. "If Phane gets the Sovereign Stone, then all is lost."

Lucky nodded. "But more immediately important, you've discovered that Phane can harm you when you view him with your clairvoyance. I would caution you not to spy on the Prince again. He was able to scatter your consciousness into the firmament. I've read accounts of such attacks before. What he did could have very easily been fatal, and we don't know if he withheld some of his power to spare you in hopes that you would bow to him and deliver Ruatha without war. Next time may be the last."

Isabel's hand tightened on his arm. Alexander nodded thoughtfully. "I hadn't considered that. The few moments I spent lost in the firmament were terrifying. It didn't occur to me that he could have scattered my awareness more completely. I wonder how close my point of view has to be before he can see me. On Karth, he didn't seem to notice that I was there when I was high above him. I guess I'll have to stop looking in on him until I gain a better understanding of my clairvoyance."

"That leaves us with the problem of the Sovereign Stone," Jack said. "With the Stone, Ithilian will probably submit to his rule without a fight, but that's not the worst of it. The old stories say that the Reishi moved armies by means of the Reishi Gates, which are tied to the power of the Sovereign Stone. When the Stone was lost, the Gates stopped working. If Phane retrieves it, he may be able to use the Gates again and bring as many troops as he wants into the heart of Ruatha."

Alexander was alarmed. He'd read stories about the Gates, but they hadn't worked in so long that he didn't even consider the possibility that they might come into play. If Phane gained control of them, he would be unstoppable.

"Where's the Gate on Ruatha?" he asked.

Jack pointed southwest. "It's about a day's ride from here, several miles west of the road we traveled. It stands on a stone platform in the middle of the open plains."

"Can it be destroyed?" Isabel asked.

"Doubtful," Jack answered. "The old stories say that the people of Ruatha tried to destroy it after the Reishi War but failed. Perhaps Kelvin will have some insight or magic that could help. But even if the Gates don't pose a problem, the Sovereign Stone must not fall into Phane's hands. It contains the secret of Wizard's Dust, and with that knowledge, he'll be able to build an army of wizards. Alexander, we must stop him from getting the Stone at all costs."

"I'm afraid I agree with Jack," Lucky said. "I don't know how Phane plans to get the Stone out of the aether, but I suspect he has a few ideas. I'd like to hear what Kelvin has to say. He may be able to shed some light on the matter."

"I sure hope so," Alexander said. "Isabel, I think it's time to send Slyder out with a message for the Guild Mage."

Isabel tipped her head back and closed her eyes for a moment.

Jack took out his tablet. "What do you want to tell them?"

"Blackstone Keep is ours. Phane has sent a scourgling to guard the entrance platform. Approach with caution. It is imperative that we speak as soon as possible. Signed, Alexander Ruatha."

When Jack finished writing the message, he rolled the parchment and handed it to Isabel.

Moments later Slyder landed in the middle of the table and looked up at Isabel curiously. She fastened the note to his leg and sent him on his way. The small-framed forest hawk flew low until he passed over the wall, then tipped his wings back into a dive to gain speed for his flight toward the advancing army.

***

Late that evening, Slyder returned with a note from Kelvin: "Understood. Will arrive tomorrow morning. KG."

Alexander read the little note and felt a bit of his anxiety fade. Kelvin might know how to interfere with Phane. The idea of the Reishi Gate suddenly coming to life and thousands of enemy soldiers pouring forth was more than Alexander wanted to contemplate.

He set his mind to the scourgling. Lucky didn't think his remaining potions would have any effect on the creature. And normal weapons were clearly useless against the otherworldly hardness of the beast's oily black skin. If Kelvin didn't have a way to defeat it, Alexander knew he would have to test the

Thinblade against it. He was certain that his new sword could cut through anything of natural origin but less sure about things unnatural. If the Thinblade didn't work against the beast, then facing it would probably be the last thing he would ever do.

Later that night, he walked with Isabel back to their quarters.

"I'm worried about tomorrow," she said when they came to her door.

"Hopefully, Kelvin will have something powerful enough to deal with that thing. If not, maybe I can lure it out onto the bridge again and at least get some of our people into the Keep without a fight. Eventually, we're going to have to deal with it though."

She looked up at him. "I just wish there was a way to know if your sword will work against it."

"Me too, but I think there's only one way to find out." Before she could protest, he gently pulled her to him and kissed her. She held on tightly and responded with gentle passion.

"Alexander, this is killing me. I know we agreed to wait, but I don't want to wait any longer," she said.

He smiled down at her. "Me neither, but I think it's important that we do."

"I know," she said. "When do you think our parents will get here?"

"Not as soon as I'd like," he said with a smile and kissed her again. "Good night, Isabel. I love you."

"I love you, too," she said before she reluctantly released him and opened the door to the room right next to his.

It had been a challenge for them both, spending their nights with nothing but a wall and their agreement between them. With every passing day, Alexander felt his love and desire for her grow stronger and his resolve to wait for their wedding weaken, but he knew that they should be wed first and that meant waiting for their families to arrive. Of all his concerns, this one was the least urgent yet the most distracting.

The next morning, he stood watching the scourgling while awaiting Kelvin's arrival. He could see the army camped below. It looked like a small force from this altitude. They'd arrived just after dark and made camp by the light of torches and fires. Alexander knew that Kelvin would take time to make preparations for the scourgling before he made his way to the top of the bridge platform, but he was impatient for the Guild Mage to arrive nonetheless.

Two hours after dawn, the bridge sentries reported movement on the spur road below. Isabel sent Slyder for a closer look and reported that Mage Gamaliel was approaching and he had six wizards with him. Clearly, Kelvin took the threat posed by the netherworld beast very seriously. Half an hour later, Kelvin and his six wizards cautiously and slowly came into view. They quietly moved onto the bridge platform and spread out behind the scourgling. The netherworld beast was oblivious to them; it stood stone-still, waiting for an opportunity to get to Alexander.

Alexander and his companions watched as the wizards advanced on the demon. When he saw Kelvin and the others, Alexander made up his mind that the risk to them might be too great. He hoped that once safely inside the Keep, they would be able to discover a means of killing the beast.

He reached into the Keep Master's ring and brought the bridge into existence. All seven of the wizards stopped and waited for the beast to make the next move. It held still for just a moment as if it expected the bridge to disappear, but then started charging across it toward Alexander.

"At least it's stupid," Alexander said with a sidelong glance at Isabel. A moment later the bridge vanished and the scourgling tumbled silently toward the spur road below.

Alexander brought the bridge back into existence and called out for Kelvin and his wizards to cross. He scrutinized the colors of each man as he passed under the arch into the paddock and found each to be honorable, dedicated—and very powerful.

Alexander felt much better having them at the Keep. They could begin exploring some of the areas devoted to the study and creation of magic. He'd left the shields guarding those areas in place to protect both those doing the exploring and the areas being explored. Alexander didn't know enough about magic to make sense out of what he was likely to find in those places.

He clasped Kelvin's hand. "I'm happy to see you alive and well. I feared the worst when the north wing of the palace collapsed."

"I took precautions to protect myself and the men who stood with me. Unfortunately, Commander P'Tal also survived," Kelvin said as he shook Alexander's hand with a firm grip.

Alexander nodded. "P'Tal was here until a few days ago. He left just after Phane sent the scourgling to take his place."

Alexander sent the bridge away before he turned to address the other wizards.

"Welcome to Blackstone Keep. We've taken up residence in the barracks on the north side of the paddock. Captain Alaric's Second will see to your quarters. We've done some preliminary exploration of the Keep's interior, but I've restricted access to the areas once used for the study of magic. I'm hoping to enlist your assistance in the exploration of those areas," Alexander said with a smile.

The wizards all nodded eagerly. This was a place of legend and they were excited by the prospect of discovering its secrets.

"This is a place of wonder," Alexander said. "But before we can begin exploring, I need your counsel and assistance on a number of important matters. First, of course, is the scourgling. It seems immune to blunt force—Abigail's arrow shattered on its chest without effect."

"Fortunately, it isn't very smart. Twice I've lured it onto the bridge and let it fall. The first time, it returned to its post within the hour, and I expect it'll be back on the bridge abutment within a few minutes. I've considered facing it with the Thinblade, but I'd rather exhaust all other options before I take that risk."

All eyes snapped to the sword on his belt at the mention of the Thinblade.

Kelvin spoke excitedly, "You've recovered the Sword of Kings? This is the best of news. Lord Alexander, may we see the blade?"

The wizards looked on like a group of children seeing a new toy for the first time. Alexander drew the blade and held it up for their inspection. All seven leaned in and looked closely, moving their heads to see the edge and murmuring to one another about the magic of it.

"We must get word of the Thinblade out as soon as possible. More than anything else, it will rally the territories of Ruatha to your cause," Kelvin said.

"I agree, but there's much more to discuss before we take any action," Alexander said as he led them to a big table set up in the middle of the paddock for an impromptu King's Council.

CHAPTER 4

All were present, including Erik and Chase. Many of the Rangers looked on as they went about their duties. Decisions of importance would be made at this table, decisions that could well determine the fate of Ruatha.

"There are many important items we must discuss, so I'll lay them all out for us to consider and then I hope we can make plans to deal with each in turn."

Alexander spoke at length. He talked about the scourgling and the little demon that had brought it to Blackstone Keep. He discussed the need to explore the Keep and look for anything of power that could be used in the coming war. He spoke of Headwater and the army Jataan P'Tal would raise.

He told them about his clairvoyant experience with Phane and recounted every word the Reishi Prince had uttered. He told them about Karth, Tyr, and Andalia. He told them how Phane claimed that he could train Alexander; told of his offer to let Alexander rule Ruatha if he surrendered; and told them how Phane had scattered Alexander's awareness into the firmament.

He saved the most important news for last, revealing that Phane was heading to the Reishi Isle to retrieve the Sovereign Stone and that the Reishi Gates may come into play if the Prince was successful. When Alexander finished, the newcomers to the table sat in stunned silence for several long moments.

"It seems that we do indeed have much to consider," Kelvin said. "Let us set aside those things we can do little about. Have you considered his offer of alliance?"

Alexander nodded. "I have—and I reject it outright. Phane cannot be permitted to rule the Seven Isles under any circumstances."

Kelvin nodded. "I agree completely. His claim that he can train you is interesting but beyond our ability to verify. His apparent ability to attack you when you send your awareness into his presence is troubling but easy enough to avoid."

Alexander nodded and Kelvin continued. "Karth and Andalia are beyond our influence at the moment. The exploration of the Keep requires little discussion. Headwater's alliance with Phane is of great importance and will require substantial troops and preparations to defend against. They will most likely attack New Ruatha as soon as they can assemble their army. We must take immediate action to organize and field our own army or risk losing the Glittering City."

"I recommend we get word to Glen Morillian to send what troops they have to New Ruatha as quickly as possible," Anatoly said.

"I agree," Alexander said. "Headwater will move quickly and they have Commander P'Tal to lead them. How can we get word to Glen Morillian?"

"Lord Alexander, if I may?" one of the wizards asked.

Alexander nodded. "Of course, I want to hear any suggestions."

"I am Wizard Hax. I believe I have a spell that may accomplish this task. In my conversations with Mage Gamaliel, he recounted Wizard Kallentera's use of a dream-whisper spell. I was intrigued by the concept, so I have very recently studied this magic. I can send your message to Wizard Kallentera tonight."

"Excellent," Alexander said. "Tell him to send all the troops they can spare to New Ruatha, while maintaining sufficient forces to hold the forest road and defend Glen Morillian. Next, we need to get word to New Ruatha and the Wizards Guild."

"Lord Alexander, I am Wizard Sark. I can return to your forces on the plains below and accompany riders to New Ruatha with instructions for the army and the Wizards Guild to make ready for war."

"How will you get past the scourgling?" Alexander asked.

"My focus of magical study is the manipulation of air. I can float safely to the ground without using the bridge."

Alexander smiled. "Magic never ceases to amaze me. Tell the assembled force to hold their position. I'll want most of them to help explore and secure the Keep. Have Regent Cery keep the rest of the army in New Ruatha."

"I would also have you supervise the moving of the Wizards Guild to Blackstone Keep," Kelvin said to Wizard Sark. "There are many items and books within the Guild that cannot be permitted to fall into enemy hands. I'd feel much better if those items were secured here beyond the enemy's reach."

"I agree," Alexander replied, "and the more wizards we have here, the faster we can determine if there's anything within these walls that can help us win the war or at least win the coming battle with Headwater."

Alexander looked around for more input before moving on. "I'm satisfied with our plan for defending against Headwater. Does anyone have anything else on this subject?"

Jack cleared his throat to gently draw everyone's attention. "Wizard Sark, may I ask you to deliver a letter for my apprentice Owen at the Bards Guild? I have a couple of songs that will tell the story of Alexander and the Thinblade, the conquest of Blackstone Keep, and the murderous indifference of Phane and his netherworld minions. Owen will get these stories into circulation to begin forming the opinion of the masses."

"Of course, I will deliver them to the Bards Guild myself," Sark said.

"Very good." Alexander was anxious to get to the more pressing matter. "My biggest concern is the Sovereign Stone. As I understand it, the Stone is in the aether and beyond reach. Any idea how Phane expects to retrieve it?"

"That's hard to say," Kelvin said. "I suspect he plans to use the powersink built into the Reishi Keep. The stories of the Reishi War say that a great deal of power was stored in the Reishi Keep. If Phane can access that stored magical energy, he'll be able to use it to reach into the aether and draw the Stone back into the world of time and substance."

"What's a powersink?" Isabel asked.

"The name is a bit of a misnomer," Kelvin said. "A powersink is usually incorporated into a structure, and the mechanics are quite complex but the result is simple. Essentially, a wizard can access the firmament through a powersink, and the link will remain open and dormant for later use by another wizard. In this way many wizards can access the firmament through a single powersink. The wizard controlling the powersink can wield a much greater connection to the firmament than any wizard could ever hope to command on his own. With a working powersink at his disposal, Phane will be able to cast a spiritwalk spell, even though such magic is beyond him otherwise."

A quintessential-looking wizard, with long white hair, a white goatee, and simple grey robes said, "There is one story from the Reishi War that says the powersink in the Reishi Keep was tainted by a very powerful witch who was allied with Mage Cedric. If that story is true, then Phane will most likely fail in his attempt to retrieve the Sovereign Stone."

"Is there any way to determine the truth of that story?" Alexander asked.

"Perhaps," Wizard Ely said. "I will need to make some preparations, but I believe I can discover if the Reishi Keep is tainted or not."

"What you're considering carries great risk, does it not?" Kelvin asked.

"The risk is great, but the knowledge is worth the risk," Wizard Ely replied.

"What exactly is the risk?" Alexander asked.

"If the Keep is tainted, then the witch's spell could spread to my connection with the firmament through the divination spell I would cast. If it does, I could lose my magic permanently," Wizard Ely said simply.

"What are the chances of you gaining the information we need without harm?" Alexander asked.

"Even odds," Ely said.

"That's too great a risk. Let's hold off on that and explore other options," Alexander said. "I would not risk you if we can find another way."

"As you wish, Lord Alexander," Wizard Ely said with a nod to his authority. "I will study the problem and see if I can find an alternative."

"What's the worst case if Phane gets the Stone?" Abigail asked.

"If Phane retrieves the Sovereign Stone, he will subjugate the Seven Isles. He will learn the ancient secret of Wizard's Dust, and he'll have the Reishi Gates to move his armies. For myself, I will fight his tyranny with my last breath," Kelvin said, shaking his head, "but with the Stone, Phane will win."

"If he can't make the Reishi powersink work, is there another way for him to get the Stone?" Abigail asked.

Kelvin took a deep breath as he thought about the question. "Possibly. There are other powersink structures in the Seven Isles. He may be able to find one that he can use to cast a spiritwalk spell. But without a powersink, such a spell is beyond all but a naturally born and well-trained spiritwalker. To my knowledge, such a wizard has not been born in over three thousand years. They are most rare. Other than that, I doubt there is any way for him to reach it."

"Is there a way for us to get the Stone?" Alexander asked. "I'd feel better if we could lock it in the Bloodvault rather than risk Phane finding a way to retrieve it from the aether."

Kelvin frowned. "I know of no way to accomplish such a thing. I doubt any wizard in my guild could cast a spiritwalk spell, even with the benefit of a usable and highly charged powersink."

"Perhaps there is another way," said a wizard in simple brown robes. "I am Mage Landi. I know of fairies that live in the Pinnacles who can use their magic to shift into the aether. In the ancient stories, it was said that some few wizards were able to attract a fairy as a familiar. What I'm suggesting is unlikely to work, but I believe, with the proper preparation, it is possible."

Kelvin looked intrigued by the idea. "A bold suggestion, Mage Landi. My understanding is that the fairies are wary of outsiders. Attracting a fairy as a familiar would be a most difficult task. What do you propose?"

"In truth, I would need to make a more thorough study of the matter before I could make an informed recommendation. However, I believe I could summon a fairy, and we could simply ask if what we desire is possible."

"What do you mean when you say you can summon a fairy?" Alexander asked.

"Simply that, Lord Alexander. I can magically bring a fairy here to speak with us on the matter. I am a conjurer. My magical calling is the art of attracting and bargaining with creatures of all kinds."

"What would you need to summon a fairy?" Kelvin asked.

"I have everything I need to prepare the spell, except a pinch of fairy dust and we have an ample supply at the guild house."

Lucky spoke up. "I have a small quantity of fairy dust with me now. You're welcome to it."

Mage Landi smiled his thanks, then turned to Kelvin. "I can cast the summoning spell tonight after dark."

Kelvin nodded. "Very good. Is there any danger involved?"

"None, except the possibility that the fairy will reject our request," Mage Landi said.

"That leaves the matter of the scourgling at the gate. Any suggestions how we might kill it?" Alexander asked.

The table fell silent. Wizard Ely broke the silence after a long moment. "To my knowledge, such a creature cannot be destroyed by force. It will return to the netherworld once it has completed its task or if the one who summoned it sends it back or if it is banished. I do not believe that any here have the capability to banish the beast and so the only option that remains is to contain it."

Kelvin nodded. "I agree. A scourgling is probably not even vulnerable to the Thinblade, and I would not risk your life to discover the truth of that. Our only real option is to contain it within a magical circle."

"How do we do that?" Isabel asked.

"First we must decide where we want to trap the beast," Kelvin said. "If we contain it within a circle constructed out of doors, then we risk the circle being tampered with or being naturally damaged by the elements. The alternative is to find a more permanent prison within the walls of Blackstone Keep. Such a place would likely hold it much better but presents far more challenges and greater risks."

Isabel looked at Alexander, then back to Kelvin. "I don't want that thing to get in here, not even to imprison it," she said. "If it somehow escaped its cage, it would be able to get to Alexander. If we find a way to trap it outside, then at least we can defend against it if it gets loose."

"I agree," Abigail and Anatoly both said at once.

"What if we built an enclosed structure down on the plain and lured it inside?" Alexander suggested. "We could post a guard detail to ensure that nothing tampers with the magic circle, and the enclosure would protect the circle from the weather."

"That sounds like a good plan," Kelvin said.

He turned to Wizard Sark. "Add that to your list. Instruct Commander

Perry to begin construction of a suitable structure and assign Wizard Jahoda to oversee the project. When you get to the guild house, send a fast cart with a supply of silver and gold adequate for a permanent circle. The construction should be complete by the time the metals arrive. Select three wizards to accompany the wagons containing the contents of the guild and ask Regent Cery to provide a force of a thousand to ride guard. You remain in New Ruatha to take command of the remaining wizards and put them to work assisting in preparations for war."

"I always feel better when I have a plan," Alexander said. "Now for the part that I'm sure you are all eager for. I'd like to begin exploring some of the more sensitive areas of the Keep today." Alexander pulled a handful of gold rings set with small black stones from his pocket and spilled them onto the table. "I found these in the Bloodvault, along with a very large book written in a language that I can't read. Each of these rings will allow you to see the Keep in your mind's eye and activate some of the shields and other capabilities, such as the bridge. I've given one to Lucky and I'd like each of you to wear one while you explore, so you can get through the shields you encounter and also so you don't get lost."

Alexander passed the rings out to all of the newly arrived wizards, except Sark, who sighed, "It is with regret that I cannot stay and help you explore, but time is our enemy. I must leave as soon as possible."

Jack gave him a tube full of papers for Owen, and Alexander walked him over to the bridge arch with Kelvin.

"Any further instructions before I depart?" Sark asked.

"I don't think so," Alexander said. "Thank you. And be careful; Headwater has powerful allies. Take what precautions you can to ensure that your journey is safe."

"I will, Lord Alexander. Expect preparations for imprisoning the scourgling to take a week or so. Wagons from the guild should arrive within two weeks."

Wizard Sark shook hands with Alexander and Kelvin, then unceremoniously stepped off the edge of the bridge abutment and fell into the open sky. Alexander watched in amazement as the wizard sailed away from the wall of the mountain, turning in a gentle arc toward the army encampment far below. He fell fast at first, but once he neared the ground, he slowed and landed on his feet in a fast walk, never breaking stride until he was standing in front of Commander Perry.

CHAPTER 5

The rest of the day was spent exploring the Keep. They broke into groups of three with a wizard in each group. Alexander wanted a preliminary assessment of the contents of the mile-long hallway that formed the backbone of the protected areas once used for the study and practice of magic. They dubbed this long corridor the Hall of Magic.

The only wizard who stayed behind was Ely. He asked Alexander if he could study the book that had been found in the Bloodvault. When Kelvin suggested that Ely was the best scholar in the guild and would have a better chance of deciphering the contents than any other, Alexander quickly agreed.

Kelvin and Isabel went with Alexander to explore the central tower. Alexander's other companions and a number of Rangers formed several groups, each guided by a wizard and each tasked to explore the various rooms and halls that radiated away from the Hall of Magic.

When Alexander's group approached the sentinel at the end of the long hallway leading to the central tower, Alexander noted that its eyes were still glowing with the color of sunlight on new-fallen snow.

Kelvin stopped several feet away from the stone statue and appraised the ancient guardian for several moments.

"What can you tell me of this?" he asked.

"When we first came to this part of the Keep, there was a line on the floor just about where you're standing, and the archway beyond was sealed over with stone. When I stepped over the line, a magical shield formed behind me and the sentinel challenged me with three tests.

"First, it demanded proof that I had the Keep Master's ring," Alexander said. "Second, it demanded that I forfeit the life of one of my companions."

Kelvin frowned with slight alarm. "How did you overcome such a challenge?"

"I was terrified at first and it took me a while to reason through it, but I finally understood that Mage Cedric was testing my loyalty to the Old Law. As such, I had no right to forfeit any life but my own, so that's what I offered," Alexander said. "The sentinel was satisfied with my answer so it moved on to the third test . . . and attacked."

Kelvin tensed a bit and looked at the stone statue with renewed suspicion. "I don't see any battle damage, so how is it that you managed to survive?"

"It didn't take long to realize that it was using the sword forms I learned from the skillbook. Once I understood, I was able to recognize each attack and employ the counterattack best suited to meet the sentinel's advance. After I'd met each and every attack series and combination in the skillbook with a successful counterstrike, the sentinel stopped its attack and pronounced that I had passed the test. A moment later the wall under the arch at the end of the hall vanished, allowing access to the central tower."

"Clearly, Mage Cedric was intent on protecting the contents of the central tower from any but you," Kelvin said. "Have you tried to command the sentinel since you passed the tests?"

Alexander frowned. "The thought hadn't crossed my mind. Do you think it would obey?"

"There is every possibility that Mage Cedric left it here to serve you once his tests had been met. I suggest you command it and find out."

Alexander thought for a moment, then faced the sentinel. "Sentinel, raise your sword."

The black stone blade spun up to the on-guard position. The statue once again froze in place. Alexander looked at Isabel and then at Kelvin.

"Sentinel, what are your capabilities?" Alexander asked.

"I can be commanded by you alone. I will guard any portal you command me to guard and prevent all others from gaining access." The voice sounded hollow and far away, but the eyes glowed slightly brighter when it spoke.

"Very good," Alexander said. "Lower your sword and stand here until I return. Challenge anyone else who attempts to pass." The sentinel lowered its sword and its eyes went slightly dimmer.

They proceeded into the large circular room that formed the entry chamber of the central tower, and Alexander led the way down to the Bloodvault. Kelvin spent several minutes inspecting the magical structure and cast a number of spells to gain more insight into the nature of its construction.

"This is truly an amazing piece of work," Kelvin said. "I've never seen such complex magical energies at work in any other construction. I could study this for weeks and still not have sufficient understanding to recreate the effect."

"Do you think Phane could get inside it?" Alexander asked.

Kelvin looked at it for a long moment before slowly shaking his head. "No, I don't believe such a construction can be breached without the cooperative effort of many very powerful wizards. It isn't so much a function of the power that one wizard can bring to bear but more that the energies involved are bound together in such a way that attempting to undo one line of binding force only strengthens and magnifies several others. Only the combined efforts of several wizards could simultaneously unravel all of the strands of this very intricate web of magical force. Even then, it would probably take many months of trial and error before they could hope to succeed."

"Good. I was hoping you'd say that," Alexander said. "Now we just have to convince the fairies to help us and hope that Phane can't use the powersink and we have a chance."

Alexander didn't mean to sound so discouraged but he felt helpless at the prospect of Phane heading toward the Reishi Isle. Everything depended on the powersink being tainted. He desperately wanted to know if it was, but he just couldn't justify the risk to Wizard Ely. He consoled himself with the knowledge that knowing wouldn't change anything. Either way, Alexander was powerless to stop Phane from making the attempt. He could only wait and see and plan for the best.

Alexander sealed the Bloodvault again, and they returned to the entry hall of the central tower to begin the long climb to the top. The tower was a series of slightly smaller rooms stacked one on top of another. The room immediately above the entry hall was a comfortable-looking sitting room and audience chamber.

Plush carpets that didn't appear to have aged at all in the intervening millennia covered the floor; a long, well-made, simple black oak table with cushioned high-back chairs lining both sides occupied the center of the room; a large hearth surrounded by oversized plush chairs took up one section of the rounded wall; and a set of three couches facing a three-sided table occupied the remaining space.

The stairway leading up to the next level was sealed with a wall of black stone very similar to the wall that protected the Bloodvault chamber.

"Kelvin, can you see this wall in your mind's eye through your Keep ring?" Alexander asked.

Kelvin closed his eyes and found the place where they stood in his mental map of the Keep. "I can see it but I cannot unseal it."

Alexander nodded. "I figured there would be some areas that would only be accessible with the Keep Master's ring." With a thought, he sent the wall away, probably to the same place where the bridge resided when it was not in this world.

Level after level, they climbed through all manner of chambers. There were countless rooms filled with bookshelves, others looked like laboratories, and still others were studies. There were simple rooms with nothing but a magical circle inlaid in gold in the floor and others that were nothing more than well-appointed sleeping chambers.

After many dozens of floors, they came to a level with transparent stone windows and three balconies that were only accessible once Alexander sent away the stone walls filling the archways.

One of the balconies faced west and offered a stunning view. The Keep spread out below to the paddock. Alexander had to squint, but he could just make out the stone-still form of the scourgling standing on the abutment of the bridge. The plains spread out farther still and the blue of the ocean many leagues away was just visible on the horizon.

Bridges extended from the other two balconies, each stretching hundreds of feet in a gentle arch across open expanses of empty sky. The balconies were already higher than most of the other towers and buildings that covered the surface of the mountaintop, but there were a few spires that reached higher still.

One of the sky bridges reached out to join another tower just a few levels below its conical top. The second led to a giant, flat platform that was several thousand feet long and at least a thousand feet wide. Aside from the towers, it was the highest point on the entire Keep and looked big enough to assemble an army in formation. Alexander made a mental note to return to the platform and investigate further.

They continued to climb. Level after level, the central tower rose into the sky. Each level was filled with all manner of instruments, apparatus, libraries, writing rooms, sitting rooms, and empty chambers that looked like they were designed to contain the magical energies of spells, should a new or experimental magic go wrong.

Finally, they reached a room just short of the top chamber of the tower. Alexander had to dismiss another stone wall to gain entrance. It was a small study, no more than thirty feet in diameter. Comfortable chairs, a hearth, a writing desk, a small shelf of books, and a bed filled the room. A bound oak door opened to a circular balcony that wrapped around the outside of the tower. The view was breathtaking.

They walked around the entire balcony and took in the spectacle of the Keep and the plains below. From their vantage point, they could appreciate the sheer size of the Keep. It stretched away from the central spire for miles in every direction. The surface was covered with buildings, roads, towers, small fields, and assembly areas. But Alexander knew the vast outer surface area of the Keep was only a small part of its true capacity; dozens of levels of rooms and halls riddled the interior.

There was only one more level of the tower, the very highest level of the entire Keep, and they soon discovered that the staircase leading up to it was barred by a magical shield that would not let anyone pass, except Alexander. He could not deactivate it. He could not even assist Kelvin to pass. Clearly, the highest chamber in the tower was meant for the Keep Master alone.

Alexander ascended to the simple little room with caution as well as a sense of excitement. He was somewhat disappointed to find that it was nothing more than a bare room with a magical circle surrounding its center point inlaid in heavy gold. In the middle of the circle was a large meditation cushion with the bleached bones of a crumpled skeleton unceremoniously piled on top.

All around the walls hung heavy tapestries depicting scenes of beauty. It was a peaceful, quiet place. Alexander spent a few moments walking around looking at the tapestries, until he noticed the faint aura of magic coming from one. It took him a minute to realize that it was actually coming from behind the tapestry. He pulled it aside and found a portal to another room.

He was puzzled because he knew the wall was nothing more than a foot of stone separating him from the sky beyond, yet the room was clearly there. Upon further inspection, he found that the portal was more of an opening in the fabric of the world than an actual door. He looked into the twenty-foot square room and marveled at the capacity of magic to leave him speechless and breathless at the same time.

Cautiously, he ventured into the little room that existed outside of the world. As he crossed the threshold, the light came up a bit and the detail of the room became visible. It was a simple place with a table, chair, bed, and bookshelf. There was a small fireplace and a comfortable chair with a table beside it. Otherwise the room was bare and slightly cold.

On the table was a letter written on fine parchment and sealed with wax. The seal was marked with the glyph of the House of Reishi. His hand went to the mark on his neck and then to the hilt of the Thinblade. He drew his sword and compared the glyph on its pommel with the mark in the wax—it was a perfect match. A thrill ran up his spine. Mage Cedric had left him a letter, probably the last thing he ever did in this world. Alexander could only guess that the bones in the circle were the remains of the Old Rebel Mage.

He sat down in the chair and broke the seal. The tingle of magic raced through him. For a moment he was alarmed but there didn't seem to be any other effect, so he relaxed. When he opened the letter, he discovered that it was written in a language he didn't recognize, but after a moment the words suddenly became clear to him.

He read the letter with a sense of awe and reverence. He knew it had been written two thousand years ago and left here for his eyes only.

"You are the heir to the throne of Ruatha, the first of your line to claim the throne in millennia. But you are much more than that—you are the greatest hope for the people of all the Seven Isles. Be true to the Old Law.

"I have fought Phane for decades and his father before that. He is cunning and evil beyond measure, but he can be defeated. His arrogance and self-centered narcissism are his weaknesses. He does not trust anyone and will betray those who are foolish enough to trust him. Use this to your advantage.

"If you are reading this, then you have found the first of the three Bloodvaults. The second is at the base of this tower. Your sword is there, along with several rings that will allow others to command the Keep. You will also find a book that will explain the workings and capabilities of Blackstone Keep. The seal on this letter has imparted the ability to read the book. Study it well, and the Keep will serve your cause.

"The third Bloodvault is hidden well and is for you to find. It contains the greatest treasure of all, but it will do you no good until you are ready to claim it. Only then will you have the insight to find it.

"I am sorry that I couldn't spare your world the horror that you now face. I gave all that I am to this cause—and I failed."

The letter was signed: "Barnabas Cedric."

Alexander sat quietly staring at the letter. Cedric had sacrificed everything and accomplished a great deal in his lifetime, yet he went into the afterlife believing that he had failed. Alexander read it again with quiet sadness. The man who had given the future a chance deserved more than a lonely death with nothing but his regret to comfort him in his last hours. Alexander folded the letter and carefully slipped it into his tunic.

He returned to the little room below and found Kelvin sitting by the bookshelf carefully leafing through a book. Isabel was outside on the balcony looking at the horizon.

"Cedric's remains are up there. He left a letter for me." Alexander handed the parchment to Kelvin. The Guild Mage took it carefully and read it through, then read it again.

"It saddens me to know he died alone and with the belief that he had failed. I would give much to let him see the esteem he is held in today. For me, this letter only serves to deepen my commitment to defeating Phane."

Alexander sat down. "Me, too … I found the letter in a room that isn't really there. It's like it's a place in another world with a doorway leading from this world."

Kelvin nodded. "It's called a Wizard's Den. Arch mage wizards are able to cast such a spell. Once cast, it creates a chamber separate from this world that can only be accessed by the command of the casting wizard. If it's left open when the wizard dies, it will remain with the doorway open indefinitely. Did you see any books?"

Alexander nodded. "There was a small shelf with a couple dozen or so. Should we take them with us?"

Kelvin considered for a moment. "If he left them in his Wizard's Den, then they were for you alone. It's best to leave them there for now."

They made their way back into the bowels of the Keep, taking care to close every passage in order to protect the libraries and workrooms Mage Cedric had left behind. Each would require more careful inspection another day. It was starting to get late, and Alexander wanted to be ready for the summoning of the fairy.

When they reached the entry hall, he ordered the sentinel to guard the central tower and prevent anyone from going either up or down from the main room. The sentinel obeyed without question. Alexander reached into the Keep Master's ring and found the four doorways leading into the large round room at the base of the central tower. He sealed them with the magical stone that had filled them the day Alexander had discovered this place.

As they returned to the paddock, they found several other groups of explorers along the way. There was a great deal of excitement on the part of the wizards. They had discovered huge libraries filled with books and scrolls of spells, magical research, writings on magical theory, discussions of the nature of Wizard's Dust and how it interacted with the consciousness and the firmament, histories of the war and the time before, and even stories and fables. By all accounts, it would take a thousand wizards a hundred years to pour through all of the volumes they'd found. The library wings were vast, and the books were all intact despite long years of disuse.

Rooms in another wing were clearly storerooms for items of magical power. The wizards were in agreement that those specific rooms should be carefully protected, first from thieves, but more importantly from those without the proper training to discern the purpose of any given item. Some items were apparently very potent and dangerous, but there were no labels explaining what they could do. It was agreed that careful and deliberate cataloguing of the items within that wing was of the highest priority.

Still other rooms were designed as laboratories. Lucky was especially excited about one in particular that he'd picked out to serve as his new workshop. He was nearly giddy with the possibilities it presented. It had clearly been used in the distant past by a practicing alchemist. It was well stocked with glassware and had plenty of table and shelf space as well as bins of raw materials. A few of the ingredients were even still viable.

Other rooms were laid out as classrooms and lecture halls. A few were sleeping rooms for wizards who were working late and needed a few hours of sleep to clear their heads. Small meditation chambers were interspersed here and there, and a number of cozy little study rooms where a wizard could be alone with his books and his thoughts were tucked in between the larger rooms.

A few rooms were set up as small cafeterias, meeting rooms, and storage rooms.

One hall in particular generated significant comment and discussion. It was lined with eight rooms, each with a heavy gold magical circle inlaid into the floor for containing summoned creatures. Within two of the rooms, creatures from the netherworld remained imprisoned even after all these years. In both cases, the demons were excited to see the descendants of their captors and made determined attempts to breach the magical circles. Fortunately, the containment fields held. Unfortunately, the creatures resorted to inhuman shrieking that sent chills into all within earshot.

Alexander discovered that he could erect a shield where each hall met the central Hall of Magic. He felt better knowing that no one could get to those rooms without his permission.

CHAPTER 6

A hearty dinner awaited them when they emerged from the Keep. There was a great deal of lively discussion and storytelling about the discoveries that had been made. Much had been learned, but, as was to be expected, there were now many more questions than before. The new questions, however, were more specific, and those who raised them had clear ideas about how to go about finding the answers.

With Isabel at his side, Alexander sat quietly and listened to the wizards recount the wonders of the Keep. Once dinner was done and darkness began to settle, he started to feel anxious about the summoning that would soon take place. It was a vital part of his plan—he needed the assistance of the fairies, but he had no idea what to expect from the reclusive little creatures. Until today, he had only heard about fairies as legend and story. They were the stuff of his childhood imagination and now his entire world might depend on the aid of a magical creature that, until very recently, he didn't even believe actually existed.

He was lost in thought when Mage Landi quietly approached.

"Lord Alexander, may we speak about the summoning?"

Alexander looked up absently for a moment before the present came back in a rush. "Please," he motioned to a nearby chair, "sit and tell me what to expect."

"I've made preparations on the other side of the paddock," Mage Landi said. "Lucky has provided me with the required fairy dust, and I've done the preliminary work. This is a bit of a delicate process for a number of reasons, so I wanted to confer with you before we begin."

"Anything I can do to help," Alexander said. "Keeping the Sovereign Stone from Phane is vitally important."

"The presence of the scourgling poses a problem," Landi said. "Fairies are creatures that exist both in this world and in the aether. Within the aether, a demon that is in this world is represented as a rift that leads to the netherworld. Such a rift is a danger to a fairy; the one summoned will probably be afraid and extremely wary."

"Will the summoning risk the fairy's life?" Isabel asked.

"No, but she will be frightened nonetheless," Landi said. "The only true risk occurs when a fairy actually touches a creature from the netherworld. In such cases, a fairy's ethereal essence can be drawn into the netherworld and her physical form will simply wink out of existence. With the scourgling safely on the other side of the chasm, the fairy will be at no more risk from the beast than we are, but she may suspect that we are actually in league with the scourgling. It's important to impress on her that we are aware of it and that we fear it as well."

"That won't be a problem," Alexander said wryly.

Mage Landi smiled. "Indeed. The next issue is of a more personal nature. Fairies are creatures of the light. They respond to love above all else and they are quite sensitive to the aura of it. Please understand, my analogy is not entirely accurate, but I believe I can communicate the important points more readily by leveraging magic that you are familiar with.

"Alexander, when you read the auras of two people who are feeling love for one another, there is a different quality to their colors, is there not?"

Alexander nodded thoughtfully. "Sometimes when I saw my parents together, the quality of their colors was always more vibrant and clear than otherwise. I never fully understood the cause until just now."

"The fairies can see love in much the same way and are drawn to it," Landi said. "For that reason, I would like Lady Isabel to participate in the summoning. The clear bond of love between you will resonate with the fairy and put her at ease more readily than any other thing."

A thought occurred to Alexander. "Does the summoning spell compel the fairy to come to you? Does it force her against her will?"

"No. There are different schools of thought in the field of conjuration and summoning. Some wizards, such as necromancers, follow a darker path. They use binding magic to compel service against free will. I bargain openly and honestly with those I summon. By offering that which a creature values, they come willingly and hear me out. If the price I offer suits the creature's interests, we agree to help one another. If not, we part ways."

"I'm glad to hear that," Alexander said. "Is there anything I can bring to the table that will add to our bargaining position?"

"Love for Lady Isabel and reassurance that the beast at our door is the enemy."

Alexander stood and offered his hand to Isabel. "That I can do. When do we start?"

They walked to the far end of the paddock. In the corner, Mage Landi had cleared a patch of ground and drawn three circles in the hard-packed dirt, each overlapping evenly with the other two. In the middle of each circle was a blanket folded into a small square. A candle was burning at each of the three points of intersection which described a triangle. A heavy wooden stake about two feet tall had been pounded into the ground in the center of the triangle. Resting on top of the stake was a small silver saucer with a circle of white powder surrounding the center point.

Mage Landi directed Alexander and Isabel to each sit in a specific circle and he seated himself in the third.

"Do not disturb the lines of the circles," he said as he cautiously opened a small paper envelope and gently tapped out a fine iridescent powder into the center of the silver saucer.

"I will need a single drop of blood from each of you. Lady Isabel, you must give your blood first. Prick the ring finger of your left hand and squeeze a drop onto the fairy dust in the center of the saucer. Lord Alexander, you must do exactly the same immediately after Isabel."

They carefully followed the Mage's instructions. Alexander could see Abigail and Jack watching from a short way off, but he paid them little mind as he focused on doing his part in the summoning.

"Very good. Now hold hands and do not let go until the summoning is complete. Focus on your love for one another and hold those feelings in your heart."

Mage Landi closed his eyes and began chanting softly. He spoke in a language like nothing Alexander had ever heard before. It was intricate and soft with gentle and lilting intonations. The mage repeated a complicated verse seven times over, one right after the next. When he stopped speaking, Alexander could almost hear the words of the verse in his head. Mage Landi waited silently for the count of three breaths before speaking a word of power. The small ring of powder surrounding the fairy dust burst into flame and melted. As the contents of the silver saucer combined, the flame grew higher, burning brightly with iridescent colors for several minutes. Alexander held Isabel's hand and focused on his love for her as he watched the flames dance.

Abruptly the flames died, and a scintillating ball of pure white light spun into existence. It floated gently down and quite suddenly transformed into a fairy. Standing on the little silver saucer was a perfectly proportioned, three-inch-tall woman with dragonfly wings. She glowed faintly with soft white light that undulated with just a hint of color.

Her aura was clear and strong and encompassed all the colors of the rainbow. She was beautiful and stood proudly, as if she were ten feet tall. She looked all around for just a moment before she spun into a little ball of scintillating light again. She was so bright that Alexander couldn't look directly at her; she was so beautiful that he tried to anyway.

From the spinning orb of light, Alexander heard a clear, lilting voice with perfect pronunciation and just a slight accent that reminded him of what he always thought royalty should sound like.

"Darkness is near," she said.

Mage Landi nodded to Alexander.

"The darkness is our enemy but you are safe from it here," he said.

"Love is also near," she said. "Your blood is sweet with it." She stopped spinning and floated a foot over the little silver saucer, wings beating in a blur as she looked toward the scourgling. "The darkness is at bay. It does not approach."

"The darkness cannot pass the chasm. You're safe here," Alexander said.

The fairy looked back to Alexander. "Why does the King of the small people call upon the fairy folk?"

Alexander was perplexed. Before he fully thought it through, he blurted his question.

"How are we small people when you're only three inches tall?"

"You are small in time, not in stature," she answered without affront.

"You mean you live longer than we do?" Alexander asked.

"Yes. Time is of no consequence to us, but this cannot be the reason for your summoning."

Alexander felt a little foolish. He had far more important matters to discuss, and he was indulging his curiosity.

"I'm in need of your help. There's an item of great power trapped in the aether. I need to retrieve it before another does or the world will fall into darkness."

She spun back into a ball of scintillating light and floated another foot higher into the air.

"I cannot help you. I will not. The risk is too great and you are not ready."

"Without your help, many will die."

Alexander felt a shiver of fear race through him. He realized that this was yet another battlefield and he had no idea what the rules were.

"Those many will die anyway." She stopped spinning and gently floated down to eye level again. "Death is the natural end of the small people."

"That's why we need your help so desperately," Isabel said. "We're doomed to die, and for that we love life all the more. There is one who would bring death to many before their time. Please help us stop him."

"I felt him wake," the fairy said. "Darkness follows him with hunger."

"If he retrieves the Sovereign Stone from the aether, then darkness will fill the world," Alexander said.

At mention of the Sovereign Stone, she spun back into a scintillating ball of light. "I have looked at the Stone you speak of. It has great and terrible power. It would be best to leave it where it is."

"I wish we could, but Phane, the one followed by darkness, will not stop until he has it. I have to prevent that," Alexander said. "I know of no way to do that other than with your help."

She stopped spinning and floated close to Alexander. She scrutinized him for a long moment before she went to Isabel and looked at her just as closely. She floated back to the silver saucer and landed facing them. "You ask more than you know. The cost will be great, to both of you."

Alexander felt Isabel squeeze his hand, and he squeezed hers in return.

"We're willing to pay the cost if it will save the future from darkness." Isabel nodded her agreement.

"Very well. Both of you must come to our home in the Pinnacles and stand before the Fairy Queen. She will decide." With that the fairy spun back into a scintillating ball of light—then she was gone, leaving them sitting in the dark of night.

Alexander and Isabel walked silently back to their quarters, still holding hands.

"What's wrong?" she asked.

"I'm just wondering about the price. I hope we can afford it."

"Whatever it is, we have to." She stopped and turned Alexander toward her. "You said it yourself: If Phane gets the Stone, everything is lost. What price is too high?"

He shook his head slowly; he couldn't bear to put words to the price he feared.

"Alexander, tonight was a triumph. You'll see." She stood on her toes and kissed him, and for a long, blissful moment, he lost his ability to focus on anything else.

CHAPTER 7

He slept fitfully and woke with a start just before dawn. He dreamt he was standing in Mason Kallentera's workshop, talking with the court wizard of Glen Morillian. Mason told him that a force of ten thousand Rangers would leave for New Ruatha in two days' time.

After several moments of pondering the strange dream, Alexander realized it was a dream-whisper spell. He rose with a renewed sense of purpose; his plans were progressing. Unfortunately, all he could do for the moment was explore the Keep and make preparations for a journey to the Pinnacles.

He realized with sudden dismay that he would have to leave his army on the eve of its first battle. They would be looking to him to lead and he would be absent. He needed a general he could count on, a man he could trust.

The Rangers had set up a large conference room as the royal dining hall. All of Alexander's friends and all of the wizards sat around the table finishing breakfast when Alexander broached the subject.

"Isabel and I have to leave as soon as the scourgling is contained. Anatoly, I need you to take command of the army and lead the battle against Headwater."

Anatoly looked up sharply and met Alexander's eyes. "No," he said firmly and went back to his breakfast.

"Anatoly, I need someone I trust," Alexander said, trying to sound reasonable.

"I agree," Anatoly said. "Find someone else. My place is beside you." Alexander opened his mouth to protest, but Anatoly cut him off with a look that Alexander had seen many times under the tutelage of the old man-at-arms. "Your father, my best friend, charged me with protecting you and your sister. I will not fail him."

Alexander took a deep breath. "Then who do you suggest?"

"General Markos is a capable man," Anatoly offered.

"I don't know General Markos," Alexander said. "I need someone I can count on absolutely."

Abigail interrupted. "You don't have to decide immediately. Maybe time will present you with a better choice."

"Maybe," Alexander said. "But I'm worried about what my absence will do to the morale of the soldiers. This will be their first battle. They need a leader to rally around, and I can't be there."

Jack cleared his throat gently. "Am I correct in assuming that you mean to go to the Pinnacles to find the Fairy Queen?"

Alexander nodded. "The Sovereign Stone has to be the first priority. Unless someone has another way, I have to go to the Valley of the Fairy Queen to get the Stone—and the sooner the better. As it stands, Phane could reach the Reishi Keep within a few days. If he can't make the powersink work, he'll start looking for an alternative. The day he finds one is the day we lose."

"Perhaps I can be of assistance in this matter," Jack said. "I can work up a story to circulate through the troops that will both alleviate their discontent over your absence and present the enemy with a false trail to chase."

"What do you have in mind?" Alexander asked.

"In truth, I'm not quite sure of the specifics, but I'm very certain that the less Phane learns about your true plans the better. I can create a false story about a mission vital to the success of our cause that only you can accomplish. I'll have to think on the details a bit though. I need something you're going after that's important enough for you to leave your army. I would welcome any suggestions."

"The third Bloodvault is important," Kelvin mused.

Lucky nodded. "Especially if we had reason to believe that it contained the secret of Wizard's Dust."

Jack smiled like the sunshine. "That will do nicely. The means of disseminating this story is vitally important. The public story must be that Lord Alexander has departed on a secret mission that may hold the key to victory. Only a select few know of his purpose and destination. At the same time, we carefully leak the false story and a destination that will lead our enemies far afield. My experience with large groups is that rumors spread faster than wildfire."

"I like your idea, Jack, but I'm still left without a viable general," Alexander said.

"I see wisdom in Abigail's advice," Jack said. "Time will present you with the right person for the job."

"I hope you're right; things could go very badly without the right leadership."

After breakfast, Alexander and Isabel headed out to explore the Keep. Many wizards had requested Kelvin's assistance with various items and rooms within the Hall of Magic so he didn't join them. He was the foremost expert on the discipline of magical enchantment, and they had discovered rooms full of items that he was uniquely qualified to identify.

Anatoly caught up with Alexander and Isabel at the entrance to the Keep.

"Alexander, I hope you aren't too angry with me for defying you, but you must understand that my first duty is to protect you. Besides, I've never led an army before, so you would do well to find another."

Alexander appraised his old mentor for a moment. "I understand your position, but I still need a general. There's no one I trust to get the job done more than you. Hopefully, another will present himself in time."

"For today, may I join you?" Anatoly asked.

"Glad to have you along," Alexander said. "We saw a platform yesterday that rises up above the rest of the Keep on the south side, and I want to take a look at it."

The Keep was as empty as always until they reached the Hall of Magic, where they started seeing a few people here and there. Each wizard had a couple of Rangers to help with exploring and cataloging the contents of the Keep. Alexander led the way to the end of the long hall, and with a thought, he opened the door to the base of the central tower. He was becoming accustomed to the power of the Keep Master's ring and was beginning to see the Keep itself like an extension of his own mind and body.

He led the way past the sentinel and up through the central tower until they reached the balcony level that led to the two sky bridges. He opened the door to the long arching pathway that led to the giant platform and stepped out into the sky. The views of the Keep were spectacular from the bridge. They could see towers and spires rising high above them and hundreds of grandly constructed buildings covering the surface below. The place was truly a city of vast and magnificent complexity. Alexander still found wonders at every turn. He hoped the platform wouldn't be an exception.

Where the bridge met the edge of the giant platform, the stone melded together as if it were all cut from the same giant block. The platform's surface was made of the same ubiquitous black granite as the rest of the mountain and it was smooth and level. The edges had no railing or even a curb, and the fall was hundreds of feet to the buildings below. Aside from multiple towers rising up into the sky, this was the highest place on the mountain.

"What do you suppose this was used for?" Alexander asked.

"It might have been an assembly area," Anatoly said. "But I'm not sure why they would have picked the highest part of the Keep to assemble their troops."

They spent a few minutes walking around on the huge platform before they found an open area. As they drew closer, they discovered that it was at least a hundred-foot square cut into the surface. The floor below was over a hundred feet down. A staircase led from the top, down along one wall, around the corner and down to the floor.

They descended with caution and curiosity. Once they were outside the field of sunlight that fell through the opening, Alexander took his vial of night-wisp dust from its tube and held it high as they made their way into the dark, giant chamber. They found huge stalls, one after the other, lining corridors easily a hundred feet wide and almost as tall. In the first stall was another hole leading down to another level. Alexander made a note to come back and inspect that area later.

They pressed on into the darkness and found that most of the place was nearly empty. The floors of each stall were littered with the desiccated remains of some form of structures, but from what little was left, it was nearly impossible to determine what had once been there. They found an occasional bone from a cow or a horse and sometimes a deer or an elk, but those bones were old and brittle from centuries of exposure.

When they reached the far end of the long corridor, they discovered a second giant passage leading down to the level below. Around the corner was another passage up to the platform above. They took the stairs down and found that the south end of the second level was open to the sky.

Light poured in, making it easier to explore the nearby stalls. In the first stall, Alexander saw the shape of something that caught his imagination, and he pulled it from the decayed debris. It looked like a giant scale nearly two feet long and a foot and a half wide and reddish brown in color. It was lightweight, yet strong. The outer surface flaked away easily, but the core of the scale was intact and looked like reddish-black metal. With a jolt of excitement and awe, Alexander knew what used to live here.

"Dragons," he whispered as a chill raced through him.

Anatoly and Isabel looked at him, and he offered them a look at the metal that was at the core of the scale. Their eyes grew wide at the truth of Alexander's statement. He pulled up his tunic to look at the dragon-scale chain shirt he wore underneath. The color and quality of the metal was identical to the core of the giant scale that he held.

"Kelvin will want to see this," Alexander said excitedly. "We'll have to find another way to the paddock that doesn't involve the central tower. I want to keep that off-limits for the time being, but we need to get some Rangers up here to search for more scales."

They made their way back down another long, wide corridor looking into each stall with renewed interest. Now that they knew what they were looking for, they discovered many more dragon scales and even a tooth. It was like wandering through a childhood fantasy.

They returned the way they came with one scale each and the tooth.

Alexander sealed the central tower and started walking briskly down the Hall of Magic, calling out to the first person he saw. It was Mage Landi, who had teamed up with Jack and Abigail to explore a secondary corridor off the main hall.

"Have you seen Kelvin?" Alexander asked from a distance.

"In fact, we were just going to see if we could find him," Landi said. "We've made a rather remarkable discovery that I believe he'll want to see."

Abigail was bubbling with excitement. "It's a workshop like nothing I've ever seen before. There are smithies and foundries and tools for hundreds of workmen, with all the raw stock of iron, lead, and copper we could ever use."

Alexander, Isabel, and Anatoly smiled with excitement of their own as they each held up a dragon scale.

Isabel giggled at their looks of astonishment. "We found dragon scales. Hundreds of dragons used to live in the Keep. There are lots more where we found these."

"Mage Gamaliel will be doubly pleased," Landi said. "Come, I believe he's helping Lucky identify a few items in his new laboratory."

They entered a large room with a high ceiling to find Lucky looking around with a wistful expression of simple happiness and Kelvin holding a rectangular box of carved bone in both hands with his eyes closed. He was chanting softly under his breath.

The room was in a state of ordered disarray, much like Lucky's smaller workroom back at Valentine Manor. It was clearly the alchemical workshop he had claimed as his own, and it was obvious from the clean surfaces that he had done a lot of work to make the place usable. It was filled with tables at odd angles, each one covered with boxes, books, or arrangements of glassware. Some looked like they hadn't been used for thousands of years, but a couple were clean and looked like they had just been set up. One was busy bubbling and sputtering with three small burners powering the apparatus.

Lucky motioned for silence when they entered, and he waved them over. Kelvin was deep in concentration, and Lucky clearly didn't want him to be disturbed during the casting of his spell. His eyes widened and he smiled with pure joy when he saw the scales they each carried. It was all they could do to wait for Kelvin to finish his identification spell. When he opened his eyes, they were standing in front of him holding up their treasures.

Excitement danced in his eyes from the knowledge of the identification spell, but when he saw the scales, his look of surprise and wonder made everyone laugh.

He took the scale from Alexander with gentle, almost tender, reverence and inspected the metal at its core. "Blackstone Keep does not disappoint. I've often dreamt of exploring this place but I never dared to hope for such profound discoveries."

"There's a lot more where these came from," Alexander said. "I also found a tooth." He held up the sharp, spike-like tooth. It was six inches long, thin, and as white as bleached bone.

Mage Landi smiled. "It seems that our discovery of the entire hall of workshops is the least of today's finds."

Kelvin laughed. "I doubt that very much. A good workspace and the proper tools are the foundation of magical creation." He carefully set the scale down and picked up the little bone box he had been inspecting. "However, this may be the crown jewel of the day."

He spoke a string of words in an old language and the lid popped open to reveal seven narrow little vials of glowing white dust as pure as fresh snow. Each was only a couple of inches long and less than half an inch in diameter, but the contents was priceless.

"Wizard's Dust!" Mage Landi and Lucky said in unison.

"Indeed. And there's enough here for seven new wizards," Kelvin said. "I have not mentored an apprentice through the mana fast in eleven years, yet I have a dozen men ready for the trials."

Mage Landi spoke cautiously, "Perhaps you should consider taking the mage's fast. I realize it would consume all seven vials, but an arch mage may serve our cause better than seven novices."

Kelvin shook his head. "I briefly considered that. Without an arch mage to act as my mentor, I would risk death. And my services, such as they are, are needed. Seven new wizards will be of greater value in the long run anyway."

Both of the mages looked to Alexander. "Mage Gamaliel, I trust your judgment. Do what you think is best."

"I'll send word for the apprentices as soon as we eliminate the threat of the scourgling," Kelvin said. "For now, we should make plans to collect all of the dragon scales and have them brought to the workshops. I can use them to make powerful armor and weapons for the soldiers of our army."

CHAPTER 8

The next six days were spent working.

They found five levels in the dragon's aerie, each with room for a hundred dragons to make their home. There were also human barracks on each level, presumably for quartering handlers or possibly even dragon riders. A dozen Rangers set up a small outpost at the aerie and worked tirelessly in search of scales and teeth. They found a route that could accommodate horses and they cobbled together a small cart to haul the scales back to the workshops in the Hall of Magic.

Lucky spent the majority of his time preparing potions for the journey to the Pinnacles. He found a number of important ingredients that were still viable sealed in magically preserved containers. With the abundant glassware of his new workshop, he was able to keep a dozen potions cooking at a time. When Alexander poked his head in on him, Lucky was happily working away at one project or another. He had even set up one of his tables as a small kitchen and always seemed to have a pot of something to eat simmering over a burner.

Alexander spent some time studying the Keep Master's book and made a number of important discoveries about Blackstone Keep. The shields protecting it also served to prevent enemies from using spells like clairvoyance to view inside the Keep or to enter the Keep through magical means. The bridge platform was the closest they could get.

He also discovered that the Keep had a number of platforms that were meant to serve as wizard-powered weapons positions. They tapped into a wizard's connection with the firmament, expanding the link while shielding the wizard's mind from the temptation of limitless creation, then assisted him in vividly visualizing a powerful magical attack that could reach to the plains below.

There were two such positions near the bridge platform and three more, one each on the north, south, and east points of the Keep. Alexander went to one of the west positions overlooking the bridge platform with Kelvin and attempted to activate the weapon but discovered that he needed to establish a conscious connection with the firmament in order to make it work. He could only touch the firmament during deep meditation—but Kelvin had no trouble making it work.

The platform was a simple half-circle balcony that jutted out from the wall of the Keep and looked down on the bridge platform and the plains. The balcony was bordered by a low wall with a pillar in the center extending a foot above the height of the wall.

Kelvin placed a hand on each handprint carved into the top of the wall to either side of the small pillar and established a connection with the firmament. Moments later a burst of white-hot magical fire sprang forth from the top stone of the pillar and stabbed down toward the scourgling. It hit the beast full in the chest, knocked it over backward in a somersault, and sent it tumbling across the platform. Alexander was elated with the power of the weapon but dismayed when the scourgling bounded to its feet and loped back to its position at the edge of the abutment. At least they had a way to defend against most enemies.

The Keep Master's book also spoke of the lower levels of the Keep. There were places deep below the more commonly used areas that were shielded against all but those of arch mage power. The book was evasive about the contents of those levels but stressed both the raw power and the profound danger of the things to be found in those dark places. Alexander was happy to find that the central tower was the only way to access the lower levels. He sealed it closed, posted the sentinel as guard, and declared it off-limits.

Isabel reported that she'd been watching the construction of the scourgling's prison through Slyder's eyes and it was nearly finished. They'd made preparations for their journey, and Alexander was anxious to be on their way.

He was worried about the Sovereign Stone, so he sought out Wizard Ely to ask if he had any way of telling if Phane had succeeded in retrieving it. Ely gave it some thought and study before he agreed to cast a divination spell designed to answer one question with a yes or no answer. He cast the spell twice.

First he asked, "Has Phane attempted to use the powersink in the Reishi Keep to retrieve the Sovereign Stone?" The answer was yes.

Alexander felt tingling dread push at the edges of his mind while he waited for the wizard to cast the spell a second time.

Second he asked, "Does Phane have the Sovereign Stone?" The answer was no.

Alexander felt a great weight lift at hearing the news. He still had a chance to retrieve the Sovereign Stone and put it permanently out of Phane's reach.

***

Seven days after Wizard Sark had left, the Rangers standing sentry at the bridge summoned Alexander. When he arrived, he saw another wizard on the bridge platform watching the scourgling warily.

"That's Wizard Jahoda," Kelvin said as he came up alongside Alexander. "It appears that the trap is set. We need to coordinate our plan to ensure success. Can you have Isabel send her hawk with a message?"

"Of course. Let's go find her," Alexander said.

Kelvin waved acknowledgement to Jahoda, who waved back before disappearing down the mountain road.

Half an hour later, Slyder returned with a message from Jahoda. It said: "The trap is set. All that is required is the bait."

Isabel looked stricken when she read the note. She handed it to Alexander with a hard look. "You knew you would be the bait all along, didn't you?"

He nodded somberly. "I'm the one the demon was sent to kill. It won't go anywhere except toward me."

Her green eyes flashed with anger. "What if the trap doesn't work?"

"It'll work. It has to," Alexander said, taking her in his arms.

"Alexander, it's too big a risk," she whispered.

"There is no other way. We can't stay here and fight this war at the same time. As long as the scourgling is at our gates, we're trapped. We already know we can't kill it, and there's no one here who knows how to send it back to the netherworld, so the only choice we have left is to contain it. And I'm the only one who can lure it into our trap."

Kelvin interjected gently, "Lady Isabel, if there were another way, I would offer it, but I know of none."

She looked up at Alexander with a touch of frantic fear in her beautiful green eyes. It made his heart hurt to see her like this, but he knew this was the only way. And deep down, he also knew that she understood.

"The pieces are in place. How do I get down there without going through the scourgling?" Alexander asked.

"I believe Lucky has what we need," Kelvin said. "I requested that he prepare a featherlite potion. It will reproduce the spell that Wizard Sark used to get to the ground."

They found Jack, Abigail, and Anatoly in Lucky's new lab, helping him clean and organize the place to his liking.

Abigail took one look at Isabel and turned to her brother. "So you're the bait then?"

He nodded without a word.

"I was afraid of that," Anatoly said.

"Wizard Jahoda is well trained," Lucky said. "He will have constructed a very sturdy trap for the scourgling. In any event, I have prepared a number of items for you, just in case things don't go as well as planned."

He went to a cupboard and got a set of four vials in a little wire rack and placed them on a table in front of Alexander. "The first is the featherlite potion that Kelvin asked for. The second is a potion of obscuring. A moment after you consume it, your appearance and the basic essence of your nature will be temporarily obscured. For about an hour, no one will recognize you for who you really are, not even the scourgling. If the trap fails to contain it, consume this potion and run for the Keep with all possible speed. The final two are familiar to you. One is a potion of healing and the other is a jar of healing salve."

"Thank you, Lucky. You're always thinking ahead," Alexander said before he turned to Isabel. "Feel better about this now?"

"A little," she said, giving Alexander a very direct look. "Promise you'll come back to me."

Alexander brushed her cheek with the back of his fingers and smiled. "I promise," he whispered.

Then he turned to everyone else and said, "Once the scourgling is contained, I'll lead half the army up here. It's liable to be a long day getting all of those soldiers into the Keep and finding quarters for them. I'm going to station the rest on the plains below for now. I'm not sure at the moment where they'll do the most good, but I suspect they'll be of more use in battle with Headwater than exploring the Keep. Let's go make the final preparations."

He went to his quarters to get his potion pouch and then headed to the bridge abutment. The scourgling stood stone-still across the chasm, waiting for an opportunity to kill him. It would have its chance today—hopefully the last chance it would ever get. Alexander could see Wizard Jahoda's magical platform on the plain below.

Pointing to a place off to the north of the bridge platform, he said, "I need a squad of men and a horse waiting for me at that position. Wizard Jahoda needs to be at the trap and ready to activate the spell when I arrive. Have him send the soldiers with my horse from there once he's ready," Alexander said.

Jack was writing quickly. "Anything else?" he asked. When Alexander shook his head, Jack tore the note from his tablet and handed it to Isabel. She fastened the note to Slyder's leg and sent him off to find Jahoda.

Kelvin sent two of his wizards to man the weapon positions overlooking the bridge platform. They had all taken a turn familiarizing themselves with the magical weapons using the scourgling for target practice.

Time passed slowly, and then the squad of soldiers came into view far down on the plain below.

Isabel opened her eyes and looked at Alexander. "Your horse is in position and Jahoda is ready."

"I guess it's time," Alexander said as he took the featherlite potion from his pouch.

Isabel stopped him. "I love you," she said softly before she kissed him.

"I'll be right back. I promise," Alexander said before he quaffed the potion. "So how do I do this?"

Lucky smiled with a shrug. "Step off into the sky and think of where you wish to fall. The potion will guide you there and slow your descent when you get close to the ground. You'll land just like you jumped off a table."

"All right then, Kelvin, signal your wizards," Alexander said.

Kelvin blew an old-looking battle horn one time. A moment later, argent-white bolts of energy arced from each of the weapon positions and found their mark on the chest of the scourgling. It tumbled backward and rolled twenty feet across the platform. The moment it gained its feet, two more blasts of searing-hot magical energy lanced out and knocked it back farther still.

Alexander gave Isabel one last look and stepped off the bridge abutment into the open sky. It was a terrifying feeling. He fell like a rock. For a second he was afraid he would hit the wall of the Keep, but then he remembered Lucky telling him to think of where he wanted to go. He looked at the small squad waiting for him below and focused on that place.

His fall began to gently arc away from the mountainside and his free fall transformed into more of a glide. He was still moving faster than he had ever moved before, with the exception of his time in the firmament—nothing was faster than that. He passed the level of the spur road as his controlled fall carried him away from the Keep. The ground rushed toward him with alarming speed and then he felt a sudden lightness overtake him and he slowed. He hit the ground in a headlong run, stumbling for a few steps to keep his footing. He was only a hundred feet from the dozen soldiers sent to escort him to the trap, and they were coming fast. They reined in and Alexander recognized the squad leader.

"Captain Sava, it's good to see you again."

The soldier puffed up a bit at being recognized by name. "It's my honor, Lord Alexander," he said. "I understand we have an enemy coming for you."

Before Alexander could answer the question, one of the other soldiers called out and pointed. All eyes followed his finger and saw the scourgling in free fall. It hit the west side of the mountain and bounced out again into the open sky.

Alexander took his horse's reins and mounted in a hurry. "Easy girl, I need your speed today," he whispered to the healthy and strong-looking mare, then he turned to Captain Sava. "Lead the way with all possible speed."

The captain gave a curt nod, wheeled his horse around and bolted in the direction of the trap. They ran with abandon driven by fear and need. The horses could sense something dark behind them even though the only noise the scourgling made was the thud thud thud of its long loping strides. Alexander glanced back and saw how close the beast was and spurred his horse to run faster still.

He heard the scream of a horse and the terrified cry of its rider when the scourgling swatted the animal on the rump with one great clawed hand. Alexander glanced back and saw the beast stumble over the fallen horse and fall headlong onto the ground. A moment later, it bounded to its feet and renewed its pursuit.

Alexander raced toward the platform. It was a stone square, thirty feet in diameter and bordered by walls on two opposite sides. The magic circle was inlaid in gold and it nearly touched each edge of the platform. From his direction of approach, Alexander could run between the two walls, forcing the scourgling to follow him across the circle. Wizard Jahoda was standing in the far corner, waiting to spring the trap.

Alexander heard another horse go down behind him and his own steed poured panic into her gallop and added another step of speed. He leaned into her neck and whispered reassurance and encouragement. She ran like the wind. Another horse squealed in shock and pain as it crumpled from a swat on the rump by the netherworld beast. His soldiers were placing themselves between him and the beast to slow its approach. Alexander felt a mixture of pride, horror, and sadness at their sacrifice.

He rode on, straining to hear the footfalls of the monster behind him. Another horse fell with a horrible, sickening cacophony of breaking bone, rending flesh, and shrieks of fear.

Alexander hit the platform and rode across it with every bit of speed his terrified steed could muster—but it wasn't enough. Midway across the circle, the scourgling swatted Alexander's horse on the right hindquarter. Its huge clawed hand tore through the animal's flesh to the bone and the horse pitched sideways. Alexander flew out of the saddle and sailed through the air with the broken mass of horse tumbling after him. He hit the hard stone, tucked into a tight ball, and rolled. The momentum of the roll brought him to his feet—just the way Anatoly had taught him during his hand-to-hand training so many years ago.

He didn't look back. He didn't stop. He didn't hesitate. The moment he came to his feet, he sprinted the last three steps toward the edge of the magical circle. A step from it, he felt a huge blow fall on his left shoulder blade that drove him tumbling to the ground. He tucked and rolled clear of the platform and onto the grass of the plain, but this time he didn't come to his feet. He could feel the broken bones in his shoulder. If the trap didn't work, he was going to die very soon.

The scourgling barreled forward. Jahoda pronounced a word of power, and the netherworld beast crashed into an invisible barrier like a bird into a window. It rebounded and tried again, but the magical circle held.

The trap had worked. The scourgling was contained and the siege of Blackstone Keep was lifted.

Alexander fished around in his pouch for his potion of healing. Captain Sava and Wizard Jahoda came to his side.

"Don't move, Lord Alexander. I'll send for a wagon to take you to our camp," Captain Sava said.

"It appears that the magical circle is holding. Lie still while help is summoned," Jahoda said.

Alexander drank the potion and smiled up at the wizard. "Pleasure to meet you, Wizard Jahoda. I'm going to take a nap for a while. Tell them not to move me until I wake."

***

Alexander woke to a small army assembled around him. All of his friends, including Kelvin and Erik, were present. The scourgling stood at the edge of the circle and watched Alexander impassively as if it were waiting to be released so it could complete its task, but not really caring if it did or not.

Isabel was sitting next to him, looking at him with love and worry.

"Am I going to live?" he asked groggily.

She smiled down at him as a tear slipped from her eye. She hastily brushed it away.

"I believe you will," Lucky said. "But I'm afraid you'll have to wait a couple of days before you set out on your journey. Your shoulder was badly broken and will take some time and a bit more magical attention to mend properly. Be thankful for Kelvin's armored shirt. Without it you would have lost your arm at the shoulder and probably your life from loss of blood."

They helped him into the back of a wagon and Lucky gave him another potion of healing. He drifted into a dreamless sleep and woke after full dark. His shoulder was feeling a bit better but it was still stiff and sore. Isabel and Abigail both sat up when he woke. His sister handed him a cup of water and Isabel got him a bowl of stew from a pot on the small campfire just outside the tent.

"Lucky said you'd be hungry when you woke," Isabel said. "How are you feeling?"

"Well enough, considering," he answered. With a sudden jolt, he remembered the soldiers who had ridden with him. "How many died?" he asked.

"Three dead," Abigail said. "And two badly hurt. Lucky tended to their wounds and says they'll recover, but both were injured more seriously than you, so it might take some time."

"I need to speak with Captain Sava," Alexander said, trying to get up.

Abigail stopped him with a gentle hand on his good shoulder. "Alexander, you're not going anywhere. Lucky said you're supposed to rest and that's what you're going to do."

"Your sister's right, Alexander. Besides, it's the middle of the night. Captain Sava is probably asleep. You can talk to him in the morning."

Alexander relaxed back onto his cot. "I guess it can wait. Has the army started moving into the Keep?"

"Not yet," Abigail said. "Kelvin said you would want to be there when they cross the bridge, so he's ordered Mage Landi to secure the Keep until you return."

"Good. I want to look at each and every person who goes into Blackstone Keep to make sure there aren't any spies or infiltrators."

"All of that can wait until tomorrow," Isabel said. "Finish your stew and go back to sleep. Everything will still be here in the morning."

CHAPTER 9

He woke just after dawn. His shoulder was stiff and it hurt, but the magic Lucky had given him had mostly mended the broken bones. He got up and found Abigail and Isabel sipping hot tea by the fire in front of the tent. Abigail poured him a cup when he emerged with is arm in a sling.

A cordon of solders stood guard around his tent, which was pitched in a wide open space in the center of the entire encampment with hundreds of other tents arranged in neat clusters. Alexander looked around and saw that Captain Sava was one of the guards standing in the circle around him. He waved the man over to the fire and motioned for him to sit.

"Captain Sava, please convey my condolences to the families of the three men who died yesterday. They died protecting me and I will never forget that."

"I'll see to it personally, Lord Alexander," Captain Sava said. He looked a bit startled when Isabel handed him a steaming cup of tea.

"Can you tell me how the two injured men are doing?" Alexander asked.

Captain Sava nodded. "I looked in on them early this morning. Both were sleeping soundly and looked to be on the mend. Master Alabrand gave them powerful magic and said they would both be well enough to ride in a week or so."

"That's good to hear," Alexander said. "I wanted to thank you and your men for your help yesterday. I underestimated the power of the scourgling. If it weren't for you and your men, I probably would have died."

Captain Sava sat up straight. "Thank you, Lord Alexander. We're proud to play our part."

"Tell me about the three men who died," Alexander said quietly. "I'd like to know a little bit about them."

Captain Sava looked surprised for just a moment. He nodded self-consciously before recounting his friendship and service with the men. Alexander listened quietly and let the knowledge burn into him.

Three men died on his order.

He made a quiet pledge to himself that he would never forget them even though he never even knew them. He and the captain talked for several minutes before Jack, Lucky, Kelvin, and Anatoly came up to the fire.

"How's the shoulder feeling?" Lucky asked.

"Much better, but it's still a little stiff."

"It'll take a few days to get your full range of motion back. The less you use it, the faster it will heal, so I recommend you keep it in that sling—at least for today," Lucky advised.

Alexander nodded his agreement. It still hurt and he knew it would be counterproductive to push himself. He was anxious to be on his way to the Pinnacles, but the fastest way to get on the road was to let his shoulder heal.

"I'd like to address the officers and a few of the men and then speak with the commanding officer before we return to the Keep," Alexander said.

Captain Sava stood. "I'll relay your orders to Commander Perry right away."

"Thank you, Captain."

Alexander tried to get up, but Isabel said, "Just relax for a few minutes and have some breakfast."

"Breakfast?" Lucky said with an unabashed smile.

They ate hot porridge with nuts, dried berries, cream and honey. It was hearty and filling, and Alexander felt much better for having taken the time to eat.

When Alexander was ready, Captain Sava led him through a throng of soldiers to a wagon in the middle of the crowd. He carefully climbed up onto the wagon, and the murmuring of the soldiers died quickly as all eyes turned toward him. He looked around and appraised the men for a long moment before he drew the Thinblade and held it aloft for all to see. There was a moment of silence, then the soldiers erupted with a thunderous cheer.

He sheathed his sword and motioned for quiet. "Soldiers of Ruatha, yesterday we lost three of our own to the enemy. They died protecting me. I ask that you remember them and their families in your prayers."

The soldiers fell deadly silent and all heads bowed in respect for their fallen. Alexander waited a moment before he continued.

"Headwater is mustering an army to attack New Ruatha as we speak. This will be the first battle of the Reishi War fought on Ruathan soil in two millennia. It will be our first test, and we will prevail because we must. Blackstone Keep is secure and well defended. Some of you will be assigned to garrison the Keep, while others will be assigned to patrol the surrounding area and guard the netherworld beast that Wizard Jahoda has trapped like a bug in a jar. The rest will return to New Ruatha with me to bolster the troops defending the Glittering City.

"Headwater outnumbers our forces by double, but they do not have the strength of the Wizards Guild behind them nor do they have the support of the Rangers of Glen Morillan. Ten thousand light cavalry are on the march from the Forest Warden to add to our forces, with many thousands more being trained and equipped to join us soon.

"Remember the Old Law in the challenging days to come. It is the core of our purpose and we must remain faithful to it. Most of all, remember those that fall for our cause. They have given everything so that we might have a chance at a future worth living."

Alexander stepped down from the wagon, and Captain Sava led him to a tent quickly filling up with officers awaiting his orders.

"Lord Alexander, I am Commander Perry. It is an honor to meet you."

Commander Perry was a tall man with an impeccable uniform. His hair was close-cropped blond and his face was gaunt with deep-set, dark-blue eyes. Alexander looked at his colors and saw a man of discipline and structure who wanted nothing more than to know his place in an ordered world.

"Commander, you have a disciplined and well-ordered force," Alexander said. "Forgive my haste, but time is of the essence. I need you to select two thousand men to garrison the Keep and assist the wizards with its exploration and defense. Next, I need a force of five hundred to set up a fortified encampment at the base of the Keep to control access to the road. Wizard Jahoda will be walling in the scourgling, and once he's finished, I want a hundred good men assigned to guard its prison. Finally, the remainder of your force will be returning to New

Ruatha with me to face the army of Headwater. We'll be leaving tomorrow morning; I'll need a hundred men on horse to serve as my advance party and escort."

Commander Perry smiled almost serenely. He was a man with clear orders and the capability to carry them out. "By your command, My Lord."

"I'm heading back up to the Keep. You may begin sending men up on my heels."

The commander nodded curtly, turned to his officers and began issuing orders. He didn't seem very friendly but he was sure of his place and carried himself with the confidence of a leader.

Captain Sava followed Alexander out of the tent. Alexander noted a dozen men fanned out around him, watching the other soldiers. When he headed for the horse pickets, they all moved with him. Clearly, Sava had taken his assignment to heart. Alexander carefully scrutinized the colors of each man in his new guard force and saw that they were all honorable soldiers who were proud of being entrusted with the safety of their King.

Not twenty minutes later, they were riding up the road that wound around Blackstone Keep, across the spur road, and then up to the top of the bridge platform. Alexander set a moderate pace to protect his shoulder. He could still feel the dull ache and stiffness and didn't want to cause any further delay by pushing himself and injuring it again. Without breaking stride, he brought the invisible bridge back into this world with a flick of his mind. His guard followed behind him in a single file across the long, narrow bridge.

There was a crowd in the paddock waiting for his return. He dismounted and called everyone within earshot to come closer. Once they had gathered, he stepped up on a small mound that used to be the corner post of a corral.

"Within the hour, a force of two thousand soldiers will be coming up that road. They will help in the defense and exploration of the Keep. Welcome them and help them find quarters," Alexander said and then motioned to Erik as he stepped down.

"It's good to see you in one piece, Alexander," Erik said. "I was terrified when that thing jumped off the bridge platform. I never imagined it would do that."

"I have to admit, I didn't expect it either," Alexander said as he guided Erik away from the milling crowd. "Erik, I need you to take command of the Keep garrison. Your primary responsibility will be the security of Blackstone Keep. Defer to the wizards in all things magical and help them explore this place and make it ready to take in more people—possibly a lot more. I hope it won't come to it, but if need be, this Keep will be a refuge for the people of Ruatha against Phane and his minions."

"I understand. Do you really think we'll have to hole up here?" Erik asked.

"I hope not, but I want to be ready just in case," Alexander said. "I know this isn't the kind of battle you had in mind, but it's important."

"Alexander, I've learned a lot in the past few weeks. I saw a lot of good people die, and my fantasies of glory in war died with them. I'll fight if need be, but I understand that the Keep might be the only safe place for our people to go. It'll be ready."

"Good man. Rely on the counsel of the wizards. This is a place of magic first and foremost."

Alexander spent the rest of the day posted at the arch where the bridge met the paddock, welcoming soldiers into Blackstone Keep. He scrutinized the colors of every person to enter and he was glad he did. Over the course of the afternoon, he discovered and detained three spies who were dishonest and evasive when questioned.

During the entire process of vetting each and every person who entered the Keep, there was always a wizard nearby. Captain Sava and his squad were fanned out all around to provide security. Sava didn't ask permission or seek approval for his actions but simply deployed his men as he saw fit to ensure that Alexander was well protected.

Erik and his Rangers choreographed a complicated process of moving soldiers into barracks and assigning quarters and duties. Erik was precise and organized. His Rangers were equally disciplined. The soldiers understood their orders and responded with efficient obedience. By nightfall, all two thousand were in the Keep, the bridge was secure, and the place was bustling with activity.

***

Alexander rubbed healing ointment on his shoulder before going to bed and woke the next morning with anticipation and excitement. He came to the breakfast table wearing his riding gear and carrying his pack, his bow, and a quiver of arrows.

It wasn't long before the table was full. Breakfast was porridge with honey and dried fruit. Once everyone had eaten their fill, Alexander cleared his throat like he'd seen Jack do so many times before. The table fell silent and all eyes turned to him.

"We're going to New Ruatha first. I want to ensure that we have a suitable general to lead the battle with Headwater, and I need to talk to Regent Cery and Wizard Sark for a few minutes. After that, we're going to the Pinnacles. No one outside this room is aware of our real destination and no one must find out. Jack has prepared a rumor that we're headed for some ruins in the highlands near Kai'Gorn to find the third Bloodvault, which we believe contains the secret of Wizard's Dust. Hopefully, that will distract the enemy enough to give us safe passage."

They spent the next two days in the saddle. Alexander got to know Commander Perry a bit better and came to respect the man. He had a precise and ordered mind. He'd been a soldier for his entire adult life and clearly intended to pursue his chosen calling for as long as he could ride.

Once they reached the northern outskirts of New Ruatha, Alexander pointed out a small hill to the northeast of the city. "Commander, I think it would be best if you build a fortified camp there for your forces. The battle lines are probably going to be drawn in the valley to the south and that position will force them to defend their flank while they attempt to advance. Make your camp big; I'll be sending you some more men to bring your regiment back up to strength, and I'll see if Wizard Sark can send you some magical assistance as well."

"Very good, Lord Alexander," Perry said with a crisp salute.

He took a dozen men with him back toward his main force and sent the rest of the advance force to scout the hill. Alexander and his companions continued on into New Ruatha with a dozen men under Captain Sava's command.

Regent Cery met Alexander at the gate to the palace. "Lord Alexander, it's good to see you. The beacons of Blackstone Keep have given the people of New Ruatha hope and our enemies pause." He gestured to the black granite mountain on the northern horizon and the beacon lights that Alexander had activated. Even at this distance, they shined brightly.

Alexander dismounted and shook Regent Cery's hand. "What news of Headwater?"

"They're on the march. Half their force is headed our way while the rest are still being recalled from the outer reaches of the territory. My scouts tell me they will be assembled in time to serve as reserve forces. I recommend we retire to the war room. My generals have maps with enemy positions and strengths. Your father is there as well; he arrived at the head of a column of ten thousand Rangers from Glen Morillian just this afternoon."

Alexander and Abigail shared a look. "By all means, please lead the way."

As they walked through the palace, Alexander was struck by the art, color, and lavish furnishings of the place after spending so much time in the austere and utilitarian halls of Blackstone Keep.

He was happy to see that his father and mother were both in the war room along with Wizard Sark and half a dozen officers, including General Markos. There was a large table with a giant map of the entire territory of New Ruatha and the areas on the periphery.

Bella looked up and smiled with relief and happiness as she rushed to embrace her children. "You're safe," she said, hugging them both tightly at the same time. "I've been so worried, especially since we heard about the scourgling."

Alexander flexed his shoulder a bit at the mention of the netherworld monster. It still hurt but only a little and his range of motion had returned almost completely. "With the help of Wizard Jahoda, we were able to trap the beast in a magical circle. With any luck, it'll stay there until Phane is killed and then it will return to the netherworld."

Duncan approached with a broad smile. "I see you've found your sword, Son. I'm proud of you, proud of you both." He hugged Alexander and Abigail in turn.

"You must be hungry," Bella said. "Come and have something to eat before we get down to business. You'll make better decisions on a full stomach."

Alexander smiled and nodded. His mother had a way of reassuring him like nothing else. He always felt safe and cared for in her presence. They ate a meal and talked of little things. It was a brief respite from the more pressing matters that had been weighing on Alexander for so many days. He took the time to simply enjoy the company of his family and allowed himself the indulgence of forgetting his duty for a few minutes.

CHAPTER 10

All too soon, the meal was over and everyone found a place around the big map table to listen to General Markos brief Alexander on the position and strength of the enemy forces and the friendly forces.

General Markos spoke with precision and care in his presentation. His officers filled in details here and there. In broad terms, a force of fifty thousand enemy soldiers was less than a week away from the outskirts of New Ruatha. Their forces were mostly infantry, with only a couple thousand cavalry and few archers. New Ruatha had thirty thousand infantry, ten thousand archers with ample arrows and well-made longbows and another ten thousand heavy cavalry in addition to the ten thousand Rangers that had just arrived. General Markos expressed confidence in their superiority given the current enemy forces but also expressed concern about the rest of Headwater's army that was being assembled. Once they joined the battle, New Ruatha would be outnumbered nearly two to one.

"Thank you, General," Alexander said. "I believe I can add a small piece to your map. I've ordered Commander Perry to take the hillock here." He pointed to the little hill northeast of New Ruatha that had a commanding view of the valley where the battle was likely to take place. "I've assigned half of his original force to garrison Blackstone Keep, so he'll need additional troops to bring his regiment back up to strength. Please see to it that twenty-five hundred soldiers are dispatched to his command tomorrow morning. Wizard Sark, do you have a wizard you can spare to assist Commander Perry?"

"Of course, I have just the man for the job. He'll depart with the soldiers in the morning," Wizard Sark said.

General Markos nodded. "That's a good position. If we draw our battle lines here in this valley," he pointed at a space just south of the hillock and due east of New Ruatha, "the enemy will have to defend against our front and protect their flank from Commander Perry on the north. The further they advance, the more exposed their flank will become."

"That's my hope. Prepare the valley for battle. Deploy the infantry to form a shield line here, supported by pikes." Alexander traced a line north to south on the map between the Ruatha River and the hill that Commander Perry was busy fortifying. "Assemble the archers and wizards behind the shield line. Deploy half of the heavy cavalry to the north of the hill so we can use it as a flanking force. Their target is the command leadership, any wizards they can find, and the enemy food and water supplies. Hold the remaining heavy cavalry in reserve to serve as a rapid-reaction force and use them to respond to any unexpected enemy movements."

"Where would you like my light cavalry?" Duncan asked.

Alexander appraised his father for a long moment. "I've been giving that some thought. Gentlemen, have any of you commanded men in a large-scale battle before?"

He already knew the answer. The last real war fought anywhere on

Ruatha was the border war between Highlands Reach and Southport on one side and Kai'Gorn on the other. Aside from that there had only been minor skirmishes.

The officers all shook their heads—all except Duncan.

"Father, you commanded a regiment in the border wars. I need that experience now. I'm assigning you as Commanding General of the Ruathan Army. All territorial forces will report to you." Alexander paused for a moment to give his father an opportunity to respond.

Duncan nodded thoughtfully. "Duane is my Second. He's a bit headstrong, but more than capable of leading the legion of cavalry I brought from Glen Morillian." He looked at Alexander a bit suspiciously. "If you want me to command your army, that must mean you have other plans."

Alexander smiled at his insight. He had never been able to hide anything from his father. "I do. I have a vitally important task that can't wait. This battle will be fought without me."

Several of the officers looked at each other a bit nervously.

"I understand that the soldiers are expecting me to lead them, but I must attend to another matter. However, now that I see the lay of the land, I believe I can do a bit of both. Tomorrow we'll go to Duane's position and take his force around to the north and flank the entire enemy army. We'll divide into a hundred war parties and make lightning raids on every weak spot we can find. Hit and run until all of the territories in Headwater are afraid of the mere mention of the Rangers of Glen Morillian. From there, the six of us will leave on our errand, but not before the men see me lead them into battle."

"Lord Alexander," Regent Cery said, "Your presence here will greatly galvanize the soldiers, and I fear that your absence will unravel their resolve. Would it be possible to postpone your errand until this battle is won?"

"No. What I have to do simply can't wait. I'm confident in our forces. We have a sound plan and my father has far more experience than I do at fighting a war."

Alexander looked around the room at each of the faces. "One last thing. Wars are won by attack. If you have the chance to hurt the enemy, take it. Be aggressive and be bold. Let it be known that any who side with Phane will never know a moment of peace from this day forward.

"Regent Cery, please assemble the delegates from the nine territories. I need to speak with them, and then I'd like a secure suite of quarters where I can spend some time with my family and get a good night's sleep."

"Your quarters are already prepared and the delegates await," Regent Cery said with a smile. "I made preparations for your arrival the moment I heard you were on your way."

Alexander and Isabel walked into the council chamber, and the room fell silent. Isabel wore the Medallion of Glen Morillian for all to see, but she didn't take her seat. Instead, she stood beside Alexander as he stepped up behind the chair at the head of the table. He waited until the representative from Headwater started to speak before he drew his sword and slowly pushed it through the table top. He eyed every one of the delegates in turn.

"I am the wielder of the Thinblade, the Master of Blackstone Keep, bearer of the Mark of Cedric, and the rightful King of Ruatha. Deliver this message to those whom you serve. Stand with me and I will count you as my friend. Stand with Phane and your life is forfeit."

He pulled the sword from the table and pointed it at the delegate from Headwater. He was a squat little man with a pot belly, stringy hair combed over a balding pate, and beady eyes that were set too close together for his round face.

"Tell your master that he will survive only if he surrenders immediately and abdicates his authority. Otherwise, I will take his head with my very sharp sword."

Without another word, Alexander sheathed the Thinblade, turned on his heel, and strode from the room. He spent the rest of the evening talking quietly with his parents and friends about everything that had happened since they left Glen Morillian. It had been only about a month, but it seemed like so much longer.

When he told his parents about his plan to go to the Fairy Queen, Bella seemed startled and alarmed but didn't offer any objection. Alexander didn't press her, but her reaction wasn't lost on him either. His mother was a wise woman who had trained with a witch coven in the mountainous forests east of Highlands Reach. He made a note to himself to question her about it before they said their goodbyes tomorrow.

The next morning on their way to the Rangers' encampment, Alexander rode next to his mother. They were quiet for several minutes after they left the city. He knew she was waiting for him to ask her about her reaction to his plan. He thought it over carefully before he began. His mother was very smart, and he had learned from long experience that it was always wise to have his thoughts in order before he started a conversation with her on any subject of importance.

Finally he said, "You were startled to hear my plan to go to the Fairy Queen for help."

She looked at him and nodded, but didn't offer anything more for several minutes. Alexander waited patiently.

"The fairies don't see the world the same way we do. They may ask a price greater than you are willing to pay for their help." She looked over her shoulder at Isabel, and Alexander felt a little flutter of fear settle in his gut.

"What do you mean? And what does Isabel have to do with it?" Alexander asked with more edge to his voice than he wanted.

His mother looked over at him and smiled gently. "You love her." It wasn't a question. "I'm glad you've found someone who brings you joy. She's a strong woman and she clearly loves you. If you go to the Fairy Queen, she will test that love in ways that may break your heart."

"I don't understand." Alexander was starting to worry that he had committed himself to a course of action that would cost him dearly.

"The fairies value love above all else, so their price will almost surely have something to do with love. I don't know what it will be or if it will hurt you or Isabel, but I fear it will." Bella looked at her son with worry and compassion. "I don't know any more than that. The fairies keep to themselves and rarely allow outsiders into their valley. What I've told you I learned from my coven mother during my training."

Alexander was silent for several minutes. He weighed the potential cost and felt the burden of his duty bear down on him without mercy. He loved Isabel more than anything, but he had to stop Phane from getting the Sovereign Stone. If he failed at that, nothing else would matter. He would never have a chance at a life with Isabel. And countless thousands of others would never have a chance to live or love either.

He remembered the summoning. Isabel said she was willing to pay any price. Alexander desperately hoped that it would not be too great a price, but he realized that he had to pay it no matter the cost to him personally. There were so many other lives depending on him.

"Whatever the price, Isabel and I will bear it together," he said.

"I know, Alexander. That's what I'm afraid of." Bella smiled at her son. "You've always been so determined once you make a decision. You're like a force of nature. I knew when you told us your plan that I wouldn't be able to talk you out of it, but it's important that you prepare yourself. The Fairy Queen will test your heart.

"On another matter," Bella continued, "your sister seems to be quite fond of the young bard. What do you think of him? Is he worthy of Abigail?"

Alexander looked at his mother and saw that she was serious. He hadn't really considered the question before. They had traveled together and he knew Abigail and Jack had become close friends, but he hadn't asked his sister how serious her feelings were. But then, his mother was always much more sensitive to such things than he was. When he faced the question, he couldn't help but smile.

"He is. Jack has helped me in many ways. His advice is sound and his knowledge is valuable. He's stood by our side at every step of the way and his colors are clear and strong. But mostly, he makes Abigail laugh and he treats her with respect."

"Good. Lucky said as much when I asked him," Bella said. "Abigail deserves someone who will make her happy." Then she laughed and said, "Anatoly even likes him."

They crested a small rise and saw the Rangers' encampment spread out in neatly organized units below. Isabel spurred her horse into a gallop when she saw her brother. She was off her horse and talking excitedly to Duane when Alexander and the rest of the party rode up. A number of Rangers took their horses to a picket line, and Duane stepped up to him with a crisp salute.

"Lord Alexander, it's good to see you well," Duane said. "I trust Isabel hasn't been too much trouble." He gave his sister a playful look; she poked him in the ribs.

Alexander took his hand. "It's good to see you, too, Duane. How are your parents?"

"Father is busy training soldiers and mother is organizing the distribution of supplies. They both seem to be in their element. In truth, I think they both look years younger now that they have things of importance to focus on."

Alexander smiled. "I'm glad to hear it." He took a deep breath. "Duane, I need to speak with your officers. How quickly can you assemble them?"

Duane gave Duncan a little glance of confusion before answering. "Give me ten minutes." Alexander nodded and Duane strode off, calling out orders.

Alexander stood with his father and Anatoly. Jack was nearby talking with a Ranger about their journey to New Ruatha, and Lucky had wandered over to a cook fire surrounded by another group of Rangers. Bella drew Isabel away to have a private word with her.

Alexander turned to his father and asked, "How ready are the Rangers?"

Duncan frowned. "Not ready enough. Each company has a number of seasoned Rangers, but the majority of them are young and inexperienced. They have heart and they're proficient with their weapons but few have actually been in a fight."

Alexander nodded at the sober assessment. "Is Duane ready to lead the legion?"

"He's as ready as he's going to get," Duncan said. "He has some good officers with long years of experience to rely on and he's well trained. All that's left is the test of battle and that one can't be simulated. If he isn't ready, you'll find out soon enough."

CHAPTER 11

Bella stepped behind a tent with Isabel in tow. "My dear, I need to speak with you about Alexander's plan with the fairies."

Isabel looked at her future mother-in-law with wide eyes. She knew Alexander respected his mother a great deal, so she desperately wanted her approval. The private nature of the conversation had her feeling a little nervous. She nodded for Bella to continue.

"The currency of the fairies is love," Bella said. "I fear that the Fairy Queen will test your love for my son."

"I'll pass her test," Isabel blurted out and then blushed.

Bella smiled and put a reassuring hand on Isabel's arm. "If the test is simply a measure of your love for Alexander, then I believe you will, but it may be more difficult than that. I'm telling you this because I want you to be prepared. My son loves you. I can see it when he looks at you."

"I love him too, Lady Valentine," Isabel said earnestly.

"I know. Hold on to that love. Whatever the Fairy Queen demands, you must keep your love for my son alive in your heart. I don't say this to protect his heart—as much as I want to. I say this because it will be very dangerous for you both and for Alexander's plan if your love for him falters in the presence of the fairies. They would see such a thing as a sign that Alexander is not worthy."

Isabel looked a bit wild-eyed at the prospect that her feelings for Alexander could put him and his plan to save the Seven Isles in jeopardy, but when she searched her soul, she found a calm certainty that reassured her and filled her with confidence.

"I love Alexander and there's nothing in the world that will ever change that," she said with her head held high.

Bella nodded. "My son has chosen well."

They came out from behind the tent just as Alexander was climbing onto a wagon to address the assembled officers. The crowd fell quiet as all eyes turned to their King. He appraised the crowd for a moment before he drew the Thinblade and held it high for all to see. There was a hush, then a murmur, and then a deafening cheer. Alexander sheathed his sword and motioned for silence.

"The war has begun. A force of fifty thousand marches on New Ruatha. The city has adequate defenses in place to repel the attack, but Headwater is mustering another force of equal size. If that force is allowed to join the fight, New Ruatha will be greatly outnumbered."

He paused for a few moments as he assessed the Rangers arrayed before him.

"Your task is to stop Headwater from fielding their second army. You will divide your forces into companies of a hundred Rangers each and move into the lands controlled by Headwater. You will raid their supply trains and depots, assault the small units moving to assemble with the main force, and attack the noble estates that are supplying the food and equipment necessary to support their army.

"Force them to keep their soldiers near Headwater to defend their own homes. Kill what enemy you can, but that is not your primary purpose. You must simply prevent them from sending their second army to New Ruatha. Make them afraid. Hit them hard and fast, then run away before they can muster a counterattack. Bleed them a little at a time. Cut them from the shadows and vanish. Never give them a fair fight. Never stand your ground. Ground means nothing. Lives mean everything.

"Your first standing order is to survive. Do not risk an engagement that you cannot win. Do not attack where they are strong. Use your speed to find the places where they are weak and hit them without mercy. When they send forces to attack you, run away and circle around to take them apart a piece at a time.

"Our purpose is not to prove our valor on the battlefield. We are not here to seek glory in war." Alexander paused and looked down for a moment, remembering those who had died by his command. When he continued, he spoke more quietly, "I used to believe that war was about glory and triumph, but I have since learned that war is about death and pain.

"Make it the enemy's death. Let them suffer the pain. I command you to survive today's battle so that you can fight the battle tomorrow. Then survive tomorrow so you can return to your families. The enemy is fighting for ambition and power. They seek subjugation and plunder. Their cause is small and unworthy. They deserve to lose.

"We fight for the safety of our families. We fight to preserve a world where love and life can thrive. We deserve to win. Prepare your Rangers. We ride in an hour."

In unison, a hundred officers saluted, fist to heart. Duane stepped onto the back of the wagon and began calling out orders. Less than an hour later, the legion of Rangers was moving north to skirt the enemy forces and drive deep into their territory.

Alexander sat on his horse and watched the units moving off across the open plain. "I'll be riding with your company, Duane," he said. "Oh, and you've been promoted. My father will be commanding all of the forces of the Ruathan army, so you're in command of this legion now."

Duane was genuinely surprised. "Thank you for your confidence." He looked like he was about to say more but thought better of it.

***

They rode for nearly a week before they reached the lands governed and protected by Headwater. The legion separated into a hundred companies and each went their separate way according to their assigned areas of operation. Rally points were defined and standing orders were issued.

A day later, Alexander lay on his belly, with Duane on his right and Isabel on his left, looking over the crest of a small hill. Their company of Rangers was mounted and ready to ride but hidden from the road beyond. Scouts had reported that a food convoy was traveling up the road from the estate of a minor noble beholden to Headwater. It was late afternoon and they'd been waiting an hour or so for the supply train to come into sight.

The convoy was a hundred wagons long, packed heavily and moving slowly, with an escort of twenty soldiers on horseback. This would be the first engagement for the company of Rangers, and Alexander was glad to see that the odds were stacked decidedly in his favor.

When they returned to the company, Duane split the force into two units so they could attack from different directions. Several minutes passed, then Isabel opened her eyes, breaking contact with Slyder. She nodded to Alexander and Duane. Alexander gave the command and each unit spurred their horses into a gallop. Alexander led his unit around the front side of the hill to charge directly at the advancing column, while Duane led his unit over the top of the low hill to come at them from the side.

The enemy soldiers saw Alexander first and formed a column of cavalry four wide and five deep. They were armed with heavy spears and shields. Alexander led fifty Rangers in a loose formation. The enemy clearly thought their heavy weapons and larger horses would give them the weight they needed to defeat the lighter armor and smaller horses of the Rangers.

The Rangers fanned out to give the enemy less of a target. The enemy didn't break formation; they charged with raised shields and lowered spears. Alexander drew his sword. It felt light and sure in his hand. He watched the soldiers hurtling toward him, and calm settled into his soul. He was in a fight and he had a blade in his hand—but not just any blade. He held the Thinblade, the Sword of Kings.

The Rangers loosed a volley of arrows. Most were deflected by the enemy's shields but a few found their way to their targets. Abigail drove her arrow straight through the shield of a lead rider and into his chest. The enemy cavalry expertly avoided the fallen in their midst and re-formed into a column.

A moment later a volley of arrows from Duane's unit caught them on the flank and thinned their ranks by half. The column broke under the chaos and the soldiers charged into the larger force of Rangers without the strength of a cohesive formation.

Alexander picked his first target and barreled toward the onrushing soldier. They locked eyes and the enemy raised his shield and his spear in preparation for the strike. By unspoken agreement, they would pass each other on the right. The engagement happened with blinding speed. Alexander slapped the flat of his blade against the haft of the spear to push the point past his shoulder and then swept his blade into the enemy shield. He knew the Thinblade was a thing of wonder and surpassing power, but he was shocked at how terrifying that power actually was in a fight.

His blade hit the face of the enemy shield and sliced through it at a diagonal angle, cleaving the soldier's arm off between the elbow and wrist. Then it caught the soldier across the chest and cleaved him cleanly in half. His arms came free as the blade passed through him like a sharp knife through paper. He came apart in a spray of blood, pieces of his body thudding to the ground one after the other.

The soldier behind him watched the spectacle in terror and surprise. He was so shocked by what he'd just witnessed that he was unable to make a clean strike with his spear. Alexander leaned over the neck of his horse and the second enemy spear passed just inches over his back. The moment the tip passed, he sat up and swept his blade back toward the enemy and cleaved his head off with a single stroke.

The charge faltered and the next enemy Alexander faced didn't have much momentum behind him. He moved in on horseback and expertly jabbed at Alexander with his long spear. The point glanced off Alexander's dragon-steel chainmail and tore his shirt. He flicked the Thinblade through the haft of the spear and took off the first three feet, then spurred his horse forward and thrust through the enemy's shield and into his heart.

He turned to see a spearman intent on running him through topple off his horse from a clean stroke by Anatoly's war axe. The battle was over as suddenly as it had begun. A few of the Rangers sustained injuries but none were lost in the fight. The enemy soldiers were dead to the last man, most with arrows sticking out of them. Duane set to work rounding up the men driving the wagons and securing the horses of the fallen soldiers. Lucky tended to the wounded Rangers, and Isabel scouted the horizon through Slyder's eyes for any additional threat.

Alexander stood before the group of teamsters. They were unarmed and looked like simple workmen. They had fear in their eyes.

"Who will speak for you?" Alexander asked.

There were several nervous moments of silence before a burly man with grey hair raised his hand.

"Very good. Stand up and tell me your name," Alexander commanded.

The man stood. He was shorter than Alexander but outweighed him and had broad shoulders and a barrel chest. "I'm called Arlo," he said nervously.

"Hello, Arlo. My name is Alexander. I am the King of Ruatha." The man's eyes widened. "Headwater is making war on New Ruatha and I've come to see to it that Headwater loses."

"Lord Alexander, I'm just a teamster," Arlo said. "I drive a wagon to support my family. I don't want no part of any war but I have to do what the Teamsters Guild tells me or I'll lose my chit."

"What do you mean you'll lose your chit?" Alexander asked with a frown of confusion.

"Elred Rake, Master of Headwater, has decreed that no man with a skilled trade can work unless he belongs to a trade guild. If I don't do as I'm told by the guild, they'll take my chit away from me and no one will hire me to drive their wagons." He held up a copper coin with a horse stamped in the face of it. "I need my job. Guild jobs are the only ones that pay well enough to feed my family." The men all around nodded in agreement. A few held up similar copper coins.

"Elred Rake won't be running Headwater for very long." Alexander drew his sword and held it so the men could get a good look at it. There were murmurs and gasps from the crowd. "People have the right to do whatever work they can get so long as they obey the Old Law. As for you men, I have no desire to harm you, but these supplies are meant to feed the soldiers advancing on New Ruatha. I'm curious, where exactly were you taking these wagons?"

Arlo hesitated. "If I tell you that, I'll be killed by Rake for sure."

Alexander pointed the Thinblade at him in silent threat. The man started trembling.

"Please don't kill me, Lord Alexander. I have kids that need me," Arlo begged as he fell to his knees.

Alexander lowered the blade and spoke more softly. "Arlo, I don't want to hurt you, but I need to know where these supplies were being taken. You are serving a master who is waging war against the Old Law. He's serving the interests of Prince Phane. I'm trying to protect the people of this island against the suffering that will engulf us all if Phane wins. You have a choice to make. You can side with me and serve the Old Law and the cause of life or you can choose to serve Elred Rake and Prince Phane. There is no middle ground. And Arlo, as much as it pains me, I will kill you if you choose to serve my enemy; then I will make one of your fellow teamsters kneel over your corpse and I will ask him where you intended to take your cargo. I'll have the answer to my question—but you'll still be dead."

Another man stood up. "Lord Alexander, my name is Bradley. Please don't kill him, he has a family he's trying to protect. If he tells you what you want to know, Rake will hurt his kids and make him watch."

"Sounds like Elred Rake isn't very well liked," Anatoly observed. Many of the men nodded their heads.

"What do you propose, Bradley?" Alexander asked.

"I'll tell you what you want to know on two conditions." Bradley looked nervous and afraid, but he held his ground and didn't waver from Alexander's glittering gaze.

"What are your conditions?" Alexander asked with a hint of menace in his voice.

"Let these men live and give me safe passage to New Ruatha. I just want to live my life. I hate Rake and all his rules and meddling. I just want a place where I can work and earn a living. I don't have a family, so Rake can't do nothing to me if I betray him."

Alexander smiled and nodded. "Bargain struck. These men can leave, on foot, with water and food for the walk back to wherever they came from. You will show us where you were headed and then I'll send you to New Ruatha."

Bradley smiled. "Thank you, Lord Alexander."

Another man stood, then another, then several more. Seventeen of the hundred teamsters stood and looked around at each other for a moment before one spoke. "Lord Alexander, can we come live in New Ruatha, too? None of us have families, so Rake has nothing on us. We all work hard and we just want to make an honest living."

Alexander scrutinized their colors for a moment. They were all simple people without ambition or guile.

"Very well, you will all be given safe passage to New Ruatha. As for the rest of you, I will allow you to return to your homes, but know this: Headwater is waging war against Ruatha; if you continue to act in service to Headwater's aggression, your life and liberty will be forfeit," Alexander said.

A few of the men still sitting looked with hate and anger at those who had chosen to flee Headwater, but most looked envious at the thought of being free of Rake and the trade guilds. Once the majority of the teamsters were sent on their way, Alexander spoke to the rest.

"We'll be taking these supplies to a rally point where we can resupply the Rangers operating in the area. You will help move these wagons under supervision of the Rangers and then you will be escorted to New Ruatha. Bradley, you will take me to the destination of this supply train. Once I'm satisfied, you'll be given safe passage as well. We have a few hours of light left. I want these supplies well off this road before dark."

Duane snapped a salute and started issuing orders. Within minutes, the teamsters and the Rangers were organized and driving the wagons off the road and toward a preset rally point that would serve as a good forward base of operations.

***

Bradley led Alexander and his companions to the enemy supply depot. He said he'd made three similar trips from the outlying estates to bring food, weapons, and tools for the war. The supply depot was huge. They stopped well short and Isabel sent Slyder in to take a closer look. She reported that it was a giant staging area with at least a thousand soldiers guarding it. From the way she described it, Alexander surmised that it was the central supply depot for the entire Headwater army.

They made it back to their base of operations by late afternoon of the next day. Duane had secured the area with a trench and a low berm wall just inside it. The wagons were lined up neatly and the Rangers were busy conducting an inventory of the captured supplies. Duane met Alexander at the entrance of the fortified encampment.

Alexander dismounted, appraising the work that had already been done. "Looks like you've been busy," he said, taking Duane's hand.

He nodded. "I've sent out scouts to look for any enemy activity in the area. Looks like most of Headwater's soldiers have been called to the main assembly area, so the small towns and estates in the area are relatively unprotected. I've sent forward observers to watch over three different roads and sent riders to find the other companies working nearby to let them know about this forward base."

"Outstanding," Alexander said. "We have a target. Bradley has shown us the location of a huge supply depot. It looks like it might be the main staging area for food and equipment for their entire army."

Duane whistled. "Did you see what kind of garrison they had?"

"Looked like about a thousand soldiers," Isabel said. "Mostly it's just workers moving wagons and huge herds of meat on the hoof."

"That's a pretty light guard for such a valuable target," Duane mused. "Either they don't expect us to attack this far inside their borders or they have some form of magical protection. I suspect they'll increase their guard forces as soon as they get wind of our operations."

"I agree," Alexander said. "So we need to move quickly. Send word to the companies in the area to assemble here. We'll attack as soon as we have an adequate force."

"I'll dispatch riders at once," Duane said.

Moments later, six men on horseback thundered out the narrow entrance as Alexander and his friends made their way to the makeshift mess area.

Ranger companies began arriving the next afternoon. They each reported on their activities during the previous days. They were able to fill in details about the surrounding area and the forces still protecting the many small villages and estates. Several of the six companies reported successful raids against supply trains and a few smaller garrisons.

They had followed Alexander's orders to the letter. Hit and run. Attack by surprise and retreat before the enemy could mount an effective defense. From the reports, Alexander knew it would only be a matter of time before a much larger force was sent to defend the supply depot.

By evening, he had a force of six hundred Rangers assembled at his forward base. He invited the commanders to dinner. They ate well from the stores of captured food before Alexander began his briefing. All of the Rangers were eager to strike out at such an important target and understood the urgency. Once Headwater realized they had an entire legion of Rangers wreaking havoc within their borders, they would no doubt deploy some of the soldiers they'd assembled to secure their own territory. The first place they would defend was their supply depot.

Plans were made for the attack. The six companies would depart the forward base before dawn in two units and attack the supply depot with fire from two directions. As soon as the enemy mounted a defense, the Rangers would retreat and circle around to attack again from another angle. Isabel reported that the soldiers guarding the depot were mostly infantry with only a few horses; Alexander's troops would be able to use speed to their advantage and hit them repeatedly without facing heavy opposition.

CHAPTER 12

Alexander went to his tent with the feeling of calm certainty he always got from having a plan.

He understood that knowledge was often the deciding factor in any conflict, so he chose to use what magic he had to gather what information he could. He sat on a cushion while he quieted his mind and relaxed his body. He'd grown familiar with the process for reaching the state of empty-mindedness that was his doorway to the firmament, but it still took several minutes. Sometimes he was simply unable to impose the serenity on his consciousness that was required but he was getting better at it with practice.

Soon he was drifting on the surface of the firmament, with the music of existence playing in the background of his mind. He allowed his awareness to float there on the leading edge of the wave of time and simply experienced the totality of creation.

After a few moments, he focused on a specific person. He felt the familiar rush of his awareness condensing from the whole of reality to one location and found himself floating near the top of a large tent. It was well lit with a number of freestanding brass lamps. The floor was lined with thick carpets and there was a sturdy folding table surrounded with plain-looking yet well-made chairs. Alexander saw the man he was seeking almost immediately and realized that his timing was perfect. Jataan P'Tal was meeting with the enemy commanders.

The man at the head of the table was a big man, six and a half feet tall with broad shoulders. He had dark brown eyes and medium-length, dirty brown hair with just a little grey showing at the temples. He wore a well-trimmed mustache over crooked teeth and looked like he hadn't shaved for two days.

To his left sat a younger man of average height and slight build with sharp features and droopy dark brown eyes. He had long black hair tied back in a ponytail, a waxed mustache, and a braided goatee with a bead dangling from the end.

Jataan P'Tal was to the big man's right, sitting next to the giant. The other four chairs were filled with officers of the Headwater army.

One of the officers was giving a report: "New Ruatha has sent Rangers into our territory to disrupt our supply lines and interfere with the assembly of our forces, but they won't stand and fight. I have several reports of raids where the Rangers showed up from out of nowhere, attacked and fled before our forces could fight back." The officer paused for a moment before continuing. "Master Rake, I recommend we consider redeploying some of our forces to defend the more vital estates."

"No," the man at the head of the table said. "Send a legion to secure the supply depot. The nobles can fend for themselves. Once we have New Ruatha, I'll buy their loyalty back with plunder."

"Dexter, what word from the front?" Rake asked the man to his left.

Dexter's voice was as droopy and languid as his eyes. "Ruatha has deployed their forces in a defensive line across the valley. The commanders on the ground claim they will suffer heavy losses if they charge the line. It seems Ruatha has a large number of archers to support their infantry and there are also several wizards working with them to defend the city. By all accounts we will not be able to break their line without additional forces."

Elred Rake turned to Jataan P'Tal. "What of Prince Phane? Is he going to send us any assistance or does he expect us to carry the day for him and then hand over the spoils for the privilege of fighting in his name?"

Jataan P'Tal regarded the Master of Headwater calmly for a long moment. Several of the soldiers seated around the table fidgeted nervously at the tension building in the room.

"Prince Phane is otherwise occupied. We will defeat New Ruatha with the forces at our disposal, and then you will bow to Prince Phane when he comes to collect your tribute."

Rake's face reddened with anger. He stood and started pacing.

"That's not good enough!" he shouted. "I'll withdraw my entire army right now unless you give me a reason not to. What is Phane doing that's more important than conquering Ruatha?"

Jataan P'Tal regarded him calmly. "Very well, Master Rake. If you must know, Prince Phane is going to the Temple of Fire on Tyr so that he may use the ancient powersink located there to retrieve the Sovereign Stone from the aether and reunite the Seven Isles under the banner of the Reishi Sovereign."

Rake stopped pacing and stared for a moment. Alexander saw the cold calculating nature of the man. His colors fluctuated from fear to deceit to shrewd opportunism. "All right, I'll accept that for now, but Phane will pay a heavy price when he comes to collect."

"Master Rake," Jataan said wearily, "you have already been promised the rule of the entire Isle of Ruatha provided you can deliver it to Prince Phane. What more do you want?"

"I want his help defeating that upstart king, that's what I want," Rake said with exasperation. "If I could conquer the Isle of Ruatha without Phane's help, I would have done it already. When you showed up, you said Phane would help us win this war but so far all he's sent is you."

The giant belched and all eyes turned to him. He shrugged without a word.

"More comes," Jataan said.

Elred Rake's eyes narrowed. "What do you mean?"

"Prince Phane has everything well in hand. There is a sizeable force of Andalian cavalry assembling for transport to Kai'Gorn as we speak. Once they arrive, the forces of Ruatha will face an enemy on two fronts. Then, when they are spread thin and fighting for their lives, Prince Phane will use the Sovereign Stone to awaken the Reishi Gates and half of the Reishi Army Regency will pour forth into the heart of Ruatha. So you see, Master Rake, Prince Phane is sending much more. For the moment, it's enough to keep the Rangers and the forces of New Ruatha occupied and distracted while Prince Phane makes the preparations necessary to crush them once and for all."

Elred Rake sat down heavily at the scope of the preparations that were being made outside of his control. He was used to being at the center of important decisions and he was coming to see that he was only a small part of a much bigger picture. Alexander saw the fear swell within him at the clear loss of control he faced, only to watch it be replaced with cunning opportunism.

He nodded with a smile. "That's all you needed to say, Commander P'Tal. Now that I know the score, I can play my part with a smile."

"I'm glad to hear it," Jataan P'Tal said. "I recommend you send the infantry and archers forward to the front and keep your cavalry in reserve to respond to any surprises the enemy may present. Your decision to leave the petty nobles to fend for themselves is wise. They have already delivered most of the supplies they have and can offer little in the way of further support. However, the situation with your supply depot has me concerned, especially with a legion of Rangers roaming around your backyard looking for soft spots. I recommend you distribute your supplies to ten smaller depots and increase the garrisons assigned to guard them."

Rake frowned. "I don't like to divide things up like that. I much prefer to keep all the supplies together so I can keep an eye on them. Central authority is the guiding principle of my whole territory." He took a deep breath like he was considering the suggestion before slowly shaking his head. "No . . . I think it's much better to just send a legion of infantry to guard it and keep it all in one place."

Jataan P'Tal shrugged. "Suit yourself, but understand this: Prince Phane doesn't care one bit about your guiding principles—he wants results."

Rake tried, unsuccessfully, to mask his irritation at P'Tal's tone before he answered, "Phane will have his results." He stood, and the officers at the table stood with him. "Gentlemen, I believe we've decided on our course. Tomorrow, a legion of infantry will be dispatched to the supply depot, two legions of infantry and a legion of archers will march to the front, and my cavalry will remain encamped here."

Alexander let his focus slip and his awareness faded back into the firmament. He gently returned to his body. So many times he'd wished for magic that could be used to attack but he was somewhat humbled by the sheer power of what he'd just accomplished. He got up and dug his journal from his pack, sat down at the field desk in his tent, and wrote for an hour. First he recorded all that he'd learned about the enemy's plans. Then he wrote a letter to his father. He dripped hot wax on the parchment and sealed it with the butt of his sword.

He lay down to sleep feeling a sense of urgency to depart for the Pinnacles. The Rangers' mission was vital but not nearly as important as preventing Phane from getting the Sovereign Stone. If the Reishi Prince was successful at the Temple of Fire, it would be a race to see who could get to the Reishi Keep first. Alexander decided to separate from the Rangers after the raid on the supply depot and make haste to the Pinnacles and the Fairy Queen. He couldn't allow lesser concerns to distract him. Everything would be won or lost with the Sovereign Stone.

***

They rode out well before dawn. The Rangers were loaded down with torches, flasks of oil, and quivers full of arrows wrapped in oil-soaked burlap.

Every one of them had been briefed the night before and understood the vital importance of the mission.

Before they left, Alexander and Isabel pulled Duane aside for a private conversation.

"After the raid, we're going to part ways," Alexander said. "There's something I need to do that's vitally important and time is running out."

Duane nodded reluctantly. "I understand. We'll do our part to keep the enemy from overrunning New Ruatha."

"Before we leave, send a dozen riders with this letter to my father. This must get through," Alexander said, handing Duane the letter he'd written the night before.

"It will, you have my word," Duane said. "Take care of my sister."

Alexander smiled. "Always."

They rode hard for the better part of a day before they came to a rise overlooking the enormous supply depot. There were thousands of wagons and hundreds of tents and corrals. Boxes, crates, barrels, and bushels of supplies were stacked haphazardly all across the little valley. Slyder took to wing from Isabel's shoulder and flew out over the enemy position to take a look at the defenses.

When Isabel's eyes snapped open, she said, "They're already fighting another enemy on the far side. The better part of the Headwater guard force is moving to engage a group of about two hundred men on foot who look like they're trying to steal food. The north and west sides of the encampment are mostly undefended."

"I wonder who the men attacking the depot are," Alexander mused. "I suppose it doesn't matter. Is Duane's force in place?"

Duane was leading the other contingent of three hundred and was approaching from the west while Alexander led his contingent to attack from the north.

Isabel nodded and Alexander looked over his shoulder to the captain of the first company. "Send up the signal," he commanded.

The captain issued an order and a whistler arrow went up into the sky shrieking loud and long for all to hear. A moment later, they heard Duane respond in kind before both forces charged the supply depot.

They met light resistance on the perimeter. There were only a few sentries, and they fled the charge when they saw the Rangers thundering toward their positions. Alexander led his regiment into the supply depot and gave the command to spread out into squad-sized units and set the entire place on fire. He saw smoke start to rise from the west side of the depot; Duane had begun his attack as well.

They swept through the rows, setting fire to every wagon, tent, and stack of crates they came across. Soon the way behind them was a wall of flame rising high into the sky. Black smoke billowed up from the conflagration, blotting out the evening sun. They were almost two-thirds through the depot and had joined with Duane's forces in the middle when they encountered resistance. The enemy soldiers had abandoned their fight with the thieves and organized a counterattack against Alexander and his forces.

The soldiers used the narrow roads between the supply wagons and piles of crates to choke off the Rangers' mobility. They used heavy round shields to ward against arrows and long pikes to block certain pathways, corralling them toward a central assembly area that was open enough for the enemy to bring its superior numbers to bear.

Alexander was the first to arrive in the wide-open area. It was easily a thousand feet square, and the exits were all clogged with men armed with shields and pikes.

It was a trap—superior numbers in front and fire behind. Alexander chided himself for having led his forces into such a dangerous place, but when he looked over his shoulder and saw the bulk of the enemy supplies going up in flames, he knew that they had struck a deadly blow against the army now arrayed against New Ruatha.

Then he saw the bright orange hair of Rexius Truss behind a wall of infantry, and his worry over the odds they faced faded into the background. He looked left and right and saw that the Rangers had formed up on his position and were awaiting his command.

"Archers, send fire at them," he called out.

The Rangers drew their fire-ready arrows and started sending volley after volley of flame into the assembled soldiers. The enemy began to advance under the cover of upturned shields. Once they were close enough, they unleashed a volley of crossbow bolts. Alexander's horse took a hit to the throat and fell to the ground, gurgling blood as it died. He felt a twinge of guilt before his anger took hold and he drew his sword. The feel of the blade in his hand calmed his nerves and settled his resolve. Not a moment later, Anatoly was beside him with his war axe in hand.

Many of the Rangers had lost their horses in the crossbow attack; several had been killed. Alexander watched those remaining regroup and prepare for the advancing enemy with the professionalism and precision that only comes from long hours of training. He held his sword high and called out at the top of his lungs:

"Charge!"

The Rangers still on horseback split into two groups. The first switched to their spears and leapt forward toward the enemy's shield-wall while the second unit continued to send arrows in a high arc over the leading edge of the enemy and into the less protected ranks beyond. A hundred Rangers on foot followed Alexander into the fray behind the light cavalry.

The enemy braced for the cavalry with pikes held high. The crash was deafening. The carnage was terrible. Hundreds of horses fell, but the Rangers who remained mounted broke the enemy line and crashed into their rear ranks.

The battle that ensued was chaotic and bloody. The Rangers stabbed at enemy soldiers with spears and swords, delivering punishing damage. The enemy infantry used pikes and swords to attack the mounted Rangers, bringing them down one at a time.

Alexander crashed into the crowd of enemy swarming around the mounted Rangers. Anatoly was at his side. The big man-at-arms didn't try to engage the enemy, he didn't advance to attack, but instead guarded the area to Alexander's left and rear while Alexander swept into the enemy with abandon.

The first soldier brought his shield up and pointed his sword at Alexander. He slashed the sword in half with a flick of his wrist and then swept through his shield, arm, and six inches into his chest. The dying man fell backward in shock and disbelief.

The soldier just to the right and behind the first man fell next when Alexander thrust straight through his shield and into his heart. He swept his sword out the side of that soldier and cleaved the next onrushing man in half.

He heard an enemy fall to Anatoly on his left and brought his sword to bear on another charging soldier, bringing his blade across and cleaving the enemy's shield in half, along with his arm. The man screamed and fell, and Alexander moved on to the next soldier. Lessons from the skillbook flowed freely, guiding his hand.

He swept through the enemy with single-minded purpose, leaving a swath of carnage in his wake. Men fell in pieces and crumpled in pools of bright red death. The stunning destructiveness of Alexander and his deadly sword drew the attention of the enemy, causing them to flee his approach. The ranks thinned in front of him, but closed in behind him, cutting him off from the bulk of the Rangers.

"Mind your surroundings," Anatoly barked as he dispatched another soldier.

Alexander called out without looking back, "I am." His all around sight was giving him the lay of the entire battlefield. He could see that he was cut off, but he didn't care. He was one with his blade and he knew with calm clarity that these men could not stand before him.

He killed more than thirty men on his measured charge toward his real target. They fell easily. They had no defense against the immeasurable power of the Thinblade. Even without the teachings of the skillbook, Alexander would have been deadly with the Sword of Kings in hand, but the mastery imparted by the skillbook's ancient magic coupled with the cutting power of the Thinblade made him unstoppable.

He saw the tide turn with the look of fear on Truss's face. There were few men left willing to face Alexander and his blade. Those clever enough to attempt to flank him met Anatoly and his very bloody war axe. The big man-at-arms waited patiently for the enemy to come and then dispatched them with practiced ease. He kept Alexander's back safe while Alexander stalked toward the knot of soldiers protecting the enemy commanders.

Their trap had turned against them. The assembly area was blocked by fire on one side and the pathways leading out were choked with men on the other. Alexander pushed on. Arrows rained down around him from the Rangers in the rear providing archery support.

With broad strokes, he cut down the three men standing between him and Truss. When he saw Wizard Rangle hiding behind a cluster of soldiers, he realized his mistake.

Rangle raised his hand and white-hot fire bloomed from his palm, streaked out in a tightly focused jet of flame, and struck Alexander full in the chest. It blew him off his feet. The Thinblade slipped from his hand. His tunic burned into smoke, but the searing heat of the wizard's spell was absorbed by Alexander's dragon-steel shirt.

His eyes were dazzled by the brightness of the attack, but his all around sight told him he was in trouble. It took him a moment to regain his feet. When he did, he was surrounded by a cordon of enemy soldiers. The battle raged all around. He heard Isabel from somewhere in the distance cry his name. Everything was moving in slow motion. Anatoly stood his ground, but there were easily twenty soldiers armed with short spears surrounding the two of them, not to mention Wizard Rangle.

Alexander's vision cleared to see Truss holding the Thinblade high in the air with a maniacally triumphant and murderous look of glee.

"I have the Thinblade. *I* am the King of Ruatha!" he shouted. He pointed it at Alexander and smiled. "After I kill you, I'll have my way with Isabel. She will die badly."

Rage welled up within Alexander like nothing he'd ever felt. He faced Truss as if his anger alone could destroy the petty little man. Truss charged with abandon, bringing the Thinblade up for a mighty downward stroke that would cleave Alexander from shoulder to hip.

Alexander surveyed the scene with his all around sight. Anatoly stood at his back with his axe at the ready facing off against a dozen men with spears all holding their positions. Rangle stood relaxed, content to allow Truss to finish Alexander.

The Rangers were rallying around Isabel and charging into the remaining enemy infantry. The soldiers on the ground had lost cohesion and couldn't mount a defense against the column of Rangers driving through them toward Alexander.

Then he saw something he didn't expect. The soldiers blocking two of the closest paths leading out of the assembly area were being attacked from behind by the thieves.

Truss closed the distance. Alexander waited. Truss raised the Thinblade and brought it down on Alexander. He raised his left arm to block the blade, knowing that it would not cut him. It bounced off his arm, slipped out of Truss's hand and flipped back toward the petty little noble in a tight circle, slicing off his left hand just above the wrist before the blade plunged into the dirt just in front of Alexander. Truss screamed in disbelief and pain as his hand flopped to the ground.

Alexander snatched up his sword and casually kicked Truss's hand into the circle of men just as a volley of arrows thinned their ranks. Truss screamed again in rage and agony a moment before the cordon of soldiers turned to face the column of charging Rangers. Alexander saw the real threat out of the corner of his mind's eye. Rangle was moments away from launching a bubble of liquid fire into the cluster of soldiers surrounding Alexander.

He heard Anatoly level a great stroke of his axe at the few advancing soldiers behind him and the crash of horses through infantry, but he narrowed his focus down to the wizard.

A soldier lunged at him with a spear. Alexander flicked his blade at the haft of the weapon, slicing it neatly, then reached out and snapped the point of his blade at the top of the man's head. It sliced through his helmet and several inches into his skull. On the return stroke Alexander tossed the Thinblade to his off hand, drew the throwing knife from the back of his belt and hurled it at Rangle. The blade flew straight into the bubble of liquid fire, splashing the searing contents onto the wizard. There was a scream and a whoosh from the sudden conflagration. A moment later, the column of Rangers broke through the infantry and surrounded Alexander and Anatoly.

They each mounted up behind a Ranger, and Alexander directed them toward the path out of the assembly area. He looked around for Truss but didn't see the one-handed little rat anywhere. The remaining infantry scattered in an effort to escape the burning supply depot. Rangers who had lost their horses doubled up with others and they galloped out onto the open plain to find a raggedy-looking collection of men and women hauling whatever food they could carry away from the burning depot.

Alexander called a halt several hundred feet from the blazing supply depot and dismounted. A man dropped his bag of food and stepped up to face Alexander. He was average height but he was slender and his face was gaunt. He was dirty and unshaven. His colors radiated desperation and need.

"We only want what food we can carry," he said. "We helped you when you were trapped back there. Please just let us keep the food." He was clearly exhausted and looked like he needed a good meal or two.

"Thank you for helping us," Alexander said. "What's your name?"

"I'm called Corbin," he said. "We just want the food we took, that's all."

"Corbin, my name is Alexander. You can keep the food you took. From the looks of you and your friends here, you could use it. Where are you from and why were you willing to face a thousand soldiers to steal food?"

"We're from Headwater," Corbin said. "None of us belongs to a trade guild, so we can't work. We're hungry and our families are hungry. When we heard that Rake was stockpiling food here, we came to get some. We didn't know there'd be soldiers."

"How many people are there in Headwater without guild chits?" Alexander asked.

"I don't know, maybe one in three," Corbin said. "Rake likes to make it difficult for people to work, so he can control things. People will do whatever he says for fear of losing the right to work."

Alexander felt his anger building. "Corbin, you take all the food you can carry. When you get back to Headwater, you tell anyone who will listen that Alexander Ruatha is coming to take everything from Elred Rake. Once he's dead and gone, anyone will be able to work without needing permission from a trade guild."

Corbin frowned. "I wish I could believe that, but Rake has control of everything in Headwater. He'll never let it go as long as he draws breath."

Alexander nodded with a grim grin. "I intend to see to it that he stops drawing breath. You tell people what you saw here today."

Alexander remounted, and he and the Rangers thundered off into the dusk. They rounded up a few stray horses that had fled the burning supply depot and wound up with a few more mounts than Rangers. When they stopped to make camp, Alexander ordered a head count.

Once he was off his horse, he was confronted by Anatoly, Abigail, and Isabel. All three looked angry. He stopped and waited for them to speak.

Abigail broke the silence. "Don't you ever charge off into a bunch of enemy soldiers like that ever again! You could have been killed. You almost were. If Anatoly hadn't been crazy enough to follow you and watch your back, you would have died a dozen times."

Alexander could see the anger and worry and relief all tangled up within his sister.

Isabel went next. She held him with her eyes as she approached and hugged him fiercely. "Please don't get killed. I love you and I need you. You don't need to take risks like that. We're here to help you and protect you. Let us!" She stepped back and brushed a tear from her cheek.

Alexander turned to Anatoly, expecting a long lecture from his old mentor. But he didn't get one. Anatoly took a deep breath. Blood was crusted on his breastplate and his bracers. "Watch the battle in your mind, Alexander. There are many lessons for you to learn from. The first of which is that you gave the enemy far too many opportunities to kill you today. Don't be so careless. Your sword is a fearsome weapon, but it will not save you from a well-placed arrow."

Alexander nodded. He remembered the battle. He was so sure of himself and his sword. The men he faced didn't have a chance. They fell before him like wheat before the scythe, but that didn't stop others from closing in behind him. His advance had been reckless, mostly because he was trying to cut his way to Truss. He allowed his desire to kill the petty little rat blind him to the bigger picture.

He nodded somberly. "You're right. I'm sorry. I got caught up in the battle and let myself become distracted."

They washed up and changed into clean clothes before eating a cold meal and going to sleep. The head count came to Alexander just before bed: four hundred and eighty-nine. The battle had cost one hundred and eleven Rangers their lives. Alexander wrestled with the cost versus the value of destroying the enemy supplies. He fervently hoped their sacrifice would save a great many more lives by depriving Headwater's army of vital food and equipment.

CHAPTER 13

The next morning the camp was abuzz with stories of the battle and of Alexander's charge into the enemy. Many of the Rangers thought he'd been heroic, but he realized after a night's sleep that he'd been reckless, needlessly risking his life—and with it, the future. This was just one battle. There was much more fighting to come and he understood in the clarity of the new dawn that he was the only one who could stop Phane from getting to the Sovereign Stone. That was the real fight.

Alexander and his companions sat around a breakfast fire with Duane and his Second. After the meal, it was time to part company with the Rangers.

"Duane, your Rangers fought well yesterday," Alexander said. "We hurt the enemy badly and now they'll be looking for any supplies they can get their hands on. I want you to make sure that they don't get them. Split back up into company-sized units and resume the original mission. Conduct raids and harass the enemy. Prevent them from moving supplies to the front. They'll be sending infantry to the supply depot. Avoid them. The real threat is the legion of cavalry Headwater still has at their main assembly area. They may come looking for you."

"We're faster than they are," Duane said. "We'll be like ghosts in the night. They won't even be certain we exist until we come out of the shadows and attack. By the time they're sure we do exist, we'll already be gone."

"Good man. Send word to my father of our success yesterday. Knowing the enemy will be running short of supplies will help him formulate his strategy."

"I'll send riders this morning. Safe journey, Alexander."

Jack cleared his throat. "Duane, please send these pages to Owen with your riders. As terrifying as it was for some of us to watch Alexander's attack yesterday, I'm quite sure it was far more frightening for those who faced him on the battlefield. Word of his deeds in that battle will go a long way toward bolstering the confidence of our soldiers, while at the same time striking fear into the hearts of the enemy. Owen will see to it that the events of yesterday are known to all."

Duane chuckled. "It will be done, Master Colton."

Isabel hugged her brother before she mounted up and then they were on their way. Duane offered to send a guard force with them, but Alexander declined, preferring the company of his five companions. They could move faster and draw less attention with a smaller number. Alexander needed speed, especially after discovering that Phane had a new plan to recover the Sovereign Stone.

Unfortunately, the fastest path to the Pinnacles was along the road to the east coast of Ruatha through Buckwold and Warrenton. They could go south through the forest, but that way was wild and dangerous and they would have to travel on foot. The road was much faster, but it would also take them through enemy territory.

They gave Headwater a wide berth, preferring to avoid the city altogether. With the assistance of Slyder, they were able to stay clear of the small

squads patrolling the area as they made their way through the lands controlled by
Rake and his trade guilds.

They encountered a company of Rangers operating on the eastern edge of
the territory and were able to replenish their provisions and trade a few stories.
The Rangers told of the poverty and general despair of the outlying communities.
Work was scarce and what work that could be had was only permitted to members
of the trade guilds. Those who couldn't get membership in a guild were left to
fend for themselves.

It was heartbreaking to Alexander. Headwater was at the center of the
Ruathan trade routes. It could be a fabulously wealthy territory with more than
enough bounty for everyone to share if people were just allowed the freedom to
work. Rake wanted power and clearly didn't care how much suffering he had to
cause to get it. No wonder he sided with Phane. They were cut from the same
cloth.

***

Things changed once they passed into Buckwold. The people were free to
be productive. The few they encountered along the way were busy tending to their
work and didn't give the travelers more than a passing glance. It didn't look like a
territory girding for war so much as for the coming spring planting season. The
farmlands were rich and fertile and the range land was well kept. The biggest
difference Alexander could see between his own home on the Valentine family
estates and the estates of Buckwold was the livestock. Instead of cattle, these
people raised sheep and goats.

They still moved cautiously, using Slyder to scout ahead so they could
avoid anything that even resembled a patrol. Buckwold was on friendly terms with
Headwater, and Alexander didn't know the degree of that friendship. On the
surface, it appeared to be an economic arrangement but it could very easily go
deeper, and Alexander wanted to avoid any confrontations that might slow him
down.

After learning about Phane's plans to go to the Temple of Fire on Tyr, he
had felt the urgency to get to the Pinnacles build with each passing day. He hadn't
spoken of the results of his spying, mostly because they'd been traveling from
dawn to dusk and it wasn't pressing that his friends know about Phane's plans just
yet.

A day inside Buckwold, they came to a small village just off the main
road leading from the city of Buckwold to Headwater. Alexander decided it was
worth the risk to gain some insight into the people and politics of Buckwold, so he
headed into town. It was a medium-sized village that served as a trade hub for the
wool, farm produce, goat meat and cheese that the western communities of
Buckwold brought to market every year. Nearly a dozen small roads fed into the
village so people could bring goods for shipment to the other territories of Ruatha.

Near the center of town they found a reputable-looking inn with a stable
and they inquired about a room for the night. It had been nearly a week of travel
across the open range since the battle at the supply depot, and they were all tired of
sleeping on the ground and eating travel rations.

The inn was a well-built structure with a large, two-story central building and three wings leading off the sides and back, all lined with rooms for rent. Off to one side was a big barn with an ample paddock. The people in town were friendly enough but kept to themselves, and there was no sign of soldiers or evidence of any interest in war.

Alexander and Isabel went into the inn while the rest waited outside. The main room was big with a high ceiling and a second-level loft over the kitchen in the back half. The room was filled with tables and there was a smattering of patrons here and there. Alexander was careful to keep his sword concealed under his cloak. He and Isabel didn't draw much more than passing notice from those eating lunch.

The bartender was a big man with broad shoulders, a round belly, and a balding head. His apron was slightly stained and he was busy cleaning a glass mug when Alexander and Isabel stepped up to the bar.

"Good afternoon, can I help you?" he said with the simple hospitality of a shopkeeper who understands that courtesy is the first part of good business.

"Yes, thank you," Alexander said. "My friends and I have need of lodging for the night and boarding for our horses. There are six of us."

"I'd be happy to accommodate you. The price is a silver sovereign for each—that includes dinner and breakfast plus boarding, hay and oats for your animals."

"Fair enough," Alexander said as he produced half a dozen silver coins from his money purse.

The innkeeper smiled and eagerly took the money. The place didn't look like it was even close to capacity; Alexander suspected this was a slow season. The inn had probably been built to house the farmers and herders during the summer months when the trade routes were the busiest.

"Right this way," he said as he gathered a handful of brass keys from a lock box behind the bar. He led them through the main room and into a long hall of the back wing and showed them the first six rooms, three to a side. Each room was small but clean. They each had a bed, desk and chair, oil lamp and a washbasin.

"More generous accommodations can be arranged if you like—for a higher price, of course," he offered.

"No, thank you," Alexander said with a smile. "I'll just be happy to sleep in a bed for the night."

The innkeeper handed Alexander the six keys. "Just show your key to the stable master and he'll take care of your horses. Same with the wait staff, just show 'em your key and they'll get you a meal."

They had a quiet night; the inn was less than a quarter full. The other guests were mostly travelers just passing through from other parts of Buckwold. Alexander was able to overhear a bit of gossip about the war here and there, but the people seemed to believe that it was very far away and wouldn't affect them directly. They were far more concerned with the disruption of the trade routes through Headwater.

Alexander woke the next morning to the noise of people in the main room of the inn. He carefully looked out his door and saw that the central hall was over half full with soldiers, all eating breakfast and telling stories. They wore the crest of Buckwold. Their presence here had Alexander curious as well as concerned. He gathered his friends in his room.

"Looks like we have some company. I'd love to know what they're doing here."

"We could just have a bite to eat and keep our ears open," Lucky suggested. "We might learn something."

"Do you think it's safe?" Abigail asked. "They might have orders to look for us. It's a good bet they're on their way to help Headwater."

Isabel opened her eyes with a sharp breath. "There's a legion camped on the outskirts of town. My guess is they arrived last night."

"That changes things," Anatoly said. "We might do well to slip out the back and be on our way."

Alexander shook his head. "I really want to know more. If Buckwold is a willing participant in this war, then they might be able to supply Rake with food. If they're in it just to protect their trade routes, then we might be able to persuade the Baron of Buckwold to change sides."

Anatoly mulled it over for a moment. "I suppose it would be useful to know where they stand, but let's try to avoid a bar brawl."

Alexander nodded his agreement with a humorless smile but still checked his sword in its scabbard.

They found an empty table near a cluster of officers and ordered breakfast from the overworked serving staff. They kept quiet while listening to the conversations all around. A number of things quickly became apparent. These were the officers of the legion camped outside the village and they didn't really want to be involved in a war that Headwater had started. More importantly, they spoke of war in terms of glory and heroics. It was apparent that these men had never fought in a real battle before. They thought this would be a great adventure to tell stories about over a drink at the ale house.

Jack leaned across the table to speak quietly to Alexander. "Perhaps a song would educate these men about the foe they face," he said with a wink.

"What did you have in mind?"

"I thought I might regale them with the tale of Lord Alexander and the battle of Headwater's supply depot. I've been working on it for several days now and I believe it's quite good," Jack said with a smile.

"What, exactly, will that accomplish?" Anatoly asked.

"If I'm not mistaken, Alexander was thinking about introducing himself to the commander of the legion. A little groundwork might be in order."

Anatoly looked at Alexander sharply.

He shrugged. "The thought crossed my mind. If we can make friends, they might reconsider their support for Headwater or at the very least give us safe passage to the Baron of Buckwold so we can make our case to him."

"This is risky, Alexander," Abigail said. "I thought you were in a hurry to get to the Pinnacles."

"I am, but this won't take long and Buckwold is along the way. If we can isolate Headwater and deprive them of support, we can defeat them without losing too many more soldiers. We're going to need all the men we can get before this is over."

Abigail narrowed her eyes at him. "What do you mean? What haven't you told us, Alexander?"

He took a deep breath. "I looked in on Jataan P'Tal and saw him in a meeting with Rake and his generals. It seems that Phane has made a deal with Andalia to send cavalry up through Kai'Gorn."

Anatoly looked worried. Fighting on two fronts was always a dangerous proposition.

Alexander spoke in a whisper to keep the soldiers nearby from hearing. "That's not the worst of it. If Phane can get the Sovereign Stone, he's planning on using the Reishi Gate to send half the Reishi Army Regency through. I sent my father a letter detailing the plan, but I'd feel a lot better if we could defeat Headwater outright as quickly as possible. Without support from Buckwold, they'll fall much more easily."

Anatoly thought it over for a moment. "You realize that we'll have to fight our way out if this doesn't work, and then we'll be on the run from a legion of enemy soldiers."

"I don't think it will come to that. The officers here don't really want to fight. If we can offer them a way out, I think they'll jump at it."

"All right, but I suggest we get our things together first and maybe have Lucky go collect our horses so we can make a quick exit if we need to," Anatoly said.

Alexander nodded his agreement.

They spent the next ten minutes clearing out their rooms and moving their packs to their horses where Lucky had tied them to the railing in front of the inn. Jack circled around and entered through the front door while Alexander, Anatoly, Isabel, and Abigail found an empty table near the exit.

Jack spoke to the innkeeper for a moment. The man was more than happy to have a bard offer a song. Entertainment had a way of making people thirsty.

Jack stepped up onto a table with a little tin whistle and started playing without any introduction. The tune was an old one that most people had heard as children. Within a minute or so, he had the attention of every person in the room. "Lords and ladies, I have a song I'd like to sing for you, if I may?" The crowd urged him on. Music was almost always welcome and he accepted their urging with a gracious bow. "This is a song of young Lord Alexander, the King of Ruatha." Jack paused to gauge the reaction.

A man from the crowd shouted. "He's our enemy!" Another yelled, "He attacked Headwater and cut off our trade routes." But the commander shouted them down. "Let the man sing. We might learn something."

Jack bowed deeply to the commander. "I learned this song just a week ago from a bard who bore witness firsthand to the events of the battle for Headwater's supply depot."

He began his song. His voice was clear and carried to every corner of the hall. The men listened with rapt attention as he put the story of the battle to a tune. The melody was a common one that Jack had adapted for his purposes and the words flowed easily.

He sang of the plan and the desperate need of the new King to defend his capital city from the invasion of Headwater. He sang about the luck of discovering the location of the central supply depot for the whole army of Headwater and then he sang of the battle.

His account of the bloody charge by Alexander wielding the Thinblade through dozens of soldiers was factually accurate but sounded like an exaggeration. He sang of the bravery of the Rangers and their willingness to risk everything for their King. He sang of the fear in the hearts of the soldiers of Headwater at seeing the fearsome power of the rightful King of Ruatha with his ancient sword in hand.

When he finished, there was dead silence. The faces all around were somber and almost worried. After several long moments, the commander clapped slowly and the crowd responded with a tepid applause, more for Jack's masterful delivery than the content of the lyrics. He gave a bow and withdrew to the bar for a cup of tea.

Alexander watched the crowd. Their mood had shifted noticeably. Once he started to hear the officers openly expressing doubts to one another, he casually sauntered over to the table with the legion commander and his senior officers. Anatoly stood and took a position by the door. Isabel and Abigail both positioned themselves to be ready to respond if a fight should break out.

CHAPTER 14

Alexander stepped up to the head of the long table and cleared his throat. When he had everyone's attention, he smiled and turned to the commander. "I wonder if I might have a word with you."

The commander stood and appraised Alexander for a moment before he spoke. "My name is Commander Kern, what can I do for you?"

He was clean shaven, had medium-length black hair, and was just over six feet tall with a medium build. He offered Alexander his hand in greeting.

Alexander examined Kern's colors as he shook his hand. He was an honorable man with a sense of loyalty and duty.

"My name is Alexander. I'm concerned about Buckwold going to war. The way I hear it, Headwater invaded New Ruatha, so I guess I'm wondering why Buckwold is getting involved."

The commander shook his head and motioned for Alexander to sit. "The simple answer is because the Baron chose to get involved," he snorted. "More likely, his administrator gave the order but we're duty bound to obey. Besides, we need the trade routes through Headwater to move our goods."

Alexander nodded his understanding. "I know how important trade is. I grew up on a ranch south of the Great Forest along the trade road between Southport and Highlands Reach. If that road had been shut down, the whole range would have shriveled up and blown away. It was a lifeline for everyone who lived along it."

"Glad to hear you understand the need to keep the trade routes open. I just hope the rest of Buckwold comes around. My family are sheepherders. If those routes close, they'll fall on hard times," Commander Kern said. "Besides, the way I hear it, the pretender to the Ruathan throne is hopelessly outnumbered, the bard's song notwithstanding," he motioned toward Jack at the bar. "As for the Thinblade, everyone knows it was lost during the Reishi War, but you can't blame a man for writing a song about it," he said with a chuckle.

Alexander considered his next words very carefully. "Commander Kern, you strike me as a man who would prefer to avoid war if possible. Is that a fair assessment?"

He nodded. "I suppose it is, but like I said, it's not my decision. The Baron's made up his mind."

"Would you welcome an opportunity to persuade him to reconsider?"

The commander frowned a bit suspiciously. "Where are you going with this?"

Alexander took a deep breath while he appraised the man sitting next to him. The rest of the men at the table had fallen silent and were looking at Alexander with suspicion. He decided to be bold. While holding the men's eyes, he very deliberately reached up and pulled his cloak collar down to reveal the mark burned into the side of his neck.

Kern's eyes widened and he froze for a moment like he was trying to decide what to do. Alexander's hand was on the hilt of his sword under his cloak.

"Commander Kern, do you serve the Old Law?" he asked pointedly.

Kern frowned as he made his decision. "Of course, but I serve the Baron of Buckwold first. Who are you?" he asked.

"I told you, my name is Alexander and I'm offering you a way to avoid war right here and right now." Alexander spoke softly but with deadly seriousness. He could see the fear bloom in the commander's colors when he made the connection. "You have this one chance to protect your lands and your people, Commander. Consider your next decision very carefully."

The commander looked around and saw a room full of his officers. Most of them were not even aware of the very tense conversation taking place at his table, but those nearby were all looking at Alexander with varying degrees of realization.

"You're hopelessly outnumbered," Commander Kern said with less than complete confidence. "What's to stop me from killing you right now and ending this war?" Alexander could see uncertainty shimmer in the man's colors.

"My death won't end this war because I didn't start it—Phane did. But more importantly, I wouldn't be here if I feared you. I can see that you're a good man. You clearly want what's best for your people. Siding with Phane and Headwater will buy you slavery at best and destruction at worst. Side with me and serve the Old Law. Help me reunite Ruatha. Please."

He held the commander's eyes with his own while he made his plea, but he watched the rest of the room with his all around sight. Most of the men were still oblivious but the man to his left was slowly going for his sword. Alexander tightened his grip on the hilt of the Thinblade.

Commander Kern hesitated like a man torn between duty and conscience before giving his answer. "What would you have me do?"

Before Alexander could answer, the man to his left stood and drew his sword. He tried to bring it around in one stroke across Alexander's chest, but he wasn't fast enough. The Thinblade came free of its scabbard, sliced up through the heavy wooden table, and clipped the officer's sword off three inches from the hilt, the blade clattering noisily onto the table. Alexander brought the Thinblade up and over the man's head, then dropped the flat of the blade down onto the startled officer's right shoulder. He looked over at Commander Kern while keeping his mind's eye on the officer who'd just drawn on him. The officer stood stone-still, looking at the edge of the Thinblade. Commander Kern stood slowly with his hands open and visible.

"Make your choice, Commander Kern, but know this, if you choose war, it begins for you right now." Alexander held him with glittering golden eyes.

The room was standing as awareness of the conflict spread from the officers' table like a wave. Some drew weapons; others just looked at the commotion.

"Stand down," Commander Kern said loudly enough for all to hear.

His men sheathed their weapons but remained on their feet, watching the spectacle unfold.

"I choose peace, Alexander. In truth, we have no desire for war. If you can offer a way to avoid bloodshed, then I will hear you out."

Alexander felt the acuteness of his all around sight. He could see everything in crisp detail within the confines of his mind. He shifted his focus to the man on his left, who stood motionless under threat of the Thinblade. "Who do you serve?"

He stood mute for a few moments before Commander Kern looked at him. "Answer the question," he commanded.

"I serve the Baron of Buckwold," the man lied.

Alexander watched his colors flare. He turned his glittering eyes on him.

"You lie," Alexander whispered with menace. "I can see right through you. Speak the truth. Tell all here whom you serve or I will take your head." Everyone at the table tensed at the very real prospect of bloodshed.

The officer whimpered, "He'll kill me if I tell."

"I'll kill you if you don't." Alexander visibly tensed his sword arm before the officer answered.

"I serve Elred Rake," he said quietly but still loud enough for all at the table to hear.

"Who gives you your orders?" Alexander asked. He could see anger play across Commander Kern's face at hearing his officer's betrayal.

The man deflated in defeat. He was broken. Alexander saw it in his colors and on his face.

"I get my orders from Administrator Nero."

"What?" Commander Kern said hotly. "Who does Nero work for if not Baron Buckwold?"

The officer hesitated. Alexander looked at him pointedly before he answered.

"Nero serves Elred Rake."

"Dear Maker," Commander Kern whispered. "Baron Buckwold took ill nearly a month ago. He's delivered all of his orders through Nero."

Alexander sheathed the Thinblade and offered his hand to Commander Kern. "I am Alexander Ruatha and I offer Buckwold my friendship."

Commander Kern took his hand and the tension in the room faded. "Thank you, Lord Alexander. I fear Buckwold may have been duped into supporting this war for the benefit of Headwater. I must return to Buckwold and expose this fraud."

"I agree," Alexander said. "I would ride with you to Buckwold and make my case to your Baron myself."

***

Commander Kern put his Second in command of the legion with orders to remain where they were no matter what messages came from Headwater. He selected a score of men to ride escort and they made haste to Buckwold.

The countryside was fertile and well managed. Commander Kern was proud of his homeland and took pleasure in answering the questions Alexander asked while they rode.

The territory was equally divided between farming and ranching in the northern plains, mining and timber in the highlands, and fishing from the port of Buckwold. They had rich resources and industrious people. In spite of many attempts by Rake to insinuate his tendrils into their affairs, they rejected the system of trade guilds used by Headwater.

Baron Buckwold was an independently minded man who respected the free will of others. Buckwold was allied with Headwater only as a matter of necessity. They had much to trade but could only do so by using the trade routes through Headwater. The more Alexander heard, the more he liked Buckwold. They would make good allies—they viewed the world in much the same way he did.

They rode hard for three days before arriving at the city of Buckwold in the middle of the afternoon. It was a sprawling community on the edge of the eastern ocean. The citizens lived in sturdy houses made of thick-cut timber and they took care of their property. The place was busy with trade. The people moved with purpose. The sea air was filled with promise and hope.

Alexander felt good about his prospects of establishing an alliance with Buckwold. If he could isolate Headwater, then his father could defeat their army with much less loss of life and be in a position of strength to defend against Andalia from the south and the Reishi coming through the Gate.

Chapter 15

Commander Kern became much more serious as they approached the center of the city. He knew the coming conflict was going to decide his fate one way or the other, but he didn't hesitate. He led them straight to the palace perched atop a bluff overlooking the ocean. It was a beautiful estate with manicured gardens and a low sprawling complex of buildings. The trees were windblown but hardy and the buildings themselves were built with the same thick-cut timber that the rest of the city was constructed of, only with much greater artistry and grandeur.

They turned their horses loose in the large paddock just outside the palace gate. When they strode into the large enclosed courtyard, a horn sounded.

A number of soldiers were stationed around the grounds and on three-story towers connected with catwalks ringing the courtyard. They wore different uniforms than the men of Commander Kern's legion. Alexander surmised that they were the palace guard.

A soldier with the markings of high rank came out of the main building trailed by an officer of lesser rank and gave Commander Kern a frown.

"Why aren't you with your legion, Commander? You should be to Headwater by now." Then he noticed the others with Kern and motioned to his adjunct, who hurried off into the main hall of the palace.

Alexander studied the officer's colors and found him wanting. He looked like a man who had risen in rank by sabotaging those of greater merit in order to clear the field and win promotion by default. He was self-serving and less than honest, with a streak of cowardice.

"General Randal, there is treachery at court," Kern said. "I have returned to reveal a traitor to Buckwold."

Before the general could respond, a man sauntered out from the main hall, followed by the adjunct officer and a dozen palace guards armed with crossbows and long swords. He was a tall man with narrow features and close-set, dull brown eyes. He wore a black goatee and mustache, and his stringy black hair was tied back in a loose ponytail.

He asked with arrogance and superiority, "And who might that be, Commander Kern?"

Alexander could see the fear flare in Commander Kern's colors, but to his credit, he drew himself up, took a deep breath and leveled his finger at the man standing on the porch.

"You are the traitor, Nero. You serve Elred Rake."

Administrator Nero regarded Commander Kern for a moment while he calculated. Alexander watched his dark and muddy colors undulate through fear, then anger, and finally settle on deceit.

"Nonsense. I am the faithful servant of Baron Buckwold, and you have disobeyed your orders, Commander Kern." He turned to General Randal. "General, relieve him of his command and detain him to answer for his disobedience, then send an officer to assume command of the First Legion and have them make all possible haste to Headwater." He issued the orders like a man who expected to be obeyed.

General Randal stepped forward. "Commander Kern, surrender your sword." Alexander watched satisfaction ripple through the general's colors.

Commander Kern stood his ground. "I will surrender my sword if the Baron commands it, but I will not take another order from this traitor."

The general sputtered in surprise for a moment. Nero's eyes narrowed and he looked around, furtively appraising the situation. Alexander looked around, too. With his all around sight, he took inventory of the soldiers arrayed throughout the courtyard. In addition to the twelve men standing behind Nero, there were easily twenty men on the towers and catwalks, all dressed in the uniform of the palace guard.

The men on the catwalk had the colors of men who were loyal, well-disciplined soldiers doing their job, but the dozen men standing behind Nero clearly served him. Commander Kern had twenty hand-picked men from his legion who showed no sign of backing down. They stood behind their commander, tensely looking around at the tactical situation.

General Randal raised his voice, as if speaking louder gave his commands more weight. "I gave you an order, Commander. Surrender your sword!"

"And I gave you my answer. I will see the Baron if I have to fight my way to him." Commander Kern had passed the point of anger and fear and arrived at steadfast resolve. Alexander grinned ever so slightly as his hand found the hilt of his sword under his cloak.

"As you wish," Nero said. "Guards, seize him!" The dozen men behind him started forward.

As one, the twenty soldiers standing with Commander Kern drew their swords. They didn't advance and they didn't speak, but their bare weapons spoke volumes. Nero's men stopped and looked around hesitantly.

General Randal's face turned red with anger. "You will be held for treason if you don't stand aside at once. Commander Kern, you are ordered to surrender your sword!" he bellowed.

Alexander got the impression that General Randal had never actually commanded men in battle. No one flinched.

Commander Kern raised his voice so that everyone in the courtyard could hear him. "There is treachery in the palace. Nero is a traitor and he has usurped the authority of our Baron. I ask only that I be given an audience. If Baron Buckwold commands that I surrender my sword, then I will obey. Will you men, who have sworn to serve the Baron and his family, stand by and allow this man," he pointed at Nero, "to speak for Baron Buckwold?"

The men on the catwalks lowered their weapons, but a moment later, another platoon of twenty men poured into the courtyard from a side building. Nero smiled in a self-satisfied way at seeing his reinforcements arrive. Kern's men spread out to face the threats from both sides.

Alexander focused his all around sight on the newly arrived men and saw in a glance that they were loyal to Nero and spoiling for a fight. He weighed his options and tried to call on his precognition but nothing came forth. Things were spiraling out of control and he wasn't sure if there was a way to avoid bloodshed.

"You men are all guilty of treason against the Baron of Buckwold," Nero said with just a hint of panic. "If you surrender now, your families will be spared. Otherwise, they will be charged with treason as well."

Some of the soldiers faltered a bit at the threat against their families, but Kern didn't budge. Alexander saw his anger flare, then Kern drew his sword and pointed it at Nero. He took a deep breath and yelled, "Charge!"

Everything happened very quickly. Nero's smug confidence evaporated. He squeaked and ran away into the main hall. General Randal looked around in confusion as twenty of his own soldiers lunged toward him. Jack tossed up the hood of his cloak and shimmered out of sight. Lucky casually pulled a jar from his bag and threw it between Kern's soldiers and the newly arrived reinforcements. It shattered and a cloud of thick, white, noxious smoke rapidly filled the area, blocking the view of half the crossbowmen on the catwalks.

The dozen men on the porch fired their crossbows into the crowd of soldiers. Kern's men were equipped with medium round shields that took the brunt of the attack, and only three fell.

Isabel drew her sword and said, "Right behind you, Alexander."

Anatoly said, "On your left," as he unslung his war axe.

Abigail nocked an arrow, smoothly drew it back, took aim for only a split second and killed one of the crossbowmen on the porch. Nero's men were drawing their swords as they retreated.

Alexander kept his grip on the hilt of his sword but didn't draw. "Commander, lead the way."

They swept forward past a sputtering and indignant General Randal. The soldiers loyal to Nero retreated into the main entry hall of the palace. It was easily a hundred feet square with a high vaulted ceiling made of beautifully carved timbers. The floor was polished hardwood and the furnishings were exquisitely handcrafted woodwork. Under other circumstances, Alexander could have spent an hour admiring the quality of the craftsmanship.

Nero's soldiers retreated down one of several broad corridors that led from the main hall, but Kern ignored them. "The Baron's chambers are this way," he pointed toward another wide corridor and several of his soldiers raced ahead. They made their way through halls and chambers, then up a flight of stairs and down another broad hallway. When they came to a four-way intersection with another wide hallway, they were attacked by Nero's reinforcements, who had circled around and set an ambush.

The two soldiers moving ahead of the rest of the platoon were cut down quickly by surprise, then twenty men with swords and shields came around the corner and advanced.

Alexander looked at Isabel to his right and Anatoly to his left. Both nodded. He drew his sword and stepped out in front of Kern's soldiers to meet the oncoming attack. An arrow whizzed past him and buried in the eye socket of a soldier; Abigail had the first kill.

Deadly calm settled on Alexander. He was in a fight and he had the Sword of Kings in his hand. He swept into the enemy with fury and rage. He sliced down through the shield and arm of the first man in a diagonal stroke and brought his blade up again to cleave the next man in two. A soldier stabbed him and drove hard into his gut but the dragon-steel chain stopped the sword from penetrating. Alexander cut him in half with another sweep of the Thinblade. He waded into the enemy with Isabel covering his back and Anatoly guarding his left side. His all around sight and the magic of the skillbook guided him through the enemy. He moved with precision and economy of motion, striking with deadly speed.

The fight lasted only seconds before the bulk of the enemy platoon lay broken and dismembered, scattered across the hallway slick with blood. Five men fled to avoid joining their companions in the afterlife. Alexander was splattered with droplets of blood and his blade was dripping red. He turned, golden eyes glittering with anger, to face a stunned platoon of soldiers all staring at him with awe and fear.

Commander Kern approached somewhat tentatively. Alexander schooled his anger and picked up a scrap of a dead man's cloak to wipe his sword clean before returning it to its scabbard.

"Take me to the Baron, Commander," he said quietly.

Commander Kern nodded and swallowed hard before motioning for two of his soldiers to take point. Soon they were at the outer doors to the Baron's chambers. There were a dozen palace guards standing ready and waiting to meet any intruder. Alexander surveyed their colors and saw they were honorable men. He let Commander Kern take the lead.

"Stand aside," Kern said, "we need to see the Baron."

The guard captain held his ground. "The Baron is not to be disturbed, by order of Administrator Nero."

"Nero is a traitor. The Baron may be in danger," Kern said. "Who's in there with him?"

The captain hesitated with a frown. "Administrator Nero was appointed by the Baron. He's a trusted advisor."

"Who's in the Baron's chambers?" Kern asked again with more edge to his voice.

"His personal physician is attending to him," the captain answered. "The Baron is very ill and must not be disturbed."

"Captain, you and your men will stand aside or we will enter by force." Commander Kern was losing his patience. The palace guard tensed and raised their weapons. Clearly they were not willing to abandon their post and permit access to the Baron without orders.

Alexander stepped forward and put a hand on Commander Kern's arm to forestall any further threats. When the guard captain saw the blood splatter on Alexander's face and cloak, his eyes widened and his weapon came up a little higher. Alexander stopped just short of the spear point and leveled his glittering eyes at the man.

"Captain, you are to be commended for your loyalty to the Baron," Alexander said, "but you may have allowed him to come to harm even as we speak. May I ask, who does the Baron's personal physician report to?"

The captain frowned before he answered, "Administrator Nero. All of the Baron's affairs are handled by him."

Alexander nodded. "Nero is a fraud. He works for Headwater, not Buckwold, and he's manipulating your entire territory into a war that will cost you dearly. Please, Captain, no more blood needs to be spilled today. I can see that you are a loyal servant of your Baron, but you've been duped. Allow us to pass and I give you my word that we will not harm him."

The captain looked incredulous. "You're a stranger covered in blood. Why should your word count for anything?"

Alexander drew the Thinblade and cut the captain's spear off a few inches from his forward hand, then pointed his blade at him. The captain looked at the clean cut across his spear haft, then at the Thinblade, and his eyes widened.

"I am the King of Ruatha. Do you recognize this blade from the old stories?"

He nodded. His men stood stock-still, staring at the Thinblade.

"I give you my word that we will not harm the Baron," Alexander said. "Now, stand aside or I will add your blood to the stains on my cloak."

The captain considered the situation for a moment, all the while looking at the impossibly thin blade pointed at him. Then he nodded. "Stand down," he said over his shoulder to his guard force. They obeyed and Alexander sheathed his sword.

"Open the door," Alexander commanded.

The captain blinked. "I can't. It's barred from the inside. We can knock, but the physician is the only one with the authority to permit entry."

"Very well, then," Alexander said, "knock and ask him to open the door."

The captain knocked loudly. There was no answer. He knocked again and still there was no answer. Finally, after several minutes of insistent pounding, a small window opened. An angry-looking man peered out at the guard and those behind him.

"What is the meaning of this?" he snapped grumpily. "The Baron is not to be disturbed. He's very ill and you've woken him from a much-needed rest."

The captain looked nervously back to Alexander and Kern. Both of them nodded for him to continue.

"Open the door. The Baron has guests who will not be denied an audience."

The man behind the door looked indignant. "I am the Baron's personal physician. He is not well. Go away!" He punctuated his statement by slamming the little window.

"Captain," Alexander said, "describe the locks and the bar holding this door shut."

The captain blinked for a moment before answering. "There's a bar across the doors here," he motioned across the double doors at about chest height, "and pins on each door that slide into holes in the floor."

"Thank you. Now stand aside," Alexander said, drawing his sword.

First he slipped the blade under the door and ran it across the two metal pins. He could feel just a slight tug of resistance as the Thinblade passed cleanly through the half-inch steel rods. Then he slipped the blade into the crack between the two doors and ran it up through the bar, cutting it neatly in two. He sheathed his sword and pushed the double doors open.

The room beyond was a well-appointed entry hall with corridors leading off to the other rooms in the comfortable suite.

"Commander, have your men secure the chambers and detain the staff," Alexander said. "I suspect that Nero will be coming with more men soon. We may need some time to speak with the Baron."

The soldiers quickly pried the sheared pins from the holes in the floor so the locking pins could be used again and then barred the door with half of the cleanly cut bar. The palace guard looked on as they were once again locked out of the Baron's chambers.

Kern's men were quick, thorough, and efficient. There were no soldiers within the Baron's suites, just serving staff and the physician with his assistants. They protested loudly but obeyed when the soldiers showed them steel. Within minutes, the entire suite was searched, all the staff were detained under guard in a large sitting room, and the Baron was found sleeping deeply in his bedchamber.

Alexander could see at a glance that something was very wrong. His colors were twisted and tortured. There was a quality to his aura that Alexander had seen before. It took him a moment to place it.

"Lucky, his colors look like those surrounding the deathwalker root," Alexander said.

Lucky nodded and went to the Baron's side. He was an older man with white hair all in a tangle from sleep. He looked frail, like someone who'd been bedridden for too long. Lucky smelled his breath and looked at his eyes before nodding.

"They've been feeding him a tincture made from deathwalker root. A skilled herbalist would be able to keep him in a stupor indefinitely with regularly administered doses, but it's very dangerous; too much and his heart could easily stop in the night."

"Can you do anything for him?" Alexander asked.

"The most important thing we can do is prevent him from taking any more. I can make a tea that will cleanse his system and drive the toxin out more quickly, but ultimately, time is the best medicine."

"How long before he's conscious and aware?"

Lucky shook his head while he thought it over. "A day, maybe more; he has a lot in his system and it will take time to flush out."

Alexander nodded, "Stay with him and do what you can. I'm going to talk with that physician."

"Wait," Commander Kern said, "are you saying he's been poisoned?"

Lucky nodded, "Essentially, yes, but not with lethal doses. It looks more like they wanted him alive but incapacitated."

Kern flushed with anger. "Nero has been running things since Baron Buckwold fell ill. He's orchestrated this whole thing to get Buckwold fighting for Headwater."

Alexander nodded with a humorless grin. "Yes, but he's failed. Now he'll pay for his crimes."

Abigail and Isabel came into the room in a rush. "We have a problem," Isabel said.

CHAPTER 16

"There's a company-sized force of palace guards massing in the south courtyard," Abigail said.

"How easily can they get in?" Alexander asked.

"This level is a good twenty feet off the ground with a balcony on three sides," Isabel said. "There are no stairs and the only way in is the one we came through, but they have ladders."

"We need more time," Alexander said with exasperation. "If they attack, can we hold them off?"

Abigail and Isabel shook their heads in unison.

Jack cleared his throat. Alexander turned to him with a little grin at the bard's familiar mannerism. "You have a suggestion, Jack?"

"Perhaps a ruse," Jack said. "Commander Kern, would the palace guard attack if they believed we were holding the Baron hostage?"

Commander Kern looked mildly shocked at the suggestion. The idea of holding his Baron hostage was something he had never considered but he answered nonetheless. "If they thought we would kill him, they would attempt to negotiate. Their first duty is the protection of the Buckwold family."

Alexander chuckled, "It would certainly buy us the time we need. Any objections?"

Commander Kern looked distraught. "Lord Alexander, I've served Buckwold my whole life. I can't hold the Baron hostage."

"It's just a ruse," Alexander said. "We have no intention of harming him, just using the threat to buy him time to wake up. Once he's awake, he can make up his own mind."

"Do you give me your word that you won't harm him?" Kern asked.

Alexander considered for a moment. "If he decides he wants to be my friend, then I will not harm him in any way, but if he chooses to be my enemy, then we're at war. I'll leave that decision to him."

Kern looked trapped by indecision. Jack stepped in and offered a nudge.

"Commander Kern, is the status quo acceptable? As it stands now, your entire territory is being played like a puppet by a liar and a traitor. Your Baron has been poisoned, and you are on the brink of a war that will not serve your people. Lord Alexander offers you the chance to restore your Baron's health and with it his authority over Buckwold."

Commander Kern deflated a bit. "It would seem that I have to choose between a bad choice and a worse choice." He considered for only a moment more. "Very well, your ruse will prevent a battle and give the Baron time to recover. How should we proceed?"

"We should have a demand of some kind," Anatoly said. "Hostage takers usually want something in exchange for the hostages. Might as well make it look authentic."

Alexander almost laughed when the thought came to him. "We'll demand that Commander Kern's legion be recalled immediately in exchange for the release of the Baron."

"That would certainly give them something to think about, but Nero will never recall the legion," Kern said. "In fact, I'd wager that he's already sent a new commander to take my place."

"I'm sure you're right, but it won't matter because we just need enough time for the Baron to wake up," Alexander said. He looked around for any other objections.

"I just hope the Baron will hear you out once he awakens," Anatoly said, "or we could be in a tight spot."

"I'm willing to risk it," Alexander said. "Anatoly, Abigail, can you do an assessment of our tactical situation just in case Nero decides to order an attack? We'll go make our demands, and then I want to talk to the Baron's physician."

Alexander went to the entry hall with Isabel, Jack, and Commander Kern. He could hear soldiers milling about outside, so he carefully opened the little window in the door. When he saw the guard captain, he called him over.

"Captain, we're holding the Baron hostage," Alexander said. "You will relay my demands to the person in command. Is that understood?"

Betrayal, humiliation, and anger played out across his face. "You gave me your word the Baron wouldn't be harmed," he said indignantly.

"Captain," Alexander snapped, "he will not be harmed, provided my demands are met. The legion formerly led by Commander Kern is to return to Buckwold. When it arrives, the Baron will be released; otherwise he will be killed. Do you understand my demands, Captain?"

The young officer stared back with hate in his eyes. "I understand," he spat at Alexander before he turned and strode off to deliver the message.

Alexander closed the little window. "If Nero orders an attack, will the palace guard obey?" he asked Kern.

He thought it over for a moment. "I doubt the rank and file will, but I don't know how many of the palace guard are loyal to Nero."

Alexander nodded. "We have to be vigilant. Nero would probably prefer that the Baron die in this confrontation. That way he can blame me and rally the people of Buckwold against Ruatha. Go tell your men to expect an assassin."

Commander Kern suddenly looked worried. "This is a dangerous game, Lord Alexander."

"Commander Kern, war is the most dangerous game there is," Alexander said. "When you're done, meet us in the Baron's bedchamber."

Alexander, Isabel, and Jack went to the sitting room where the staff was being detained.

"What if the court has a wizard?" Isabel asked quietly along the way.

Alexander looked at her sharply. "That would be a problem. We'll ask Kern about it."

They stopped at the threshold of the room. Six of Kern's soldiers stood along the walls, watching the eight people sitting fearfully in the center of the room. He appraised their colors and only one stood out from the others.

The physician had magic.

Alexander's hackles raised a bit. He couldn't tell from the colors what the physician's calling was, but his level of power was less than that of a wizard.

"Sergeant," Alexander said to the squad leader, "bind that man and bring him into the other room."

The sergeant motioned for two of his soldiers to tie the man's hands behind his back and walk him into the next room.

"See to it that the rest of these people are treated well," Alexander said over his shoulder.

The soldiers sat the man down and Alexander appraised him for a long moment before he spoke.

"Are you a sorcerer or have you survived the mana fast?" he asked.

The physician looked startled at the question but regained his composure quickly. He was a medium man in almost every respect: average height and build with medium-length, very ordinary brown hair; eyes of the most common shade of brown; and a round, soft-looking face.

He looked up defiantly at Alexander without a word. Alexander sighed and drew his sword. He held it close to the man's face.

"You will answer my questions or I will have no further use for you." Alexander fixed him with his glittering eyes.

He looked from Alexander to Isabel to Jack and found no help. He swallowed hard and nodded tightly. "I'm a sorcerer," he said.

Alexander sheathed his sword.

"What magic are you capable of?"

The man hesitated for a moment with a furtive glance at the Thinblade. "I can make myself look like another person if I've seen them before."

Alexander and Isabel shared a look before she took up the line of questioning. Alexander stepped back and watched his colors. Jack stood silently in the background observing intently.

"Did you pose as the Baron to give Nero authority over the affairs of Buckwold?" she asked.

He squirmed for a moment before he answered. "Yes, but it was Nero and Rake that made me do it. I didn't want to."

Alexander watched the subtle shift in his aura as he gave up the pretense, and the weight of the burden of deceit sloughed off his conscience.

Isabel frowned. "How did they make you do it?"

"Well," he hesitated, "they threatened me."

Alexander saw he was still hiding something. "Was that all?"

He looked down and spoke very softly. "Rake also promised to pay me a thousand gold sovereigns."

"Besides Nero, who else is involved?" Isabel asked.

"Just a couple dozen men in the palace guard. Mostly soldiers Nero brought on staff to help him with security."

"Aside from enlisting Buckwold's aid, was there anything else Nero was doing that we might like to know about?" she asked.

"Not that I know of, but they didn't tell me everything."

Isabel looked at Alexander and shrugged.

"Just one last thing," Alexander said, "let me see you change into someone else."

"All right. But it takes a few minutes. Who do you want me to look like?"

"How about me," Alexander said.

The man stared at Alexander very intently for several long seconds and then started whispering a chant over and over again. After a couple of minutes, his appearance very abruptly shifted and Alexander saw himself sitting in the chair in front of him. It was a remarkable likeness, but the physician couldn't disguise his aura. There was a distorted quality to the man's colors that revealed he was masking his true appearance. That was what Alexander was hoping for. He nodded his approval. They left the man alone in the room and closed the door.

"We've got to do something about him," Isabel said. "He's way too dangerous. There's no telling what kind of trouble he could cause."

"I was thinking the same thing," Alexander said. "I'd feel a lot better if he was unconscious. I'm going to stay here and keep an eye on him. You two go get Lucky and have him bring some deathwalker root. Jack, I'd like you to stay with the Baron while Lucky's away from him."

They hurried off. Alexander opened the door to find that the man looked like himself again. He stood in the doorway, arms crossed, and watched the man until Isabel returned with Lucky.

"Isabel told me about our friend here," Lucky said. "I think your instincts are correct." He fished around in his bag and produced a tin cup, then a water skin, and finally a jar of deathwalker-root flowers. He quickly mixed enough tincture to make the man sleep for a good eight hours.

The physician watched intently with a bit of fear.

"I think I'll rest easier if you're out cold. Drink up," Alexander said.

The man tried to resist but they held his head back, pinched his nose, and poured the tincture down his throat. In ten minutes he was asleep. They tied his hands and feet and laid him down on the floor, then posted two guards with orders not to open the door for anyone unless Alexander was present.

They returned to the Baron's bedchamber to find Anatoly and Abigail looking worried as they discussed their tactical situation with Commander Kern.

"We're surrounded by about three hundred soldiers," Anatoly reported. "They're well armed and well trained. If they attack, we won't be able to hold them off."

"I saw Nero with General Randal on the far side of the courtyard," Abigail said. "It looked like they were making plans. Alexander, I doubt we have long before they come for us."

"It looks like they have a battering ram in the hall outside the door," Anatoly added. "They'll probably come through the door and up ladders from the courtyard at the same time."

"My men will find it difficult to kill the palace guard," Commander Kern said, "especially since we know that most of them are loyal servants of the Baron."

A soldier entered with a worried look. "They say they have an answer to your demands, Lord Alexander. A representative of the court is at the door."

"This is moving much quicker than I'd like," Alexander muttered to himself. "Lucky, how's the Baron?"

Lucky shrugged helplessly. "He may not wake until this time tomorrow. I'm sorry, Alexander, but there's nothing I can do that wouldn't put him at greater risk."

"I guess we'd better go see what their answer is," Alexander said, heading toward the entry hall with everyone but Lucky trailing behind him.

He carefully opened the little window in the door and saw an officer of the palace guard waiting impatiently. "Well?"

"Administrator Nero refuses to meet your demands," he said. "The Baron was adamant about protecting the trade routes through Headwater. Furthermore, Administrator Nero demands you show proof that the Baron is alive or we will assume he's dead and your act of war against Buckwold will be met with the full force of our army."

Alexander smiled humorlessly. "As you well know, the Baron is ill. It will take some time to prove he's still alive without further jeopardizing his health. I'm sure the palace guard wouldn't want to act rashly and provoke a fight that could result in his death." Alexander closed the little window and went to the room where the serving staff was being held.

"Sergeant," Alexander said, "take these people to the Baron's bedchamber."

Alexander and his friends walked well ahead of the group of servants being herded along behind them. "Commander Kern, is there anyone in the palace who would be willing to help us if they learned the truth of Nero's treachery?"

"Just about everybody," Kern said.

"Anyone the palace guard would obey over Nero?" Isabel asked

"Perhaps Lady Buckwold, the Baron's daughter," Kern said. "She is first in line for succession. Her two brothers are still too young and the Baron has been grooming her for the position. She and Nero have been at odds for some time now."

Alexander looked over his shoulder at Jack. "How do you feel about running an errand?"

Jack smiled. "I live to serve," he said with a flourish. Abigail shook her head and rolled her eyes but couldn't help grinning.

Alexander had the servants each come up and sit on the bed next to the Baron. One by one, he asked them the same question: "Is the Baron alive?"

One by one, they said, "Yes." Once all of them had seen the Baron and verified that he was still alive, Alexander had Kern's men escort them to the entry hall and hold them there. When they were gone, he turned to Commander Kern.

"Where can Lady Buckwold be found?"

"Either in her private chambers or in her offices; given the situation, I'd say her offices."

"Can you draw a map?" Alexander asked. "One that shows how to get there from here?"

"I can do better than that," Commander Kern said. "Come with me." He led them into another chamber within the Baron's private residence. It was a map room with maps of the palace, city, and territory. Kern walked to the wall map of the palace grounds and pointed to the building that housed both the private residence and the offices of Lady Buckwold.

"Can you find your way from here, Jack?" Alexander asked.

He studied the map closely and traced the route. Then he traced a second and a third route. When he was satisfied, he nodded. "When I find Lady Buckwold, what would you have me say?" Jack asked.

"Tell her that her father is alive but Nero is about to order an attack," Alexander said. "If she doesn't intervene, the Baron may not survive the battle.

Tell her Nero is a traitor who has been poisoning her father and we need a day to flush the poison from his system."

"The truth it is," Jack said with a wink.

They returned to the entry hall. Alexander opened the little window and called out to the nearest guard. "Clear the hall of your soldiers and we will offer proof that the Baron lives."

Alexander could see the frustration in the colors of the guard. He was clearly working with Nero, but the rest of the men were loyal to the Baron and moved quickly to clear the hall. Alexander opened the door and told the servants to file out to the guards and report on the condition of the Baron. Jack tossed up the hood of his cloak and faded out of sight. Only a slight wavering in the air could be seen as he passed through the door on the heels of the servants.

The afternoon faded into dusk and then to darkness. Alexander watched the palace guard argue with Nero, who clearly wanted them to proceed with the attack. But the testimony of the servants gave the soldiers pause. They were sworn to protect the Buckwold line regardless of Nero's emphatic orders to attack.

The courtyard was lit with torches all around. It was a dark night shrouded in heavy clouds that blacked out the moon and stars. The torches sputtered in brief gusts of wind. Soldiers milled about waiting for orders to attack or to stand down.

After an hour of waiting for a sign from Jack, Alexander noticed a commotion in the courtyard. Nero marched one of the servants out in front of the soldiers. Alexander could see fear in her aura. She spoke with a tremor and glanced furtively at Nero as he prodded her on.

"I saw the Baron. He was dead," she said. "The criminals told us they would hurt our children if we didn't lie to you." She hung her head after she gave her false testimony and a guard led her off into the palace.

CHAPTER 17

Nero raised his voice to address the soldiers. "The Baron is dead! He's been murdered! You must avenge him now. Attack and leave no one alive. There is no more reason for delay. The enemies of Buckwold have killed the only reason to withhold our vengeance."

General Randal stepped up next to Nero and commanded, "Make ready for our assault!"

The soldiers were roused to anger by the revelation of the Baron's death and began donning helmets and strapping on shields.

One of Kern's men came rushing through the Baron's bedchamber and onto the balcony. "Lord Alexander, Lady Buckwold is at the door. She's demanding to be let in to verify the condition of her father."

Alexander smiled fiercely at the news just as another soldier rushed out to the general and spoke hastily in his ear. Alexander could see the anger flare in Nero's colors when he was told the news. He snapped orders to prevent Lady Buckwold from entering her father's suite at all costs, then grabbed General Randal by the arm and pulled him close to reiterate his orders to attack.

Alexander turned and ran for the entry hall. He threw open the little window and saw Lady Buckwold standing not ten feet from the door. He tossed up the bar and pulled the pin from the floor. The Baron's daughter entered silently with Jack trailing behind her still less than visible. Just as he dropped the bar back into place, Alexander heard a breathless and exasperated guard rush into the hall and yell to stop her.

She stopped in front of Alexander and appraised him with a stern expression. She was a plain-looking woman, not ugly by any means but not beautiful either. Her hair was dark blond and naturally wavy. Her eyes were slate grey and her skin was a touch too pale. She stood just over five and a half feet tall and, while she wasn't fat, she was big-boned. She wore a long, plain grey dress made from coarse cloth.

"You are the man responsible for this," she said. It was not a question. Jack became visible behind her and Alexander gave him a brief look of thanks.

"I am," Alexander replied. "Please come with me, Lady Buckwold." She didn't hesitate when he turned and strode off toward the Baron's bedchamber. She followed him wordlessly through the halls. Kern's soldiers looked slightly shamed by the reproving looks she gave them as she passed.

Alexander led her straight to the Baron. When she saw her father, she went to his bedside and took his hand. She choked back a sob at seeing him alive and breathing slowly and deeply. Then she stood and faced Alexander.

"Master Colton tells me that my father has been poisoned by Nero."

Alexander nodded gravely. "Nero is a traitor to Buckwold and Ruatha. His loyalties lie with Elred Rake and Prince Phane. Your father should wake from the poison sometime tomorrow."

Before she could respond, a soldier stuck his head into the room and shouted, "The palace guard is advancing!"

A look of thunderous anger overtook her severe expression and she marched out onto the balcony and up to the railing. In a clear and loud voice, she spoke to the palace guard moving under cover of shields and carrying ladders toward the building.

"I am Lady Buckwold. My father lives. I command you to stand down."

The soldiers slowed, then stopped as they looked up at her on the balcony. A murmur of confusion rippled through them.

Nero stood far in the back and shouted, "Attack! You must attack!" But his commands were lost on the palace guard—they had sworn to protect the Buckwold line.

General Randal approached the front of the company of soldiers. "Lady Buckwold, are you being threatened? Perhaps they have coerced you into making such a statement. We have it on good authority that Baron Buckwold is already dead."

"He is alive! I have seen him with my own eyes and held his hand in mine. You will order your men to stand down. Is that clear, General?"

"Yes, yes, of course, Lady Buckwold," General Randal said, then turned and started issuing orders to withdraw.

Alexander smiled when he saw Nero's colors change from rage to fear.

Lady Buckwold returned to her father's chambers and faced Alexander. "Explain yourself. You have come into my home and are holding the Baron of Buckwold hostage, yet you claim that his most trusted advisor is a traitor. You sent an emissary who is clearly imbued with powerful magic and a very persuasive tongue to enlist my aid. I have given it and now I will have my questions answered."

Alexander studied her colors. She was a strong woman who lived a life bound by duty. She held her emotions very close and didn't often permit them to intrude.

"Lady Buckwold, my name is Alexander Ruatha," he said as he drew his cloak back to reveal the distinctive hilt of the Thinblade. Her eyes widened a bit and her severity faltered just slightly.

"Headwater has thrown their lot in with Prince Phane and they have attacked New Ruatha. When I discovered that Buckwold had been duped by Nero into supporting Headwater, I decided the best course was to uncover the treachery and allow Buckwold to determine its own fate. From the brief time I've spent with Commander Kern and his men, I've learned a great deal about your people. They are industrious and productive; they seek peace and trade. I respect that, and I serve the Old Law. Your people have the right to self-determination guided by a clear understanding of the facts."

She regarded him for a moment before her expression softened. "My father often spoke of the time when the House of Ruatha would be remade. He will be pleased to meet you, Lord Alexander."

"I will be pleased to meet him, as well," Alexander said. "Master Alabrand, my court alchemist is watching over him. Please stay with your father. You'll be safe here. Now, if you'll excuse me, I have other matters to attend to."

"Lord Alexander, surely you don't believe the soldiers will attack now that they know I'm here and my father lives."

"No, but Nero may try something more desperate. I need to find out what he's planning." He turned and left without offering an explanation.

Before Lady Buckwold could ask any more questions, Isabel stepped forward. "Lady Buckwold, my name is Isabel Alaric, daughter of the Forest Warden of Glen Morillian and Alexander's betrothed. Please, sit with me. I'd like to hear about Buckwold."

On his way to a quiet sitting room, Alexander chuckled at Isabel's skillful interference. Anatoly followed without a word and stationed himself at the door. Alexander tossed a pillow on the floor to use as a meditation cushion.

It took several minutes to find the place of empty-mindedness that led to the firmament. Once his awareness slipped free of the boundaries of his body and spread out across the endless ocean of possibility, he quickly focused on Nero. He knew he would be planning his next move and Alexander didn't want to miss it.

His awareness coalesced in the upper corner of a room that looked like a wizard's workshop. There were three men present. One was Nero, the second was a wizard, and the third was a soldier dressed in the uniform of the palace guard.

"Administrator Nero, I'm not sure what one man can accomplish. There are twenty soldiers guarding the Baron," the wizard said.

"Wizard Raj, this is my very best man. He will protect the Baron while the palace guard storms the building. I'm confident he can keep the Baron safe during the assault."

Alexander could see his colors shift and twist as he lied to the wizard.

"I think it's too great a risk. We would do better to wait until morning and attempt negotiation," Wizard Raj said.

"I appreciate your input, as always, but I've made my decision," Nero said with exaggerated patience. "Can you get my man into the building undetected or not?"

"Of course, but I'm still not convinced I should. Your plan seems rash and desperate. I don't believe we're at that stage yet."

Nero drew himself up with a look that teetered between panic and rage. "Wizard Raj, you were in the council chamber when Baron Buckwold conferred upon me the authority to act in his name, were you not?"

Wizard Raj frowned with a sigh. "I was."

"Very well then, I command you to use your magic to get my man inside that building."

Wizard Raj looked angrily at Nero, but he relented. "Very well, Nero, but you're making a mistake. If you cost the Baron his life, you will answer to me."

"I'm just trying to save the Baron," Nero lied with feigned exasperation. "We are on the same side, Wizard Raj. Now, when will you be ready and what can I do to help?"

"I'll be ready in an hour. All I require from you is your absence."

Alexander returned to his body. When he walked back into the Baron's bedchamber, Isabel and Abigail stood after seeing the look on his face.

"What is it?" Isabel asked.

"Nero is sending an assassin. Commander Kern, have your men find a room without a window in the servants' quarters. We're going to move the Baron and put the physician in his bed as a ruse."

Kern smiled and nodded before leaving to scout the building for a suitable place. Within fifteen minutes, they had moved the Baron into an out-of-the-way room and put the sleeping physician into his bed.

Anatoly, Lucky, and three of Kern's soldiers stood guard over the Baron while Alexander, Abigail, Isabel, and Jack took positions in the four corners of the Baron's bedchamber and waited in the dark. Half a dozen soldiers waited in the next room with Lady Buckwold. The rest played the part of standing watch all around the royal suite.

The night wore on. The palace guard maintained their cordon around the Baron's suites but didn't advance. Alexander stretched out with his all around sight and watched for the enemy to arrive. When he did, it was altogether unexpected.

A mouse darted into the room from a crack in the corner. It came to the center of the dark room and stopped. Its colors flared brightly to Alexander's second sight as it transformed into a man. He stood still for a moment as if he was trying to orient himself before slowly drawing a dagger from his belt and carefully, quietly approaching the Baron's bed. Without hesitation, he put his hand over the sleeping man's mouth and sliced his throat deeply.

Alexander and Jack flooded the room with light from their vials of night-wisp dust. The assassin looked around frantically for a way out but found none. He was trapped. A moment later, Lady Buckwold stood in the doorway looking at his bloody hands as he stood over her father's bed and the corpse that lay there.

"Surrender and you might survive," Alexander said. "Resist and I will cut you in half." He drew the Thinblade and leveled it at him to punctuate the threat. The assassin slumped to his knees, his knife clattering to the floor.

"Please don't kill me," he pleaded with a sob. "Nero made me do it."

Alexander watched the colors of a liar ripple through his aura.

"How exactly did Nero make you do anything?" Alexander asked with menace in his voice, still pointing the Thinblade at him.

The man's face contorted with anger and malice as he gave up the pretense. "You're a pretender to the throne. When Prince Phane conquers the Seven Isles, Master Rake will rule all of Ruatha and I will be rewarded for my loyal service."

"I doubt that," Lady Buckwold said. "You have murdered a man in his sleep while attempting to assassinate the Baron of Buckwold. According to the Old Law, your life is forfeit." She held him with her severe gaze for a moment until his anger transformed back into fear. Then she continued, "However, if you assist us with the apprehension of Nero and all of his accomplices, I may be able to persuade my father to let you live."

He struggled with his situation for a moment before he hung his head. "I don't want to die," he whined.

She turned to a soldier who stood nearby. "Remove his weapons and bind his hands." The assassin didn't resist. Once he was bound, she marched him out onto the balcony and pushed him up against the railing.

"General Randal," she called out across the courtyard. Several moments later the general approached with his adjunct officer.

"Yes, Lady Buckwold?"

"Go get Wizard Raj and the members of the council. And be quick about. I'll be waiting."

He blinked a few times before he turned to his adjunct and commanded him to round up the people she had requested. Alexander and Isabel stood in the shadows behind her, watching silently.

The wizard arrived first. He looked up with a frown and shook his head. When he started to speak, she raised her hand sharply. "Wizard Raj, you will have a chance to speak, but not yet." They waited until, one by one, members of the council of nobles arrived. They all looked like they'd been roused from their beds. Once they were assembled, Lady Buckwold addressed them.

"General, Wizard, and Nobles, Buckwold has been the victim of treachery. Nero is an agent of Elred Rake. He has been poisoning my father with deathwalker root for over a month now. This man," she motioned to the miserable-looking man standing next to her, "is an assassin sent by Nero to murder my father in his sleep. I witnessed his crime myself." She turned to him. "Confess."

He squirmed under her accusing glare before he turned to the men assembled below the balcony. "Nero was sent by Master Rake to ensure that Buckwold would side with Headwater against New Ruatha. He sent me to kill the Baron. Wizard Raj cast a spell on me that transformed me into a mouse for a few minutes. Once I made my way inside, I carried out my orders, except the man I killed wasn't the Baron." He hung his head. "Please don't kill me," he whimpered.

The men standing below looked shocked and worried about the treachery. But Alexander could see that they were more concerned about the events of the past month and how their actions might be viewed in light of this new information. He remained in the shadows.

"General, you will order the palace guard to stand down. My father is alive and safe, and I have it on good authority that he will wake sometime tomorrow evening. Next, you will send fast riders to deliver orders to Commander Kern's legion to stop and hold their position until further notice. Finally, you will issue an order for Nero's arrest. Do you understand your orders, General?" she asked pointedly.

He nodded nervously.

"Wizard Raj, explain your actions."

He stepped forward and bowed respectfully. "My Lady, I offer no excuses. Against my better judgment, I obeyed Nero's command to get that man inside the Baron's suite." He pointed to the assassin. "Nero said he needed his man inside to protect the Baron while the palace guard stormed the building. After I cast the spell, two men came to my chambers and attempted to kill me, I presume to keep my knowledge of Nero's involvement a secret. I'm grateful to learn that the Baron survived my mistake."

"Very well then, you will help General Randal find Nero. Nobles, my father never gave Nero the authority he's been wielding for the past month. An imposter played the part of my father and, with the aid of magic, duped us all into accepting Nero as the Baron's spokesman. I would like to introduce to you the man responsible for delivering us from Headwater's treachery." She motioned to Alexander, and he and Isabel stepped out of the shadows and up to the balcony railing.

"I give you, Lord Alexander Ruatha, our rightful King and wielder of the legendary Thinblade, and his betrothed, Lady Alaric, daughter of the Forest Warden of Glen Morillian. Lord Alexander saw through the lies of Nero and his minions. He is not an enemy of Buckwold, but a friend and an honored guest. Until my father awakens from his long sleep, we will remain within the safety of the Baron's suite. Once he has been made aware of the events of the past month, I suspect he will have a few things to say to you all. Until then, we are not to be disturbed."

The rest of the night and the next day passed quietly. They spent time talking with Kern and Lady Buckwold about their homeland. Alexander offered news of the war and revealed much of what he knew about Phane and his machinations but withheld all mention of the Sovereign Stone. Jack told stories about the events of the past few months that held everyone in thrall. Alexander remembered many of the events Jack spoke of but they seemed somehow more glorious in his stories.

Late in the afternoon the Baron woke. Lady Buckwold was at his side and Alexander was in the room along with Jack and Lucky. The Baron was groggy at first and took several minutes to fully wake. When he did, he looked up at his daughter. A single tear slipped from her eye. He gave her a quizzical look before frowning and looking around the room at the unfamiliar faces. He sat up with effort.

"What's happened?"

"Nero poisoned you with deathwalker root. You've been asleep or in a stupor for a month. He tricked the nobles into thinking he was acting on your behalf and committed our army to war against New Ruatha in support of Headwater."

He gave her a look of alarm. "Where's Nero now?"

"On the run. He's being hunted by the army and Wizard Raj."

He turned his gaze to Alexander and Lucky. "Who are your friends?"

Lady Buckwold stood. "Father, this is Lord Alexander Ruatha and Master Alabrand. They brought Nero's treachery to light."

Alexander stood and his cloak slipped away from his hip revealing the hilt of the Thinblade. Baron Buckwold stared at it as if he wasn't sure he could believe what he was seeing, and then he smiled.

"So the legend has come to pass," he whispered. "Help me up," he said to his daughter.

He was a bit unsteady on his feet but managed to stand with her help. He extended his hand to Alexander. "My name is Carson, this is my daughter Elise. I just have one question for you, Lord Alexander. Do you serve the Old Law?"

Alexander smiled as he took his hand. "I do."

Carson Buckwold appraised him for only a moment. "Good enough. I pledge the support of Buckwold in service to my King. I'd bow, but I'm afraid I'd fall over."

Alexander chuckled softly. "I'm just glad to find another friend."

Buckwold smiled knowingly. "I was born into power. It's a lonely life. There are precious few you can trust and even fewer who can truly understand your burden. Come, I have something to show you."

With the help of his daughter, Carson Buckwold led them into a room in one corner of his suite. It was a comfortable little library. Once the lamps were lit, Buckwold pointed to the tapestry that hung in the center of one wall between two bookshelves. It was very old but held its color well. It was a picture of two men standing arm in arm. When Alexander looked closer, he saw the hilt of the Thinblade at the hip of one of the men.

"This is the first Baron of Buckwold standing with his dear friend, the King of Ruatha." He smiled. "I've often looked at this tapestry and wondered about those times. There are several books in this room that tell stories about the origins of Buckwold. I've read them all. When I felt the warning spell and knew Phane walked the Seven Isles again, I hoped for your rise with all my heart. I've also read stories of Phane and I fear for the future if he succeeds."

They talked late into the night. Alexander told him of the war and the battles he'd fought. He told him about Blackstone Keep and the details of Headwater's treachery. Buckwold listened intently and questioned him intelligently, then pledged two of his three legions to help defeat Headwater and to support Ruatha after that battle was won.

When he learned how Commander Kern had assisted Alexander, he promoted him to the rank of general and gave him command of the two legions. He sent a letter to his brother-in-law, the Duke of Warrenton, explaining the situation and gave Alexander assurances that Warrenton would support him and Ruatha.

Alexander slept well that night and woke the next morning anxious to be on his way. The Baron wanted him to stay longer, but Alexander explained that he was on a mission of great importance. Carson didn't ask any further questions or press the issue. Instead he ordered horses and supplies made ready and gave Alexander a letter of safe passage through Buckwold and Warrenton.

They had a hearty breakfast together and Alexander and his companions were on the road by midmorning.

CHAPTER 18

"I don't like the looks of that place, Prince Phane," the ship's captain said, eyeing their destination as Phane stood next to him. The big man held the ship's wheel tightly to guide the galleon into the calmer waters of the little cove. It was midday, but the sky was dark with swirling clouds that seemed to rotate around the volcanic peak of the central island of Tyr. The occasional spurt of lava that splattered into the sky from the broad crater gave the clouds a reddish tinge.

Phane smiled at the captain reassuringly—but after spending several weeks in the company of Prince Phane, the smile was anything but reassuring.

The captain had first ferried the Prince to the Reishi Isle. During that voyage, they had come under relentless attack from the sky by wyvern riders armed with magic and steel. The riders had tried repeatedly to sink the ship, but Phane had lashed out at them with ferocious magic that either drove them away or sent them into the cold embrace of the black waters. Several wyverns and their riders died during those attacks.

When the ship reached the Reishi Isle, they took refuge in a tight little cove surrounded by rocky spires that reached from the water into the sky. The captain remembered the reassuring smile Phane had given him then. For five days he and his crew had huddled under the protective cloak of Phane's magic while the wyvern riders searched for them and while Phane traveled inland with half a dozen men to find the Reishi Keep.

The Prince had returned alone, empty-handed and furiously angry.

On their voyage away from the Reishi Isle, the wyvern riders attacked again. This time Phane engaged them with rage and glee. He struck out at them with dark magic that made the air feel heavy with hate. Unwholesome shadows formed out of the thick sea air and chased the wyvern riders toward the horizon.

Now the captain was again looking at a place he would rather be sailing away from. He'd heard the rumors about the central island of Tyr. Rumors of dragons. No one sailed near the island, not just for fear of dragons but for fear of the island itself. It was a live volcano.

At night its radiant fire could be seen for miles. Sailors who passed too close told stories of rivers of molten lava flowing into the sea and bringing the ocean itself to a boil. Others told of giant rocks and globs of lava being cast high into the sky only to come crashing down into the ocean. Smart sailors avoided these waters.

He eased his ship into the cove and commanded the sails to be furled and the anchor dropped. All the while, Phane stood on the bow looking intently at the volcanic light show playing out across the angry black clouds swirling overhead.

"We're ready to launch the longboat, Prince Phane," the captain said tentatively.

Phane ignored him for a moment before turning without a word and taking his place on the small landing craft. The Prince sat quietly watching the glowing summit of the island while the sailors rowed and the captain manned the tiller.

When they made landfall, Phane stood without a word and stepped off the boat onto the rocky shore. He wasn't three steps away from the boat when the air near him turned deathly black. With a thump, Kludge appeared out of the cloud of now rapidly fading darkness.

"Ah, Kludge, what news do you bring?" Phane said, stopping for his familiar with a smile of genuine fondness. The little creature hovered slightly lower than eye level in front of Phane, wringing its clawed little hands while its batlike wings flapped furiously.

"Master, Karth is secure," Kludge said with grating subservience, "and the few surviving members of the House of Karth have been scattered into the jungle. Your army is assembled. They will move to Ruatha the moment the Gate comes to life. Andalia is beginning to transport cavalry to Kai'Gorn and should have a sizable army in place within the month."

Kludge descended a bit and his voice took on a slight whine. "News from Ruatha is not what you hoped for, Master. Commander P'Tal reports that Headwater's army has been deprived of supplies, and Buckwold has allied with the fugitive. He was last seen by an agent of the Reishi Protectorate riding south from Buckwold toward Warrenton."

Phane frowned darkly. Kludge wrung his hands. "How soon will Headwater fall?" Phane asked.

"Within the month, Master."

Phane nodded as he considered the news. "No matter. Headwater has served its purpose. Once I have the Sovereign Stone, the army on Karth will pour forth and crush Ruatha. What of the scourgling? Why has my servant failed to kill the fugitive?"

"Master, it seems that your servant has been trapped within a magic circle."

Phane chuckled. "This upstart is proving to be quite resourceful. Shame he can't be persuaded to join with me. He could be useful. Did Commander P'Tal offer any insight into the fugitive's purpose in Warrenton?"

"Only that Buckwold and Warrenton are closely allied by blood and friendship—where one goes the other will follow. Commander P'Tal also reports a rumor that the fugitive is on a mission to retrieve a book explaining the process for making Wizard's Dust."

"So he's not after Warrenton's support," Phane mused. "Yet he goes south from Buckwold amidst rumors of a quest for the secret of Wizard's Dust." He stood in deep thought for several long moments. "Walk with me, Kludge."

He turned away from the longboat and started up the treacherous path leading to the top of the volcano. Halfway up the path, he stopped suddenly. "He couldn't possibly be that bold," he said to himself. "It's doubtful that she would help him, but . . ." His voice trailed off as he worked the problem over in his mind. "Better to be safe," he said to himself before looking over at Kludge. The little monster flapped its wings faster and rose another foot into the air to meet Phane's eyes.

"Kludge, go to Commander P'Tal and instruct him to take an adequate force to hunt down the fugitive and kill him once and for all. Then take this," he handed Kludge a vial of black liquid he produced from his robes, "and go to the scourgling. Splash it across the lines of the magic circle, and my servant will be free to complete its task, should P'Tal fail. Return to me when you're done."

"As you wish, Master," Kludge said. He touched his ring, and the air around him darkened into an inky blackness. There was a thump and Kludge was gone.

When Phane looked up, he took a sharp breath. Perched on the edge of the volcano's crater was the silhouette of a dragon. He froze and cautiously extended the tendrils of his magical awareness into the mountain. What he saw made his blood run cold. Phane was an arch mage, perhaps the most powerful wizard anywhere in the Seven Isles. One dragon was no match for him.

But when he heard the dragon roar and saw her take to wing, he turned and ran for the boat. He wove protection spells around himself as he ran and used his wizardry to sense the coming attack. Dragons didn't like to be disturbed and he had just walked into a lair occupied by hundreds of the ancient magical beasts.

He sensed the shadow descending on him from behind and turned to face the onslaught. The fire came only a moment after he raised a magical shield. The heat of dragon fire washed over him in spite of the bubble of magical energy that prevented the flames from actually reaching him. He saw the magnificent creature soar overhead and then he saw a second and a third leap from the lip of the volcanic crater.

He ran with all the speed he could muster and then added magic to his stride and ran faster yet. He reached the longboat and found the sailors paralyzed with fear just as the dragon made another pass. He shielded the little boat with his magic, and the dragon roared overhead into the gloom of the late afternoon.

"Cast off," Phane commanded as he stepped aboard. "Now!"

He turned to the dragon that was wheeling for another pass and spoke words of power that made the air tremble. A black rope of dark energy streaked from his hand toward the dragon and coiled around her, binding her wings to her body. She toppled over in midair and plummeted to the sharp, craggy rocks below.

The men rowed with strength fueled by panic. Another dragon breathed fire at the little boat, but Phane was able to protect them with his magic once again. He looked back to see another five dragons take to wing off the summit of the volcano. Then the captain called out in terror and anguish. When Phane turned, he saw the galleon ablaze from dragon fire. Burning men were leaping into the water and the ship was listing. A moment later, another dragon plunged into the water not twenty feet from the little longboat. The splash tossed the boat into the air and sent Phane flying.

The Reishi Prince did what he'd always done when faced with defeat. He ran away. He called the door to his Wizard's Den into existence in the path of his trajectory and he tumbled roughly into the tiny magical room. The portal was a good thirty feet off the surface of the water, floating in midair as if frozen in space.

The men who had manned the capsized longboat were floating in the ocean below. Phane looked at the approaching dragon and judged that he had the time he needed. He held on to the wall and leaned out the door, sending his magic out to take hold of the first man he saw. He pulled him up through the air into his Wizard's Den. He saw the dragon fire coming toward him when he closed the door to his magical sanctuary, but he was safe, and he had the sacrifice he needed for yet another summoning. He smiled graciously at the doomed sailor.

CHAPTER 19

Alexander and his companions made good time to Warrenton. The territory was much like Buckwold in their trade and governance; they were prosperous and free with constables who didn't overstep their bounds yet demanded obedience to the Old Law.

Near the border, they encountered a squad of soldiers riding patrol. The soldiers were courteous and respectful while taking an active interest in the business of those passing into their territory. When Alexander produced the letter from Baron Buckwold guaranteeing safe passage, they were even more respectful and offered to ride as escort. Alexander politely declined.

He estimated they were about a day's ride from the city, but he didn't intend to pay Warrenton a visit. He'd spent enough time in Buckwold and was feeling a renewed sense of urgency to reach the Pinnacles. Everything hinged on who retrieved the Sovereign Stone first.

It was midday when Alexander saw the tail of a big cat flick out of the high grass. He called out and reined in his horse just in time to avoid the animal's ambush. Alexander knew that big cats sometimes wandered out of the mountains or forest to prey on livestock, but the few times he'd encountered them, they had stayed well clear of horses and people. They usually just wanted a calf for a meal. This one was different.

It came fast and spooked the horses. Alexander held on as his horse reared to defend against the charging cat. It was a magnificent creature, easily three feet at the shoulder and six feet long with golden fur and bright yellow eyes.

It leapt for the throat of Alexander's horse. The big mare lashed out with her hooves, but the cat launched itself high enough to avoid her desperate attempt to fend off the predator. The cat clamped its fangs into the soft flesh of her throat and sank its front claws into either side of her neck while raking the chest and belly of the dying horse with its rear claws. The horse started to topple over, screaming in pain and terror.

Alexander half fell and half jumped clear as his horse crashed to the ground in a jumble with the cat. He hit hard.

The cat didn't waste a moment with the dying horse, but instead fixed its yellow eyes on Alexander. He shook his head to dispel the stunned feeling and tried to take a breath but the wind was knocked out of him. All he could do was struggle to breathe and watch the big cat prepare to spring. As he fumbled to draw his sword, he thought vaguely to himself that the cat's colors weren't quite right.

Abigail sent an arrow into its shoulder; it howled and flinched sideways, giving her a murderous look. Anatoly gained control of his horse and charged the cat. Isabel drove an arrow into its haunch. The cat leapt into the air toward Alexander, but Anatoly caught it on the hindquarter with the sharp spike on the back of his axe. The cat spun and twisted in midair with such speed and violence that Anatoly lost his grip on his axe. The cat tumbled to the ground and came up limping and hurt. Abigail and Isabel each sank another arrow into the bleeding animal, but it didn't seem to notice.

Alexander succeeded in drawing a breath and his sword at the same time. He regained his feet only a moment before the cat pounced again. This time he was ready. He slipped to the side and cleaved the head and right shoulder of the big cat free of its body. It crashed to the ground in a broken heap.

He stood gasping for breath and looking at the scene of carnage with shock and bewilderment as he schooled the pounding in his chest. Wild animals didn't behave like that. It made no sense until he saw it—a thin filmy shimmer of discoloration rose up from the dead cat and almost took form. It hovered for just a moment as a beastly face of contorted malice coalesced. Its eyes glowed with a menacing red, but they were the only part of the insubstantial creature that had any semblance of solidity. It locked eyes with Alexander before it shrieked soundlessly and darted straight for Isabel.

Alexander watched in helpless terror as the demon possessed her horse. Isabel put her hand to her horse's neck to comfort the spooked animal, and before Alexander could warn her, she made a connection with the animal's mind—a mind now possessed by a creature from the darkness.

She screamed with horror and pain in a way that made Alexander's soul squirm. The horse bucked. Isabel was a skilled and experienced rider, but her mind was recoiling from the contact she'd made with the mind of a demon and she was tossed free and hit the ground hard.

Alexander wanted nothing more than to race to her side, but the possessed horse was blocking his path. It reared and lashed out with its hooves. This time Alexander knew what he was facing. He flicked his blade across the horse's legs and lopped them both off just below the joint. The horse screamed in pain. When it fell forward and tried to break its fall with what was left of its legs, it screamed again. The next moment, Alexander sliced through its brainpan. The horse slumped over and the demon rose again.

Anatoly was already on the ground retrieving his axe. Lucky had dismounted to attend to Isabel. That left Jack and Abigail still on horseback.

"Dismount!" Alexander called out urgently. "A demon is possessing the horses." Abigail and Jack wasted no time clamoring down from their steeds. Anatoly's horse was the next to be taken. With resignation, he stepped between the animal and Alexander. It charged. Anatoly picked his moment and sidestepped, swinging his axe at the back of the horse's neck. It fell forward and died quickly.

With sickness in his heart, Alexander stepped up to Lucky's horse and killed the beast before it could be taken by the demon. He gave Abigail a look that spoke volumes. They'd grown up riding horses together. Both of them loved the animals, but now they were a threat.

Her anguish turned to resolve and then to cold anger. She said "I'm sorry," as she sent an arrow into her horse's heart. Jack's horse was last. The demon took it and turned to charge Alexander but it never made it. Abigail took careful aim and released her arrow into the side of the animal's chest. It stumbled to the ground and fell over.

Alexander watched the demon rise up from the last of the horses. It held his gaze with murderous hate and soundlessly shrieked again before passing straight through his body. He felt a chill that made his skin crawl as the netherworld creature moved through him and then faded off into the distance.

The battle lasted less than a minute but there was death all around. In the stunned silence that followed, worry for Isabel flooded into Alexander and he raced to her side.

She was unconscious. Lucky looked worried but not half as worried as Alexander was when he saw the taint in her aura. She'd made contact with the mind of a demon, and the foul creature had stained her beautiful colors.

"How badly is she hurt?" Alexander asked as he willed the frantic terror welling up inside him into the recesses of his mind.

Lucky was all business. "Nothing is broken but she hit her head. She won't be ready to travel until tomorrow at best. I need to get a healing potion into her, but I want to let the salve do its work first before I sit her up."

Alexander nodded, struggling to swallow the lump in his throat. He couldn't stand the fact that she was hurt but he was distraught over the taint in her colors.

"Alexander," Anatoly said, "what just happened?" The big man-at-arms looked at the dead animals all around.

"We were attacked by another demon," Alexander said, standing up to face his friends. "I think it was like the zombie demon except this one possessed animals instead of corpses. It was in the cat when it attacked. When it died, I saw the demon go into Isabel's horse." He took a deep breath to steady his voice for what he had to say next.

"She touched it with her mind and now her colors are wrong." In spite of his best efforts, his voice broke a bit as he put words to his greatest worry. The look on his friends' faces was one of sorrow and fear. Abigail wiped a tear from her cheek.

"What do you mean her colors are wrong?" Lucky asked with alarm.

"Her aura is tainted. It's like that thing left something behind inside her when she tried to talk to her horse. I wasn't fast enough. I should have warned her."

"Could you see the demon?" Jack asked.

Alexander looked at him sharply and nodded. Jack looked to Abigail and Anatoly in turn. Both shook their heads. "It would seem that you are the only one who could see it, Alexander," Jack said.

"I should have warned her," he said in anguish.

Abigail grabbed him roughly by the shoulder and turned him to face her. "Nonsense, the whole thing lasted all of a minute. You didn't have time because you were fighting for your life."

"She's right, Alexander," Jack said. "You can't beat yourself up over it. Isabel will be fine. She's strong, and Lucky will take good care of her."

Lucky stood up with a look of less confidence. "Alexander, I can heal her physical injuries but I'm worried about the taint the demon left behind. Touching the mind of a creature from the netherworld is not a trivial matter. I've read accounts of wizards who've done such things." Lucky shook his head sadly. "Most of those accounts end badly."

Alexander felt panic build inside him. He couldn't lose Isabel. She was his best reason for drawing breath. She filled him with joy. The sheer power of his love for her humbled him. In all his life, he'd never felt anything so profound, so all-encompassing, or so beautiful.

He knelt next to her with a sob. He tried to fight it but the fear of loss overwhelmed him and he simply cried. He held her hand for several minutes while tears streamed quietly down his cheeks and dripped onto her tunic. Slyder landed next to her and looked at her, then at Alexander, and then back at Isabel. The bird cocked his head and gently nudged her. When she didn't react, he sat down next to her in the grass to wait for her to wake up.

Alexander's friends left them alone. Anatoly quietly put everyone else to work gathering supplies and repacking the contents of their saddlebags into their packs. An hour later, they had camp made with a small cook fire and a shelter for Isabel.

They carefully moved her inside. Lucky tended her injuries but she still didn't wake up. The afternoon wore on. She was fitful and restless but wouldn't wake. Cold dread began to settle into Alexander's soul. By dark he was despondent. He felt so helpless. He could see her rich, vibrant, wholesome colors struggling with the base, muddy, hateful colors of the demon's taint. It was like watching oil grapple with water in an effort to force a mixture that wasn't natural.

He stayed with her through the night, hoping she would wake, but she didn't. His panic grew, threatening his sanity. The idea hit him with the force of a lightning bolt. He sat up with sudden realization. There was slim chance of it working but he had to try. The opportunity to take action washed away all of his fear and despair and replaced it with fierce, desperate hope.

He crossed his legs, held her hand between both of his, and closed his eyes. His determination was so great and his need so terrible that he ruthlessly calmed his mind. He recognized, acknowledged, and discarded his thoughts with cold severity as he schooled his breathing and drained all tension from his muscles.

In just a few minutes he was in the state of empty-mindedness that was his doorway to the firmament. And then he was there, floating on the sea of potential that was the source of reality. He didn't waste a moment listening to the music of creation, but instead brought his awareness into focus a few feet above his head. He looked down on Isabel's restless body and examined the taint working to overpower her mind. And then he plunged his awareness into her.

At first he was simply within her body. When he focused, he could see the details of her insides. He would have been fascinated by the implications of such vision, but he had more pressing concerns. He searched within her to find a way to help her. Then he found it—a point within her head just at the top her spine.

When he touched it with his awareness, he felt an icy darkness draw him in as though he was passing through a doorway into another realm. He went willingly but not recklessly. He visualized a lifeline: a string of awareness and magic that linked his consciousness to his physical body. He made it real with an act of will and plunged into the darkness.

It was cold and lifeless, filled with dread and despair, without form or substance. In many ways it was like the firmament except there was no crest of the wave to manifest into reality, only endless, unformed darkness. There was also no hope or potential, only the anguish of unrealized possibility, desire unfulfilled.

Alexander was in the netherworld.

With a stab of fear, he realized that Isabel was there too, and she was completely unprepared for such an experience.

He felt the frustration, pain, and rage of stunted and malformed minds deprived of any chance of ever realizing the possibilities that they could only imagine. When they brushed up against him, he felt their hate and their fury but they recoiled from the light of his nature and the radiance of his living soul. He knew instinctively that his light would fade under the relentless assault of the darkness and so would Isabel's. He had to find her quickly. She had already been in the darkness for so long.

For a brief moment he tried to expand his awareness the way he did in the firmament. He tried to be everywhere at once but saw in an instant the folly of doing that in the netherworld. When the light of his living soul was concentrated in one location, he could fend off the darkness, but when he tried to expand his awareness, his light dimmed. The numbing coldness that flooded into him in that one brief instant was enough to cause him to pull back to a single bright point.

But it was also enough to let Isabel know he was with her. Off in the distance, through the murky darkness, he saw a brief flare of light. He moved through the unrealized potential of broken souls, driving them aside with the light of his very real existence fueled by vital life energy and love.

When he found her disembodied awareness, she was huddled into a ball of fear surrounded by a swarm of howling dark spirits trying to drive her farther and farther away from life. Alexander plunged into the fray. His weapon was the light of his life powered by his boundless love for Isabel. He brought his soul to hers and surrounded her with his light, sheltered her with his love, and defended her with righteous fury.

She clung to him and opened the essence of her being to him. He rushed in and washed away all of the fear and doubt and then opened himself to her completely. He held nothing back, allowed her into every crevice of his soul and rejoiced in the love she gave him in return. The darkness shrank back as their light joined and shined with piercing brightness.

The sudden flare of light where no light should ever be drew the attention of the beasts that lurked deeper in the darkness. Alexander saw shadows of their malice stirring in the deep. He took hold of Isabel and began to trace his lifeline back to his starting point.

The beasts from the depths saw their quarry attempting to escape and gave chase. When Alexander burst free of the netherworld and back into Isabel's mind, he didn't let go of her soul; he stayed with her in the confines of her own mind. She was still terrified and the passage to the darkness was still open within her. He knew he had to find a way to help her close that doorway or she would be forever lost.

He visualized a room with a door and imposed his vision on her nightmare. She stood with him in the room, looking at the open doorway leading into the netherworld. Specters of broken souls with unspeakable appetites beckoned them to enter.

"You have to close the door," Alexander said.

"I don't know how. I'm so afraid."

"It's all right, I'm right here with you. See yourself walking to the door and pushing it closed. This is your mind, your dream. You can make anything you want happen here."

As was the nature of dreams, one moment she was standing next to
Alexander and the next she was closing the door and bolting it shut. There was an
otherworldly howl of rage from beyond the door. Isabel backed away quickly into
Alexander's arms. Her fear was palpable.

The door was still there and the darkness knew it.

"It's time to wake up now."

"Don't leave me, Alexander."

"I'm right here with you. I'll be right beside you when you wake."

She nodded and he carefully disentangled his consciousness from hers
and withdrew to a point above her and then into himself.

Abigail was sitting in the little makeshift shelter looking worried. When
he opened his eyes, she breathed a sigh of relief.

He gently shook Isabel's shoulder and she came awake with a start. Her
eyes opened wide and she threw her arms around him. He held her while she wept.

After several minutes, she whispered, "I was so afraid."

"I know. You're safe now." He drew her back and looked at her colors.
The taint was still there but more faintly.

She shook her head and wiped away tears from her cheeks. "It's still
there. I can feel the darkness trying to draw me in."

"You have to resist. We'll figure out how to get rid of the doorway for
good, but for now you have to be strong."

She nodded and looked up into his eyes. When their eyes met, he saw
more there now. They always had an easy bond but there was much greater depth
to it now. They had shared themselves with each other in a way that transcended
love. Each was intimately aware of the very essence of the other's soul and each
accepted and embraced the other with full knowledge and complete trust. Their
souls were mated in a way that few others would ever experience.

CHAPTER 20

Lucky tried to question Isabel but Alexander knew she didn't want to talk about it yet. She needed distance from the experience, so he asked Lucky to wait awhile before asking his questions.

They set out after breakfast. Everyone was exhausted, but Alexander knew they had to keep moving. He kept an eye on Isabel. She was brave and strong, but he could see the fear in her that had never been there before. She could stand and face any enemy without flinching, but this was different. She knew there was something inside her that was wrong and she couldn't do anything about it.

They weren't able to cover much ground because they were all so tired, but they made it to the outskirts of Warrenton where they found a small inn and rooms for the night. A solid night of sleep and a warm meal would do them all good. It was a simple little place made from rough-cut timber, but it was well cared for and the proprietors were hospitable enough.

They paid for three rooms, each with two beds, and went to the main hall for the evening meal. They listened to the conversations around the room while they quietly ate their meal of roasted pork. Jack chatted up the barkeep and learned a bit about the happenings around Warrenton. It seemed that the talk of the town was the treachery of Headwater against Buckwold.

Alexander found it amazing that word of events in Buckwold had traveled so fast, but then he remembered his father's words: "Nothing moves as fast as a rumor." The general sentiment of the people was one of solidarity with Buckwold and by extension with New Ruatha. Alexander was pleased to find that Carson was right about the long-standing friendship between the two territories.

Alexander and Isabel shared a room but slept in separate beds. After the experience of the previous night, he wondered if they were already married in a way more profound than any ceremony could match, but he kept his thoughts to himself. More than anything, they both needed sleep and he knew Isabel was still afraid of the darkness within her.

In the dead of night, Alexander was jarred awake by a scream of sheer terror. He was up and out of his bed in an instant, sword in hand and scanning the room and beyond with his all around sight. Isabel had pushed herself into the corner and was curled up into a ball, panting with fear. Alexander sheathed his sword and went to her, gently offering his comfort. She threw her arms around him and wept.

Anatoly knocked. "Is everything all right?" he asked through the door.

"Yes, thank you, Anatoly. Isabel had a nightmare," Alexander said without moving to open the door.

"It was so real," she said. "The door was open and I was standing in front of the darkness. I could see hateful faces form and fade. Then I saw Rangle. He looked right at me and laughed as tendrils of darkness shot out of the portal and tried to pull me in. I struggled and fought until I was able to slam the door shut and throw the bolt." She held onto him and took comfort in his presence for several long moments.

"Will you hold me?" she asked in a small voice.

"Of course. Lie down and try to get some sleep. I'm right here," Alexander said as reassuringly as he could in spite of the worry and dread that filled him. The situation was more dangerous than he first thought. If the darkness could try to claim her in her dreams, she wouldn't be able to sleep. Eventually, she would be too exhausted to resist. He tried to sleep but his worry kept him awake. Isabel drifted off but woke with a start a few hours later. She didn't scream but she cried for a few minutes.

"I'm afraid, Alexander," she whispered. "I've never faced anything like this before. I've always been able to see my enemy and fight them head-on. This doesn't have a form or a body, and it's inside me. How can I kill something that's a part of me?"

He held her tighter. "I don't know, but I promise you I'll do everything in my power to find out. I think we should talk to Lucky about it. He may know of a way to help." He felt her nod in the darkness. They didn't sleep much for the rest of the night. Isabel was afraid to fall asleep, and Alexander was afraid that if she did, she would get drawn into the darkness again. When dawn came, they were both exhausted.

They bought some supplies after breakfast and made a few inquiries about the path to the Pinnacles. Most people thought going into the wild mountains was a foolish thing to do, but told them the way to get there nonetheless. By midmorning they were on the road that skirted around the city of Warrenton. They decided not to buy horses because they would have to abandon the animals once they reached the mountains. Also, in the back of everyone's mind was the thought that the demon was still out there somewhere.

Once they were on the road, Alexander decided it was time to talk about the experience of sending his consciousness into the netherworld and Isabel's ongoing struggle with the darkness. He gave her a look. She understood and nodded, taking a deep breath before she began.

"Lucky, I need your help," she said.

"Of course, my dear, anything I can do."

"When I touched the horse's mind, I made contact with the mind of a demon instead," she began, but before she could continue everyone stopped dead in their tracks. She pressed on with her story now that she had everyone's undivided attention. "Somehow it created a portal to the netherworld within my mind and I was drawn into the darkness. That's why I couldn't wake up."

Lucky couldn't help himself. "How did you get back?"

Isabel smiled and took Alexander's hand. "Alexander used his magic to come in and get me," she said simply to looks of astonishment and alarm all around. "He saved me."

"You did what?" Abigail said. "What have I told you about being more careful? Don't get me wrong, Isabel, I'm glad he saved you, but," she turned back to her brother, "this is exactly the kind of thing you need to let us help you with."

"She was dying. When the thought came to me, I just did it," Alexander explained without any hint of apology.

Abigail stared with her mouth agape at her brother and shook her head in dismay.

"Please continue," Lucky said intently.

Isabel nodded. "It was a cold and terrible place filled with fear and despair. I was lost and adrift. Disembodied beings of pure hate and malice assailed me for what seemed like a very long time. I could feel my connection to the world of the living slipping away, and then Alexander was there. He found me and brought me back. I have no idea how he did such a thing, but he did." She smiled up at him. "The trouble is—the doorway to the darkness is still there in my mind. Alexander showed me how to close it, and it doesn't seem to have any power over me when I'm awake but when I sleep, it opens up and tries to draw me in. I'm so tired, but I'm afraid to go to sleep and I'm afraid it's only going to get worse."

Lucky took a deep breath. "This is troubling indeed. I can give you some deathwalker root to help you sleep without dreams. At least you'll be well rested, but we need to find a way to permanently destroy the connection between your mind and the netherworld. That is a much more challenging problem. Let me think on the matter."

Isabel nodded with a smile. "Thank you, Lucky. I feel better knowing that I can sleep without being lost to the darkness."

***

By nightfall they were well past Warrenton and just a couple of days away from the treacherous path into the Pinnacles. Isabel slept through the night with the help of the deathwalker-root tea that Lucky prepared for her. She woke the next morning feeling much better.

That afternoon she stopped dead in her tracks after a moment of looking through Slyder's eyes.

"We're being followed. Looks like a dozen men on horseback but they're keeping well back. I'm sending Slyder to take a closer look."

An hour later she reported again. "It's Nero and a dozen soldiers."

Anatoly grunted. "The coward doesn't want to fight us. He's probably just a scout for Phane."

"Keep an eye on him, Isabel," Alexander said. "We should make it to the mountains by tomorrow afternoon. If he follows us into the Pinnacles, we might just have to set an ambush for him."

Nero kept his distance, and the six travelers made it to the foothills of the Pinnacles on the evening of the next day. From where they stood, they could see the sharp, craggy mountains jutting up from the surrounding forests. They were white at the peaks and looked like giant ivory fangs gnashing at the sky. Alexander understood from the ominous look of the place why the locals thought it was a bad idea to venture there.

It was a few hours from dark when they moved from the plains into the low rolling hills covered with the ancient trees that made up the eastern edge of the Great Forest.

Warrenton relied on the timber from the foothills of the Pinnacles. As Alexander and his companions hiked into the forest on the wide, well-cut road, they passed several timber crews and saw a few operations in progress. By dark they had traveled several miles and stopped for the night at one of the frequently used campsites along the road. It was a quiet evening except for the coming and going of work crews.

The next morning after breakfast, Isabel sent Slyder to have a look at Nero. "Looks like he's waiting at the trailhead. I wonder what he's waiting for."

"Might as well take advantage of their delay and get some distance on them," Alexander said as he hoisted his pack.

They made good time, considering that they were traveling on foot uphill along an increasingly narrow pathway. The well-cared-for roads gave way to little-used trails and then to animal tracks through the thick brush and timber. They pushed on toward the south and the teeth of the Pinnacles until they found a mountain spring an hour before dark and made camp.

After dinner, Isabel said, "It looks like Commander P'Tal and a company of soldiers are about a day away from Nero's camp at the trailhead. That puts them two days behind us."

"We should be all right if we press on," Alexander said.

"That's assuming we can find another way out of these mountains when we're done here," Anatoly said.

Alexander nodded. "I'm hoping we can find a way down to Highlands Reach. From there we can go to Southport and get a ship to take us to the Reishi Isle."

"I guess that makes more sense than backtracking through New Ruatha, although it would be good to see how we're doing against Headwater," Anatoly said.

"I'm sure father has things well in hand, especially with the help of Buckwold," Abigail said.

CHAPTER 21

They spent the next two days hiking uphill through thick forests. Isabel reported that Commander P'Tal had joined Nero and they were pursuing slowly. She brought Slyder back to help navigate through the mountains. The terrain was steep and treacherous and there were many opportunities to wander into box canyons that would cost them precious time.

As they gained altitude, the air cooled and the forest diminished. In the lower foothills, the forest was composed of giant trees that reached hundreds of feet into the sky with trunks ten to twenty feet thick. At higher elevations the trees became smaller. The tallest were only forty feet high with trunks no more than a foot in diameter. The forest was thinner and the underbrush was lower and less dense. It made for easier travel.

They came into a broad valley with a shallow but fast-moving mountain stream running down the middle. The valley floor was almost a mile wide and stretched for several miles due south. Strewn throughout were giant boulders standing up to forty feet tall. The tops of the trees just reached the height of some of the larger rocks. The boulders were covered with moss and lichen and many had bushes and even a few small trees growing on top. It would have been an idyllic setting if not for the column of smoke rising about a mile upstream.

Isabel sent Slyder to take a look. Alexander saw a look of alarm and worry ghost across her face just before she opened her eyes.

"It's a half dozen ganglings and they have a woman tied up on a roasting spit," Isabel said. "It looks like they're just waiting for the fire to die down to coals before they start cooking her."

"What's a gangling?" Jack asked.

"They're a primitive race of giants that live in the wilds," Lucky said. "They stand about ten feet tall with very long arms. They're strong but not very smart, typically live in small communities of twenty or thirty, and usually inhabit caves. Unfortunately, they're not terribly reasonable."

Alexander sighed. "We have to go right past them, and I don't like the idea of leaving that woman to become their dinner. Maybe if we help her, she could point us in the right direction. I'm starting to feel like we're wandering aimlessly in these mountains."

"It would be a dangerous fight," Anatoly said. "Ganglings are big and strong and they throw rocks. We might do better to slip past them."

"Yeah, probably, but I won't feel right if we don't try to help her," Alexander said.

Anatoly nodded with a knowing little smile. "I figured as much. We should use ranged weapons as much as possible. One good thump of their oversized fists and you'll be out cold—until they start cooking you, anyway."

"Is there any high ground nearby?" Alexander asked Isabel.

She nodded. "There are actually three big boulders around their campsite. We should be able to get on top of one without much problem."

"How well do they climb?" Alexander asked Lucky.

"Quite well, actually; these mountains are their home."

"All right, let's head their way," Alexander said. "Keep an eye on them, Isabel. Jack, be ready to sneak in and untie the woman while we attack."

They approached the cook fire carefully as the woman cried out for help. She sounded terrified and desperate. They slipped around to the south side of the camp so they would be able to make their escape once Jack freed her. When they reached the cover of the southernmost boulder, Alexander stopped and divided the party into two groups.

"Isabel, Abigail, and Lucky will go up the back side of that rock and take over-watch positions. Don't start shooting until the ganglings attack. Anatoly and I will approach from the right side of the boulder. Jack will approach cloaked from the left. All we want is to get the woman and get away. We don't have to kill them, we just have to keep them from killing us."

Everyone nodded their agreement and they split up. Anatoly and Alexander waited a few minutes for everyone to get into position. Anatoly slung his axe and got his slingshot out of his pack along with a handful of lead-shot bullets.

Alexander chuckled. "Always another weapon stashed somewhere."

Anatoly nodded. "I always told you to keep a weapon handy. I practice what I preach. Unfortunately, these aren't going to do much more than give those things a headache, but I may be able to discourage one or two before they get close enough to warrant a blade."

Alexander and Anatoly approached slowly and silently. There were six ganglings. Each stood nine to ten feet tall with unusually long arms and oversized hands and feet. They were manlike in that they had two arms, two legs, and a head, but that's where the similarities ended. Their tight leathery skin was ash grey and completely hairless. Their snout was slightly pronounced and their forehead sloped back from the bridge of their nose. They had grey eyes without pupils and sharp-looking canines that showed a bit even when their mouths were closed. Their colors were more complex than those of a typical big animal but not by much and they revealed a violent and even cruel nature.

Once they were within easy slingshot range and separated a bit, Alexander gave the nod to Anatoly. The big man-at-arms whipped the slingshot around his head once, then twice, and released his heavy lead bullet. It sailed soundlessly toward the gangling nearest the woman.

The fire was about ready and the gangling was making sure her leather bonds were tight and wet to prevent them from burning through before their meal was cooked. The lead shot smacked him in the side of the head and he toppled over with a thud. The woman looked around frantically before she saw Alexander and Anatoly. The look of hope and salvation Alexander saw in her eyes made the risk more than worth it.

He loosed his arrow at the nearest gangling, driving it into the flesh of the giant's thigh. It tipped its head back and roared in rage, pain, and surprise. The other four ganglings were up and looking for the threat. Abigail and Isabel released their arrows in tandem. Abigail's shot straight down from the top of the boulder and lanced through the belly of one of the ganglings, out its backside, and into the ground. The giant slumped to its knees and toppled over with a wail.

Isabel's arrow sailed gracefully off the boulder and stuck six inches into the shoulder of another.

It roared at her as it dug into a bag on its hip and pulled out a rock about six inches in diameter. It took a hop step and threw the rock toward Isabel. She ducked and it shattered against the stone face of the boulder behind her, showering her with shards of gravel.

The two uninjured ganglings threw rocks at Alexander and Anatoly, who quickly ducked as the rocks whizzed over their heads. Alexander watched the angry ganglings close ranks around their wounded and roar in warning while Jack led the frightened and grateful woman away from the camp.

Alexander and Anatoly carefully retreated from the angry giants and met Abigail, Isabel, and Lucky behind the big rock. Jack and the woman came up a moment later. They heard the furious roar of several ganglings, no doubt at discovering that their dinner had escaped.

"Thank you. Thank you so much," the woman said. "My name is Marla Tasselheim. We have to get far away from here before the ganglings work up the anger to come after us."

Marla was just over five and a half feet tall, with brown hair and plain, yet intelligent, brown eyes. She had a strong jaw and a broad mouth that fit her broad shoulders and sturdy body. Her smile was genuine and bright. She wore simple brown robes and she wasn't armed.

Her colors were a bit unusual. Alexander knew what magic looked like in another, and Marla definitely had magic, but it was of a type and a quality that he'd never seen before. Fortunately, her colors also revealed good character.

"Do you know your way around these mountains?" he asked.

She nodded. "I've lived in these mountains all my life, although I don't usually come down this far."

"Excellent. Why don't you lead the way?" Alexander suggested.

They moved quickly but quietly away from the gangling camp. Roars of anger and indignation could be heard behind them. Once they made it through the little valley and into one of the narrow canyons that fed the mountain stream, they slowed a bit to catch their breath.

"My name is Alexander. You've met Jack. These are Abigail, Isabel, Anatoly, and Lucky."

"It's very nice to meet you all," Marla said. "I'm so grateful to be free of those monsters. I can't tell you how helpless I felt tied to that spit, watching the fire burning down to hot coals." She shook her head with a shudder. "Thank you again for saving me." She stopped and looked Alexander very directly in the eye. "I mean it, Alexander. You saved my life and you have my gratitude."

"I'm just glad it all worked out," he said. "Perhaps you could help us?"

"Of course, anything I can do," Marla said.

Alexander took a deep breath, measuring how much to tell her. "We're seeking the Fairy Queen."

Marla's eyes went wide with alarm as she shook her head. "From time to time, men come into the Pinnacles looking for the Valley of the Fairy Queen. A few find it. None return. I would hate to see you lost to her ancient magic, Alexander."

He nodded. "Thank you for your concern but it's a matter of great importance, and she's the only one who can help me. Can you guide us there?"

"I can, but I'm not sure I should," Marla said. "Please understand, sending you into the Valley of the Fairy Queen will probably get you killed. You just saved my life. At the very least, I have a duty to protect you from wandering into a place of great danger."

"I've been invited by a fairy to come to the Fairy Queen with my request," Alexander said.

Her eyes widened a bit, this time in surprise. "Such a thing is unheard of. The fairies don't want much to do with anyone but their druids."

"Druids?" Abigail asked.

Marla nodded. "Druids serve each of the great powers and tend their temples. Some druids serve the fairies. I serve the dragons," she said proudly, taking a chain from under her robes and holding up a gold medallion in the shape of a dragon.

"Dragons?" Alexander said. "I thought dragons didn't like people."

"They don't in general," Marla said. "But they make exceptions for a few of us." She smiled with genuine pride and love.

"Marla, Master Grace and I are Rangers," Isabel said. "In times past, the Rangers and the druids have cooperated to preserve and protect the forest. Please help us now."

Marla frowned. "Perhaps we should present your request to my patron. If she gives you safe passage through the Pinnacles, then the other great powers are honor bound to recognize her word. I would feel much better about leading you to the Valley of the Fairy Queen knowing that you'll be safe from her whims."

"By patron, do you mean dragon?" Jack asked a bit hesitantly.

Marla smiled like the sunrise. "Yes. Her name is Tanis and she's the most magnificent creature you will ever see."

"And she won't eat us?" Alexander asked.

Marla laughed. "Not if I introduce you to her."

Alexander looked to each of his friends. They all looked a bit dubious but they nodded agreement nonetheless. "I've never met a dragon before. Lead the way."

CHAPTER 22

Marla led them into the more rugged and rocky mountains that rose above the forests. She seemed to know her way and was surefooted enough to travel along paths that Alexander would never have tried on his own. They moved relatively slowly due to the poor footing and the steep grade, but they managed to cover a good distance before dark. She stopped at a small cave with the rivulet of a waterfall trickling down the wall beside it. It was on a steep switchback trail cut into the side of a mountain.

"We'll be safe here for the night," she said. "I've stayed here many times."

They cooked a camp stew over a small fire and had biscuits with their dinner. Marla ate her fill and then some. She was clearly hungry and genuinely seemed to savor each bite of her meal. It reminded Alexander of Lucky.

Marla took a deep breath and relaxed against the rock wall at her back. "Thank you. I haven't had a decent meal in days. I feel so much better now."

"A meal always brightens my spirits as well," Lucky said. "How did you come to live in the Pinnacles?"

"I was born in Highlake City," Marla said. "I've lived in these mountains my whole life."

"I thought Highlake City was just a legend," Jack said with sudden interest.

"We work pretty hard to keep it that way," Marla said. "It's a small, self-reliant community, and we don't venture out of the Pinnacles often, if at all. I've never been out of the mountains myself."

"Is that where we're headed?" Jack asked. "Highlake City, I mean."

"Not directly," Marla said. "I'm taking you to the Dragon Temple high in the mountains. If Tanis grants you safe passage, I'll guide you to Highlake City and introduce you to the druids who serve the fairies. They are the only ones who can safely guide you into the Valley of the Fairy Queen."

"I guess the path is the path," Alexander said.

"May I ask why you need to see the Fairy Queen? I understand if you don't want to tell me, but Tanis will definitely ask and she won't help you if you don't answer her truthfully."

Alexander was silent for a long moment while he stared into the fire and thought about what he was trying to do. Now that he had more information about the fairies, he realized he would need some help to get there. Marla was his best bet, so he decided to trust her.

"I need their help to retrieve the Sovereign Stone," he said without looking up.

Marla stared at him incredulously. She tried to speak but stopped short, then opened her mouth again but couldn't find the words she wanted. For several moments she just looked into the fire silently while she pondered what she'd just learned.

"This is about Phane, isn't it?" she asked finally.

Alexander looked up and met her eyes. He nodded with resignation. "He's trying to get the Stone. If he does, the world will suffer for a very long time. I have to stop him but I need the fairies' help."

"That changes things," Marla said, now deadly serious. "The Druid Council has been concerned since the warning spell. They've been debating whether we should remain isolated here in the mountains and hope that Phane will be too preoccupied with the rest of the Seven Isles to bother with us or if we should make contact with the one who has claimed the throne of Ruatha and offer our services in the fight. It's been a bitter debate. No one wants war but many believe war will find us if we hide, so we might as well find it first."

"Where do you stand?" Jack asked.

"Tanis is opposed. She would prefer to remain isolated in the Pinnacles. I heed the will of my patron, but I fear that war is coming anyway."

Alexander looked from one face to the next for their buy-in before he went any farther. Each knew the stakes and each nodded their agreement to his unspoken question. Marla watched the silent exchange with a mixture of trepidation and curiosity.

"Marla, my name is Alexander Ruatha," he said as he slowly drew the Thinblade and gently pushed the blade into the rock wall up to the hilt. "I lead the forces sworn to the Old Law that stand against Phane. Will your patron hear me out?"

Marla blinked, then looked from Alexander to the Thinblade and back to Alexander. "You saved my life. She'll hear you on the strength of your actions alone. She may not agree to help you, but she's still your best chance of reaching the Fairy Queen safely."

Alexander nodded thoughtfully. "You wouldn't happen to know where the Fairy Queen stands on the issue."

"She is opposed to war as well, but it's important to point out that the great powers are communities just like any other. There are both fairies and dragons that are in favor of taking war to the enemy before he brings it to us. But the Dragon Queen Tanis and the Fairy Queen Ilona are both strongly in favor of isolation."

"That complicates things," Abigail said.

"Hopefully, the Fairy Queen will be open to reason," Isabel said. "The fairy we summoned said she'd hear us out before she makes her decision."

"There's another matter that bears mentioning," Anatoly said. "We have a hundred soldiers chasing us. They're about two days behind."

Marla shook her head. "I doubt they'll be a problem. As soon as one of the great powers gets wind of a bunch of soldiers moving into the Pinnacles, they'll take action."

"One of the soldiers is very dangerous," Alexander said. "He doesn't look like much, but he's a battle mage. The men with him might be ordinary soldiers, but he's not."

"When we get to the Dragon Temple, I'll inform Tanis of the threat and she will decide how to best handle the situation. In any case, your enemies will have a very difficult time following you through these mountains."

Just before dawn, Isabel woke screaming. She caught herself a moment after she realized she was awake but her scream woke the entire camp. Alexander took her in his arms. She didn't cry, but it was clear that she was shaken by her nightmare. The portal to the netherworld was still there and it was still trying to draw her in while she slept.

"I'm afraid I'm almost out of deathwalker root," Lucky said. "I cut her dose back last night to make it last a bit longer. I'm sorry, my dear."

"It's all right, Lucky," Isabel said. "Maybe the fairies will be able to help." She took a deep breath as she regained her composure.

After breakfast they resumed their journey along the treacherous trail. It wound through rocky mountain passes and along narrow ledges with sheer rock faces on one side and thousand foot drop-offs on the other. Each step took them higher into the Pinnacles, yet the mountain peaks stood thousands of feet overhead.

About midday Isabel pointed out several ravens flying above them. "They've been following us for most of the morning. I didn't think much of it at first, but now I'm wondering if that demon could possess birds as well as cats and horses."

Alexander looked up at the ravens and saw in a glance the telltale colors of magic. He nodded. "Something's not quite right about them. We'll keep an eye on them and see if they keep following us. If it's not the demon, then maybe someone else is using them to track us."

"If I may ask," Marla said, "what is this demon you speak of?"

"Several days ago we were attacked by a demon that possesses animals," Alexander said, still looking up at the ravens. "It attacked as a big cat. When we killed it, the demon left the corpse of the cat and took our horses, one by one. We killed them all, and the demon left. We haven't seen it since but I have good reason to believe it's still hunting us."

Marla frowned. "That sounds like a grimthrall."

Both Alexander and Isabel turned to her. "What can you tell us about it?" Alexander asked.

"They are minor demons that possess animals," Marla said. "Usually they must be summoned, but sometimes they find their way into the world of life without help. They are not very smart, but they do have the hunting and fighting instincts of the animals they possess."

"There's more," Isabel said as she pulled the animal charm necklace from under her tunic. "This necklace is a gift from the Guild Mage of New Ruatha. It allows me to speak to animals with my mind. When the demon took my horse and I tried to calm her, I touched the mind of the demon instead." She shuddered at the memory. "It opened a passage in my mind to the netherworld and drew my soul into the darkness. Alexander saved me, but the portal to the netherworld is still there and it opens up and tries to pull me in when I sleep. That's why I screamed this morning."

Marla looked at her with a mixture of awe and incredulity. She shook her head as if the circumstances she found herself in were beyond her experience, and then she frowned at a sudden thought. "Is that why you've been taking deathwalker root?"

Isabel nodded. "Lucky's been giving me deathwalker-root tea so I can sleep without the nightmares and the threat of losing myself to the netherworld."

"I believe I can help you," Marla said. "There's an herb in the mountain valleys that induces a dreamless sleep in much the same way that deathwalker root does. The path to Highlake City takes us through a valley where it grows."

"Can you describe this herb you speak of?" Lucky asked.

"It's a flowering vine that sends out many shoots and is covered with small broad leaves of bright green and tiny little white flowers. It's quite common in the valleys of the Pinnacles and is used for many medicines."

"Hmm, that sounds like skymeadow creeper vine," Lucky said. "In many ways it's preferable to deathwalker root for inducing sleep since the chances of an overdose poisoning are much less."

"How far away is this valley?" Alexander asked.

"If we continue toward the Dragon Temple, it will be three days; otherwise we can reach it by tomorrow afternoon," Marla said.

"Let's head for the valley, then double back to the Dragon Temple," Alexander said.

"Nonsense," Isabel replied. "We're almost to the Dragon Temple and that's far more important than my nightmares."

"What if you get lost in the darkness again and I can't save you?" Alexander asked.

"I won't. If nothing else, I just won't sleep. I'm sure Lucky has something in his bag that will help me stay awake," Isabel said.

"You plan on going three days without sleep?" Alexander said. "I doubt it. And besides, you won't be able to travel very far if you're exhausted."

"Be that as it may, we need to get to the Dragon Temple," Isabel said. "The Sovereign Stone has to be our first priority."

"I don't like this, Isabel," Alexander said softly.

"Me neither. But it is what it is, and that's what we have to deal with."

Alexander couldn't help but smile at the simple truism. It was a common piece of advice offered by his father while he was growing up.

"Can't argue with that," Abigail said to her brother as she started up the trail.

For the rest of the day, Isabel walked with a lighter step and Alexander with a heavier heart. He was worried about her. He hated the fear she felt and the helplessness he felt, but mostly he worried how she would suffer once Lucky ran out of deathwalker root. For now it was allowing her to sleep; without it, she would quickly become exhausted, or worse—she might get lost in the netherworld again. He just hoped she would make it to the valley unscathed by the darkness infecting her mind.

CHAPTER 23

Late in the afternoon after a grueling day of walking uphill, they rounded a bend and saw the Dragon Temple in the distance. It was both magnificent and ominous. The trail led along a steep ridgeline up to the flat-topped mountain that looked like it had been sheared off to create a platform. On each of the four corners of the open-air temple was a life-size stone statue of a dragon looking down on the platform. There was no building or structure, just an altar and a wide open space where a dragon could easily land.

Beyond the Dragon Temple were seven stone peaks that looked like fangs. Alexander caught his breath when he saw a dragon soaring gracefully before it flared its wings and landed in the open mouth of a cave in the steep face of one of the mountains.

Marla smiled.

Alexander absentmindedly checked his sword in his scabbard.

They arrived at the Dragon Temple just before dark, and Marla led them down a flight of stairs into a small shelter beneath the platform. It was a set of rooms with ample space for ten or twelve people to sleep comfortably. There were cots and a table with chairs. One small room had some food stores, water, and a bit of firewood. The place looked like it was used infrequently but often enough to keep stocked.

"We can sleep here tonight," Marla said. "The dragons won't come to the temple during darkness, so we'll have to wait until morning."

Alexander woke in the middle of the night to find Isabel sleeping fitfully. He could see that she was dreaming, so he gently shook her. When she didn't waken, he shook her harder and she woke with a start, looking frantically around for a threat. When she regained her wits, she fell into Alexander's arms and cried quietly for a few minutes.

"It had me," she whispered. "I tried to fight it, but it had me and was pulling me in again. Alexander, I don't ever want to go back there."

"Just a couple more nights and you'll be able to sleep without fear again," Alexander said. "Hopefully, the Fairy Queen will be able to help you. Now try and get some rest."

She dozed fitfully for the rest of the night, coming awake several times. By morning she and Alexander were both exhausted.

When they walked up the little staircase to the top of the platform at dawn, Alexander was momentarily overcome be the sheer wild beauty of the view. The air was cold and the sun was just cresting over the horizon. The snow-covered mountains of the Pinnacles shone brightly in the morning light and the green of the forest blanketed the world to the north and west.

"The dragons will be stirring," Marla said. "Now is the best time to request an audience. I need all of you to stand here." She motioned to an area behind the altar.

"Tanis will land over there if she chooses to answer my call. Do not address her unless she addresses you first. Dragons have a strong sense of propriety and they expect to be respected by humans who visit their temple."

They did as she said, but Alexander still checked his sword. Marla went to the altar and opened a cabinet built into the square stone platform. She produced a cask of oil and poured a good quantity onto the bowl-like top of the altar. She withdrew her dragon medallion and kissed it before she began her incantation. After a few moments of soft, lilting chanting that sounded almost like a song, a small ball of fire materialized over her outstretched hand. With one final word, she cast the flaming sphere into the oil and it ignited with a whoosh.

Marla stood back and waited with her head held high. It wasn't long before several dragons could be seen soaring gracefully around the mountains in the distance. Then there was a roar that echoed and reverberated off the peaks. Alexander could see the thrill of excitement building within Marla's sturdy frame while she waited for her patron.

A dragon that was half again as big as any of the others emerged from the side of a mountain peak high above and glided smoothly toward them. She grew in size as she neared, the sun glinting off her golden-brown scales. She landed on the platform before the altar with a lightness that belied her size.

She was truly magnificent. Standing on her hind legs, Tanis towered a good forty feet over them. Her wings nearly reached to the statues perched a hundred feet apart on both sides of the temple platform. Her snout was long and her teeth looked razor sharp. She had a horned ridge that ran down the length of her spine and a long tail ending in a bone spike. She was beautiful and terrifying all at once. Most impressive were her eyes. They were golden brown with flecks of gold scintillating in her catlike irises, and they communicated a deep intelligence and a profound, ageless wisdom.

Alexander was caught between awe and terror. He looked up at the Dragon Queen and simply marveled at her presence in the world. He'd read stories about dragons in his childhood but even the vividness of his rich imagination failed to do them justice.

Tanis was truly worthy of worship. She was beyond human troubles or the mundane considerations of governments and nations—altogether above such things for reasons that were all too apparent.

More than anything else, her colors left him breathless. He'd never seen a creature or a person with such a rich, clear, powerful aura as Tanis. She was a creature of profound magic that radiated from her in waves of flowing color.

He wondered if he would be able to persuade her to help him or if he even had any right to. When he looked at his friends, he saw a mixture of reactions. Everyone had a look of awe but each was mixed with different emotions. Isabel was filled with innocent joy at seeing such a magnificent creature, Abigail looked like she was trying to reconcile her understanding of reality with the presence of such a creature, Anatoly had a look of wariness, Lucky smiled with simple joy, and Jack was clearly taking notes in his head for his next song.

Marla stood tall and proud before her patron but did not speak. Tanis looked at her for only a moment before her scrutiny turned to Alexander and his friends. She regarded them each in turn and then focused on Alexander. Her eyes narrowed and she sniffed at the air before she tipped her head back and roared with such sudden fury that it froze them all to the spot.

More frighteningly, Marla tensed at the roar and her colors turned to fear and dismay but still she said nothing. In the distance other dragons emerged from the mountains and began to approach but they remained high in the sky, circling over the temple rather than landing.

When Tanis spoke, her voice was a deep, resonate rumble that Alexander could feel in his chest. "Why have you brought dragonslayers to my temple?" She brought her head down and stared intently at Marla.

The druid stumbled back a step and shook her head in denial. "I have not, My Lady. These travelers saved my life. In return, I have agreed to help them seek passage to the Valley of the Fairy Queen. If they are dragonslayers, then they have deceived me."

Tanis sniffed at the air and turned her eye to Alexander. "Bragador—I smell Bragador. How is it that you came to wear her scales, human?"

Alexander stepped forward, threw his cloak back and lifted his tunic to reveal the mail shirt he wore. "This armor is a gift given to me by the Guild Mage of New Ruatha and made from the scales of the dragon Bragador. He acquired those scales in a bargain after having met her tests."

Tanis eyed him for a moment, then she saw the hilt of the Thinblade and withdrew her head and spread her wings. "How is it that you possess the Sword of Kings? There are few weapons capable of piercing the scales of a dragon, and that is one of them."

"The Thinblade was left for me by Mage Cedric so that I might reunite the Isle of Ruatha," Alexander said as he stepped up beside Marla. "Lady Tanis, I have no desire to harm you. My only reason for coming before you is to ask your help in reaching the Valley of the Fairy Queen. I am in great need of her assistance."

"Lady Tanis, they saved my life," Marla said. "I gave my word that they would be safe in your temple."

She folded her wings with a skeptical look. "Very well, Priestess, your word will be honored until I have reason to act otherwise."

"Thank you, My Lady," Marla said. "I have much to report."

Tanis nodded her approval and Marla continued. "Lady Tanis, this is Lord Alexander Ruatha, heir to the throne of Ruatha. He comes in search of the fairies in hopes that they will help him retrieve the Sovereign Stone." Tanis's eyebrow raised a bit at that but she didn't interrupt. "They are being pursued by many soldiers who serve Prince Phane."

Tanis frowned deeply and eyed Alexander more closely. "Why have you brought your war into my mountains?"

Alexander drew himself up and looked the dragon in the eye. "I do not bring war. Phane does. I have no wish to be a king or to fight the enemy that I face, but I've been chosen by powers far beyond my control to stand against him. A great many lives depend on the outcome of this struggle, so I will do what is necessary. Right now that means retrieving the Sovereign Stone before Phane does; if he gets to it first, the world will fall into darkness, and he will not stop until every one of the Seven Isles is under his boot."

"He will not challenge me," Tanis said.

"Perhaps not at first, but once he has built an army of wizards, he will subjugate even you. His lust for power is as without limit as his malice."

"I think your fear of him has distorted your estimation of his power," Tanis said. "Even with an army of wizards, he will find waging war against the Pinnacles to be more trouble than it's worth."

"Lady Tanis, as much as I would like to have your help against Phane, that's not why I've come before you," Alexander said. "I'm here only to ask for safe passage through the Pinnacles so that I may seek out the fairies and enlist their aid."

Tanis actually laughed—a great rumbling sound that reverberated through the stone of the mountain itself.

"What makes you believe that Ilona will help you? She is even less interested in the wars of men than I."

"I've spoken to one of her fairies and have been invited to present my request to the Fairy Queen," Alexander said.

Tanis looked a bit surprised to hear that. "It would seem that you are at the center of momentous events, human. I will not aid you in this war but I am indebted to you for saving my priestess, so I will grant your request for safe passage."

She reached into her mouth, broke off the tip of a tooth and carefully placed it on the altar. "Take this tooth. Present it to any of the powers within the Pinnacles and they will allow you to pass without harm. But be warned, there are many dangers in the mountain wilds that recognize no authority. My talisman of safe passage will be of no use with them."

Alexander took the piece of Tanis's tooth, which was about six inches long and as sharp as a spear at the point. He bowed formally and said, "You honor me. Thank you for your generous hospitality within your home."

She snorted at the flattery, then turned to Marla. "Be well, Priestess, and be more careful with your life. It is dear to me," Tanis said before she launched herself into the air with one great stroke of her wings. She wheeled away from the temple platform and tipped into a gentle dive to gain speed before she started her ascent toward her mountain lair.

"You have my love always, Lady Tanis," Marla said to her departing patron. She looked at Alexander with a smile and a tear of joy and pride in her eye.

"You were right," Alexander said. "She is the most magnificent creature I've ever seen. Thank you for introducing us to her."

Chapter 24

They made good time traveling downhill away from the Dragon Temple. It was a clear and bright day with still air and a warm sun. Alexander was tired but he pressed on, trying to gain as much ground as possible. Every step brought him closer to greater safety for Isabel. He knew she wouldn't get much sleep tonight, so he wanted to get as close to the meadows as possible. Once they reached the skymeadow vine, they could make camp and she could rest. After that he could turn his attention back to the purpose of his journey, but as long as Isabel was in danger, he just couldn't focus on anything else.

During the afternoon, Isabel pointed out the five ravens floating high in the sky. When Alexander looked at them, he saw the same color of magic he'd seen the day before. He was sure of it now—the birds were tracking them. He suspected that Commander P'Tal had enlisted the assistance of another wizard, maybe even more than one. Alexander worried that the journey to the Dragon Temple had allowed the soldiers to gain ground on them and decided to look in on them once they made camp.

They wound down the mountains and into the deep valleys. The air warmed and the foliage returned. The trees were short and slender. The ground cover was low and hardy and the rock of the mountains frequently protruded through the dirt.

Here and there they found cold, narrow little mountain streams running from the higher peaks and meeting to form small, fast-moving rivers. They came into a valley late in the afternoon with a stream meandering down the middle and cliffs rising sharply on both sides.

The valley floor was covered with a thick carpet of green and speckled with wildflowers of every color. It was stunning in its simple beauty, and Alexander found himself drifting away from his worries and into his childhood daydreams while they walked. Then he heard an odd buzzing sound and his focus snapped back to the present.

In the distance, he saw a cloud of insects swarming toward them and then he saw the dark and unnatural colors of the demon. He stared in confusion for a moment. It was one thing for a creature of the netherworld to possess a horse or a cat but quite another to possess thousands of bees. Everyone stopped and looked at the angry cloud as it undulated through the air toward them.

Alexander broke through his confusion and shouted a warning. "Demon!" he yelled, pointing toward the swarm.

Anatoly cursed. Lucky started rummaging around in his bag.

Alexander watched the bees with a growing sense of helplessness. He'd faced many enemies in the past several months but none like this. He felt an instinctual need to draw his sword but knew it would do no good. He quickly ran through an inventory of all of the weapons he had at his disposal but none was equal to this enemy.

He stood helplessly and watched it come.

Lucky produced a couple of flasks of oil and a fire pot from his bag, then he too looked around with a growing realization of helplessness. The fire he could muster wouldn't be enough.

Then Isabel screamed and slumped to her knees with her hands on her head. Alexander ran to her. She was huddled on the ground and trembling. Her breath came in tight gasps and her eyes were shut tight.

The cloud of bees approached.

"Isabel, I'm here with you. Be strong. Resist the darkness. It has no power over you unless you let it in."

Alexander wasn't even sure if the things he said were true, but he needed so badly to believe they were that he said them anyway.

Lucky quickly dumped the flasks of oil around Alexander and Isabel. "It's after you, Alexander. Fire may keep it at bay."

Alexander nodded as he drew up his hood and wrapped his cloak around himself and Isabel.

Lucky couldn't cast spells in general but there were a few minor spells he was capable of. One of those few was the ability to create a very small flame from the tip of his finger that lasted only long enough to light a candle. He used that simple spell now to ignite the ring of oil around Alexander and Isabel. It went up with a whoosh and surrounded them in brightly burning fire.

The rest of the party scattered. The bees came for Alexander, and he and Isabel huddled under his cloak as they swarmed around them. The fire protected them from the sides and kept the bulk of the swarming bees away, but many were still able to get to them and deliver their tiny, yet startlingly painful, attack.

Alexander focused on the dispassionate place in his mind where the witness lived and watched the little explosions of sharp pain detonate throughout his body as, one by one, the bees found their way past his hasty defenses.

Worst of all, he could feel Isabel flinch in his arms every time one of the bees stung her. She whimpered at the dual attack of the proximity of the demon and the stabbing pain of the stings.

Marla saved them.

Alexander felt a wave of heat overhead and heard the popping and sizzling of burning bees. The stench was gagging and the heat was oppressive. Orange light washed over them as Marla directed a jet of flame from her outstretched hands and bathed the swarm of bees with her magical fire.

A moment later, the swarm broke and the demon came free of its host. It looked straight at Alexander with its hateful red eyes and shrieked soundlessly before turning and fleeing into the mountains, no doubt in search of yet another creature to possess.

They made camp on the spot and built a fire while Lucky attended to Alexander and Isabel. Both had been stung countless times and were in great pain. He used numbweed and healing salve to treat their many wounds and they both drifted off to sleep for an hour or so while the medicine did its work. When they woke, it was nearing dark and dinner was ready.

"How are you feeling?" Alexander asked Isabel.

"More afraid than anything. When that thing got close, the door opened and I couldn't close it. I could feel the darkness trying to draw me in, and it was all I could do to keep from losing myself again."

"We have to find a way to get rid of that cursed door, once and for all," Alexander growled. "I wish there was something I could do."

"There is, Alexander. You're doing it right now," she said as she gave him a tighter hug, and then they got up for their dinner of a simple but well-seasoned camp stew.

Alexander itched all over from the bee stings, but the welts were fading fast and the pain was almost entirely gone.

"You have terrifying enemies, Alexander," Marla said quietly after the meal was over.

"I can't argue with that," Alexander said wryly. "How did you create that fire?"

"I'm a Priestess of the Dragon," she said with a proud smile. "Fire is one of my areas of study, although I must admit, I rarely have cause to cast that particular spell."

"Thank you," Isabel said. "The demon possessing those bees was also in my mind trying to claim my soul. If you hadn't driven it off when you did, I fear I would have been lost to it."

"You're welcome, Isabel. I don't want to get your hopes up, but the Druid Council may be able to help you. If they can summon that demon and then banish it, I believe the door within your mind may vanish. I can't be sure because I've never heard of a case such as yours, but it stands to reason that the demon is actively keeping the connection to the netherworld open within your mind and that it can only do so if it remains in our world."

"How is a demon banished?" Alexander asked.

Marla frowned a bit. "My understanding is limited because the power to do so is beyond me, but I know a little about the process. Demons are not supposed to be in this world, so their presence creates an imbalance. That imbalance draws them toward the netherworld if a passage is created.

"Certain members of the Druid Council may be able to create a place where the veil separating the world of time and substance from the aether is blurred. If done in the proximity of the demon, it will be drawn into the aether where it will eventually find its way back to the netherworld."

"And once it's gone, it won't be able to hurt Isabel anymore?" Alexander asked.

"I believe that to be the case," Marla said.

"I think she's right," Lucky said. "I've read of banishings before where the victims of a demon recovered quickly after the demon was sent away."

"Thank you, Marla," Alexander said. "If you can help Isabel, I will be forever in your debt."

"I'll do whatever I can to help," Marla said. "You made a friend when you saved my life, and I'm coming to see the choice that lies before the entire world. You are a man who would risk your own life with no promise of gain to rescue a stranger. Your enemy sends creatures from the world of the dead to haunt the living. I know which side I would choose to stand with."

"What of Tanis?" Alexander asked.

"She is my patron and I will obey her in all things, but I will also help you as much as she will permit me to. She sees things from a much longer perspective than we do. She has lived for many hundreds of years and will live for many hundreds more. Our wars and governments are fleeting and ephemeral to her, so she pays them little heed. I fear this conflict is different, and I believe there will come a time when she will see the necessity of taking sides."

"I hope you're right," Alexander said. "We can use all the help we can get. Phane is dangerous and resourceful. But most of all, he's relentless. He'll never stop until he subjugates the entire Seven Isles."

Before dark, Alexander found a small patch of soft moss in the meadow and sat down to meditate. It had been some time since he'd left his father to fight the battle against Headwater and he was starting to wonder about the outcome.

He relaxed his body and inhaled the cool but fragrant mountain air. Methodically, he went about clearing his mind of thoughts, acknowledging each one as it came to him and then dismissing it.

Soon he was in the state of empty-mindedness that was his portal to the firmament. This time it took only ten minutes or so before his awareness was floating gently on the ocean of endless possibility.

He listened for a time to the infinitely intricate music that represented all things happening at once. It was complex and graceful but mostly it had become a sound of beauty to Alexander's mind. Here, anything could happen and he could see any event by simply focusing his attention on it. The power of his clairvoyance still amazed him but not nearly so much as the vastness of the firmament.

He focused on the city of New Ruatha, and his awareness coalesced above the Glittering City. It looked intact and was as busy as usual in the early evening. He redirected his focus to the valley east of the city where his army had made their stand. His awareness moved with impossible speed; the world rushed by in a blur until he was hovering over the valley many miles to the east of New Ruatha.

It was scorched and marred, muddy and trampled. There were markers of mass graves for the fallen, but soldiers were no longer on the field. The battle had been fought and apparently Ruatha had won. Again, Alexander focused his awareness, this time high above Headwater.

What he saw caused him to recoil slightly. The city was on fire. The Ruathan army was surrounding the city in a cordon, but they hadn't advanced; it didn't appear that they were planning to attack so much as lay siege.

The fires appeared to be the result of a total breakdown in the government. Alexander's heart ached for the innocent caught in the city, but he knew that Headwater must be taken and those allied with Phane must be rooted out and captured or destroyed. Headwater was situated in the heart of Ruatha and could not be allowed to support Phane.

Alexander pictured his father in his mind's eye, and he plunged back into the formlessness of the firmament for only a moment before his awareness coalesced in the command tent of the Ruathan army. His father and mother were both there and they both looked tired. Hanlon and Emily Alaric were there as well. That was good news, as they would have brought the bulk of the Ranger army that Hanlon had hastily raised. General Markos was there, as was Wizard Sark.

"Commander Alaric reports that Rake has fled north into the wilds with his legion of cavalry," General Markos said. "He's also captured about half a legion of foot soldiers fleeing from Headwater. He's requesting orders and additional support."

Hanlon smiled and winked at Emily.

"Seems your son has done well, Hanlon," Duncan Valentine said.

To General Markos, he said, "Have General Kern send a regiment of cavalry to support Commander Alaric. Detain the enemy soldiers on the spot and send sufficient supplies to keep them alive but not enough to make them fat. Have Duane send scouts to keep track of Rake."

"Understood," General Markos said. "Headwater is still refusing to surrender unless we recognize the authority of the trade guilds to govern the right to work."

Duncan shook his head and sighed. "So be it. Wizard Sark, I'd like you to coordinate with Warden Alaric and develop a plan to kill the leaders of the trade guilds, in their sleep if possible. I don't want to destroy the city; there are too many innocent people living there. Maybe if we eliminate the agitators, the rest of the people will listen to reason."

Alexander withdrew out of the command tent and floated high above the city for a few moments, taking in the sweeping army of Ruatha. There were nearly a hundred thousand soldiers arrayed against Headwater. Legions from New Ruatha, Northport, Glen Morillian, and Buckwold were all working together under his father's able command.

Satisfied with the progress he saw, Alexander shifted his focus to Blackstone Keep. His awareness came to rest above the bridge platform. He surveyed the surrounding area and saw a force of nearly three legions on the plains below. One was close to the base of the giant black Keep and the other two were camped in fortified positions around the Reishi Gate in the distance.

His message of warning about Phane's threats had been received and heeded. When he turned his attention to the Keep, he saw the bridge was not present and the paddock was bustling with activity even in the dark of early night. Rangers were working to organize and distribute large stockpiles of supplies that had only recently arrived.

Satisfied that his allies were working effectively toward his goals, he directed his attention elsewhere. He thought of Phane and was suddenly floating high above a rough cove off a volcanic isle. What he saw next was difficult to understand at first. Thirty feet off the water, frozen in space, was a portal cut into the fabric of space with a small room behind it.

Phane sat in a comfortable chair, looking out the door as if he was waiting for something. Alexander looked around and saw a dragon perched on the lip of the volcano's crater looking down toward Phane. Before Alexander could look closer, Phane suddenly looked straight at him. Alexander shifted his awareness back into the firmament and away from Phane before the Reishi Prince could take any action.

Alexander didn't know for sure if Phane could hurt him when he was using his clairvoyance, but the Reishi Prince had been able to scatter his awareness before and it made him wonder if Phane could do even more if he wanted to. Better safe than sorry.

The last stop on his journey brought him to the camp of Commander P'Tal. He was surprised to see that the Commander of the Reishi Protectorate had only a large platoon of soldiers left and many of them looked bruised and battered. Alexander wondered what had done his enemy such damage. Unfortunately,

P'Tal, Nero, Grudge, and Truss were all alive and well. There were also a couple of others at the fire with them. One was clearly a wizard. Alexander approached and listened to their conversation for a moment.

"They're camped in a meadow a day away," the wizard said, "and it looks like they have the assistance of a guide who appears to be taking them to the lake city high in the mountains."

"I'd prefer to catch up to them before they make it there," P'Tal said. "If their detour to the Dragon Temple is any indication, they will be well received by the druids in the lake city."

Truss twitched a bit. "I never even believed in dragons. It's hard to accept that one would attack us because the pretender asked it to. There has to be a better explanation." Truss sounded afraid.

"I'm sure there is, Duke Truss," the wizard said. "Dragons don't take orders from men."

"That seems like a pretty big coincidence then . . ." Truss said, but before Alexander could hear the rest of the sentence, his awareness slammed violently back into his body.

CHAPTER 25

He felt pain tear through him and a moment later he understood why. A mountain lion was on top of him, preparing to strike. His arms were pinned and he couldn't breathe from the weight of the cat pressing down on him. He felt helpless and foolish. He saw in a glance the colors of the demon.

An instant before the big cat could clamp its fangs into Alexander's face, an arrow buried deep into its shoulder, no doubt from Abigail's bow. The cat flinched, but didn't let up. In the back of his mind, Alexander was once again grateful for the armor shirt he wore. Without it, the cat's razor-sharp claws would have already torn deeply into his chest.

Isabel arrived first. She hadn't even taken the time to get her sword but instead dove at the big cat with a dagger in hand. With her left arm, she caught it around the neck and crashed into it with her shoulder as she drove her dagger deep into its ribs on the opposite side. The cat stiffened.

What Alexander saw next defied reason. The colors of Isabel's necklace flared, and the demon possessing the big cat came free as the animal slumped over. But rather than running away, the demon slid toward Isabel and it seemed to be resisting.

She screamed a blood-curdling scream that made ice flow through Alexander's veins. He watched in slow motion, helpless to do anything, as the demon flowed into his love. She stiffened and slumped over lifelessly. With his heart in his throat, he scrambled to her side, heedless of the wounds on his arms and legs.

She was trembling but still breathing. He shook her and tried to wake her, but she wasn't there. Curiously, the demon's colors weren't there either. Alexander wasted no time. He gently laid her down and sat next to her, taking her hand in his.

"The darkness has her," Alexander told his friends. "I'll be back with her or not at all."

With that, he closed his eyes and ruthlessly schooled his mind. He had become better at it but it still took longer than he wanted. Once he was floating in the firmament, he immediately coalesced his awareness above himself and plunged into Isabel.

This time he knew exactly what he was doing and where to look for the portal within her mind. He found it easily and lunged into the darkness, leaving a thread of light to follow back to the world of time and substance.

The netherworld was cold and lifeless, a place of unrealized potential where souls could imagine all of the possibilities life had to offer but never create anything more than a fleeting dream of what could be. It was a place of frustration, despair, and rage. The broken and hateful souls that swirled in the murky darkness lusted for life—to exist in that world or take it from those who rightfully lived there.

This time Isabel was much easier to find. She was struggling with a creature of darkness and malice. Alexander saw at a glance that it was the grimthrall. She had somehow drawn it into her, and it had drawn her through the portal to the netherworld.

Now they were locked in a mortal struggle. Worse, there were a number of other broken souls stirring in the darkness, alerted to the prospect of feasting on the fear, despair, and hopelessness of a living soul unfortunate enough to have been cast adrift in the darkness.

Alexander wasted no time. He willed himself toward her and focused on his love of life and his love for her. In this place, light was the greatest weapon he had. His living soul was the source of it, and his love for Isabel and his own life were the fuel that powered its brilliance.

He joined the battle with fury, crashing into Isabel's soul and once again joining with her in a way that was more profound and complete than words could ever convey. She embraced him and flooded into every recess of his being. He opened himself to her without hesitation. In their joining, they magnified each other's light and the demon fled with a soundless shriek.

Alexander took hold of Isabel's soul with his will and traced his path back toward the place where they had both entered the netherworld—the portal within Isabel's mind.

But even as they fled the darkness, the darkness gave chase.

They burst forth from the netherworld into the confines of Isabel's psyche and turned as one to face the portal. She needed no guidance this time. She saw it as a door and stepped toward it to slam it closed, but before she could reach it, three shadows of despair emerged from the darkness.

In that moment, Isabel's eyes snapped open and Alexander slammed back into his body. She gasped as the three shades escaped through her psyche and swirled into the sky. With a shriek that could freeze a man's heart, they vanished into the night.

Alexander had seen creatures from the netherworld before but never anything like this. These three demons were darker and more hateful than anything he'd ever witnessed. And they were loose in the world.

He turned back to a panic-stricken Isabel and took her in his arms as she wept.

"What have I done? Oh, Dear Maker, what have I done?" she cried.

Alexander tried to console her, but for a time she could only say those words over and over, so he just held her and let her cry. When she stopped, he held her at arm's length and looked closely at her. Her eyes were as clear and piercing green as ever and her colors were strong and bright, yet somehow deeper and more complex than before.

"Are you all right?" Alexander asked, looking at her with deep concern. Lucky was kneeling next to him, scrutinizing her eyes.

"I'm safe, Alexander," Isabel said with a sob, "but I fear I've doomed the world." She started crying again.

"Shhh . . . it's all right," he said, taking her in his arms again. "Tell me what happened."

"I made mental contact with the grimthrall when I attacked the cat," Isabel said through her sobbing. "I'm not sure why I even tried it. I guess I was hoping I could push it out of my mind. Instead the darkness of the netherworld drew it in. As it passed through me, it took me with it into the darkness.

"We fought, but this time I was more prepared. I remembered the last time and I focused on our love to create light against the darkness. I fought against the demon for what seemed like a long time, and then you were there and you brought me back again."

Before Alexander could speak, she put a finger to his lips and continued, "But this time, something followed us. They were waiting for us there, waiting for us to lead them here. The shades are loose in the world, Alexander."

He felt his blood run cold and saw the despair and dismay in her beautiful green eyes.

"When they passed through me, I learned their names: Shivini, Rankosi, and Jinzeri. Oh, what have I done?" she said.

"You survived," Alexander said firmly. "What of the portal? Is the doorway closed?"

She nodded. "It's not just closed, it's gone, except I feel like I could bring it back if I tried to."

"Well, don't," Alexander said. "I can't see the taint of darkness in your aura anymore, so maybe you're safe."

"I may be safe, but I've let loose three of the most terrifying creatures imaginable," she said with utter misery.

"No, you didn't," Alexander said. "I did."

She looked at him with a hard frown. "What do you mean?"

"Could you have found your way back without me?" Alexander asked.

A look of realization ghosted across her face. "I don't think so."

"Isabel, I'm the one they needed. You were just the bait," Alexander said. "What's more, they were waiting for us. They were waiting for you to get pulled through into the darkness and for me to come in after you. This isn't your fault. In fact, I'd wager that the shades were the ones who pulled the grimthrall into the netherworld in order to draw you in."

"What do we do?" she asked with a small voice.

"We press on to the Fairy Queen," Alexander said firmly. "I'll see if I can warn the wizards. If Phane can see my presence during clairvoyance and if I can manifest within your psyche, maybe I can use my powers to communicate with one of the wizards somehow."

"In the meantime," Lucky interjected, "I must caution you all. Do not say the shades' names aloud; they can hear you. The old stories say they will come as if summoned when their names are invoked aloud three times in succession."

"What else do you know about them?" Abigail asked.

Lucky shrugged. "Most of what I know is from legend and story. The last Reishi Sovereign learned their names and discovered a means of summoning them to do his bidding. For a century during the Reishi War, the shades terrorized the world at the behest of Malachi Reishi. He used them to spy on his enemies and assassinate them when he felt it was necessary.

"Mostly he used them to sow the seeds of fear and distrust. The shades can possess people and even some magical creatures. One of the greatest instances of poetic justice in all of history is the death of Malachi Reishi at the hand of a creature from the darkness that he first introduced into the world."

Isabel interrupted. "Why didn't they possess me? They were already in my mind."

"They are said to be limited in that regard," Lucky said. "They can only possess by surprise or invitation. Since you were in the midst of a battle, your guard was up, as was Alexander's."

"What do you mean by invitation?" Jack asked. "Why would anyone invite a demon into themselves?"

"The word invitation has a very specific meaning in this context," Lucky said. "The shades are drawn to the darkness within a person. If you act in a way that is contrary to your conscience, with malice, deliberate hurtfulness, or self-destructiveness, they see those character traits as an invitation.

"In short, if the darkness is great within you, they find it much easier to enter and take possession. A person of pure heart cannot be possessed because the light of their soul repels the demon. However, the shades are very cunning and manipulative. During the Reishi War, they often worked to sully the integrity of their ultimate target and lead them into corruption and evil. Those who are good of heart and stray from convictions they hold dear are the most vulnerable to invasion by a shade."

"Since they're loose in the world without a master, what are they likely to do?" Alexander asked.

Lucky sighed, "That I cannot say. Only two are known to have summoned a shade: Malachi Reishi and Nicolai Atherton. Malachi used them to great and terrible effect during the war and there is no record of him ever losing control of his summonings.

"Nicolai Atherton summoned a shade to kill Malachi Reishi and place the Sovereign Stone beyond reach by pushing him bodily into the aether, which resulted in Mage Atherton's death, as you know. Left to their own devices, I suspect they'll cause harm when and where they can."

"What are the chances they'll join forces with Phane?" Anatoly asked.

"That's hard to say," Lucky said. "Phane knows much more of them than I do. He may be able to bind them to his will."

A terrifying thought occurred to Alexander like a lightning bolt. "Can the shades retrieve the Sovereign Stone?"

Lucky nodded gravely. "I believe they could if they wished to. A shade can move into the aether from this world and back again at will. If they stay for too long, they will be drawn back into the netherworld but they can shift back into the world of time and substance. If they went to the spot where Malachi Reishi was shoved into the aether, they could shift into the aether, grab the Sovereign Stone, and shift back."

"Dear Maker," Alexander whispered. "Phane has failed at the Temple of Fire. It seems that a family of dragons has taken up residence there and they weren't too happy when he arrived. If he learns of the shades, he may try to enlist their aid."

Marla frowned in confusion. "Perhaps it isn't my place to ask, but how could you know such a thing?"

Alexander smiled. "It's complicated. Suffice it to say that I'm capable of clairvoyance. I can project my awareness anywhere I like and watch what's happening. When I was meditating earlier, I was looking in on our friends and enemies.

"In short: My father has Headwater under siege; Rake has fled into the northern wilds with Duane in pursuit supported by a regiment of cavalry from Buckwold; Erik is busy stocking and organizing the Keep; P'Tal is a day behind us and he's lost a large number of his men, apparently to a dragon attack." Marla smiled at that. "And Phane is stuck in a magical room floating thirty feet off the ocean about half a mile from the coast of the central island of Tyr. It looked like he was waiting for something, and it also looked like there were several very unhappy dragons watching him like a hawk."

"A magical room?" Abigail asked.

Alexander nodded, "I believe it's a Wizard's Den. It's a portal frozen in space thirty feet above the water. Beyond the doorway is a small room with Phane sitting in a chair looking out his front door. There's an open portal to a similar room in the topmost level of the central tower of Blackstone Keep. Kelvin said it was Mage Cedric's Wizard's Den."

Lucky nodded to confirm Alexander's assessment. "A Wizard's Den is a constructed spell of great power and profound complexity. It's said that only an arch mage is capable of casting such a spell. It creates a space separate from the world we live in—sort of a pocket reality. Once inside, the wizard can close the door and he's beyond the reach of any magic or power known to exist. He is no longer in this world, although he can open the portal at will from either side and step through like you or I would walk through a common door."

"With a few angry dragons watching over him, it might be a while before he can get back to his mischief," Anatoly said.

"True, but he might be able to enlist the aid of the shades from where he is," Alexander said. "If so, we could have a problem. We have to hurry, and I have to send a warning to the wizards at Blackstone Keep about the shades. We can't afford to have them caught off guard."

It was fully dark and Alexander was beaten up and bloody from the attack by the mountain lion. He was exhausted but felt a desperate urgency to warn the wizards about the shades. Maybe they would know how to defend against them.

He struggled for longer than usual to find that place of empty-mindedness where he could slip into the firmament but eventually found his awareness floating on the ocean of possibility. He didn't spend much time listening to creation's song but instead coalesced his awareness in a room with Kelvin.

The Guild Mage was busy working over a hot oven, pounding and shaping a breastplate from the dragon scales they'd found in the aerie. He was focusing intently on his work. Alexander could see the flow of magic burning brightly in his colors as he added his will to the heat of the fire. Sweat dripped from his brow and soot stained his bare arms while he worked in the low light of the smithy.

Alexander cautiously moved his awareness closer to the big mage and gently pushed through his aura and into his body, but all he saw were Kelvin's innards. It was an unsettling experience. He moved around and tried to make contact with him but had no luck. After trying for several minutes, he floated out of the smithy and down the hall toward the library wing in the Hall of Magic, where he found a number of wizards.

The first was Wizard Hax. He was busy studying a very old-looking book and was concentrating deeply. Alexander tried to make contact with him, but failed. It was as if he wasn't even there. Hax couldn't discern his presence at all.

Next, he tried Mage Landi, who was sitting in an easy chair staring off into the distance like he was lost in the realms of his own mind. Alexander positioned his awareness directly in the line of the wizard's sight and tried to get his attention, but again he failed. He wondered what it was that permitted Phane to see him when no one else could.

Then he saw Wizard Ely snoring gently with his head down on a book. Perhaps he could reach him through his dreams. He gently pushed into the wizard and for a moment all he saw were the insides of the old man, but when he focused on reaching out to him, he quite suddenly found himself standing in a library with countless bookshelves stretching off out of sight.

He was looking at Wizard Ely. The place had the quality of a dream; time was disjointed and there were gaps in reality that led nowhere, but Wizard Ely was alert and attentive. He was a bit startled to see Alexander and frowned with a mixture of concern and curiosity.

"If you are truly Lord Alexander, then tell me where you're going and why," Wizard Ely said.

Alexander smiled. "I'm going to the Fairy Queen to seek her help in retrieving the Sovereign Stone. It's good to see you're cautious, Wizard Ely."

"Your understanding of your powers has grown. That's very good. How can I assist you?"

"I come to you with a warning. The shades are loose in the world. Shivini, Rankosi, and Jinzeri are all free of the netherworld, and I don't know how to send them back where they came from."

Wizard Ely was alarmed. "That's terrifying news indeed. I will send warning to your forces at once and speak with Mage Gamaliel on the matter as well. How did they come to be in the world?"

"Isabel touched the mind of a horse possessed by a demon and opened a connection in her mind to the netherworld. When she was pulled into the darkness, I was able to send my awareness in after her and bring her back. The first time, the creatures living in the darkness were alerted to the passageway. The second time, the shades followed us back through her mind and into our world. She said she heard their names when they passed through her psyche."

"Astonishing," Ely said, "I've never heard of such a thing. We will do what we can to defend against them. I have a warning for you as well. The scourgling has escaped and was last seen running south and east, I presume toward your location. Mage Gamaliel has dispatched three wizards and a company of soldiers, but I fear they will not be able to catch up with the beast before it reaches you. We were trying to find a way to warn you after several attempts at a dream-whisper spell failed."

Alexander felt the chill of fear flood into him. The scourgling was beyond his ability to defeat. His only hope was distance and speed. If he could get to the ocean and onto a boat before the demon reached him, he might be safe for the time being.

"Thank you, Wizard Ely. Send word to my father that my sister and I are alive and well."

"One last thing, Lord Alexander, Kelvin was angry with himself for not suggesting this before you left. He's put a message board in his smithy. His hope is that he can place messages there for you to read with your clairvoyance. At least we can get information to you if you periodically look in on the Keep."

"Tell Kelvin he's a genius. I'll look in on you from time to time."

Alexander separated himself from Ely's dream and drifted up and away from the wizard's body. The old, grey-haired man came awake and stood excitedly, drawing the attention of the other two wizards in the library. Within seconds he had apprised them of the situation and all three were headed for Kelvin's smithy. Alexander gently brought himself back to his body. His eyes came open to see Isabel watching him intently.

Chapter 26

"Alexander, you're still bleeding. Let Lucky tend to your wounds while you tell us what happened."

He nodded and lay back against his pack so Lucky could apply healing salve to the gashes on his legs. Now that he was thinking about it, the pain was more intense.

"I managed to make contact with Wizard Ely but only because he was sleeping. I had no luck with anyone who was awake. Ely said they'll start looking for information about the shades."

Once Lucky finished applying the salve, Alexander started to feel drowsy. He drifted off to sleep with Isabel next to him. His friends let them both sleep the entire night without waking them for watch. Neither of them had slept well in the previous several nights and everyone knew they were exhausted.

They both woke well rested the next morning. Isabel smiled up at him and sighed. "No nightmares. The darkness is gone."

Alexander gave her a hug and they got up to find Lucky cooking breakfast over a small fire. They spent the day traveling through peaceful little mountain valleys nestled between tall, narrow mountain peaks that reached high into the sky. Between Marla's guidance and Slyder's eyes, they were able to avoid the few potential dangers that they might have otherwise encountered.

The five ravens were still floating high in the sky watching them and tracking their movements for Commander P'Tal. Every time Alexander looked up at the black birds circling overhead, he felt a greater sense of urgency. His troubles were multiplying. He didn't know what the shades would attempt to do, but he was sure it wouldn't be good—and then there was the scourgling. After some reflection, he decided he needed to tell his friends about it. There was no telling how quickly it would track him down, but he was sure he didn't have very much time.

"Wizard Ely said the scourgling escaped," he said while they walked. Everyone stopped.

"When?" Anatoly asked urgently.

"I'm not sure. He just told me it was loose and headed our way."

"What's a scourgling?" Marla asked.

"It's a beast from the netherworld that's hunting Alexander," Lucky said. "We know of no way to destroy it, so we lured it into a trap and had it contained within a magical circle. Now that it's escaped, it'll be coming."

"That's one of the reasons I've been setting such a fast pace today," Alexander said. "I'm hoping it'll lose our trail once we make it to the ocean."

"That's a fair assumption," Lucky said, "but it may simply slow the thing down."

"At this point, I'll take what I can get," Alexander said. "Marla, how far is it to Highlake City?"

"At this pace, we should arrive by tomorrow evening."

"Any chance the Druid Council can send the scourgling back to the netherworld?" Abigail asked.

"Doubtful," Marla said. "It's one thing to banish a demon without substance but quite another to attempt such a thing with a demon that can manifest physically in our world."

"It was worth a try," Alexander said to his sister. "For the time being, speed is our best option. We should press on."

They traveled quickly the rest of the day, wasting little time for meals, preferring to eat on the move so they could cover more ground. They pushed on until darkness made it too treacherous to continue and then made camp in a wide spot on the narrow trail that wound through steep rock walls.

There was no wood for a fire, so they ate a cold dinner by the light of night-wisp dust. Alexander always marveled at the stuff. It was a pure and scintillating white that seemed to store the light of the sun for later use. He kept the vial sealed in a bone tube to prevent the light from showing through when he didn't want it. Marla was intrigued by it and inspected it closely.

As they lay their bedding out on the hard stone, the air suddenly went chill. Alexander dropped his bedding and stood, looking around for the ghost he knew was coming.

The silvery, translucent silhouette of Nicolai Atherton wavered into view not six feet from him. Alexander faced the ghost as Isabel and Marla gasped in unison. Alexander motioned that they were safe.

"Hello, Nicolai," Alexander said calmly, in spite of the icy fear running through his veins. Nicolai wasn't dangerous but he had a way of showing up just before things got interesting.

"You've freed the shades!" he said, clearly distraught. "They will seek out the Nether Gate . . ."

Before he could finish, another ghost wavered into view not far away. He was a tall, imposing figure dressed in a breastplate with the letter R emblazoned over the heart and a rich velvet cloak flowing from his shoulders. Even though his face was the transparent, silvery light of a ghost, Alexander could see the malice and madness alive in his glittering eyes.

The second ghost laughed maniacally. "The puppet of the Rebel Mage has sealed the fate of the world. You've finished the task I started two thousand years ago." He pointed at Alexander and faded out of sight, laughing hysterically.

"You must destroy the Nether Gate before the shades find it," the ghost of Nicolai Atherton said. "Everything depends on it now." The last words came from very far away as he flickered out of existence.

Alexander sat down hard. He felt defeated.

One problem after another rose up in front of him. He had no idea what the Nether Gate was, but he knew it was bad; Nicolai Atherton wouldn't have come to him if it wasn't, and whatever it was, the shades wanted to find it. The timid little voice of optimism in the back of his mind said "at least you know what they're after." Alexander snorted at the fatalistic humor of it all.

Isabel knelt next to him. "Alexander, look at me," she commanded. "What was that? Was that Mage Atherton's ghost?"

Alexander nodded and looked up at her. When he saw the intelligence and fierce passion for life in her piercing green eyes, it gave him a bit of his strength and resolve back. The challenges that lay before him seemed insurmountable, but he would never have imagined how far he would come since that horrible day in the north pasture hunting wolves. He resolved once again that, come what may, he would press on through every obstacle in his path until he could live in a world safe from the twisted ambitions of narcissists who craved power and safe from the dark appetites of netherworld creatures.

"Anybody happen to know what the Nether Gate is? Or where I can find it?" Alexander asked no one in particular. He was answered with dumbstruck silence. He put his hand on Isabel's cheek and did his best to smile at her before getting up and laying out his bedroll in silence.

"Who was the second ghost?" Jack asked.

Alexander sighed. "I presume it was Malachi Reishi," he said while he made ready for bed.

"That was terrifying," Marla said. "I never even believed ghosts were real."

Alexander actually laughed. "Says the woman who's friends with a dragon." He gave her a sidelong glance and she smiled a bit sheepishly.

"At least a dragon is flesh and blood. It's a real creature."

"True enough, but that just means a dragon can tear you apart. A ghost can only scare you to death. I'm quite sure that Malachi Reishi would have done his worst to me if he had the power to do more than mock me from the aether."

"What do you think he meant about finishing the task he started?" Anatoly asked.

Alexander shook his head. "If I had to guess, I'd say he created the Nether Gate, and the shades know how to make mischief with it and it sounds like he expects them to do just that."

"I wonder what it does," Isabel said.

"I'll bet it has something to do with the netherworld," Alexander said.

"That's a sound assumption," Lucky said. "I have my suspicions but they are almost too terrifying to contemplate."

Alexander sat up and looked at his old tutor. "Tell me."

Lucky nodded. "It may be that Malachi Reishi constructed a gate to the netherworld, much like the Reishi Gate. With such a device, he could call forth an army of dark creatures to do his bidding. My great fear is what the shades intend to do with it."

"What else?" Alexander said with the numbness of defeat. "They intend to open it." He rolled over and slipped his night-wisp light into its bone tube.

He slept fitfully, dreaming of a future ravaged by dark beasts that didn't belong in the world of the living. He felt guilt for having let them into the world, but in those moments of clarity when he weighed the cost of not acting as he had, when he thought of leaving Isabel to die in the clutches of the darkness, he knew he wouldn't have done anything differently, even knowing the consequences of his actions.

CHAPTER 27

Dawn broke over a somber camp. The crisp mountain air was chill and dry. The sky was clear and the brightness of the new day did little to lift Alexander's spirits through the gloom of overwhelming challenges—each on its own was more than he believed he could bear, but together felt like nothing short of the death of the world.

He ate his breakfast in silence and packed up his gear without a word. He could see Isabel and Abigail share looks of concern for him and his dark mood, but his sister signaled Isabel to leave him to sort through his despair without interference. She knew him well enough to know that attempting to cheer him up would fail and only leave Isabel feeling hurt for her inability to reach him.

It was Anatoly who interceded. Before they set out, he stepped up close to Alexander so he could whisper harshly into his ear. "Man up. We have challenges to overcome, so what? That's life."

Alexander snorted and nodded. This wasn't the first time he'd heard Anatoly say those words to him. When he was an adolescent and became depressed or defeatist, Anatoly would remind him about reality, usually without much sympathy.

"Fair enough," he said quietly, before turning to address his friends. "We can't do anything about this Nether Gate at the moment, so we stay the course and face one threat at a time. Who knows? Maybe the fairies will know something about it."

Alexander set a fast pace through the mountains. The sky became overcast as the day wore on but the air was still and there was no rain. He kept careful watch on the sky, noting the ravens circling overhead several times during the early afternoon. No doubt Jataan P'Tal was driving his hunting party as hard as Alexander was driving himself and his companions. To her credit, Marla didn't complain and kept pace without difficulty.

By midafternoon they were tired and hungry. They'd eaten while they walked, so no one had eaten their fill.

The trail followed a series of switchbacks that led up to a ridgeline high in the mountains. They gained altitude steadily but the peaks of the Pinnacles rose higher still. When they finally crested the rise, Alexander realized it wasn't a ridgeline but the lip of a giant crater formed by a long-dead volcanic caldera. It was easily two leagues across at the widest point and more than a league at the narrowest. The crater was filled with the deepest blue water that Alexander had ever seen. An island covered with countless buildings made of grey mountain granite rose steeply from the center.

Marla smiled with pride and affection for her home. "Welcome to Highlake City," she said with a flourish. "We have to go down to the water's edge and hire a ferry to take us across the lake."

They traveled down another series of switchbacks cut into the rock wall of the crater. As they approached the ferryboat dock, Marla pulled the dragon medallion from under her robes for all to see.

Half a dozen boats were tied up to the docks, and there were slips for half a dozen more. A small building housed the ferryboat office, and a series of rooms cut into the granite wall served as housing for the boat operators. A short, burly man stood when he saw them coming. He smiled with crooked teeth and nodded in deference to Marla when he saw her medallion.

"Good afternoon, Priestess, passage for seven?"

"Yes, thank you. Might I speak with your employer?" she said pleasantly.

The burly young man looked a little wary, apparently hoping he hadn't given offense, but he nodded and loped off toward the office shack. A few moments later a tall, narrow-looking man with graying black hair and a gaunt face came up ahead of his laborer.

"How may I be of service, Priestess?" he asked politely.

"There are a number of men following us," Marla said. "If they come to your ferry, you are to allow them passage, but light the warning fire just after they're on their way."

He frowned. "How am I to know them?"

Alexander stepped forward. "The leader is a small, swarthy man with close-cropped black hair. He's probably dressed in black."

"I will do as you request," he said courteously.

They paid the toll and boarded the boat. The short, burly man rowed the longboat across the lake to a dock on the island.

Everyone took in the pristine beauty of the mountain community. It was so isolated and untouched. The buildings of the tiny city looked like they were somehow a natural part of the scene.

As they walked through the streets, Alexander couldn't help but notice the calm and measured pace of the inhabitants. They seemed to be moving with deliberate purpose yet without any urgency or rush. The place was well kept and finely crafted, made mostly from grey mountain granite that revealed sparkling whites and specks of black when examined up close. The buildings were simple yet sturdy and built with attention to detail. They were adorned with little ornamentation, which only served to heighten the appearance of quality construction.

The people nodded in greeting to Marla as she passed and seemed to give her a measure of deference. Alexander noted a few others dressed in similar coarse brown robes and saw that they too were accorded respect. He surmised they were all members of the Druidic Orders that appeared to form the basis of what little government the mountain community had.

Marla led the way through a maze of streets that wound higher on the little mountain island until they came to the central structure built on top of the island peak at about the same altitude as the lip of the crater surrounding the entire lake. It was a large dome made of the same grey mountain granite as the rest of the structures but the architecture of the building was impressive. There were thousands of tons of stone resting on the strength of a series of arched ribs that provided the structural support for the entire massive building. Lesser buildings radiated away from the central dome. Marla stopped and took in the place for a moment before she spoke.

"The Hall of Druids," she said, gesturing to the central dome. "It's been a long time. I didn't realize how much I have missed this place."

She led them into the entry hall of a broad three-story-high building with colossal granite pillars in two rows supporting the massive, stone ceiling beams overhead. Standing behind a small oak desk centered on the entry doors was a young man dressed in simple grey robes. He nodded respectfully to Marla.

"Greetings, Priestess, welcome home. How may I be of service?"

"I must speak with the High Priest of Tanis."

"Of course, I will send word at once," he said, then turned and nodded to a collection of other young men and women seated along the wall. One came quickly and took a note into the bowels of the giant building complex. "May I show you to a waiting room and offer you some refreshments?"

"Yes, thank you, we've had a long journey."

One of the acolytes led them to a comfortably appointed room off the main hall, while another brought a tray of food and flagons of wine. It was a simple meal of nuts, berries, smoked fish, and dried venison. Everyone ate their fill, and almost on cue, another acolyte came to the chamber just as they finished their meal.

He led them through a maze of austere granite corridors and stopped at a large oak door. With a bow, he opened the door and waved them through. Marla went first, without hesitation, followed by Alexander. They entered into a simple but well-appointed sitting room with a fire crackling in the hearth and a kettle of water steaming gently nearby.

Richly stained hardwood bookshelves lined the walls, and a deep-red carpet covered the cold stone of the floor. All around the room stood well-crafted brass lamps and a number of comfortable-looking chairs and couches. Central to the room was a large table with a number of heavy wooden chairs surrounding it. There were several books on the table, some stacked one atop the other, while others lay open.

A man of medium height and build with fair skin, blond hair, and grey eyes sat at the table reading one of the volumes. He wore the same coarse brown robes as Marla and had the golden medallion of a dragon hanging from his neck, except his had a single vibrant red ruby set where the eye of the dragon would be.

He looked up and smiled politely but without joy. Alexander could see at a glance that he was a man of considerable magical capability, though, like Marla, his colors looked somehow different than those of a wizard.

"Welcome home, Priestess Tasselheim. I see you've brought guests."

"High Priest Callahadran, it's good to be home," Marla said with a much more genuine smile. "May I present Lord Alexander Ruatha and his companions."

A puzzled look came over his face followed by a frown. "I mean no offense," he said with measured courtesy, "but I thought the line of Ruatha perished millennia ago."

"Until a few months ago, I thought as much myself," Alexander said. "As it turns out, Mage Cedric hid my bloodline to protect it until now. I have reclaimed the throne, and I'm fighting to protect Ruatha from the ambitions of Phane Reishi."

He smiled again without humor. "As I'm sure Priestess Tasselheim has told you, we have no wish to participate in the affairs of the outside world. May I ask your purpose here in our secluded little community?"

Alexander caught just a hint of wariness in his colors. No doubt he was worried that Alexander might be there to press them into taking sides in the war that was raging in the distance.

"High Priest Callahadran, I have come to the Pinnacles to petition the Fairy Queen for aid. I have reason to believe that she is the only one who can help me prevent untold suffering."

Callahadran tried unsuccessfully to stifle a laugh. "Surely, you understand the danger you face if you enter the Valley of the Fairy Queen. Only her most trusted priests and priestesses are permitted to enter with any hope of returning. Whatever you hope to gain from Queen Ilona, I fear you will have to seek it elsewhere."

"I've taken them before Lady Tanis," Marla said. "Our patron has granted Lord Alexander safe passage within the Pinnacles. Queen Ilona will honor that agreement."

Anger momentarily ghosted across the High Priest's face. "On whose authority did you summon Lady Tanis?" he asked Marla pointedly.

She didn't back down. "Lord Alexander saved my life. According to our law, I am obligated to offer him guidance through the Pinnacles. His path takes him into dangerous places and so I sought to safeguard his passage by securing for him the blessing of Lady Tanis. A blessing which she offered, I should add."

He was taken aback by her last statement. "How has she blessed this outsider?" he asked with rising anger. When Alexander withdrew the dragon tooth from his tunic, Callahadran took a sharp breath and stared in disbelief at the talisman. His colors shined brightly with jealousy.

"I have no wish to intrude into your home," Alexander said. "I serve the Old Law and will respect your wish to avoid this war, although I do not believe my enemy will offer you the same respect. My only purpose here is to seek the aid of the Fairy Queen."

Callahadran drew himself up and swallowed his inner turmoil at seeing the tooth of his patron having been given to an outsider. "Very well, follow me," he said curtly and led them from the room without another word.

Again they wound through the simple granite halls of the large complex of buildings until they came to another large oak door in a different wing. An acolyte seated before the door came to her feet when they rounded the corner and bowed to High Priest Callahadran.

"Please tell your mistress that I have urgent need of an audience."

The acolyte bowed and slipped through the door. Not a minute passed before the young woman opened the door again and respectfully motioned them through.

They stepped into an open-air courtyard with a beautifully sculpted garden surrounding a large stone gazebo made from the same granite as the rest of the buildings. The night air was crisp but not too cold. The garden was in early bloom and the fragrance of dozens of different flowers mingled to create a soft and comforting scent. Several heavy brass lamps hung from stone posts jutting from the support pillars of the gazebo, providing ample light.

Seated at the table inside the gazebo was a middle-aged woman wearing the same coarse brown robe as the other druids. She was slight of build with long, silvery blond hair and hazel eyes. Around her neck hung a golden medallion fashioned in the likeness of a fairy. She stood and smiled warmly.

Alexander could see she was a genuinely good person who had lived her whole life in the peaceful confines of these mountains. She had the soft innocence of someone who had rarely encountered violence, yet her character was tempered by a deep wisdom that belied her apparent age.

"Please come and sit. You are welcome here."

High Priest Callahadran bowed politely to her. "High Priestess Clarissa, please forgive the intrusion. Priestess Tasselheim has brought guests with the sanction of my patron to seek your aid," he said with studied politeness.

"Of course," Clarissa said. "You must be Alexander and you must be Isabel. I have been expecting you, although not so soon. Your need must be urgent indeed to make such haste."

Alexander and Isabel shared a smile of relief at being acknowledged. Alexander said, "High Priestess Clarissa, thank you for your hospitality. I'm heartened to hear that you've been expecting us. Can I assume that Queen Ilona is also aware of our purpose here?"

"Yes, in fact it was she who instructed me to look for your arrival. You will stay here tonight and we will depart for the Valley of the Fairy Queen tomorrow morning. It's a journey of three days. Once we arrive, Queen Ilona will hear your petition, although I must caution you that she may not grant your request."

"I understand, but I sincerely hope that she will," Alexander said. "The future of the Seven Isles may depend on her decision."

"It has been many centuries since a fairy was permitted to bond with a mortal," Clarissa said. "Queen Ilona is loath to lose one of her own."

Marla and High Priest Callahadran shared a look of surprise.

Alexander frowned and looked over at Isabel to see worry on her face as well. "I'm afraid I don't know much about the fairies. How does bonding to a mortal cause a fairy to be lost?"

High Priestess Clarissa nodded knowingly. "Fairies are immortal and so they view the world much differently than we do. They can, of course, be killed with violence, although it rarely happens. They are wary creatures, existing in the world of time and substance while at the same time existing in the aether. When danger presents itself, they typically move into the aether to escape the threat.

"The one thing that is a certain death sentence is to form a bond of love with a mortal. When the mortal dies, the fairy bonded to them will die of a broken heart."

Alexander suddenly realized what price he was asking others to bear. But then he weighed the alternative. Phane couldn't be permitted to retrieve the Sovereign Stone.

"Forgive me, High Priestess, I understand I'm asking a great deal. If there was any other way, I would try it."

"Queen Ilona is very wise," Clarissa said. "She will determine if your need warrants the sacrifice of one of her own. She will also look into your soul and determine if you are indeed worthy of the limitless love of a fairy. I must caution you, Alexander, she may place a very high price on what you seek."

"What I ask for is priceless. I'll pay the price she asks if it will give me hope for preserving the world."

"Very well, we will depart just after dawn." With that she rose and rang a small bell. Her acolyte entered a moment later and led them to guest quarters.

They spent the night in a suite of simple rooms that were comfortable yet sparsely furnished. The rooms were built of the same grey granite and the workmanship was masterful. The stones were cut so accurately and so cleanly that a blade couldn't fit between them. The furnishings were purely functional yet built with care and attention to detail.

At dawn they were awakened by an acolyte with a platter of food. Once they'd eaten, the acolyte led them to High Priestess Clarissa. Alexander was surprised to see Marla there as well, packed and ready for travel.

"Marla, you don't need to come with us," Alexander said. "You've already done so much to help us that I consider any obligation you may feel toward us to be paid, and then some."

"I'd like to come along if I may," Marla said. "High Priestess Clarissa has consented, since I've been traveling with you."

"Of course, you're more than welcome."

Clarissa led them to a small dock where a number of well-crafted boats were moored. She stepped aboard the largest one, which was manned with a captain and a team of oarsmen, and motioned for the others to follow. Once all were aboard, they set off, moving swiftly through the calm, deep blue water.

The mountains surrounding them looked like something out of a story, pristine white against the clear blue sky and shining brightly where the sunlight fell on them. Alexander felt calm wonderment settle over him as they glided gently across the water. He sat holding Isabel's hand and focused his attention on the beauty all around.

Then he saw the fire.

"Marla, is that the warning fire you told the dock master to light if my enemies arrived?"

She nodded gravely. "It would seem they have gained some ground, although I doubt they will be able to follow us any farther. The Valley of the Fairy Queen is hidden and said to be impossible for outsiders to find."

Alexander looked up and searched the sky for a moment before he saw the ravens circling overhead. He pointed with a grim expression. "Commander P'Tal won't give up easily. He may well find his way into the valley."

Clarissa frowned. "Queen Ilona will not take kindly to uninvited guests. If your enemies choose to trespass, they may discover why so few mortals ever return from such a journey."

"High Priestess," Alexander said gravely, "perhaps we should return to Highlake City and confront them there. I have no wish to bring danger to the fairies."

"Your enemies may be very dangerous to mortals, but I doubt they pose much threat to the fairies. It would be best to stay on our current path, yet remain vigilant."

Isabel opened her eyes, breaking her connection with Slyder. "Commander P'Tal and his men are aboard three boats and they're headed straight for us."

Clarissa frowned and squinted to see across the water. "You have better vision than I. At this distance I can just make out the silhouettes of their longboats."

Isabel smiled proudly. "I have a forest hawk for a familiar. I can see through his eyes when I want to."

Alexander gave her hand a squeeze. "She and Slyder have saved us untold trouble on our journey."

Clarissa smiled warmly. "It gladdens my heart to learn such a thing. Queen Ilona will look favorably upon your bond with Slyder. Noble animals like hawks don't bond with any but those of pure heart and sound character. As for your enemies, they will find our trail quite difficult to follow."

"They're relentless," Alexander said. "Now that they have sight of us, they won't let up until they catch us."

Clarissa smiled. "The path is not clearly marked and there are many opportunities to become lost along the way. Chances are good that they will never find their way into the valley, and if they do, chances are even better that they will not be permitted to leave."

"One of them is a battle mage of great power," Alexander warned. "Even with the Thinblade, I'm not sure I can defeat him in single combat."

"A battle mage is a terrifying enemy for a mortal," Clarissa said, "but for a fairy such an enemy is of little consequence. They will simply avoid him, charm him, or send him away if he presents a threat."

Alexander frowned. "I hope you're right. He's been trying to kill me for months."

The boat pulled up next to a simple wooden dock near a little waterfall. The crew expertly guided the boat into position, leapt onto the dock with mooring lines, and tied it in place. Alexander gave his enemy one last look before stepping onto the dock. They were about an hour behind and coming fast.

Clarissa led them along a narrow, infrequently traveled path that wound behind the waterfall and into a cave. As she entered the darkness of the underground passage, she spoke a number of words in a lilting, arcane language and three orbs of light that looked like night wisps, only slightly brighter, came to life floating over her head. They provided ample illumination for the journey through the dark and damp passageway.

Once everyone was inside the cave entrance and the boat had disembarked for its return to Highlake City, she spoke another set of incantations and the stone of the entrance to the natural cave closed up behind them, forming a solid rock wall.

She smiled with satisfaction. "They will no doubt discover my artificial wall, but it will take them some time and then they'll have to break it down, which will delay them further."

Alexander smiled with wonder before turning to follow the High Priestess. She led them into a passage cut straight through the side of the caldera's crater wall that gently gained altitude for a mile before opening into the sparse forest surrounding the ancient dormant volcano.

They followed a well-made trail for the better part of the day. A few trails branched off here and there, but the ravens were still overhead, so the enemy would have no trouble following them. However, Isabel reported that Commander P'Tal had lost nearly a day trying to find a way through the rock wall.

They emerged from the underground passage just before dusk. Alexander felt much better having greater distance from the enemy. He knew P'Tal would try to make up for lost time by pressing on until full dark so he resolved to do the same. They traveled even after nightfall for an hour or so by the light of the night-wisp dust and the glowing orbs of illumination that bobbled in a wide orbit around Clarissa's head.

They made a hasty camp in a clearing off the side of the trail. Everyone was tired from the long day of travel, so they went to bed without much conversation. There were a number of things Alexander wanted to ask Clarissa, but he decided it would be better to wait until they reached the Valley of the Fairy Queen.

He fretted about the Nether Gate and the ominous warning Mage Atherton's ghost had given but worried even more about the gleeful proclamation of Malachi Reishi's ghost that Alexander had doomed the world. Of all the horror stories told about the Reishi War, tales of the shades evoked the greatest fear, mostly because they were so insidious and they couldn't actually be killed.

Stories of the shades in battle were the worst. A shade would use its host to rush headlong into the fray with wild ferocity. Once its host was struck down, it would simply possess the nearest unsuspecting enemy soldier and continue its rampage. Whole armies broke and fled from the attack of a single shade.

More than anything, Alexander feared that the shades and Phane would somehow join forces to retrieve the Sovereign Stone and open the Nether Gate, resulting in a world terrorized by Phane's naked ambition and the insatiable lust for suffering of the hordes from the darkness. He had to remind himself that his fears about the Nether Gate and its purpose were only speculation, yet his certainty was growing.

The next day began in the forest but quickly transitioned into a mountain wasteland that Clarissa called the maze. It was a barren and uneven field of giant boulders that seemed to stretch for miles. Clarissa said that the Valley of the Fairy Queen could only be reached through the maze and there was only one true path. Most of those who sought out the fairies became lost in the endless dead ends and the confusing jumble of twists and turns that the seemingly random field of scattered boulders created. The maze was devoid of life and in many places the ground was nothing but bare mountain granite.

Clarissa led the way with a confidence that Alexander found himself doubting after a while. Within an hour of entering the twisted place, he became so disoriented that he started to think he wouldn't be able to find his way out without a guide.

Even Isabel with Slyder's help was turned around and led astray. Alexander heard her muttering about the lack of sense the place made. She often stopped when Clarissa calmly took a turn that didn't seem to be the right course and tried to orient herself to the new direction only to shake her head in confusion.

They traveled through the maze for the rest of the day and into the early hours of the night. Well after dusk, Clarissa stopped in a clearing large enough for them to make camp. They prepared a cold meal before laying out their bedrolls and going to sleep.

Alexander wondered if Commander P'Tal would have as much difficulty navigating through the maze as he knew he would have without the guidance of High Priestess Clarissa.

They would arrive at the home of the fairies tomorrow, and Alexander was starting to feel a bit nervous about their reaction to his request. He was asking a great deal of them and he knew it would cost him but he just didn't know how much. He'd pledged to pay any price but as he got closer, he wondered what they would demand in exchange for helping him.

He slept fitfully and dreamt of danger swirling all around in the shadows. It was unformed, just outside of the range of his vision but he knew it was there waiting to strike. He woke several times in the night with a start, then calmed himself with the deep breathing techniques he'd learned in Glen Morillian, only to return to the darkness of his dreams.

He woke at dawn to see five ravens watching him from the rocks above. He knew at a glance that they were the enemy's spies and wondered idly, as he slowly reached for his bow, if they'd been responsible for his nightmares. He usually slept soundly and his dreams were rarely dark or fretful, although he did have more weighing on him now than ever before.

With a fluid motion he rolled to his feet, nocked an arrow, drew his bow, took quick but careful aim and released his arrow at one of the ravens. All five leapt into the air the moment his intent became clear. His arrow grazed one bird on the side of its breast and passed straight through its wing. It squawked angrily as it spiraled to the ground.

The moment Alexander moved for his bow, Anatoly came up quickly with his axe, looking around for the threat. Abigail saw the target of her brother's wrath and tried to get a shot off before the birds escaped, but she was a moment too late. They dodged behind the top of a boulder and vanished into the early morning.

Alexander stood over the injured raven as it squawked at them. Marla and Clarissa came up on either side of him and looked at the bird with a mixture of sorrow and curiosity.

"Why have you injured this bird, Alexander?" Clarissa asked.

"It has been spelled by one of the wizards tracking me. Five ravens have been following us for days. This is the first time they've been close enough to shoot at."

"I've seen these birds as well, High Priestess," Marla said. "They're not common in the Pinnacles and these have been in the sky overhead since I met Alexander."

"Perhaps I can break the spell controlling this bird and render your enemy blind to your course," Clarissa said.

She began a soft and lilting chant. Her words were more like those of a song than those of a spell. She wove a beautiful melody that echoed around the sheer stone walls of the maze. At the culmination of her spell, the raven screeched as did the four others off in the distance. Alexander watched the colors of the bird change abruptly as the spell broke and faded away. A moment later, it was just a simple raven.

Clarissa bent and cooed softly to the bird. It seemed to understand her wish to help it, almost as if she were speaking to it. The bird hobbled closer to her and she began the words of another spell. After a few minutes of soft rhythmic chanting, Alexander watched the colors of the High Priestess flare and the bird's wing was mended. It nodded at her a few times before it leapt into the air and took to flight.

"Thank you," Alexander said. "Without the ravens to track for him, I doubt Commander P'Tal will be able to find his way out of this maze. More importantly, he'll never find his way into the valley."

The rest of the day passed much the same as the previous day. They followed Clarissa through the seemingly endless maze of jumbled giant boulders. She wove and wound through the bewildering series of pathways with clear purpose. Late in the afternoon, she stopped and traced her hand along the rock wall of a high cliff that bordered the maze on one side. After a few feet, her hand fell through the rock wall. She smiled to Alexander and his friends.

"The entrance to the valley is hidden by an illusion," Clarissa said. "There's actually a crack in the stone of this cliff that reaches all the way to the top but cannot be seen even by me. Please," she motioned to the stone wall, "push through the wall into the space beyond."

Alexander looked closely at the wall for any sign of a magical aura but saw none. He felt a sense of wonder and dread. He'd come to rely on his second sight for so much. Now, for the first time that he was aware of, he'd encountered something that didn't reveal its nature with an aura. He wondered at the power of such an illusion as he passed through it into the narrow crevice. He turned and looked back into the maze as though there was no illusion at all. Apparently, it only worked from one side.

Clarissa led them through the winding crack in the cliff face and into the Valley of the Fairy Queen. The crack opened into a thick grassy meadow littered with wild flowers. The air seemed to warm noticeably the moment they stepped from the crevice into the valley itself. It was much like Glen Morillian in that the entire valley was surrounded by impassible mountains on all sides, but this valley was much smaller. The meadow stretched before them and met with a sparse forest of the biggest oak trees Alexander had ever seen. The ancient trees stood hundreds of feet taller than even the biggest fir, with trunks dozens of feet in diameter.

Clarissa took a deep breath of the fragrant air and smiled wistfully. "Welcome to the Valley of the Fairy Queen. Her temple is this way. Be warned, not everything in this place is what it seems. Please don't wander away from me," she said as she started off across the meadow.

They didn't follow a trail because there wasn't one but instead wound under the ancient oak trees through the dimly lit but lush undergrowth that carpeted the valley floor. Twenty minutes of walking brought them to the central meadow of the valley and to the Fairy Temple.

As they walked, Alexander had the distinct feeling that he was being watched. He looked around for the telltale aura of magic or life, but all he could see was a collage of colors that shone brightly in every direction. It was as if the entire mountain valley was enchanted and the aura of that magic drowned out the colors of everything else.

From the corner of his eye, he occasionally saw a flicker or a glimmer in the trees but when he turned to look, it was always gone. Aside from the obvious magic, the valley was one of the most idyllic and beautiful places he'd ever seen, even in the early dusk. He could only imagine what it might look like in full daylight.

The central meadow had a giant oak tree directly in the middle. It was easily a thousand feet tall and the trunk was nearly a hundred feet across. It was so magnificent that Alexander and his companions stopped to stare at it. The ancient tree was enormous and clearly older than any tree any of them had ever seen. Its colors were rich, bright, and vibrant. Isabel found Alexander's hand without looking and gave a gentle squeeze.

Clarissa let them all take in the giant oak for a few moments before she broke the spell of its grandeur. "Please, Queen Ilona will be waiting."

Alexander shook off the beguiling effect of the tree and followed the High Priestess to the Fairy Temple. It was simple, yet evoked a feeling of reverence for life. The temple consisted of a raised, solid granite slab with seven evenly spaced pillars along each of the long sides and four along the front and back. Stone beams rested along the tops of the pillars to form the outline of a room without walls or ceiling. Three stairs led to the interior of the open-air temple.

There was no furniture or adornments of any kind. The only thing inside the temple was a large, circular stone altar in the center. The surface was beveled and filled with water to the edges to form a perfectly smooth reflection of the tree as one approached. In the early evening sky, Alexander could just see the sparkle of starlight through the gaps in the giant tree's branches.

Clarissa stopped in front of the altar and stood with her head held high. "Queen Ilona, I bring you my love," she said with reverence and pride. Then she began to sing. Her voice was clear and strong. Although Alexander didn't know the language, he was struck by the beauty of the music she created with her voice. He glanced at Jack and saw a look of admiration for her talent. His colors shone brightly with pride. Not for himself, but that a human being was capable of making music as beautiful and soulful as her song.

Alexander felt a mixture of wonder and trepidation. Much would be decided in the coming moments. He had fought hard to get here. Now he would find out if his efforts would bear fruit. He took Isabel's hand and gave her a smile as they listened to the magical song.

Chapter 28

When High Priestess Clarissa stopped singing, she silently bowed her head for a long moment. Alexander realized he was holding his breath when suddenly a brilliant orb of scintillating light spun into existence above the pool of water that formed the surface of the altar. When she stopped spinning, Alexander saw a woman of exquisite beauty, yet only three inches tall, floating above the altar on dragonfly wings. Her hair was golden and her eyes were blue. Her skin was a softly glowing pale white.

Even with her diminutive stature, Alexander could see ancient wisdom and nobility of spirit within her. She was an enchanting creature. More than her physical appearance, Alexander was awed by her colors. They were pure and bright with an intensity that he'd seen only once before, at the Dragon Temple. Not only was she devoted to love and life but she was immensely powerful as well. Her magic seemed to flow from the realm of light itself and shined as if she had an endless supply of power to draw from.

High Priestess Clarissa bowed to her patron. "My Lady, you honor me with your loving presence."

Ilona smiled brightly and Alexander could actually see her colors flare when she directed her immortal love toward her High Priestess. "You are in my heart always, Clarissa." The bond between them was clearly profound and powerful.

Alexander knew in that moment that the only love he had ever felt that could match the intensity or sheer power of the fairies' capacity for love was what he felt for Isabel.

Ilona appraised Alexander and his friends for a moment. It reminded him of the way he looked at another person's colors, reading much more about their character than they could possibly know. The Fairy Queen looked into their souls and weighed their merit, each in turn, before she spoke. When she looked at Isabel, she glanced up briefly at Slyder sitting on one of the stone beams of the temple and smiled.

"The world is once again in turmoil," Ilona said. "Once again humanity is at the center of the strife. And again you have come to seek my aid."

Alexander stepped forward and bowed respectfully. "Our need is great. The fate of many hangs in the balance."

"Indeed. I witnessed the Reishi War firsthand. I saw the cruelty and destruction inflicted on the innocent by the wicked. I wept when Malachi Reishi and his soulless offspring slaughtered many of my sisters and daughters." Ilona stopped, looking haunted by memories of the distant past. She fixed Alexander with her penetrating gaze and shook her head sadly. "Mankind's capacity for hate and cruelty is matched only by its capacity for love and charity. I have long puzzled over humanity's preeminence in the world. You are a short-lived race destined for quick death and yet you seem to be forever at war with yourselves."

Alexander shook his head. "I have no explanation for it, except that there are those who are so selfish and so driven by an insatiable lust for power over others that they will commit unspeakable atrocities to gain that power. But they are few. Most people just want to live their lives and love their families and friends."

"Sadly, the lust for power that drives those few is the guiding hand of your history. Bitter experience has taught me to be very selective when dealing with humans. You are the first outsiders who have been invited into our home in two millennia. Your request would never have been granted were it not for Cedric's warning spell. I know better than most the danger to the world that Phane Reishi represents, yet I am wary of becoming involved again. We took sides in the last war between men, and we paid dearly for it."

"I understand and share your reluctance," Alexander said. "I didn't ask for this war or the responsibility I've been given but many depend on me, even if they don't know it. If I fail, darkness will claim the Seven Isles for a thousand years. Phane will rule as a tyrant and he will not tolerate liberty for anyone anywhere, even here."

Ilona smiled gently. "I knew Mage Cedric to be an honorable man. It seems he has chosen his champion well. State your request." She drew herself up like a judge waiting for a confession.

"I must retrieve the Sovereign Stone before Phane does, but I have no way of reaching into the aether, so I've come to ask for your help." Alexander stood and faced her forthrightly.

"You know not what you ask. No fairy would leave her home for any reason save love, and the bond of love to a mortal is certain death."

Alexander bowed his head sadly. "I know," he said quietly. "I wish there was another way."

"I believe you do. What do you intend to do with the Sovereign Stone if you were to retrieve it from the aether?"

"I plan to seal it away in one of Mage Cedric's Bloodvaults to place it forever out of Phane's reach."

"Phane is a deceiver. Perhaps you are his unwitting servant. Since he is unable to retrieve the Stone, he may be using you to achieve that which he cannot, only to take it from you before you can place it beyond his reach."

That was a possibility Alexander hadn't considered. He thought it over for a moment but decided that the presence of the shades in the world posed too great a threat. If the shades joined forces with Phane, he would have the Stone as soon as he could get to the Reishi Keep.

"Phane is cunning and manipulative, so I can't rule out what you suggest, although I don't believe it to be the case. He has tried to use the powersink at the Reishi Keep and at the Temple of Fire. He has failed on both counts." Alexander paused and took a deep breath. "Now the danger is greater because the shades are loose in the world."

Ilona's eyes grew wide and she spun into a ball of scintillating light for a moment. "How can this be so?" she demanded with clear alarm.

"It's my fault," Alexander said as he looked back to Isabel and reached for her hand. She stepped forward next to him and bowed to Ilona as she took his hand. "Isabel touched the mind of a demon that had possessed her horse. It opened a rift to the netherworld within her psyche, and her soul was lost in the darkness. I used my magic to follow her into the dark and bring her back to the world of time and substance."

Ilona spun back into a ball of light. "You have joined souls?" she said almost reverently.

Alexander and Isabel shared a look before they nodded in unison. "A few days later, the demon took possession of a mountain lion. The beast was on me, preparing to strike, when Isabel attacked it. During that attack she was again drawn into the darkness. Again, I went in and brought her back, but the shades were waiting for us. They escaped through Isabel and into the world."

"This news is far more troubling to me than the awakening of Phane."

Alexander nodded grimly. "There's more. Since this ordeal began, I've been visited by the ghost of Nicolai Atherton. He comes to offer advice and warnings. Several nights ago, he warned me that the shades would seek out the Nether Gate. Then the ghost of Malachi Reishi appeared and told me that I had doomed the world."

Ilona spun into a ball of light floating in place for several long seconds, throwing off streaks of brightly colored light. She glowed with such intensity that it hurt his eyes to look directly at her. When she stopped spinning and faced Alexander, she was a mixture of alarm and fury. She flitted up to within inches of Alexander's nose and pointed her finger at him.

"The Nether Gate is the end of everything. If it's opened, the hordes of the netherworld will pour forth to devour the world of life and love. Nothing will long stand against the broken souls of the dark. Malachi Reishi is right—you have doomed the world."

Alexander didn't flinch or retreat from her accusation but held his ground and looked her directly in the eye. He gave Isabel's hand a gentle squeeze which she returned without hesitation. "Be that as it may, I would not do a single thing differently. My love was lost in the darkness and I had the power to save her, so I did." It wasn't an apology or even an explanation; it was a challenge.

Ilona blinked and her ire evaporated in the face of Alexander's pure motive. She smiled gently and floated a few inches farther from his face. "The result of your actions is a disaster, but I cannot fault your intentions. How long have you been wed?"

"We are betrothed but not yet wed," Alexander said.

Ilona spun back into a ball of light and returned to her place above the reflecting pool of the altar. "You come before me to ask that one of my children give you her heart, yet you have not even committed your short life to the one you love." Ilona was angry. Her colors shone brightly and with intensity.

Alexander suddenly found himself on thin ice. Within the turmoil roiling through him, he found a place of stillness and instantly knew his course. He loved Isabel. He was already bonded to her in a way that was deeper and more complete than most people would ever know. He had seen her soul and opened himself to her completely. They had agreed to wait for their wedding for the sake of their families, but in that moment he realized their mistake.

They were denying each other love for the sake of formality and tradition. Life was too short and far too dangerous to hesitate in the face of such clear feelings. They were meant to be together. Alexander knew that with certainty.

Without letting go of Isabel's hand, he drew his sword with his left hand

and gently laid it at their feet. Ilona spun into a ball of light again. As Alexander turned to face a wide-eyed Isabel, the darkness all around them erupted into dozens, then scores, and finally hundreds of scintillating balls of light all spinning excitedly in the night. The meadow of the Fairy Temple was suddenly filled with fairies and awash in their magical light.

Alexander let everything else slip away and gave Isabel his entire attention. With a clear and unwavering voice he spoke his vows.

"Isabel Alaric, I love you with all that I am and all that I have. Step across this sword with me and become my wife. I pledge my heart and my soul, my life and my love to you for every day that I live."

Isabel looked back at Alexander and blinked a few times before smiling radiantly.

"I used to be afraid of marriage. I thought it meant the end of the life I wanted to live. Now I realize it's the beginning of everything. I will love you forever, Alexander."

With that they stepped across the Thinblade and became husband and wife. Alexander smiled up at Queen Ilona unabashedly and said for all to hear. "May I present my wife, Queen Isabel Ruatha."

Queen Ilona's anger evaporated and she smiled brightly and clapped her hands. "Well done," she said as all of the fairies in the meadow spun into brightly glowing balls of light for a moment before they began flitting about in an aerial dance. Then they started singing.

There were hundreds of them, all joining in the ancient wedding song. A moment later, Clarissa began to sing. A moment after that, Jack added the music of his tin whistle to the song. The music was the most enchanting and hauntingly beautiful thing Alexander had ever heard. It went on for several minutes and moved everyone to tears, even Anatoly.

The fairies danced and flitted around their heads and around the temple, all the while adding their voices to the impossibly complex song. When the music stopped, hundreds of fairies came to stand on the stone beams that rested on the pillars of the temple.

"Your capacity for love is plain for all to see," Ilona said. "We will speak of the future tomorrow. Tonight is your wedding night and you are my guests."

Several druids came out of the forest as if on cue. They took Alexander and Isabel off in different directions and the rest of the party in yet another direction. An hour later they were reunited in a medium-sized stone building with a long banquet table dominating the center. It was well lit with hundreds of softly glowing orbs of light floating and bobbing gently against the ceiling. The table was set with a feast; where the food had come from or how it had been prepared so quickly was a mystery.

Everyone was dressed in simple robes, all except Isabel and Alexander. He had changed into his banquet finery and was waiting when Isabel arrived. She was wearing a simply cut, white satin dress with a gold ribbon tying back her chestnut-brown hair. Alexander felt a lump in his throat when he saw his wife. She was stunning.

The banquet lasted into the late hours of the night. The food was plentiful and well prepared. Everyone did their best to avoid talk of the troubles they faced. Instead they enjoyed the evening. Fairies flitted about. One by one, they came up to the newlyweds and offered congratulations. Alexander got the feeling that having their impromptu wedding in the Valley of the Fairy Queen was as much a gift to the fairies as it was to Alexander and Isabel.

When the feast was over, High Priestess Clarissa led Alexander and Isabel into the woods to a simple little cottage. A fire burned in the hearth and several oil lamps softly illuminated the single room. The big four-poster feather bed in the center of the far wall was draped with white gossamer and several bouquets of fragrant wild flowers were set about the room.

Alexander and Isabel took in the room from beyond the threshold. They had both waited so long for this night and now that it was here, it seemed somehow surreal. Everything else faded away when he looked at her. With a gentle smile, he lifted her off her feet and took her into their wedding night bedchamber.

They spent the night rediscovering each other. Slowly and tenderly, yet with unbridled passion and unabashed lust, they made love for the first time. What had been a union of heart and soul was now complete. At one point, late in the night, when they held each other and lost themselves in the eyes of the other, they felt an irrevocable bond form between them. Their souls were mated. The joy in that moment was more than either had ever imagined.

Alexander woke early with the first stirring of dawn. He lay still and watched Isabel sleep for a few minutes, tracing the line of her neck and the rise and fall of her breast with each deep breath. When her eyes fluttered open and met his, he knew total certainty for the first time in his life. They were meant for each other. As long as he had her love, he could meet any challenge.

CHAPTER 29

When they emerged from the cottage, there was a fairy waiting for them. She flitted up close to Alexander and looked at him with mischief, then darted over to Isabel and gave her the same look. "Breakfast is waiting," she said and then flitted off into the forest laughing.

Everyone was already there and the table was set with a generous breakfast. They enjoyed the meal, but Alexander could feel the sense of urgency start to build within him again. He wished things could be different. More than anything he just wanted to be alone with his wife. Even as the thought formed in his mind, he heard his father's old refrain: "Deal in what is." It was a common admonishment to see the world for what it was and make decisions based on an honest and objective understanding of reality rather than a fantasy created out of hopes, desires, and wishes.

The reality was that Alexander was running out of time. His enemies were multiplying and he hadn't yet achieved his true purpose in coming to the Pinnacles. After the meal was eaten and the conversation lulled, Alexander gave Isabel a look that said more than words could. She nodded her ascent to his silent question. He took a deep breath and focused his mind on the purpose that had brought him here.

"Clarissa, I'm grateful for your hospitality and our wedding was beautiful in a way that I could have never planned or hoped for, but I have urgent need of Queen Ilona's help. Will she make her decision today?"

Clarissa nodded acquiescence to his gentle request to move the conversation away from joy and back to the turmoil of the world. Before she could answer, a ball of scintillating white light spun into existence over the table. A moment later, Ilona was floating a few feet in front of Alexander and Isabel.

"Your love is a joy to witness. I regret you have so little time to enjoy it before you return to your duty."

Alexander and Isabel both smiled sadly in agreement.

"Queen Ilona, you've given us a wedding night beyond my imaginings," Isabel said. "I will be forever grateful for the time I've spent here in your home. But Alexander is right—many lives depend on our success. As much as I would like to spend more time getting to know my husband even better," she gave him a smile, "we must act quickly. Will you help us?"

"What you seek is no small thing. Will you share your husband's love with another, Isabel? For that is what you ask."

Out of the corner of his eye, Alexander saw a little flare of jealousy in Isabel's colors, but she recovered quickly. "I have seen his soul and I know his love for me is true. Even if he loves another, I know his feelings for me will not waver."

"As you know, we consider bonding with a mortal to be a death sentence. Even a mortal who has survived the mana fast will only live for two hundred years at best. To us that is a very short time."

Mason Kallentera, the court wizard of Glen Morillian, had mentioned that the mana fast prolonged the life of a wizard but he hadn't mentioned how long. Alexander was struck with the suddenly very real possibility that he would outlive those he loved. And then he realized the absurdity of worrying about a problem that was decades away when he had so many other problems that were trying very hard to ensure he would never have to worry about outliving anyone.

Ilona continued, "You may have the opportunity to endure the mage's fast which would prolong your life for several hundred years more, but still you will die and the one bonded to you will fade from this world. If you are to take a life, I require that you give one in return."

Alexander felt his blood run cold. He fixed Ilona with a hard look, anger dancing in his golden-flecked eyes. "Exactly what do you mean?"

"You must sire a child to replace the life you will take."

Alexander froze as jealousy flared brightly in Isabel's colors. It was one thing to bond to another but something else altogether to create life with anyone but his wife. He suddenly realized the price he would have to pay and now that he was faced with it, he wasn't sure he was willing to pay it.

Before he could gather his thoughts, Isabel spoke. Her voice was measured and controlled but Alexander could hear the tremor beneath her words. "How is that even possible?"

Ilona turned to Isabel. "You pledged that you would pay any price for my help. I can see the distress this demand is causing you and I'm sorry for that, but I have a responsibility to my community to preserve the balance. What's more, Isabel, you must not only consent to this, but you must be a part of it. There is no other way."

She was stunned speechless. When she looked at Alexander, he felt a stab of guilt and heartache at the look of pain in her beautiful green eyes. He didn't know what to say but he would have done anything to ease her suffering in that moment. He took her in his arms and whispered in her ear. "We'll find another way. I can't bear to see you hurt by me, Isabel. We'll find another way."

She hastily wiped a tear from her cheek and shook her head. "This is the price your mother warned me about." Isabel sniffed back her tears and faced Ilona. "What do we have to do?"

Before Ilona could answer, Alexander turned Isabel back to him. "Isabel, are you sure about this?"

She took a deep breath and looked into his eyes. "I am your queen. I have just as much responsibility for preserving and protecting our people as you. If that duty requires a sacrifice, then so be it. I will endure what I must."

Alexander felt trapped. He needed the fairies' help, but at what cost? Before he could form his objection, Isabel stood and faced Ilona. "Tell me what I have to do." Her voice was steady but Alexander could hear the pain she was feeling. More than that, he could see the fear and misery in her colors. He reminded himself of his duty and decided to be at least as brave as she was. He stood next to her and faced Ilona.

She appraised them for a moment before nodding. A moment later, another fairy spun into existence in a bright ball of light. She flitted up to Alexander and then to Isabel, looking each of them in the eye before moving to hover next to Ilona.

"Alexander, Isabel, I would like to introduce Chloe, my eldest daughter. She has consented to the bonding." Ilona spoke the words with simple nobility, but Alexander could see the sadness in her colors and realized that she was sacrificing her own child to his cause.

Chloe was beautiful. At three inches tall she was a perfectly proportioned woman with silvery hair and sapphire eyes. She smiled warmly at the two of them. "I have witnessed the love you have for one another. The intensity of your feelings is one reason I have agreed to the bonding. The second is because I have seen the nature of the enemy you face and I know the world will suffer greatly if the darkness wins."

"Hello, Chloe, I'm honored to meet you," Alexander said solemnly.

"Alexander, you must go with Chloe. Isabel, you will come with me. We must prepare," Ilona said. "The assistance of Master Alabrand would be welcome."

Lucky looked a little surprised but stood nonetheless. "It would be my privilege to help in whatever way I can."

Alexander's friends had been quiet in the presence of the Fairy Queen. Mostly they seemed awed by the magic of the place and by her presence. Alexander shared a look with each of them. He saw sympathy in their eyes where only an hour before they had been nothing but happy for the two of them.

Alexander hugged Isabel fiercely and kissed her tenderly. "I love you. I will always love you, no matter what happens," he whispered to her.

She forced a smile and nodded. "I know. I love you, too, Alexander."

Chloe led him off into the forest of huge oak trees. She flew next to him, keeping pace with his long strides. The valley was such an enchanting place yet Alexander wasn't in the mood to marvel at the natural beauty all around him. He was worried for Isabel. She was hurting and he was the cause of her pain. Chloe brought him out of his dark mood.

"Your love for her is bigger than this. For my part, I have no desire to bring you pain. In time, you will come to see that our bond will only strengthen your love for Isabel."

"How can you be so sure?"

"I have seen it many times in the past. Fairies will only bond with one who has committed his heart to another. It is the most basic test of a potential mate. If a mortal does not have the capacity to love another mortal, then no fairy would risk bonding with him. In most cases the love between the mortals only grows stronger because the love given by the fairy is so innocent and so pure that they learn how to love more freely and give that love to their mortal mate. You will see."

"I hope you're right. I can't stand the thought of hurting Isabel."

Chloe smiled warmly. "That is why I have chosen you."

She led him to a little meadow near the edge of the valley. A stone shelf protruded from the cliff face a few feet above the meadow. The entire surface of the shelf was covered with an iridescent white powder. When he looked closer, he saw the remnants of fairy wings mixed in with the powder.

"This is where we come to shed our wings. They dry out and turn into fairy dust. You may take some for your friend. Master Alabrand has it within him to make potent magic with fairy dust."

Alexander smiled. "I'm sure Lucky will appreciate that." He emptied the coins from his coin purse into his pocket, then scooped up a handful of the magical dust and carefully poured it into the purse.

"Alexander, you must take a pinch of fairy dust and place it under your tongue. It will dissolve and then your essence will be able to pass into the aether where the bonding will take place."

He nodded and did as she instructed. The fairy dust was sweet and dissolved almost immediately. Only moments passed before he felt a surge of magic course through his body. His perspective on the world subtly shifted. He could see beyond the realm of time and substance and into the aether. As he peered through the veil, he saw dozens of fairies flitting about the forest. In the light of day, they were only visible if they wanted to be but they were always visible within the aether.

"Now come and sit with me," Chloe said. "Close your eyes and allow me to take your essence into the aether. There is no danger. You will feel pressure build in the front of your forehead, then you will hear a buzzing noise like the sound of bees that will grow louder and louder. Allow these things to happen. Finally, you will hear a popping noise and you will be free of your body."

Alexander sat cross-legged in the thick grass and closed his eyes. He used the meditation techniques he'd learned in Glen Morillian to calm his mind and relax his body. As his tension faded, the pressure in his head started to build. It wasn't unpleasant or painful, just unusual. Then the buzzing started. It rose and fell as it increased in intensity. Alexander let it flow through him until he felt it more than heard it. When it filled him completely, he heard a loud pop and he was suddenly floating over his meditating body.

It was different than his clairvoyance because he wasn't in the world of time and substance anymore. The quality of the aether was altogether different. It was a timeless place that overlapped and coexisted with material reality. It was a place where the soul existed and where spirits went before they transitioned into the realm of light or into the netherworld.

Alexander realized he was floating in the form of a brightly glowing orb of light not more than a few inches in diameter. With that thought, he looked at himself again and found that he was now a silvery image of his own body.

Chloe appeared before him as a human woman. She smiled and he heard her thoughts. "Within the aether you can take any form you wish, but your true form is the sphere of light you first manifest as."

Alexander looked around in wonder. He felt like he could go anywhere and be there instantly, very much like the firmament, except there was no ocean of potential, just a ghostly reflection of the material world.

"I'm going to move closer to you now," Chloe said. "Don't be frightened, I won't hurt you." She transformed into a simple orb of beautiful glowing light and drifted toward him. He transformed as well and then she was within his soul and he was within hers.

It was a shocking sensation as he realized just how ancient she really was. He could feel her passion for life and her boundless love flow into him, given freely and without reservation or hesitation. He resisted briefly, thinking of Isabel and his experience with her in the netherworld. This was similar, except without fear and danger all around.

After a moment, he opened himself to Chloe and bared his soul to her. She flowed into him gently and offered him her pure and unconditional love. It was a profound experience. Alexander loved Isabel but he suddenly realized that he had always kept a part of himself safely away from her without even knowing it. He thought he'd given himself over to her totally but his mortal fear was subconsciously holding back a part of himself. Chloe showed him what unflinching love really was with the innocent clarity of ancient wisdom.

Love was the source of life. It was the underlying power that flowed into the world from the realm of light. Chloe had lived long enough to learn how to love without condition or fear. She gave freely and completely without expectation. Alexander was humbled by her willingness to open herself to him and expose her vulnerability. The level of trust she gave him was daunting. He couldn't help but feel love in response.

For what seemed like a long time, they simply shared existence with one another and became accustomed to the nature of the other's essence. Alexander let his resistance go when he realized that love freely given could not be wrong and should never be feared. He discovered that his love for Isabel was not a limitation or an impediment to his love for Chloe but a complementary force. And that his newly formed bond with Chloe would only serve to help him love Isabel more freely and completely. His fear evaporated and his confidence in the underlying benevolent design of the world solidified. When he felt that limitless faith in the nature of the world take root in his being, Chloe separated from him and he gently drifted back into his body.

Everything he thought he understood about the world changed. The bond with Chloe was complete and his view of the world took on a much longer and larger perspective. Her ancient wisdom tempered his very shortsighted perspective and gave him a depth of understanding that he couldn't put into words.

She was floating a few feet in front of him, smiling gently. He heard her speak within his mind. "How are you feeling, My Love?"

He answered her without words but rather through the bond they now shared. "More grounded. I believe I have a greater understanding of what is truly important in life. Thank you, Chloe. I had no idea how small my view of the world was until you showed me. How are you feeling?"

"I'm in love," she answered simply, then flew up and kissed him on the cheek.

He looked around and realized it was early evening. The bonding had taken the better part of the day.

"Come," Chloe said in his mind, "Isabel awaits us."

"I don't understand."

"You will," Chloe responded, then darted off, beckoning him to follow. She led him to the cottage where he and Isabel had spent their wedding night. The windows were glowing softly in the early dusk. When he opened the door, he saw Isabel and Ilona talking softly. Isabel looked up and searched his eyes for a change.

He smiled and went to her. "I love you, Isabel—that will never change." Her look of relief lightened his worry for her.

"I've been talking with Ilona. She's helped me to understand what must happen," Isabel said in a small voice. "Chloe will make love with you through my body. She will merge her essence with me for the night and through us a fairy child will be born."

Alexander was speechless. He hadn't given much thought to what had to happen for him to sire a fairy child. He was more preoccupied with the process of bonding and was still a bit unsteady from the profound nature of the experience. Now that he understood, he was both relieved that he wouldn't have to physically betray his wife and a little worried about the consequences to Isabel of sharing her body with Chloe.

"I would never hurt her, My Love," Chloe said to reassure him. "I feel your love for her through our bond."

Alexander smiled his understanding to her before turning to Isabel. "Are you sure about this?"

She nodded. With that, Ilona spun into an orb of light and vanished, leaving Alexander and Isabel alone with Chloe. Isabel gave Alexander one last look before sitting down in front of a crystal chalice filled with syrupy-looking, slightly pink liquid. She turned to Chloe and said, "I'm ready."

Chloe darted up to her and kissed her on the cheek. "You honor me, Queen Isabel."

She flew to the chalice and shed a single tear into the liquid. The contents of the cup changed from slightly pink to perfectly clear with a slight glow of pure white light. Isabel took the chalice and drank the contents all at once. Chloe spun into a bright white ball of scintillating light and disappeared. A moment later, Isabel opened her eyes.

"Hello, My Love."

"Chloe?"

"Yes, My Love. Isabel is here as well."

When Alexander woke the next morning with Isabel in his arms, she was still sleeping. Chloe was curled up on the pillow next to him. What he remembered most from the night was the moment when he looked into Isabel's eyes and saw the pure white radiance of the realm of light glowing behind her piercing green eyes. It was as if, through her, he could see past the veil and into the source of creation to look on the face of the Maker of the world.

She woke and smiled gently at him.

"Isabel?"

She nodded. Chloe came awake and flew in a circle over them, then darted in and kissed them each on the cheek in turn. She smiled proudly as another fairy spun into existence next to her. She looked much younger than Chloe even though she was a fully-grown, three-inch-tall fairy. She had piercing green eyes the color of Isabel's and golden- blond hair.

"I'd like you to meet our daughter, Sara."

Sara smiled and kissed them both on the cheek. "Thank you for giving me life," she said simply. Alexander and Isabel were both speechless.

Chloe smiled brightly. "I must take our daughter to meet the rest of her family. They are most anxious." With that, both of the fairies spun into brightly glowing orbs of light and disappeared.

"Are you all right?" Alexander asked Isabel.

She smiled and nuzzled in closer to him.

"I don't remember much about last night except a feeling of profound love and a brilliantly pure light that seemed to fill me completely. I'm sorry I was jealous. I didn't understand. Now that I do, I'm grateful for the experience. I feel a deeper connection to the world than I ever did before and a deeper connection to you, too."

Alexander smiled and kissed his wife.

Chapter 30

When they wandered into the banquet hall, they found their friends all there talking quietly with Marla and Clarissa. Everyone stopped and looked at them. They just smiled their greeting and sat down at the table.

"I trust all is well," Lucky said.

"All is well," Isabel said with a smile.

Jack started playing a soft little tune on his whistle. It was similar, though much less complex than the song the fairies had sung at their wedding. Several fairies spun into existence inside the room and flitted about adding their voices to his music. Then Chloe arrived with Sara.

Isabel stood up. "I'd like to introduce our daughter, Sara." Her face flushed even as she smiled brightly. Sara flitted up to each of Alexander's friends and introduced herself.

Everyone at the table was surprised, except for Clarissa. She smiled knowingly and welcomed Sara into the world with genuine affection.

Suddenly, Ilona spun into existence above the table.

"Darkness comes," she said with deadly seriousness. "Master Alabrand, I have need of your assistance. Come quickly."

Lucky looked to Alexander. He nodded as he stood. "What's coming and how far away is it?" Alexander asked, checking the Thinblade in its scabbard.

"A scourgling is scaling the mountains that ring this valley," Ilona said. "It will be here soon. We can send it away but it will require the sacrifice of a fairy."

Alexander and Isabel both shook their heads in unison. "No, we'll leave immediately," Alexander said. "It will follow us. Phane sent it to kill me. If I'm gone, it will leave you alone." He turned to his friends. "Make ready at once."

Ilona buzzed up to him. "There may be another way. If you leave, it will hunt you and you cannot outrun it. Eventually you will be forced to face it and then you will die."

Chloe spun into a ball of light at the mention of Alexander's death. "I will not let that happen, My Love."

Ilona continued as if Chloe hadn't spoken. "With my help and guidance, Master Alabrand can create a potion that will send the scourgling back to the netherworld."

Lucky stepped up with his bag over his shoulder. "Tell me what to do," he said without hesitation. She led him from the banquet hall.

Alexander and his friends prepared to leave. The threat of the scourgling brought the reality of his duty slamming back into the forefront of his awareness. He had accomplished his goal for coming to the Pinnacles and now it was time to go. He still had a great distance to travel and time was running out.

They stood near the crevice that led out of the valley, waiting for Lucky and Ilona. Chloe spun into a ball of light every few minutes out of nervousness and fear.

"I will face the scourgling, My Love, and send it away if all else fails," she said.

"No! You will not risk yourself against that demon, no matter the danger to me," Alexander said. "I mean it, Chloe." She spun into a ball of light. He turned to the rest of his friends. "That goes for the rest of you as well. If it comes to it, I'll face that thing alone."

"You heard Kelvin," Anatoly said, "the Thinblade won't work against it. You don't stand a chance."

"Neither do you," Alexander said, "any of you. Look, if we end up fighting that thing, we're going to lose. It was sent to kill me. I won't have it killing any of you just to get to me."

Abigail pointed up toward the top of the cliffs across the valley and called out, "Look!"

All eyes turned to where she pointed and saw the dark silhouette of the scourgling only a moment before it leapt off the edge and plummeted to the ground. It crashed into the forest not a mile away with a loud thud that reverberated off the stone walls of the valley.

"Chloe, go warn your mother and the rest of the fairies," Alexander said. "Tell them not to engage that thing, just avoid it. The rest of you get into the crevice. I doubt the scourgling can fit in there."

Chloe darted up and kissed Alexander on the cheek. "If you die, I die. Preserve me, My Love," she said before she spun into a ball of light and disappeared.

"What are you going to do?" Isabel asked.

"I'll wait for Lucky or the scourgling, whichever gets here first . . ."

Before he could finish his sentence, the scourgling emerged from the forest at a dead run, its huge glistening black form moving with frightening speed in long loping strides. It spotted Alexander and adjusted course to charge straight for him.

He pushed Isabel into the gap in the stone cliff and followed her in. Not ten steps inside, he heard an impossibly loud crashing noise as the scourgling smashed into the stone with tremendous force. Alexander spun in the tight quarters and drew his sword. The scourgling was stuck in the entrance of the crevice, clawing its way in deeper and closer. It raked the stone walls with its iron-hard claws, scoring it deeply with each stroke and tearing the face of the stone away to clatter against the ground as gravel. Slowly it started working its way toward him.

An arrow whizzed over his shoulder and shattered against the demon's empty eye socket. Alexander looked back at Abigail.

She shrugged. "Had to try," she said before moving deeper into the crevice.

They backed up and got some distance from the demon when it suddenly stopped clawing its way forward, withdrew to the opening of the crevice and started climbing up the side of the cliff toward the top. Its claws left angry-looking gouges in the sheer rock face and rained chips of stone down on the valley floor.

Alexander saw Lucky come into the clearing with Ilona and Chloe. Lucky held up a glass vial to show Alexander that he had a weapon to use against the beast.

As Alexander watched the beast climb, he tried to decide on a strategy. If he tried to get to Lucky, the beast would drop down on top of him. If he went through the crevice, the scourgling would be there to face him on the other side; he also risked coming to a wide space in the crevice that the scourgling could fit into. He decided to face it sooner rather than later. At least if the potion failed, he would have the cover of the crevice to take refuge in while he came up with another plan.

He reached out for Chloe with his mind.

"I'm here, My Love."

It was a new sensation to be bonded with another. It would take some getting used to. He projected his thoughts to her. "Tell Lucky to be ready, I'm going to lure the scourgling back to the ground."

"Be safe," she said.

Lucky began to approach cautiously with both Ilona and Chloe floating above his head. Alexander started moving slowly toward the opening, all the while looking up at the beast as it continued to climb. Once Alexander came within six feet of the entrance to the crevice, the scourgling abruptly dropped from the cliff face and came crashing to the ground not twelve feet in front of him. It leapt out of the hole it had created in the meadow with such speed and force that it wedged itself into the crevice, swiping at Alexander with one giant clawed hand.

He stumbled backward and lost his balance, which saved him; the claws of the beast came within inches of his face. He regained his feet quickly and slashed in an upward motion at the next swipe of the beast's giant hand. The Thinblade struck with force but didn't even scratch the glistening black surface of its hand.

Alexander withdrew farther to be sure he was out of reach. Then Lucky was there behind the beast. He heaved a glass vial filled with a dark liquid; it shattered against the monster's back.

Nothing happened.

Alexander waited for a moment, holding his breath. Still nothing happened. The demon swiped at him again and then backed out of the crevice. Lucky retreated toward the edge of the forest, safely out of reach of the single-minded netherworld beast.

Just when Alexander decided that the potion had failed, the scourgling stopped suddenly, frozen in place. Abruptly, the surface of its glistening black skin started burning away. The bright white leading edge of the flame spread over every inch of its eight-foot-tall frame. It happened quickly—in less than a second, the entire creature was nothing but a cloud of black smoke without substance or form.

The smoke began to swirl like water flowing down a drain. For several seconds it flowed into the ground, and then it was gone. A moment later there was a thunderous, otherworldly clap of noise that stunned Alexander and left him a bit shaken. Loose rocks clattered to the ground from the walls of the crevice in the aftermath of the scourgling's banishing.

Alexander emerged into the valley, followed by his friends.

Marla stepped up next to him. "You have terrifying enemies, Alexander. Those who envy you your crown have no idea what you face on their behalf."

"Indeed," Ilona said. "It has been two thousand years since such a beast was loosed on the world. Know this, Alexander, if you fail to prevent the Nether Gate from being opened, creatures like that will roam the world freely."

Alexander took a deep breath. As if Phane wasn't bad enough, he had the threat of the whole netherworld invading the world of the living to contend with as well.

"Ilona, I know you're opposed to taking sides in this war, but I urge you to reconsider. I'm one man. I can't fight this war alone. Your help and guidance would be invaluable."

Ilona smiled. "Chloe will give you the guidance you need. As for joining the fight, there may be a few things we can do to help. I will think on the matter. I must admit, seeing a beast from the dark so close again has reminded me of the stark choice the Reishi have given the world. Farewell, Alexander. Love my daughter well."

She turned to Chloe and smiled sadly. They both spun into brightly glowing orbs of light and passed through each other, and then Ilona was gone.

They made their way through the crevice and reached the maze of giant boulders by midday. Alexander talked silently with Chloe as they traveled. She asked a thousand questions about his life. He answered every one honestly and without hesitation. She wanted to know about his childhood, his friends, his family, even his favorite color. He spent the time happily feeding her childlike curiosity with details about himself.

He asked questions as well. He was shocked to discover that Chloe was over seven thousand years old. She had a general knowledge of the history of humanity, but she'd spent most of her years living in seclusion deep in the mountains with other fairies. She'd had little contact with those in the outside world and knew humanity mostly through the druids who lived among the fairies.

He also gave her some reassurances. She was committed to him and put on a brave face, but Alexander could sense that she was afraid of leaving the safety of her home of so many years and even more frightened by the idea of war. In many ways she was like a child in her innocent belief in the power of love above all things. Yet that innocence was tempered by a deep wisdom earned through the experience of living for over seven millennia.

CHAPTER 31

Now that he had Chloe's assistance, time was the enemy. He needed to get to the Reishi Isle as quickly as possible. There was no telling what Phane was up to and Alexander didn't want to risk looking in on him again. He still didn't know if the Reishi Arch Mage could do worse than scattering his consciousness.

Just after they passed through the illusion that guarded the entrance to the valley, they stopped for lunch. Alexander noticed a marked drop in temperature. It was as though the entire Valley of the Fairy Queen was spelled to create an endless spring.

Once they finished eating, Alexander decided they needed to set their course to reach the Reishi Isle as quickly as possible.

"Clarissa, what's the fastest way to get out of the Pinnacles and to the west?"

She thought about it for a moment. "It would be best to return to Highlake City and then take the western road. It winds through the mountains into the Great Forest and finally to Highlands Reach."

Marla chimed in, "I agree. Going back to the north would take much longer. The road to the west is a more direct route."

"Good, it's decided then. We'll return to Highlake City and hope Commander P'Tal is lost in this maze for good."

Not an hour later, Isabel stopped them. "The Reishi are just up ahead around that bend. It looks like more than a dozen men with P'Tal and his giant friend. Truss is with them, too. He looks much better with a hook for a hand," she said with grim satisfaction.

Clarissa frowned. "They're in our path. We cannot get to Highlake City except by that route."

Before Alexander could decide what to do, a half dozen ravens floated into view overhead and started squawking. He knew at a glance that they were spelled. Apparently, the wizard working with P'Tal was able to find another flock of birds to press into service as spies.

He turned to Clarissa. "We have to flee. Is there another way out of this maze that will lead us out of the Pinnacles?"

She frowned in thought but it was Marla who answered, "The cataracts. If we can get the aid of the ashrays, they can guide you down to the sea."

Alexander frowned. "What's an ashray?"

"They're another of the great powers of the Pinnacles," Marla said. "They're sentient beings made of water. With their help and guidance you can take canoes down the river to the ocean. Without their assistance, the journey through the cataracts is certain death."

Alexander heard shouting in the distance and turned to see a soldier pointing toward them and yelling, "There they are!"

A moment later an arrow drove through the soldier's breastplate and into his heart. He looked down in surprise before slumping to his knees and falling over.

Abigail calmly nocked another arrow.

"Nice shot," Alexander said.

A moment later, Jataan P'Tal came around the corner. Abigail loosed her arrow at him, but he slipped aside and caught the shaft in midflight. He set his sights on Alexander and started running toward him. Alexander felt a thrill of fear; he wasn't sure if he could beat the battle mage. Chloe spun into a glowing orb of light, probably in reaction to his fear.

"Run!" Alexander commanded, drawing the Thinblade. They fled around a corner, following Clarissa as she guided them toward the south exit of the maze. Alexander brought up the rear with Anatoly right beside him. When they rounded another corner, Alexander saw a stone pillar jutting off the side of one of the boulders and smiled with relief.

With two strokes of his ancient magical sword, he cut a wedge out of the thirty-foot-tall, five-foot-diameter menhir. The chunk of rock slipped out slowly and crashed to the ground, followed by a cracking noise that reverberated in the stark and barren maze. Then the pillar of stone toppled over and crashed into the opposite wall, shattering into a dozen boulders and blocking the path, giving them a few precious minutes to get distance on their enemies.

They fled through the maze. Clarissa moved quickly and with certainty, even though there were many different paths to choose from.

Every so often Isabel stopped and looked through Slyder's eyes. She reported that the enemy had gotten over the jumble of rocks in their path and were quickly pursuing with the aid of the ravens. At each turn a jet black bird stopped and waited for the Reishi to arrive. At each turn the enemy took the proper path after their wizard consulted the bird.

Alexander looked for the ravens, but he could only catch fleeting glimpses of them. It seemed that the wizard controlling the birds had learned his lesson when Alexander brought down one of his spies a few days earlier.

Within the maze they had cover and could avoid a confrontation, but once they were out of the jumble of giant boulders, Alexander worried that they wouldn't be able to stay far enough ahead. He knew they could handle the majority of those following them, but the battle mage still gave him pause. He remembered the last time he'd faced P'Tal and how fast he moved and how hard he'd thrown the spear that would have killed Alexander if it weren't for the dragon-steel shirt he wore under his tunic.

They reached the south exit of the maze late in the afternoon. A raven was floating high overhead watching their progress.

"How far to the river?" Alexander asked Marla.

"If I remember correctly, it's about a day's travel on foot."

Alexander checked the position of the setting sun. "We'll have to press on through the night."

They set a fast pace. By the time darkness fell, everyone was tired but they kept moving with the light of the night-wisp dust and the glowing orbs bobbing around Clarissa's head. The trail wound through another sparse, high-mountain forest with narrow little trees and low, thick ground cover.

The forest was alive with the sounds of bugs and night predators but nothing big enough to pose a threat. Alexander knew the enemy wouldn't slow their pace for darkness; they were too close to their prey and they had the scent of blood. Every now and then, Chloe spun into a ball of light. Alexander silently offered his assurances that all would be well, but the threat of attack was something she had not faced for a very long time. He could feel her nervousness at being out in the world away from the safety of her valley home and her fear that he might be harmed.

They traveled through the night, setting as fast a pace as they dared. Occasionally, the light of the enemy's torches could be seen in the distance through the sparse mountain forest. Each time Alexander caught a glimpse of their torches, it refocused his need for haste. They arrived at the little forest boathouse just before dawn. When they approached, they saw a druid kneeling at the edge of the mountain river, praying to her patron. She stood quickly with alarm when she heard them coming but relaxed when she saw the telltale brown robes of Marla and Clarissa.

"Good morning and welcome. I am Priestess Ilsey."

"Good morning, Priestess, we have urgent need of your assistance," Clarissa said, withdrawing her High Priestess medallion from her robe to identify herself. "Our friends are being pursued by an enemy of great power. Can you call on the ashrays to guide them down the cataracts to the ocean? There is no other path that will guarantee their safety and they are on a mission of surpassing importance."

Chloe spun into a ball of light, drawing attention to herself. Priestess Ilsey blinked in wonder and surprise at seeing a fairy.

"High Priestess, your need must be great indeed if you are accompanied by a fairy," Ilsey said. "I have lived in the Pinnacles for my whole life and I've never before seen a child of your patron."

Alexander stepped forward and smiled. "Priestess Ilsey, I'd like to introduce Chloe. We were just recently bonded," Alexander said proudly.

Chloe buzzed in an orbit around his head and then floated up and hovered just a foot or so in front of Ilsey.

"Hello, Priestess," Chloe said. "My mother has long believed that seclusion was our greatest defense, but now that the ancient enemy is awake, she has permitted me to bond with Lord Alexander Ruatha to help him protect the world from Phane. The enemy soldiers are not an hour behind us. Will you help us, please?"

Priestess Ilsey nodded. "Of course, Chloe. It's a privilege and an honor to meet you." Ilsey turned from Chloe to Alexander and said, "Quickly, get into the boats. Once you start down the cataracts, don't try to steer; just let the ashrays guide you and hang on for dear life. It's a harrowing journey, even with the water guiding you."

Alexander nodded and they headed to the boats.

"Clarissa, Marla, you are welcome to come with us but I certainly don't expect you to. This is your home and I hope that you will stay here and protect it."

Marla stepped up and kissed Alexander on the cheek and then gave Isabel a hug. "You will always have a friend in the Pinnacles. Be safe and know that I will pray for your success."

Clarissa smiled warmly and bowed to Alexander. "You are always welcome here, Alexander. I hope that I will see you again, under less urgent circumstances."

"Once we're on our way, you must flee from the soldiers," Alexander said. "They won't follow you, but I don't know what they might do if they catch you here. Thank you both for everything, your help has been invaluable. Clarissa, please tell Ilona that I will take good care of Chloe."

Alexander climbed into a canoe with Isabel. Abigail and Jack paired up and Anatoly and Lucky took the final little boat. The river was moving steadily but not too fast. Alexander noticed the line that was stretched across the river to help boaters stop and guide them into the little boathouse.

Ilsey began the incantation to summon the ashrays. She spoke in the same lilting and softly musical way that Clarissa and Marla did when they cast spells. Not long passed before the water in the middle of the river rose up into three pillars two feet in diameter and six feet above the surface. Each of the three pillars of water formed a face and looked quizzically at Priestess Ilsey.

She bowed deeply. "Thank you for hearing my call. Will you guide these canoes safely to the ocean?"

The three ashrays looked at each other and nodded their agreement, then one turned to Chloe. It spoke with a voice that sounded like a gurgle. "You are a long way from home, Little One," it said.

She spun up into a ball of light for a moment and then went to the ashray and kissed it on the cheek. The watery surface rippled where she touched it and she giggled.

"It's been too long since we frolicked together in the waterfalls," she said as she buzzed around the three water elementals.

"Indeed," the ashray gurgled. "You have been hidden away in your valley for far too long."

Chloe stopped and hovered in front of the ashrays and her demeanor changed. "I have bonded to this mortal. Please guide him safely to the sea."

The watery face looked surprised for a moment as it looked from Chloe to Alexander and back to the fairy. "We will not fail you, Chloe."

She buzzed into a ball of light and then floated back to Alexander and landed on his shoulder.

In the growing light of dawn, Alexander could just make out the flicker of torchlight through the forest. The enemy was near. When he looked up, he saw the black silhouettes of six ravens circling overhead.

"You haven't much time," Alexander said to the three druids. "Thank you for everything. Now flee before the enemy arrives and go safely."

The druids waved their last goodbye and faded into the forest, moving quickly upriver away from the boathouse. Alexander and his friends cut their boats loose and drifted out into the center of the river. The current carried them gently downstream. When he looked back, Jataan P'Tal was standing on the dock watching them. They rounded a bend in the river before his soldiers could attack with their crossbows. For a mile or so, they drifted at a good pace. Then the sound of rushing water came to them from up ahead.

Around the next bend, Alexander saw the cataracts—a stretch of river that wasn't quite a waterfall but where it moved with terrifying speed and furious energy as it flowed down a steep and narrow channel.

He yelled, "Hang on!"

And then all sound was drowned out by the deafening torrent.

The speed would have been exhilarating if it wasn't so terrifying. They careened down the narrow channel, hanging on with all their strength. Alexander lost count of the number of times he thought his fragile little boat would shatter against the rock wall where the channel turned, but each time they negotiated the passage as if the water itself was guiding them.

They covered miles and miles in such a short time that Slyder was actually straining to keep up with their breakneck pace. Alexander felt his ears pop as they descended from the jagged mountains of the Pinnacles toward the ocean. The journey lasted for over an hour. His forearms burned from the death grip he had on the canoe's crossbeam. And then it was over just as quickly as it began. They came out of a rapids and the river widened and leveled out. Alexander could smell the salt of sea air. They slowed to a gentle yet steady pace and everyone took a deep breath.

The three ashrays rose up out of the water. "Safe journey," they gurgled. Chloe flitted over to them and gave each a kiss on the cheek. They each smiled at her attentions, then melted back into the river and were gone.

CHAPTER 32

By late morning they were floating out into the ocean, rowing slowly along the shore toward Kai'Gorn. Their canoes rolled gently on the waves out beyond the surf that lapped up against the steeply rising coastline. It was a beautiful day, but everyone was too exhausted to enjoy it. They rowed until the sun began to dip toward the western horizon, then turned their canoes toward shore and made landfall on a deserted little beach.

They camped in the secluded cove and built a big fire with driftwood before laying out their bedrolls and making a simple stew. Everyone slept well that night. They were all weary from the long day of rowing and the previous night's flight from the enemy. Were it not for the ravens circling high overhead as they rowed down the coastline, Alexander would have thought they had lost their pursuers.

They set out at dawn the next morning, feeling much better for having a full night's sleep. The day was clear and the wind was calm. Alexander gave thanks for that. He didn't like the idea of trying to row a canoe down the coastline during a storm. They would have to stay in the canoes until the rocky coastline gave way to gentler beaches where they could go ashore and set out on foot, but there was no telling how long that might be. He'd never been to the southern coast of Ruatha and only knew of it from stories and the maps he'd seen in old books.

They rowed along the rocky coastline for the entire day. Alexander frequently looked up to find the ravens still flying high overhead. He wished there was something he could do about the enemy's spies, but they were well out of the range of any bow—even Abigail's.

That night they camped in another secluded cove surrounded by high rocky cliffs. Alexander used his clairvoyance to look in on Commander P'Tal. His party was moving through the high mountain forest even as darkness fell. The commander of the Reishi Protectorate was clearly driven to make up lost time and find a way to get back within striking range.

As Alexander watched the enemy soldiers moving by torchlight through the forest, he suddenly saw something that made his fear spike. One of the soldiers in Jataan P'Tal's detail was possessed by a shade. It was apparent that no one knew they were traveling in the company of one of the most feared demons to ever walk in the light of the world. Alexander didn't know why the shade had chosen one of P'Tal's soldiers to possess, but he suspected it had something to do with him. He came back to his body gently and opened his eyes to see Chloe floating a foot in front of his face and looking at him with a curious look.

"You were gone, My Love. I was worried."

Alexander smiled at her genuine concern for his well-being. Isabel smiled as well.

"I was looking in on the enemy."

Chloe frowned. "I know you have survived the mana fast, but I do not understand how you could see so far with your mind. You were not in the aether, I checked, yet your essence was far away from here."

He shrugged. "In truth, I don't understand either. My magic doesn't work like other wizards' and I haven't met anyone who can tell me why or how to make better use of it."

"Be cautious leaving your body unattended like that," Chloe said, shaking her tiny finger at him. "There are creatures in the aether that can take advantage of an uninhabited body."

Alexander was surprised by the thought, then chided himself for not considering the possibility before. The shades were loose. It would probably be much easier for them to take possession of him if his consciousness was away. He sighed and shook his head.

"There's just so much I don't know about my magic. I wish I had an instruction manual."

"Be patient, my boy," Lucky said. "I suspect you'll come to understand your abilities with time."

"I just hope I have the time I need. Commander P'Tal's force is marching through the forest by torchlight and a shade has taken up residence in one of his soldiers." Everyone sat up straighter. "I don't think P'Tal knows he has a demon for a traveling companion. I just wonder why the shade is with them."

"The shades will seek out the Nether Gate," Chloe said. "Perhaps they believe that you or your enemy may lead them to it."

Alexander snorted. "If they're looking for me to lead them there, they'll never find it. I didn't even know it existed until the other day."

"It could be that the shade is just gathering information," Jack suggested. "We don't really know how much they know about our world. They may be totally lost and just trying to get their bearings."

"That's an encouraging thought," Abigail said. "At least that way they'll be a while looking for the Nether Gate." She turned to Alexander and said, "Maybe we can beat them to it and you can cut the thing into tiny little pieces with that sword of yours."

Alexander nodded. "Maybe we can learn something about it once we get to the Reishi Keep. For the time being, we have to stay focused on the Stone. At least the shades don't seem interested in joining forces with Phane or they probably would have made their presence known to P'Tal."

"That's a fair assumption," Lucky said, "but I would caution you not to ascribe human motives to the shades. They are not of this world. Their reasons may be beyond our understanding."

"Lucky's right, My Love," Chloe said. "Creatures of the dark have twisted minds that do not make sense to those who love life."

"At any rate, they're a long way away from here," Isabel said. "At least we have some distance on them."

Alexander chuckled. "My father always said that range is the best armor; I guess I understand that particular truism better now."

Anatoly smiled knowingly and nodded at the mention of his old friend's admonition.

***

The next day brought a steel grey sky and light rain. By midafternoon they were all soaked through and cold. The rain was just a drizzle but it was unrelenting. They rowed doggedly through the gloom. Late in the day, Alexander realized he hadn't seen the ravens. The low clouds probably interfered with their ability to track him.

Just before dusk, the rugged and rocky coastline gave way to sandy beaches and grassy dunes. Alexander was relieved to see the change in terrain. He was tired of rowing and he wasn't altogether comfortable being on the water. He could swim but he didn't want to have to. Worse, if they encountered a threat, he wouldn't be able to engage with his sword very easily when his footing was unstable. He was anxious to get back on land. With any luck, they would be able to find a town that had some horses for sale.

They beached their canoes for the last time and made camp. The driftwood was too wet for a fire, so they ate a cold dinner, but nobody seemed to care. After the long day of rowing in the rain, everyone was tired and eager for the warmth of a bedroll.

For the next two days they hiked along the coastline. Alexander was torn between two possible routes. They could go through Kai'Gorn and risk being discovered by the enemy; the magistrate of Kai'Gorn had taken sides with Andalia and Phane. If they went that way, it would allow them to stick to the grasslands and travel much more quickly even though the distance was actually farther, but they might end up in a fight they couldn't win.

The alternative was to set out north across the mountains and into Highlands Reach. The southern mountains weren't nearly as tall as the Pinnacles, but they were still too rocky and treacherous for horses. That route had the added benefit of taking them right past Valentine Manor. Alexander had to admit that seeing his home was irrelevant but it would nice, especially after the way they'd left it.

He'd just made up his mind to turn northwest and avoid Kai'Gorn, when they crested a rise in the gently rolling grassland and saw the enemy. Alexander's blood went cold at the sight of a hundred cavalry not half a mile away and headed toward them. Alexander looked around for a place to hide or to at least make a stand, but they were out in the open in virtually endless grassland bordered by the ocean. The ravens were circling high overhead. There was nowhere to run.

He looked over to Anatoly for suggestions. The big man-at-arms shook his head grimly as he calmly unslung his war axe.

"Alexander, this is a fight we can't win," Jack said.

"And yet, the fight comes," Alexander said.

Chloe spun into a ball of light for a moment.

As the enemy approached, Alexander saw that they were not mounted on horses but instead on the fabled rhone steeds of Andalia. The rhone were similar to horses, only half again bigger with a bony knot on the forehead. The men mounted on the giant steeds were armored in scale mail with large shields. Each wore a long sword on his belt and carried a lance.

"Andalian Lancers," Anatoly said. "I've faced them before. They're well trained and well armed. They don't carry ranged weapons except for their force lances which project a blast of magical energy for several dozen feet."

The company of Lancers broke in two and moved to surround Alexander and his friends. Abigail sent an arrow at the lead soldier, but he angled his heavy shield and easily deflected it away.

"Chloe, Jack, disappear," Alexander commanded. "If they wanted us dead, they would have charged. Don't let them capture you."

Jack tossed the hood of his cloak up and faded out of sight. Chloe vanished from view. Alexander heard her small voice in his mind. "I'm afraid, My Love."

"I know," he thought back to her, "but it'll be all right. Just don't let them see you."

The company of Lancers surrounded them before a group of ten approached. Most were mounted on the giant rhone, but two were riding heavy war horses. They wore the uniforms of Kai'Gorn, while the Lancers all bore the crest of the House of Andalia on their shields.

"I'm Captain Tate of Kai'Gorn," the higher-ranking officer said. He wore chain mail under a military tunic with the crest of Kai'Gorn emblazoned across it. He was armed with only a long sword and a large quiver filled with javelins. His pock-marked face was round and his teeth were crooked. He had dirty brown hair and plain brown eyes that nevertheless revealed a spark of intelligence. "You are Alexander Ruatha, I presume."

Alexander didn't respond with anything more than a glare. He appraised the situation with his all around sight and found it to be virtually hopeless. He could probably kill several of the soldiers before they ran him down, but it would cost him dearly. He scrutinized the colors of the men before him. The two from Kai'Gorn were not evil by nature but were soldiers who would follow their orders.

The Andalian Lancers were something else. They were disciplined and accustomed to violence. Andalia was clearly ruled by force and these men enforced that rule. And now they fought in service to Phane.

Captain Tate smiled grimly. "I have orders to take you into custody. If you surrender peacefully, you and your companions will be unharmed until Prince Phane decides your fate. If you resist, your friends will be killed and you will be subdued. Surely you can see you're beaten."

"What's changed?" Alexander asked. "Phane's been trying to murder me for months. Now, suddenly, he wants me alive?" Alexander watched Tate's colors carefully even though he suspected he already knew the reason.

Captain Tate shrugged. "I don't know, nor do I care. My orders are clear. You are to be taken alive. Your friends are to be taken alive as well, so long as it's not too much of an inconvenience." He leaned forward. "Surrender your weapons."

Alexander looked at his friends. Everything inside him told him to fight. His rage was crying to be released but he knew with certainty that doing so would cost him the lives of those most dear to him. For a fleeting moment, he tried to touch his magic in the vain hope that it would save him, but there was nothing there except his magical sight.

He was powerless to win this battle. He only hoped that surrender would give him the chance to stand and fight another day. He heard his father's voice in his mind, plain as day: "So long as you are alive, there's still hope."

After so long a struggle and so many encounters with death, he was faced with an impossible choice. It was Chloe who decided for him. "If you surrender, you will live and I can save you, My Love," she said in his mind.

With a deep breath and anguish in his heart, he unbuckled the belt that held the Thinblade at his waist and tossed the ancient sword on the ground before him. Anatoly nodded grimly at the choice and tossed his war axe down as well.

The commander of the Andalian Lancers smiled with malice and lowered his lance at Alexander and unleashed its magic. It felt like being hit in the chest with a war hammer—he hit the ground hard and his consciousness faded away into darkness.

CHAPTER 33

When he woke, he hurt all over. He was chained in the back of a wagon, shackled at the wrists, around the ankles, and collared with a short chain leading from the back of his neck to a bolt set into the side railing. He looked around quickly to see that everyone except Jack was in similar restraints. Alexander wore only his undershirt and trousers. The Keep Master's ring was no longer on his finger. His armor, knives, and pack were nowhere to be seen. Jack was huddled in the corner of the wagon, hiding beneath his cloak. Alexander gave him a wink and saw his colors flare slightly with hope. At least Jack was free. They might have a chance to escape.

Anatoly looked like he'd received similar treatment. He'd been stripped of his armor and weapons and was still unconscious. Isabel and Abigail were disarmed as well but they were both awake and looking miserable. Lucky was unharmed except for the abrasions caused by the shackles and the rough ride. Andalian Lancers rode all around the wagon.

"Is everyone all right?" Alexander asked.

Before anyone could answer, the nearest Lancer shouted, "No talking!"

Isabel, Abigail, and Lucky all nodded in answer to his question. It broke his heart to see his loved ones in such pain because of a birthright that he hadn't asked for and didn't want. He closed his eyes and forced his anger and pain away so he could focus his mind. He knew they would have precious few opportunities to escape and he was determined to be ready when they came.

He reached out for Chloe. She was there in his mind in an instant. "I am here, My Love." She sounded worried and fearful but also angry.

"Stay hidden, Little One," Alexander thought to her. "Did you see where they put our weapons?"

"They're locked in the crate in the back of the wagon," Chloe said in his mind. "Do you want me to push the lock into the aether and open the crate for you?"

Alexander thought about it for a moment but decided against it. They were surrounded by more than a hundred heavily armed soldiers. If he'd wanted to fight them, he would have had a better chance the moment they met. For now, they were alive, that was enough.

"No, not yet," Alexander thought to her. "The time isn't right."

They rode in the back of the wagon for three grueling days before they reached the city of Kai'Gorn. They were given one meal a day and very little water. By the time they arrived, everyone was chafed by the shackles and collars to the point of bleeding. Alexander's fury grew with each passing hour he was forced to watch his wife and sister, his protector and mentor suffer for the accident of his birth. He vowed he would not permit this to be the end of his struggle.

He caught glimpses of the people and buildings of Kai'Gorn as they entered the city. It was a rundown place filled with cowed people who scrambled to get out of the way of the soldiers as they clattered up the road.

The wagon came to a stop in the courtyard of the central keep of Kai'Gorn, a giant stone castle positioned on a bluff overlooking the broad river that flowed past it to the sea on the southern tip of Ruatha. A soldier unbolted the chains that held their collars to the sideboards, and Captain Tate ordered them from the wagon.

Alexander stumbled from the wagon and fell hard. One of the Andalian soldiers stepped up and kicked him in the ribs. He felt them crack. His next breath was a stab of pain.

Isabel shouted, "Leave him alone! You said Phane wants him unharmed!"

Alexander tried to make eye contact with her to silence her rage but couldn't muster the strength past the stabbing pain in the side of his chest. Then he heard Isabel scream and he struggled to regain his feet. He glanced up to see another Lancer drag her from the wagon by her hair.

Rage flooded into him, filling every corner of his being with indignant fury. He surged toward the man, but before he could reach him, another mounted Lancer pointed his lance at him and a blast of magical force launched him from his feet and onto his back. He lay on the cold stone of the courtyard, listening to the derisive laughter of his enemy as his consciousness faded away in an ocean of pain.

He woke chained to a chair in a dimly lit room. For a moment he didn't know where he was until he took a breath and the pain of his broken ribs racked through his body. He felt the terror of panic well up inside him before he gained control and withdrew to the place where his own personal witness lived. He took refuge in the calm stillness of that corner of his mind where nothing mattered, where he could simply observe events unfold with detachment.

The pain was still there but it was farther away. He looked around and saw Anatoly, Lucky, Abigail, and Isabel lined up along the wall, chained to chairs of their own. They wore a mixture of pain, anger, and fear on their faces. He tried to give them each a measure of his strength with a brief glance. Jack was nowhere to be seen.

A soldier dressed in the uniform of Kai'Gorn noticed that Alexander was awake and grabbed him roughly by the hair to tip his head back so he could look into his glittering eyes.

"You awake?" he asked, clearly not expecting an answer.

Once he was satisfied that Alexander was conscious, he left the room. It was only then that Alexander looked more closely at his surroundings. The stone-walled room was dirty and dark. The only light was the product of several old and poorly kept oil lamps. There were stains on the stone floor, and the one table in the room had tools of torture carefully laid out on its surface as if they were on display.

Alexander caught his breath. He could take what pain they might inflict on him—he'd endured the trial of pain during the mana fast. But the thought of Isabel or Abigail being tortured made his soul quail in fear.

When he heard the boot steps in the hall, he knew things were about to go from bad to worse. The door opened and four men entered. The first wore a gaudy, jewel-encrusted golden crown. He was an older man with graying hair and a drawn face. His skin looked like it was two sizes too big and hung on his large frame in drooping folds. He wore a heavy gold ring on each finger and had at least half a dozen jeweled chains around his neck. His heavy velvet red robes were decorated at the hem with gold filigree.

The next man through the door looked similar in facial features and frame except he was strong and fit. He wore a breastplate emblazoned with the crest of Kai'Gorn and carried a finely wrought short sword on his wide belt. Captain Tate filed in next, followed by the soldier who had been waiting for Alexander to wake up. When Alexander looked closer at the man and saw that his smock had dried blood encrusted on it, he realized that he was a torturer.

Alexander scrutinized their colors and saw the vicious selfishness of evil burning brightly in each of them, with the sole exception of Captain Tate.

The man with the crown looked at Alexander for a moment as if considering his worth. "I am Magistrate Cain. This is my brother General Cain, and I believe you have already met Captain Tate." He spoke with disdain and haughty arrogance. "It would seem that the reign of the pretender is at an end, wouldn't you say?" He looked at his brother who chuckled as he nodded in agreement.

"Commander P'Tal will be along in a few days to collect you. Apparently, Prince Phane now believes you can help him retrieve an item of importance to him, with the proper persuasion, of course." He smiled knowingly at Isabel and Abigail. Alexander felt a mixture of rage and despair well up within him. "Until then, you will be my guests." The magistrate turned to the man with the smock and snapped his fingers. The man handed him the Thinblade, still in its scabbard.

With a greedy smile of triumph, Magistrate Cain took the Sword of Kings and held it up in front of Alexander almost reverently as if it were a talisman that conferred untold power upon its holder. "It is said that the one who wields this sword is the rightful King of Ruatha. That's fitting because I expect Prince Phane to grant me command of Ruatha in exchange for delivering you into his care."

Alexander snorted derisively and looked up at the magistrate with unconcealed contempt. "At best you'll be his puppet, at worst you'll be a meal for one of his pets. Either way, you'll never taste freedom again."

The magistrate laughed. "Who needs freedom when you have power?" he said as he drew the Thinblade with a flourish. The sword came free of the scabbard and promptly slipped out of his hand and flipped through the air. It caught General Cain by surprise and sliced him cleanly in half. His torso fell away from his legs, and his hands and forearms thudded to the ground, staining the floor with lurid red splatters.

The Thinblade wound up stuck into the stone wall, blood dripping from its inky black blade. A crimson pool quickly spread across the dirty stone floor as General Cain's lifeblood drained from his broken body. The magistrate stared at the mutilated corpse of his brother with shock. He tried to speak but nothing came out.

Alexander laughed.

Cain's face turned scarlet. He backhanded Alexander across the face. "You did this!" he shouted with fury as he hit Alexander again.

Alexander smiled and spit blood at the magistrate's boots. "It's not your sword," he said, working his jaw.

Magistrate Cain seized him by the collar and jerked him up straight so he could shout into his face. "You will pay for this! You will tell me how to command the sword or I will make you suffer until you do."

Captain Tate cleared his throat. "Magistrate, I must remind you of Prince Phane's orders. He is not to be harmed."

The magistrate looked coldly at the captain and snorted. "I don't have to hurt him to make him suffer." Then he turned to the torturer. "Don't cause him any permanent harm, but make him talk."

The torturer brought a wide bucket of water and placed it in front of Alexander, then roughly tipped him over in his chair onto his knees with his chest resting against the edge of the bucket. The pressure on his ribs was agony. He could barely breathe.

Then the torturer pushed his head into the water. The suffocating feeling coupled with his injured ribs was beyond any pain he'd felt since the trials of the mana fast. He could hear Isabel and Abigail crying out on his behalf and knew that even this pain was nothing compared to the pain he would feel when the magistrate decided to use them against him. The torturer pulled his face up out of the frigid water and Alexander gasped for breath, sputtering.

"How does the Thinblade work?" asked the magistrate calmly, clearly enjoying Alexander's suffering.

Alexander ignored him, struggling to breathe. The torturer shoved his head back into the water. The pain was almost unbearable, but Alexander knew where to take refuge against it. He withdrew once again into the place within his psyche that didn't feel, that only observed. He saw the racking pain his body was enduring but it mattered less when he viewed it from the little corner of safety within his mind.

He could hear Chloe whimpering in the background of his consciousness, but he forbade her to reveal herself. Even through the distraction of torture, he knew that Phane was aware of her and intended to use her to obtain the Sovereign Stone. The last thing he wanted was to confirm her existence to the enemy.

"Find Jack and tell him where we are," he thought to her.

"Hold on, My Love," she said in his mind. "We will save you."

The torture lasted for hours. Alexander used his all around sight to watch the scene from a different perspective. He found that looking at the situation from the viewpoint of an observer helped him remain within the safety of the detached corner of his consciousness. The hardest part was seeing the tears of anguish streaming down the faces of his wife and sister. Lucky had his eyes closed and was doing his best to shut out the horrible experience. Anatoly wore a grim expression of pure coiled rage; Alexander knew things would go badly for these men when Anatoly and his war axe were reunited. He took solace in that thought.

Eventually, Alexander became so exhausted that Captain Tate stepped forward. "Enough! You risk killing him."

The magistrate turned and faced the captain with a look of cold fury. "He killed my brother!" he shouted, but Tate held his ground. "Who do you serve anyway?"

"You know very well that I am an agent of the Reishi Protectorate, Magistrate Cain," Captain Tate said calmly. "I serve Prince Phane, as do you," he added pointedly.

Magistrate Cain's face turned a deeper shade of crimson and he wheeled on Alexander in fury. "You will tell me what I want to know by tomorrow morning or I will give your women to the Lancers for sport." He kicked Alexander over onto his side and spit on him, then barked at the torturer as he walked out, "Bring me the Thinblade . . . in its scabbard."

After they left, Alexander closed his eyes and tried to breathe deeply enough to replenish his oxygen-starved body but shallowly enough to avoid the stabbing pain of his broken ribs. It was a delicate balancing act that he couldn't quite get right.

"Are you all right, Alexander?" Isabel asked with a mixture of worry and fury in her voice.

He nodded with his eyes still closed tightly against the rhythmically stabbing pain in his chest that came and went with each breath. "Broken . . . ribs," he managed through clenched teeth.

"Take shallow breaths," Anatoly said.

"Alexander," Lucky said in a tone that got his attention. "Is the blood in your mouth from being struck or did you cough it up?"

Alexander thought about it for a moment. "Hit," he said quietly.

Lucky sighed in relief. "Good. Your lungs aren't punctured. Try to rest."

He heard his friends talking softly as he faded into unconsciousness. It was much later when he woke to urgent whispers. He held still for a moment, straining to hear what was happening around him. It was dark, but with his all around sight, he could make out the silhouettes of his friends still chained to their chairs. He pushed his magical vision through the door and saw Jack kneeling just outside holding perfectly still.

Another voice whispered something to Jack but it was muffled by the door. Alexander held his breath and waited.

He heard Chloe in his mind, "We've come to save you, My Love."

Then the door slowly and carefully opened. Jack slipped inside and went to Alexander. Somehow he had the key to his shackles and collar. It was all Alexander could do to keep from crying out when the irons came off; the skin beneath had been rubbed raw. Jack carefully and gently unbound Alexander and helped him get free of his tipped-over chair.

He gratefully eased himself down onto the sticky blood coating the floor and focused on his breathing. A moment later, Isabel was at his side. He could feel the warmth of her tears as she silently cried for his pain. He took her hand and gave it a gentle squeeze.

Abigail came next. She put her hand on his head and whispered to him. "It's almost over. You'll be able to rest soon."

The trip out of the dungeon was a blur. Anatoly and Lucky carried him through dark corridors, following behind a group of men that Alexander didn't know. Chloe was there in his mind the whole way offering reassurances and the simple solace of her unconditional love.

Chapter 34

He woke the next morning on a cot. His ribs felt much better though they were still sore. Isabel was in a chair beside him with Chloe sitting cross-legged on one of her knees. He opened his eyes and looked up at them both with a smile that turned into a grimace.

"Where are we?"

Chloe flitted up to hover over his face and look intently into his eyes with worry and relief while Isabel sat forward and gently took his hand.

"We're still in Kai'Gorn. It seems Jack is well connected even here. How are you feeling?"

He tested his ribs with a deep breath and winced at the tightness and pain. "I've been better, but I guess I shouldn't complain, all things considered."

"Lucky says you'll be sore for a few days, but your ribs should be just about mended. Jack was able to get our stuff back, except for the Thinblade, so Lucky gave you a healing potion and put some salve on you before he left you to rest."

He looked up at her and saw she was wearing her animal charm necklace. Before he could ask his next question, Abigail came into the room. She sat down next to Isabel and gently put her hand on his knee.

"Be more careful," she said with a sad smile.

A moment later, Anatoly, Lucky, and Jack came in to see him.

Anatoly looked down at his charge and nodded his approval. "You handled that better than most."

Lucky pulled up a chair on the other side of Isabel and sat down to examine Alexander's wounds. When he probed his ribs, Alexander gasped slightly.

Lucky said, "After you have some food and water, I have some more healing draught for you and then you should sleep until tomorrow morning. I suspect you'll be nearly mended by then."

Alexander nodded, then looked up at Jack. "Well done, Master Colton."

Jack bowed with a respectful flourish although his face was a mixture of sadness and smoldering anger.

"It would seem that there are those in Kai'Gorn who are unhappy with the magistrate and his, apparently late, brother. I must say, Alexander, you've given me quite a lot to work with. Even as we speak, the story of how you slew General Cain while chained to a chair is burning through the citizenry of Kai'Gorn like a plague." The bard winked with a mischievous smile. "By tomorrow, every soul within a day's ride will have heard it. In these parts, General Cain was feared and hated."

"Who helped you get us out?" Alexander asked.

Jack shrugged. "My bards, of course, and a few of their acquaintances. We are everywhere, you know," he said with mock arrogance.

Alexander started to chuckle but stopped abruptly with a wince. "Tell them I said thank you."

Lucky chased everyone out so he could feed Alexander and give him
another draught of healing potion. It wasn't long before he drifted off into a
dreamless sleep.

He woke the next morning to find Isabel asleep at the little table. Chloe
was pacing in front of her, looking worried. When she noticed Alexander open his
eyes, she flew over to him and kissed him on the cheek.

"Are you better?"

He took a deep breath. His chest was still tight but he could breathe
without the stabbing pain. He nodded, "I think so."

"Good," Chloe said, "we have more trouble." She stopped and frowned at
him. "I must say, My Love, danger seems to follow you."

"I can't argue with that," Alexander said, sitting up. He was glad to see
his dragon-steel shirt on the chair next to his bed along with his ring. He was just
putting his tunic on over his armor when Isabel woke and looked up at him with
bleary eyes. She smiled brightly.

He went to her and hugged her gently. "Are you all right?" he asked,
looking closely at the fading wounds on her neck and wrists left by the collar and
shackles.

She nodded. "Lucky took good care of me. Are you hungry?"

He nodded, suddenly feeling famished. They emerged from the room and
everyone turned to look at them. His friends were in a long underground barracks
that looked like the kind of place where low-ranking soldiers lived. There were no
windows and only a single door that was barred twice with heavy oak planks.
Lanterns hanging from stout ceiling beams cast shadows across the room.

Besides his friends, there were another ten men. According to Jack, they
were men who made their living transporting goods in and out of Kai'Gorn under
the cover of night to avoid the oppressive tariffs levied by the magistrate.

The largest of them stood and nodded deferentially to Alexander. "I'm
Captain Finley Raisa, at your service."

Alexander extended his hand and the big man took it firmly but with care.
"Thank you for helping us. Master Colton has good friends."

Captain Raisa shrugged. "Jack's silver tongue has kept me out of trouble
a time or two, but in truth, I would have helped you all on my own the moment I
learned you killed General Cain. The man was a monster."

Alexander didn't bother to protest. He knew that people would believe
what they wanted to believe and in this case it served his purpose.

Lucky motioned Alexander and Isabel over to a pair of open seats at the
long table and served them breakfast. Alexander ate every bite of the well-
seasoned mixture of potatoes and sausage without a word. When he finished, he
took a deep breath and sat back in his chair, testing his ribs. They felt much better.
Lucky's magic always amazed him. He knew from past experience that broken
ribs took a long, painful time to heal on their own.

"Chloe mentioned trouble. What's our situation?"

Anatoly leaned forward. "The city's locked down and soldiers are
searching house to house. There's nearly a legion of Andalian Lancers patrolling
the area surrounding Kai'Gorn with more arriving by ship every day. Cain has
your sword. And he's planning to execute a handful of Captain Raisa's men this

afternoon in the city square. They were captured helping us escape."

"How many men do you have that can fight, Captain?" Alexander asked the smuggler.

"I can round up thirty or so, but there are more who would be willing to fight if they believed it would end the suffering we've endured at the hand of Cain and his brother."

"How many soldiers does Cain have and how many Lancers are inside the city?" Alexander asked.

"He has a couple thousand men in his royal guard within the city. The rest of the Kai'Gorn army is barracked outside the city walls. Cain has always been paranoid. As for the Lancers, I'd estimate three to four hundred within the city. They're slow and clumsy on foot; they depend on those giant horse-like things for their real strength."

"How fast is your ship?" Alexander asked.

Captain Raisa smiled proudly. "Faster than anything Kai'Gorn or Andalia has on the water."

"Can you get us to it? And would you be willing to take us to Southport?"

Captain Raisa rubbed his chin in thought as if he was doing some calculations in his mind. Alexander smiled. The man's colors were basically good, but he was clearly loyal to his ship and his crew.

"You will be well compensated for your efforts," Alexander offered.

Captain Raisa smiled and nodded, then looked over at Jack. "You said he was a smart one." He turned back to Alexander. "I can get you to Southport if you like, but I need to help my crewmen first."

It was Alexander's turn to smile. "Good man. Here's the plan. We'll assault the magistrate and his troops just before the planned execution. At the same time, some of your men will set the docks on fire along with an Andalian ship or two if they can. Lucky will tell you what he needs to make fire pots."

He turned to Isabel, "Do you have a whistler arrow?"

She nodded, "Of course."

"Good, that'll be our signal. Is Slyder nearby?"

"He's on the roof."

"Take a good hard look at the town square. I want to put you and Abigail up on a high point so you can fire down into the crowd. We'll also need to know our exits and where enemy reinforcements will come from."

Alexander spent the next hour laying out his plan. It was more than a simple rescue. He wanted to take this opportunity to cause as much damage to the Kai'Gorn docks as possible to slow the influx of Andalian Lancers.

He also wanted to kill Cain.

Captain Raisa assured him that without the Cain brothers, Kai'Gorn would fall into disarray as factions whose animosity had long been held in check by their tyranny went to war with one another.

Alexander was relieved to hear that Commander P'Tal was still a few days away. He didn't need the battle mage to contend with right now.

They made preparations all morning. Captain Raisa procured a sword for Alexander; it wasn't fancy, but the blade was sturdy and sharp. It would do. Lucky used lamp oil to make fire pots and handed out three of his shatter vials. He warned the three men charged with delivering them about the power of the liquid fire they contained. Alexander gave them very specific instructions to target two of the Andalian troop-transport ships and then the center of the dock. Once the initial fires were set, the rest of the men would add fuel to the fire with jars of lamp oil.

As they made their way to the town square, Isabel reported that at least a hundred of the royal guard were present but none of the Lancers were there. Alexander told Captain Raisa to have twenty of his men mix in with the crowd and to send the rest to the docks, armed with fire.

Isabel, Abigail, and Lucky went to a rooftop on the corner nearest their exit route, while Alexander and Anatoly, wearing long heavy cloaks to conceal their weapons, made their way into the crowd with Captain Raisa. Jack was already concealed at the edge of the square, waiting for his opportunity to free the prisoners.

A raised wooden platform stood along one wall of the square. On one end was a table covered by a white cloth that draped to the floor and was embroidered with the crest of Kai'Gorn. Behind the table was an ornately carved oak chair. On the other side of the platform was a round of wood a good three feet in diameter and nearly as tall.

A big man with a greasy black ponytail and a week's worth of stubble sat on the round of wood, sharpening a broad-bladed axe. He wore a tunic with the crest of Kai'Gorn. Twenty soldiers armed with crossbows stood along the wall behind the platform and another dozen with short spears stood in front of it. All around the town square in clumps of five or six stood the rest of the royal guard assigned to provide security for the executions.

The square was filled to overflowing with people who came to watch the spectacle. The magistrate demanded a good turnout for his executions or he would punish the city by rationing food and water. In that way, he ensured that many of his subjects were present to witness his version of justice. More importantly, enough heard accounts of the executions and lived in fear of his wrath.

Alexander, Anatoly, and Captain Raisa carefully made their way toward the platform. The crowd was talking mostly about Alexander. He listened to the gossip about his apparent slaughter of General Cain and the magic he was reputed to wield. It never ceased to amaze him how otherwise reasonable people could shape tidbits of truth into the most outlandish tales.

He supposed that Jack had helped them form their ideas about the event, but still the stories he caught bits and pieces of were almost enough to make him laugh out loud. He suspected that the events about to unfold would also be blown completely out of proportion, especially if Jack had anything to say about it. Hopefully, Alexander's visit to Kai'Gorn would break the people's will to fight.

"We are in position, My Love," Chloe said in his mind. She was with Isabel, Abigail, and Lucky. He didn't want her in the midst of a crowd, especially when he planned to turn the crowd into a riot.

"We're ready," Alexander said to Anatoly and Captain Raisa. Almost on cue, Magistrate Cain came into the town square flanked by a dozen royal guards armed with short spears. Following behind him were five men in shackles and collars, chained together in a row. Alexander was relieved to see that their feet weren't chained. That would make it easier to get them out once the fighting started.

The magistrate took his place behind the table while the dejected-looking and clearly frightened prisoners were brought up onto the platform to stand in front of the crowd. Alexander smiled grimly when he saw the Thinblade strapped to Cain's waist. He took a mental image of the positions of the enemy soldiers. Without the crowd to provide cover, this would be a suicide mission, but with the chaos that would ensue once the fighting began, Alexander was confident they would be successful.

Cain held up his hand for silence, and the murmuring of the crowd slowly died out.

"These five men are traitors! They have betrayed Kai'Gorn and the rightful Sovereign of the Seven Isles, Prince Phane Reishi." Cain spoke in an angry tone, spitting his words at the crowd.

"They helped the pretender escape after he murdered my brother, the protector of Kai'Gorn, with his dark magic. For their crimes, they will die." With that, Cain sat down to watch the executions. He waved for the three guards on the platform to begin.

Alexander waited until one of the guards unlocked the collar of the first prisoner. The moment he heard the lock click open, he thought to Chloe, "Now." A moment later the shriek of a whistler arrow streaked into the sky. The crowd turned in stunned wonder at the interruption. Soldiers looked around for a threat. The magistrate stood and his face went crimson.

A moment later, things started happening very quickly. The executioner pitched backward off the raised platform with an arrow from Abigail's bow sticking out of his chest. Alexander threw a knife and buried it in the throat of the nearest guard, then swiftly drew his sword and charged the platform.

Anatoly whipped his cloak off his shoulders and brought his axe to bear on a guard standing in front of the platform. The young Kai'Gorn soldier was caught completely off guard by the sudden attack and barely had time to raise his spear to defend against the heavy downward stroke of the axe. The spear shattered and the soldier fell, with the axe blade buried from his right shoulder to the middle of his chest.

Commotion broke out all around as Captain Raisa's men started attacking the soldiers stationed at the periphery of the crowd. A whoosh of fire from the port drew everyone's attention as the sails of an Andalian troop ship quickly caught fire and sent a plume of black smoke into the air.

Alexander leapt onto the platform and pulled the first of the prisoners past him and into the waiting arms of Captain Raisa, then in one fluid motion brought his sword up and into the gut of the first guard. He looked the man in the eye for a brief moment before kicking him off his blade and into the line of the crossbowmen behind the platform.

Time seemed to slow down. Through his all around sight he saw everything unfolding around him. A crossbowman got off a clean shot that tore through his tunic but stopped cold when it hit his armor. Abigail and Isabel sent arrow after arrow down into the line of crossbowmen behind the platform. One by one they fell.

The crowd was deteriorating into the chaos of a riot as Captain Raisa's men moved through the citizenry to strike at the soldiers and then retreat. The soldiers responded by attacking indiscriminately, which enraged the people and turned them against the greatly outnumbered soldiers.

Anatoly moved methodically through the crowd in front of the platform from one soldier to the next. He didn't offer them a challenge or a fair fight. He simply killed them as efficiently as possible. Jack leapt up onto the platform from behind the two remaining guards and cleanly knifed the first in the back. He flickered into visibility for only a moment and was gone by the time the last guard looked over to see his comrade fall. Alexander used the line of four chained prisoners as cover from the last remaining guard as he moved with purpose toward Magistrate Cain.

The magistrate stood behind his table and worked his mouth apoplectically as his face turned a deeper crimson. Alexander fixed him with his glittering golden gaze and pointed his sword in challenge. Cain drew the Thinblade just as Alexander reached him and kicked the table toward the steps at the end of the platform. It flipped over and tumbled down the five short steps, creating an obstacle for the six soldiers rushing in from the side to protect the magistrate.

Behind him with his all around sight, he saw the last guard on the platform fall from Jack's knife. A moment later the collar of one of the prisoners clicked open and Captain Raisa stepped up onto the platform to help free his men.

Alexander smiled as Cain slashed at him with the Thinblade and calmly stepped into the attack, bringing his arm up to meet the ancient blade. It turned just before it hit him, as he knew it would. The Thinblade was his. It was bound to his line. It wouldn't harm him no matter who wielded it. The Thinblade stopped cold as it hit his arm and squirmed out of Cain's grip. With his left hand, Alexander snatched his magical sword from the air. In the same moment, he drove his ordinary steel sword into Cain's heart and looked him in the eye as his life faded away.

As Cain slumped to his knees, Alexander let go of the ordinary sword buried in the tyrant's chest and grabbed him by the hair. With the flick of his wrist, he took Cain's head off with the Thinblade and turned to face the crowd with the head of their dead tyrant raised high. He pointed the Thinblade at them and all of the fighting and commotion stopped. Everyone in the town square turned to look at Alexander.

"I am Lord Alexander Ruatha and I serve the Old Law. Kai'Gorn will submit to my rule or fall."

With that pronouncement, he casually tossed Cain's head into the crowd, collected the Thinblade's scabbard, and stepped off the platform. The crowd parted for him and his men as they made their way out of the town square. Only once did a soldier attempt to challenge them, but he fell with an arrow through the chest before he could even get within spear range.

A cheer began to build behind Alexander as he reached the edge of the square and rejoined the rest of his friends. It seemed the stories of discontent with Cain's brutal rule were well founded.

"Captain Raisa, I suggest we make haste to your ship," Alexander said. "As soon as the Andalian Lancers and the Reishi Protectorate get wind of this, they're going to throw everything they have into finding us."

They fled down the street and into an alley. Captain Raisa led them through a confusing maze of back streets and alleyways until he came to a nondescript door. It opened to a staircase leading down into a cellar. As they started to file down into the dim light of the underground, Alexander heard a guard shout from the end of the alley, "There they are!" only to be silenced a moment later by one of Abigail's arrows. The next men to round the corner were far more cautious. By then the alley was empty.

Raisa led them into the cellar and through a door in the back which opened into a dirt tunnel supported by wooden beams and boards. Alexander presumed it was a smugglers' tunnel. As he moved through the dark by lantern light, he could hear the enemy soldiers in the distance giving chase but they were far behind and represented little threat. The tunnel seemed to go on for miles. Occasionally the floor became damp but mostly it was dry powdery dirt that floated up into the air to form a brown haze.

When they emerged to the light of day, they were in a secluded little cove. Anchored not far from the bank was a swift-looking midsized ship. Captain Raisa waved and the man in the crow's nest waved back. Before they headed down to the water's edge and the longboat tethered there, Captain Raisa found the end of a sturdy rope that led back into the tunnel and gave it a mighty heave. The sound of wood scraping against stone was followed by the collapse of the tunnel and a whoosh of dusty air.

By nightfall they were several leagues away from Kai'Gorn and making good time sailing up the southwest coast of Ruatha. It was the first time Alexander had ever been aboard a ship and it took some getting used to. After spending the afternoon fighting the nagging feeling of nausea, he decided that he would much rather have solid ground underfoot.

Captain Raisa was another story. He seemed to be more at home aboard his ship than he was on land. His crew was a motley bunch but they obeyed his orders without question and ran the ship with skill and precision. They treated Alexander and his friends with respect and camaraderie. The story of the rescue of their shipmates and the death of Magistrate Cain swept through the ship with great joy and enthusiasm.

It would be a good five days to Southport if they had favorable winds. That evening Alexander stood at the railing of the ship with Isabel and Chloe, watching the sunset. He still had more than his share of worries but in that moment he was content. They were safe and making good time. They'd dealt a blow to the enemy and sowed the seeds of fear and doubt in the populace of Kai'Gorn. If he could capitalize on that fear, he might be able to bring Kai'Gorn under his control and stop Andalia from sending any more of their Lancers. With Kai'Gorn under his banner, he would have control of all of Ruatha.

CHAPTER 35

Half a day out, Jataan P'Tal saw the smoke rising from Kai'Gorn. He cursed under his breath. He was down to nine soldiers in addition to Boaberous Grudge, Rexius Truss, Vasili Nero, and Elred Rake's court wizard, Dagon Cade. Wizard Cade was a summoner who had proven to be very useful; his ability to call on the creatures of the wild to do his bidding had been instrumental in capturing the pretender.

Now that he saw smoke rising from the city, he wasn't so sure he'd made the right decision. He started to think he should have had the Andalian Lancers hold the pretender where they found him until he could arrive and take command of the unit. He had a sinking feeling that his quarry had escaped yet again. It was becoming an embarrassing pattern that was no doubt beginning to wear on Prince Phane's patience.

Every time he thought about his master, a sense of uneasiness settled on him. He couldn't quite put his finger on it. It was almost like serving the Prince made Jataan feel as if he was defying his own conscience. The messages that were delivered periodically by Kludge, Phane's imp familiar, only served to magnify that discomfort. Jataan reminded himself again that he was Reishi Protectorate—his purpose was to preserve and protect the Reishi line. He had to trust that Phane would rule with justice once his challengers were neutralized.

An hour away from the city, they came upon a company of Lancers. Jataan took command and ordered them to send word out to all the other Lancers in the vicinity to make a cordon around Kai'Gorn and converge on the city. If the fires burning in the southernmost city of Ruatha were the pretender's doing, he didn't want to chance his escaping again.

Jataan P'Tal entered a city in chaos. Soldiers were moving in large groups, trying to quell the violence that seemed to be directed everywhere at once. Gangs of men armed with farm implements roamed the streets looking for anyone wearing the crest of Kai'Gorn and tearing them apart when they found them. They stayed clear of the Lancers who moved in larger units and remained mounted on their giant steeds but called out the soldiers of Kai'Gorn in open challenge, especially soldiers of the royal guard. Gruesome displays of mutilated soldiers hung from lampposts. The city was in open rebellion.

Jataan made his way through the streets with a company of Lancers surrounding him. He paid no heed to the violence going on all around but instead moved steadily toward the central fortress and the dungeon where his prize was supposed to be waiting for him. The fortress was locked down and the soldiers manning the gates refused to allow him entry. They were clearly terrified of the mobs of angry citizens roaming the streets, but they relented when Captain Tate came running up and countermanded his previous orders to keep the gates closed.

Jataan P'Tal rode into the courtyard and dismounted in front of Captain Tate. He could tell from the man's expression that the news was not good, but he was in the habit of reserving judgment until he heard the facts. He appraised the man for a moment before sighing and shaking his head.

"Report."

Captain Tate swallowed hard. "The pretender murdered the magistrate and General Cain and then escaped. The port is on fire and the city is in a state of open revolt."

"Has he left the city?"

"Yes, General Commander," Tate said. "Soldiers reported that he fled through a smuggling tunnel that led to a nearby cove. When we sent a platoon to investigate the area, they reported evidence that a longboat had recently launched. Additionally, the pretender freed five prisoners who were known to crew for a local smuggler named Finley Raisa who assisted in his escape two nights prior."

"So the pretender has a sense of loyalty to those who help him," Jataan mused. "Any indication of where he was headed?"

"No, but we presume he would head north along the coastline."

Jataan nodded absently at the obvious suggestion. "Captain Tate, have the fastest ship in the harbor supplied and ready to depart tomorrow morning at first light. Issue curfew orders to the citizenry; anyone out after dark will be killed on sight. Call the Lancers into the city and put down this revolt. Have a hot meal and suitable quarters prepared for my soldiers and officers."

"Right away, General Commander," Captain Tate said with visible relief.

Jataan turned to Wizard Cade, "I believe we could use the assistance of your birds again."

Cade nodded, "I will begin the summoning at once."

Before Jataan could turn to head into the keep, a cloud of dark black smoke began to form several feet away. He drew himself up and faced the swirling darkness. A moment later there was a loud clapping noise and the smoke faded to reveal Kludge, his wings beating furiously to keep him floating at eye level. His row of sharp teeth and his hateful yellow eyes offered clear insight into his malevolent character. Jataan P'Tal didn't like Kludge and he never turned his back on the little monster.

"Master is most displeased," Kludge said in his raspy, whining voice. "Make haste to the Reishi Keep. When the pretender retrieves the Sovereign Stone from the aether, you will kill him and his companions and return to Tyr with the Stone. Do you understand these orders?"

Jataan P'Tal nodded slowly.

Kludge smiled with malice. "Master says this is your last chance to prove your worth. Do not fail him again." Smoke began to form around the little demon until he was completely shrouded in the dark vapor. There was another loud clap and when the smoke cleared, Kludge was gone.

CHAPTER 36

Alexander coalesced his awareness in Kelvin's workshop deep in the bowels of Blackstone Keep. He scanned about until he saw the message board, then moved closer so he could read the writing. There were three numbered items. The first explained that they had a platoon of Rangers assigned to sleep in shifts to ensure that there was always someone asleep for Alexander to dream-whisper with. The second revealed that Headwater had fallen and was in the process of being reorganized to ensure that trade would flow and people would be able to work. The third said that they were working on the problem of the shades.

Alexander drifted through the Keep to the chamber where his sleep messengers were housed. There were three Rangers asleep. He drifted into one of them and insinuated his awareness into the sleeping man's dreams. A moment later he found himself standing in a field of wildflowers with the barrier mountains of Glen Morillian all around. Alexander smiled when the Ranger noticed him with a start.

"Lord Alexander, is that really you?"

"It is. I've bonded with a fairy named Chloe. We're aboard a ship a few days from Southport. Once I arrive there, I'll commandeer a warship and head for the Reishi Isle. Send word to my father that I'll be ordering Southport and Highlands Reach to move south and engage Kai'Gorn. If he can spare a legion of cavalry, have him send it south with haste. I've killed the magistrate and their commanding general, so Kai'Gorn is in disarray. The time to strike is now."

"Understood, Lord Alexander, but I believe General Valentine has already dispatched a legion of Rangers led by Commander Kevin Alaric to support the southern army. Will that be sufficient or would you like another?"

Alexander smiled. "I think one will do. It's good to see my father hasn't lost his edge. Send word to New Ruatha that we're all alive and will return as soon as possible."

"By your command, Lord Alexander. Best speed."

Alexander withdrew from the Ranger's mind and into the firmament. He floated there on the ocean of possibility for a long time before returning to his body. He was becoming more accustomed to his clairvoyance and felt more in control each time he used it. When he opened his eyes, Chloe was floating around his head and Isabel was sitting at the little table in their quarters watching him.

Chloe stopped and flew up to within a foot of his nose and gave him a stern look. "You were gone again. I was worried. I can't find you when you're away from your body like that."

Alexander shared a smile with Isabel. "I was looking in on Blackstone Keep. Headwater has fallen to us and Kevin is leading a legion of Rangers to Southport. Maybe we'll have a chance to see him."

Isabel smiled excitedly at the prospect of seeing her brother. "Really? That would be wonderful. It feels like it's been so long since I rode with my brothers. Now they're scattered all over Ruatha and I hardly get to see them anymore."

Despite the uneasiness Alexander felt at being on a ship, the trip to Southport was blessedly uneventful. After so many days spent traveling by foot or horseback, it was a welcome change to be making good speed while having the opportunity to rest. They spent a fair amount of time talking and planning their strategy going forward. There were still many obstacles to overcome but their goals seemed more achievable now that they'd eluded Commander P'Tal and were no longer being chased.

Captain Raisa was a good host and a skilled seaman. His crew treated Alexander and his friends with respect and did their best to make them feel welcome. On the afternoon of the fifth day at sea, the lookout in the crow's nest called out that a ship was approaching. Alexander and his friends came up on deck armed and ready for a fight. There was no telling whether Commander P'Tal had reacquired their location. All Alexander knew for certain was that the General Commander of the Reishi Protectorate was relentless and resourceful.

Isabel opened her eyes and smiled. "It's flying the flag of Southport and headed right for us."

"Captain Raisa, lower your sails and raise a flag of truce," Alexander said. "Let them come alongside so I can talk with their captain."

An hour later they were sailing toward Southport with a warship as escort. The Southport captain was initially wary but offered his services without hesitation once he saw that Alexander carried the Thinblade. The songs and stories of Alexander and his achievements, written by Jack and distributed throughout Ruatha by his bards, were paying off.

Southport was a different city than it had been the last time he was there. It was now on a war footing and making preparations for battle with Kai'Gorn. A sense of purpose filled the air, the docks were orderly and well cared for, the streets were cleaner, and people who couldn't find work before were now gainfully employed making ready for the coming battle to the south.

The residence of the Regent of Southport was built on the highest point in the city, which happened to be a bluff overlooking the port. Alexander and his friends made their way from the docks to the fortress, winding up one staircase after another while accompanied by a squad of Southport city guard and Captain Raisa.

They arrived in the western courtyard just as the Regent was coming out of the keep, trailing a number of functionaries and petty nobles behind him. He smiled warmly, yet Alexander saw in a glance that he was not an honest man but an opportunist who relished power and would do what was necessary to hold on to it. Alexander also knew in that glance that the Regent was probably responsible for ordering the city guard to help the Reishi Protectorate hunt him down when he fled Valentine Manor. Under different circumstances he might have taken action against the Regent, but right now he just needed a fast ship to take him to the Reishi Isle, and he didn't want to risk a delay for the sake of replacing one self-serving official.

"Welcome to Southport, Lord Alexander," he said. "I am Regent Landon. Had I known you would be visiting, I would have made better preparations. I apologize."

Alexander decided to play it smooth and avoid revealing any hint that the

Regent's power might be in jeopardy. He smiled and offered his hand. "No need, Regent Landon, you couldn't have known we would be visiting. And regrettably, we won't be staying long. I have a task of great urgency that I'm hoping you can help me with."

"Of course, Lord Alexander," Landon said. "Anything we can do to help. Perhaps we should adjourn inside and discuss your needs over a meal."

Alexander smiled again. "That would be most welcome." He introduced his friends as they made their way into the keep and to the dining room. The place was gaudy and overly decorated with expensive-looking artwork and furniture but it failed to create the impression of grandeur that the simple white marble halls of Glen Morillian or the ancient artwork of the palace of New Ruatha had so easily accomplished.

Alexander took the chair at the head of the table and motioned for Isabel to take the chair to his right. Regent Landon seated himself to Alexander's left, and while he was outwardly gracious, Alexander could see irritation in his colors. Landon was a man who wanted to be the most important person in the room and he wanted everyone else to know it. Deferring to Alexander was an ordeal for the self-serving Regent, but Alexander didn't really care. He had more important things to deal with.

The meal was excellent and quite satisfying. Servants began bringing platters of food the moment the Regent took his seat. They served thick slabs of well-seasoned, tender, juicy roast beef; roasted potatoes; and freshly baked bread with rich yellow butter. They made small talk during the meal because Alexander and his friends were more interested in eating than talking once the aroma of the hearty fare reached them and set their stomachs to grumbling.

Alexander sat back, feeling much better after his meal, and drained his flagon of wine. He took a deep breath and sighed contentedly. "Thank you, Regent. My compliments to your chef. That was an excellent meal."

Lucky nodded happily past a mouthful of crusty bread slathered with butter.

Regent Landon smiled at the praise. "My chef is the finest in all of Southport."

"I have no doubt," Alexander said. "I only wish I was staying long enough for him to demonstrate his skills at their finest."

"Oh, Lord Alexander, with a few days of preparation, he can create a feast worthy of a king," Landon said, clearly enjoying the attention.

Alexander smiled with a sigh. "I'm afraid I'll be leaving tomorrow at first light. For now I have a number of things I need to discuss with you. First, I'll need a warship for my journey, the fastest you have that can be ready to sail with the sunrise."

Regent Landon frowned slightly at the request but nodded quickly to disguise his reluctance to part with one of his best ships. "Of course, I will tell Captain Targa to make ready for departure tomorrow morning. May I ask how long you'll need his services?"

"Hopefully for only a couple of weeks," Alexander said. "Second, please provide Captain Raisa with the sum of five hundred gold sovereigns for his service. You will be reimbursed by the treasury of New Ruatha."

If the demand for a ship made the Regent frown, the request for gold made him cough and sputter for a moment before he regained his composure.

"Please forgive me, I swallowed wrong," he lied. "I will have the sum you've requested made ready for Captain Raisa immediately."

"Excellent," Alexander said. "Have the Rangers arrived from New Ruatha yet?"

"Yes, in fact they arrived just yesterday," Landon said. "They're camped in the pasture north of the city."

Alexander and Isabel shared a look and a smile. "Please send a rider to the commander of the legion and ask him to join us here, right away."

"Of course," Regent Landon said as he snapped at a servant and sent him off to deliver orders to the commander of the watch.

Alexander leaned forward with greater seriousness. "Are your forces ready to move?"

Regent Landon looked a bit surprised by the question but he answered quickly, "I have two legions prepared for battle. They can move on very little notice. Additionally, Highlands Reach has sent two legions; they are camped southeast of the city."

"Very good," Alexander said. "We've just come from Kai'Gorn. The magistrate and his brother are dead. A legion of Andalian Lancers is occupying the surrounding area and the city is in turmoil. Kai'Gorn is vulnerable and leaderless—now is the time to attack. Please summon the commanders of your forces and the legions from Highlands Reach so we can discuss the campaign."

"Of course, Lord Alexander, but are you sure that's wise?" Landon tried to ask diplomatically. "After all, rumors of Magistrate Cain's death may not be true and the Andalian Lancers are fearsome warriors. Would it not be better to let them come to us and defend rather than overextend ourselves by an attack?"

Alexander shook his head slowly. "No, Andalia continues to send more Lancers. As long as Kai'Gorn is a friendly port, the enemy will grow in strength. We need to stop them sooner rather than later. As for the magistrate, I'm pretty sure he's dead," Alexander said wryly.

"Can you be certain?" Landon asked. "Cain is a consummate liar. He may be trying to lure you into a trap."

Alexander fixed Landon with his glittering gaze. "I'm sure he's dead because I took his head myself."

Regent Landon sat up a bit straighter. Alexander saw fear flash through his colors. It looked like he was trying to discern if he was in danger. He made a mental note to have Jack do some asking around to see if Landon had made other deals that might put his plans in jeopardy.

Alexander sat back a bit and relaxed to diffuse the tension he'd created. "Cain wasn't very hospitable. He had me tortured, and he threatened to give my wife and sister to the Lancers for sport. His death was justice."

Landon feigned indignation. "I knew he was a tyrant but I had no idea he was such a monster. With him gone, you're right, of course. Now is the time to attack. It will take an hour or so for the commanders to arrive. Perhaps you and your friends would like to rest. Your quarters are ready and my staff will provide anything you require."

"Thank you, Regent. It would be nice to get cleaned up," Alexander said. "It's been a long journey." He stood and turned to Captain Raisa.

"You and your crew have my gratitude, Captain. If you choose to return to Kai'Gorn, take caution. It's going to be a dangerous place for a while."

"I was thinking about giving my men shore leave for a couple of days here in Southport, if that's all right with Regent Landon, of course."

Landon smiled graciously. "Of course, of course, you are most welcome. We have many fine establishments that are always eager for new customers."

As they followed Landon's aid to their quarters, Alexander sent his thoughts to Chloe. "Little One, I need you to spy on Regent Landon for me while we wait for the commanders to arrive."

"Of course, My Love," she said in his mind and flitted away through the aether without notice. She'd been hiding in plain sight since they arrived. Alexander was wary of revealing her presence to anyone he didn't trust—first because she was perhaps the only one alive who could retrieve the Sovereign Stone and second because he loved her and didn't want any harm to come to his new companion.

CHAPTER 37

Their quarters were lavish and well appointed, but Alexander got the impression the décor was more to demonstrate the importance of Regent Landon than to make his guests comfortable. He silenced his friends from discussing their strategy or destination for fear that spies were watching. He didn't trust Landon and was becoming more and more certain that the Regent had an agenda of his own.

Instead he took advantage of the opportunity to get cleaned up and rest for a few minutes while he listened for Chloe in his mind. He had just pulled on his trousers after a quick bath when he heard her voice, trembling with fear.

"Darkness comes," she said.

Alexander felt fear for a moment before it was overshadowed by anger. He was coming to understand that there were precious few people who gravitated to positions of power that could be trusted.

"Do not risk yourself, Little One," Alexander thought to her urgently.

"I'm not in danger," she said. "Send me your mind and I will show you the darkness."

Alexander wasn't sure what she meant but he sat down, closed his eyes, and entrusted himself to her. In a flash he was looking through her eyes and hearing through her ears. He imagined that this was what it must be like for Isabel when she looked through Slyder's eyes. Then he saw the demon.

He recognized it immediately. He'd seen it twice before, once in Southport when he'd fled his home and again at Blackstone Keep when the scourgling had arrived. It was only a foot and a half tall with leathery grey-black skin, sharp teeth, and hateful yellow eyes. Its batlike wings beat furiously to keep it hovering at eye level with Regent Landon.

Landon did his best to smile at the little monster but it was clear he wasn't comfortable. "Prince Phane will be pleased to learn that the pretender will not live through the day," he said. "I've already sent orders to my best assassin. He'll strike within the hour." Landon smiled, clearly pleased with himself.

"Master sends new instructions," Kludge said in his raspy and simpering voice. "Do not harm the pretender. Send him on his way. Master has other plans."

Landon looked suddenly alarmed, almost on the verge of panic. "But I've already given the order. He may already be dead."

Kludge wrung his clawed little hands and smiled with malice. "If he dies, you will die slowly. Call off the attack and let him leave unharmed. Master commands it."

Landon's eyes grew wide and he bolted for the door, shouting for his administrator. Alexander snapped back to his body and called for Chloe to return to him. A moment later she spun into existence in a ball of scintillating light right next to him.

Alexander burst from the bathing room with his sword in hand. "Assassin," he shouted. Anatoly was on his feet with his axe in hand scanning for danger in an instant. A moment later everyone else was up and looking for the threat.

Alexander scrutinized the large sitting room at the center of the guest chambers, looking for the telltale colors of a living aura. He was a fraction of a second too late. His warning had forced the enemy's hand. A small slot opened in the wall and the tip of an arrow showed through.

Isabel heard the sound of the slot opening and whirled to see the enemy. She dove just as the arrow was released. It was a clean shot. It would have caught Alexander full in the chest. Without his armor, it would probably have killed him. Instead, Isabel took the arrow in her left shoulder, the glass arrowhead filled with poison shattering into the wound. She screamed as it hit her and then toppled to the floor. Anatoly tossed a knife at the slot in the wall but the assassin was gone.

Alexander raced to Isabel's side. She was shock white and shivering. "I'm so sorry, Isabel. Please hold on. Lucky will save you." He hastily wiped tears from his cheek. "I love you."

Isabel forced a smile. "I love you too, Alexander," she said through the pain. "Now let Lucky work on me and go find that assassin." She put her hand on his cheek and wiped away fresh tears.

Lucky was there a moment later. "Stand aside, Alexander. I need room to work." Alexander stood up with a building feeling of panic growing in his chest.

Anatoly grabbed him by the arm and pulled him away from Isabel. "Turn it to anger. We're still in danger. Lucky will do everything that can be done for her." Before Anatoly could say more, there was an urgent knock at the door.

Jack looked over to Abigail who nodded while nocking an arrow. Jack opened the door to find Regent Landon standing in the hall with a terrified look on his face.

"Lord Alexander, I've just learned of a plot against you," he said in a rush, then he saw Isabel and realized he was too late. "Oh, Dear Maker, I'll send for my personal physician at once," he said entering the room with his aid and two guards.

Alexander turned his glittering gaze on the Regent. Landon froze in midstep. When his two guards saw the murderous look in Alexander's eyes, they both drew their swords and tried to place themselves between Alexander and the Regent. Landon and his aid turned and ran. The first guard fell from Abigail's arrow, which drove through his throat and into the wall behind him. Jack slipped up behind the second soldier, put a knife to his throat and pulled him out of the way as Alexander bolted through the door with Anatoly on his heels.

He looked down the hall to see the Regent and his aid fleeing just as Kevin and three Rangers turned the corner. At first glance, Kevin smiled when he saw Alexander, then he saw the Thinblade drawn and the Regent running away and he drew his sword.

"Stop them!" Alexander commanded.

Without hesitation, the four Rangers fanned out across the wide hall, blocking the Regent's escape. He came to a cautious stop and looked around in a panic like a trapped rat. As Alexander approached, the aid tried to place himself between Alexander and the Regent, brandishing a knife in warning. Alexander cut the man's hand off with a flick of the Thinblade and then drove the blade straight through Regent Landon's shoulder with the flat of the blade horizontal. Landon screamed. Alexander grabbed him by the collar to keep him from falling and bore into him with the glittering fury of his golden-flecked eyes.

"What's happened, Lord Alexander?" Kevin asked.

Without looking at his brother-in-law, Alexander answered, "An assassin just shot Isabel with an arrow." Both Kevin's and Landon's faces went white. "Regent Landon here sent the assassin to kill me by Phane's order, but Isabel threw herself in the arrow's path. She saved my life." Landon started to tremble from the pain and fear as Alexander held him up with the blade of his sword.

Kevin turned and gave one of the Rangers a nod. He bolted down the hall at the silent command. Alexander ignored everything around him except the man on his blade.

"How long have you been in league with Phane?" Alexander asked. When Landon hesitated, he turned the blade slightly and the man screamed. "I'll know if you lie to me," Alexander growled.

"Please, don't! Phane said he'd make me King of Ruatha if I helped him. I've been working for him since you came to Southport just a few days after he woke. I didn't want to, but he threatened me. I'm afraid of him," Landon said, breaking down into tears. Alexander saw fear in his colors but no remorse. The man was as self-serving as he was dishonest, even under stress.

"Why did Phane change his orders?"

Landon's eyes registered surprise. "How . . ." Alexander turned the blade of his sword again and Landon screamed.

"Answer me!"

"I don't know. Please, you have to believe me. I don't know. He doesn't tell me his plans. He just sends orders and threatens me if I fail. Please don't kill me. I don't want to die." Even through the pain and fear, Landon was trying to play on Alexander's reputation for simple decency. It took a special kind of criminal to keep up his calm calculation under such duress.

Alexander withdrew his sword without cutting him further. The Regent slumped to the floor just as a dozen Southport city guard rounded the corner. They drew weapons the moment they saw the Regent on the ground and Alexander standing over him with his sword. Alexander kicked the man over on his side while fixing the guard force with his fury. He strode forward past Kevin and the Rangers who fanned out behind him, weapons drawn and ready.

Alexander stopped ten paces from the soldiers and pointed the Thinblade at them. "Landon is in league with Phane. He's a traitor to Ruatha and an enemy of the Old Law. Surrender your weapons now."

The sergeant of the guard hesitated for a moment before Regent Landon shouted at them, "Attack, you fools!"

Without looking over his shoulder, Alexander said, "Anatoly, kill him." He heard the sickening thump of the axe fall across the Regent's neck a moment later even as he met the charge of the Southport guard.

The sergeant reached him first. Alexander slipped to the side of his thrust and drove the Thinblade into the center of the man's chest, then sliced laterally out his shoulder, bringing the blade across and extending his reach just enough to slice the next man's throat. He reminded himself that he wasn't wearing his armor as he lopped the tip off a spear with the flick of his wrist. The Thinblade moved with lightning speed back across the soldier and sliced a gash across his chest four inches deep. Alexander whirled into the mass of them and sliced in a broad arc, cutting three men in half with one stroke. The rich carpet soaked up the blood.

Anatoly, Kevin, and the two Rangers stepped into the fray and only moments later the dozen soldiers were nothing but scattered carnage. The fight ended as abruptly as it had started. Alexander was splattered with crimson across his bare chest and face. He looked like the fury of death itself.

He turned when he heard boots running toward them and was relieved to see a platoon of thirty Rangers thundering up the hall.

He headed back to the room where Isabel lay injured by an arrow meant for him. He shoved his worry aside and focused his thoughts on the precarious situation they were in. "Kevin, secure this hall and send orders to your forces to take Southport in my name immediately." Alexander didn't break stride or even look over at Kevin as he issued his orders. "Also send word to the commanders of the Southport legions that the Regent has been executed for treason. Any who wish to stand against me will suffer the same fate."

Kevin issued orders to his men and two of them broke away from the cordon surrounding Alexander and set off at a dead run. Alexander walked into the room past the soldier who was now disarmed and sitting in a chair looking at Abigail and her bow. He started trembling when he saw the blood splattered across Alexander's chest and face.

Alexander knelt beside Isabel. Kevin was there a moment later. She was still and her face was pale. She looked so peaceful. If he couldn't have seen her colors, he would have thought she was dead. Lucky had dressed her wound and given her some healing draught.

"Is she dead?" Kevin asked with a hint of panic.

"No, she's alive," Lucky said, "but she's been poisoned." He turned Alexander by the shoulders to look him directly in the eye. His fear spiked into sickening panic when he saw the look of despair in Lucky's eyes.

"My boy, I've given her something to slow the poison but I have nothing that can stop it. Eventually it will kill her." A tear slipped down Lucky's cheek.

Alexander sat down hard, staring in disbelief at his old mentor.

"She can't die," Kevin said, "she's my little sister. This can't be happening. You have to save her," he said urgently, taking Lucky by the robe and starting to shake him as if that would change the reality of the situation.

He stopped when he heard Isabel's voice. "Kevin? Is that you?" she mumbled.

He released Lucky and went to her side. She smiled up at her brother. "It's good to see you," she said, taking his hand.

"I'm here, Isabel," Kevin said, his eyes watery and his voice cracking.

She smiled up at him. "Alexander and I are married. The Fairy Queen presided over our wedding. It was so beautiful, Kevin. I wish you could have been there."

"Me too, Little Sister," Kevin said. "Mom and Dad will be so happy." His voice broke a bit in anguish.

Lucky put his hand on Kevin's shoulder. "She needs to rest."

Kevin looked over and nodded, sniffing back more tears. "I'll be here when you wake, Isabel," he said. She was unconscious before he finished speaking.

Alexander sat staring in disbelief. He knew Lucky was very good at his craft and he would never have made such a pronouncement unless he was certain. Alexander just couldn't make himself accept the reality of the situation. They had just gotten married. He loved her with his whole heart; he knew that losing her would break his spirit.

"Lucky," he croaked, "There has to be a way to save her." His statement was the embodiment of misery. The look on Lucky's face reflected his own suffering and only served to confirm the diagnosis.

"I'm sorry, I wish there was more I could do."

CHAPTER 38

"How long does she have?" Alexander asked.

"A few days, maybe a week," Lucky said quietly. The pronouncement was so final and so immediate that Alexander had a hard time accepting the truth of it. He knew Lucky would never mislead him about something so important, but he wanted to believe his old mentor was just plain wrong. He struggled to face the truth of the sentence, but every time he looked directly at it, he couldn't help but reject it. It felt like his sanity was unraveling.

Chloe buzzed up to him. "Do you still have the fairy dust?"

He could feel her worry for him. He nodded numbly. She buzzed over to Lucky. "I will guide you. With fairy dust you can make a much more potent healing draught. It may not save her, but it will give her more time."

Alexander shot to his feet at the sound of hope and rushed to his pack. He tore through it until he found his coin purse and held it out to Lucky like it was the most important thing in the world. Lucky looked skeptical but he took it with care and opened it to reveal the iridescent white powder. He smiled at the sight. "Alexander, this is worth a king's ransom. Fairy dust is very powerful. If anything can save her, this can."

A Ranger entered in a rush. "The commanders of the legions from Southport and Highlands Reach are here," he announced. "General Fabian of Southport is demanding an explanation. He's seen the body of the Regent and his guards and he's furious."

"Send them in," Alexander commanded, then turned to Lucky. "What do you need to make this potion?"

"A lab with glassware and some time," Lucky said. "I have all of the ingredients I need." He patted his bag.

Alexander strode over to the terrified, one-handed aid. The Rangers had collected him from the hall and brought him into the room. He was sitting on the floor in pain and fear. "Where can we find a laboratory with glassware?" he asked urgently and in a tone that would not accept anything less than an honest answer.

The aid looked up and stammered, "Three floors down. The court wizard has a workshop."

"Where is the wizard and what's his name?"

"Wizard Ulick is with the legions making preparations to defend Southport against Kai'Gorn," the terrified aid answered quickly.

"Good, you will take Master Alabrand to the workshop. Get up," Alexander commanded. "Kevin, assign a squad of Rangers to provide security for Lucky."

Kevin motioned to his Second, who quickly gathered a squad of ten men and gave them their orders. They were ready in the hall when Lucky left. He passed the commanders as they were escorted into the room.

General Fabian looked furious. He was a big man with closely cropped salt-and-pepper hair and a well-groomed thick black mustache and goatee. He was accompanied by his aide-de-camp and a subordinate officer. His fury morphed into caution when he saw Alexander. The blood splattered across his chest and face coupled with the glittering rage dancing in his eyes was enough to give anyone pause.

The next to enter was a man of medium height and build with short dirty-blond hair and grey eyes. He was clean shaven and fastidiously dressed in the uniform of Highlands Reach. His eyes were filled with intelligence and looked like they took in every detail. He wore the stern expression of a man who demanded a great deal from himself and from those under his command. He appraised the scene in the room at a glance, briefly noting Alexander's appearance, before his penetrating gaze settled on Anatoly. A slow smile broke across his face and all his sternness faded away.

"Anatoly Grace, you're looking well, my old friend," he said, striding over to the big man-at-arms and extending his hand.

Anatoly smiled warmly for just a moment. "General Talia, it's good to see you as well, sir. I wish the circumstances were different." His expression turned serious. "I'd like to introduce Lord Alexander," he said, gesturing toward Alexander with an open hand.

General Talia bowed formally and precisely. "Lord Alexander, your father led a regiment under my command during the border wars. He's an excellent commander and an even better man. It's a pleasure to meet you."

"Thank you, General," Alexander said, offering his hand.

General Talia didn't seem concerned about the blood drying on Alexander's bare chest and arms. He took his hand and returned a firm grip. Alexander appraised the colors of each of the new arrivals and determined that they were all professional soldiers, long accustomed to ordered and regimented lives. They were ambitious but only within the limits of their chosen profession.

"Gentlemen, we have much to discuss. You no doubt saw the scene of battle and the corpse of the Regent in the hall. I killed Regent Landon because he ordered an assassin to murder me." He held General Fabian's eyes for a moment with a hard look.

"It seems the Regent was working for Phane. His assassin failed, but only because my wife threw herself in the path of the poisoned arrow." Alexander had to school his voice to keep it from breaking. He withdrew into that place in his psyche where the witness lived, where emotion and feeling were distant and less important.

General Talia's eyes danced with sudden anger. "Lord Alexander, you have my condolences. Assassination is the way of the coward."

General Fabian looked shocked at the revelation of his regent's treason. From his colors, Alexander could tell the man had no idea of Landon's secret alliances. "I was unaware of Regent Landon's divided loyalties. You have my condolences for your wife's injury as well, My Lord."

"Anatoly, please brief them on the situation in Kai'Gorn while I finish getting dressed," Alexander said.

He spent a few minutes cleaning the blood off himself and putting on his shirt, armor, and tunic. He looked in the mirror and struggled to hold back the tears. Everything seemed so pointless without Isabel. If she died, he knew his drive to win and even his reason for fighting would die with her.

When he emerged from the washroom, Abigail and Jack were sitting with Isabel. She was still unconscious. Abigail gave him a worried shake of her head in response to his questioning look. Anatoly, Kevin, and the generals sat around a table talking quietly. Alexander took a chair at the head of the table.

"You have roughly four legions at your disposal. Will that be enough to take and hold Kai'Gorn?" Alexander asked.

"Given the loss of Cain and his brother and the unrest among the populace, I believe our force strength will be more than adequate to the task," General Talia said.

"I concur," General Fabian said. "Although, I believe we will suffer heavy casualties at the hands of the Andalian Lancers."

"The Lancers are formidable, but their strength rests in their mounts and force lances," Alexander said. "I recommend you engage them in terrain and circumstances where they can't make full use of their rhone. I trust that you're more than capable of finding and exploiting the Lancers' weaknesses. Once you do, kill them to the last man.

"Kai'Gorn must be taken. We cannot allow Andalia to continue landing troops there. If you can take the city intact, then by all means do so. But if you have to burn it to the ground, so be it. Once you've secured the city, commandeer every ship you can find, arm them and begin intercepting the Andalian troop transports on the water. Sink them without mercy or quarter."

General Fabian and General Talia shared a look.

"Say what you have to say, gentlemen," Alexander commanded gently but firmly.

General Talia smiled without mirth. "We have both served territories led by men who would rather not fight. When forced into battle, they choose limited engagement and half measures. As soldiers, we tend to see things in more absolute terms. For myself, I am relieved to find that my new King understands that warfare is an all-or-nothing proposition."

General Fabian nodded. "I'd rather not have to send soldiers into harm's way, but once the decision to go to war has been made, the only honorable objective is total victory."

"Outstanding," Alexander said. "I'm glad we understand each other. General Talia, you will take command of the Ruathan forces south of the Great Forest. My father, General Valentine, is the commander of all Ruathan forces; you will take your orders from him or from me. If you need reinforcements, send your request to New Ruatha. Also, send word to Highlands Reach informing your governor of the situation and my expectation of his continued cooperation."

"By your command, Lord Alexander," General Talia said. "The governor and I are on very good terms, friends even, so I feel comfortable assuring you that he will provide our forces with all of the support he has to offer."

"Excellent. Thank you, General Talia."

Alexander took a deep breath and turned to his brother-in-law. "Kevin, you will serve as temporary Regent of Southport."

Kevin blinked in surprise. "Surely there are others more qualified, Lord Alexander."

Alexander nodded somberly. "I'm sure there are, but right now I need someone I know I can trust. The post will only be temporary. For now, keep half your legion here and send the rest south under General Talia's command. Protect the people of Southport, keep the port open, and protect the flow of commerce. Coordinate with Highlands Reach to keep our southern army supplied. And send regular reports to General Valentine. Everything else will take care of itself."

"As you wish, Lord Alexander," Kevin said. His mind was clearly still on Isabel. Alexander understood completely.

"Now, gentlemen, if there's nothing else, I'm going to sit with my wife," Alexander said as he stood up.

Anatoly walked the military men out into the hall where they talked for a few minutes. Rangers took positions in the hall to provide security.

Alexander sat with Isabel late into the night. Kevin stayed as well. They didn't talk much but occasionally shared a look of fear and anguish. Lucky returned in the dark of night with Chloe. He entered quietly after a brief discussion with the Rangers standing guard outside.

Order had been restored in the keep and the city. General Fabian had called all of the officers of the Southport city guard together and informed them that Regent Landon was dead and Regent Alaric would be assuming command of the city. They were a bit surprised and confused but they followed their orders without too much question. By midnight, Kevin's legion had secured the city and was working with the city guard to maintain order and ensure a smooth transition of power. There were rumors of a petty noble or two making noises that they should have been consulted prior to a new regent being named, but they didn't pose any credible threat, so Alexander ignored them. Instead, he focused his energy on Isabel.

Lucky came up beside him and laid a hand on his shoulder. "I have the potion. It won't eliminate the poison, but it will prevent it from doing any further damage for a while. I have to caution you though, it's not a cure. Without magic of greater power than mine, she will eventually die. This potion will keep the poison from killing her until she develops immunity to the potion's magic. Once that happens, the poison will do its damage."

Alexander nodded with a mixture of hope and despair. At this point he would take what he could get. "How long will this buy her?"

"A month, maybe five weeks," Lucky said.

"Who might have the magic to heal her?"

Lucky shook his head. "I know of no healer on Ruatha who is accomplished enough to extract such a virulent poison. Perhaps Kelvin might know of a way. The wizards may have found something within Blackstone Keep capable of healing her."

Alexander nodded. "I'll send a message tonight. Will she be able to travel?"

"I don't see why not. The poison will be held in check so it won't incapacitate her until the effects of the potion are no longer potent enough to keep it at bay. As soon as her shoulder mends, she'll feel as good as ever."

"Should we wake her so she can drink it now?" Kevin asked.

Lucky shook his head. "The healing draught I gave her is keeping the poison from harming her for now. It would be best to let her sleep until morning and then give her the potion." He handed the heavy glass vial filled with milky-looking liquid to Alexander.

Before Alexander tried to sleep, he sat down to meditate. It took him longer than usual to find the place where he could enter the firmament, but eventually he found it. He coalesced his awareness in Kelvin's workroom deep inside Blackstone Keep and looked at the message board; there were no new messages.

Next he went to the sleeping chamber of the Rangers assigned to receive his dream whisperings. His message was simple and to the point. He told a sleeping Ranger of Isabel's poisoning and asked that Kelvin make it a priority to find a way to save her. Then he explained that General Talia was leading the southern army to attack Kai'Gorn, Regent Landon was dead, and Kevin Alaric was taking his place for the time being. He didn't give the Ranger a chance to ask any questions before he extracted himself from the man's sleeping mind and returned to his own body.

Alexander slept in a chair beside Isabel. He didn't want to move her from the couch because the healing draught was still doing its work and he wasn't about to leave her alone. It was a restless night. He woke often and had trouble getting back to sleep when he did. His worry for her seemed to ebb and flow like a tide, sometimes receding into manageable concern, other times spiking into a mixture of panic and despair that threatened to overwhelm him.

CHAPTER 39

He was at her side when she awakened. Chloe was curled up on the back of the couch and woke the moment Isabel did.

"Hi," Alexander said, taking her hand gently. "You saved me again."

She smiled up at him, but her smile turned to a frown when she saw the worry in his eyes. "How bad?"

"Bad. Lucky made this for you." He held up the potion. "You were poisoned. He said this will keep the poison from killing you for a month or so, but then . . ." His voice broke into a sob. She squeezed his hand.

"Alexander, I wouldn't do a thing differently," she said. "If I'm your wife, then I'm the Queen of Ruatha and I have a great duty to our people. Part of that duty is protecting you so you can protect us all." She was so strong and brave, but he could see the fear in her aura.

Alexander shook his head. "I don't care about any of that right now. I need you, Isabel. You can't die. I'm not strong enough to survive losing you," he said through his tears.

"Yes you are!" she said, firmly holding his eyes with hers. "Alexander, you have to promise me that you'll see this through even if I die. Too many people are counting on you. You can't fail them because of me. I won't allow it." She gave him a stern look. "Promise me, Alexander. Swear on your love for me that you will not give up, no matter what happens to me."

He nodded but couldn't form any words past the lump in his throat.

"I need you to say it, Alexander," she said.

He nodded again as tears slid down his face. "I promise," he said through a sob and then put his forehead on her stomach and cried softly for several minutes.

After he regained his composure, he helped her sit up to drink the potion. Her arm was still sore but she felt well enough to get up for breakfast.

Kevin woke when she sat up, and he smiled over at his sister. "How're you feeling, Sis?"

"I've been better," she said with a wince at the pain in her shoulder.

One by one everyone else trickled out of the sleeping chambers that surrounded the large sitting room. They treated Isabel gently, timidly asking how she felt and looking at her with sorrow—until she stood up with her green eyes flashing.

"I'm not dead yet!" she said. "Stop looking at me like I am!"

Alexander actually smiled. Even in the face of doom she had a fire in her that awed him. "All right, Isabel, but I think we should change our plans and head for Blackstone Keep right away. If anyone can help you, the wizards can."

"No!" she said firmly. "We have a mission to complete and I intend to help you do that until I can't. We're going to the Reishi Keep and we should leave today."

"Still as bossy as ever, I see," Kevin said to his sister with a sad smile.

"More. I am a Queen, you know," Isabel said with mock haughtiness. "Now let's go get breakfast. I'm starving."

Alexander didn't press the issue. She seemed to be feeling well enough and she was in good spirits, so he decided to set aside his desire to drop everything else and find a way to save her, although he fully intended to come back to it. He wasn't going to give up on her, no matter what she said.

When they emerged from their suite of rooms, there was an ordinary-looking man waiting for them in the hall. He bowed formally with a practiced but empty smile. "I am Administrator Crandall, at your service, My Lord. If I may, I would like to discuss the transition of power that will result from Regent Landon's death."

Alexander saw in a glance that he was a courtier who viewed words as tools of manipulation and valued power over all else.

He didn't really want to deal with such things but he knew Kevin would need a few people around him who understood the workings of the court, so he motioned for the man to follow them as they made their way to the dining room. The halls of the keep were patrolled by Rangers who took no chances. Isabel was one of their own and she'd been harmed by an assassin who was still on the loose. Kevin's Second had deftly managed to insinuate the Rangers into every facet of keep operations literally overnight. The young man looked like he hadn't slept a wink but he was steady on his feet and offered Kevin a detailed report on the status of the defenses and the extent of their coordination with the city guard.

Administrator Crandall looked a little nervous as they walked over the blood-stained section of the carpet where Landon and his guard force had been slain the night before. Alexander pretended he didn't notice the dark stains.

"Administrator Crandall, are you well versed in the workings of Southport?" Alexander asked while they walked.

"Yes, My Lord. I have served in court for many years."

"Good. I've appointed Kevin Alaric as the new Regent," Alexander said. Isabel gave him a sidelong glance. She hadn't heard that her brother had been assigned the responsibility of running a territory. "I expect you to provide him with honest and forthright advice about the operations of the city. He will require your experience and assistance."

"As you wish, Lord Alexander, but this is most unusual," Crandall said smoothly. "The nobles will expect to be consulted in the selection of a new regent and will be most resistant otherwise."

"I imagine," Alexander said, "but nonetheless, they will support and obey Regent Alaric or I will impose consequences on them and their holdings. We are at war. For the time being, I require a regent in Southport whom I know and trust.

"At my earliest convenience, I will consult with them regarding the selection of a permanent territorial governor. Until then, Regent Alaric is the Master of Southport. Your first task will be to help him secure the petty nobles' oaths of loyalty and to coordinate with each landholder to provide a steady flow of supplies to our forces in the south."

Clearly this wasn't going as Crandall had planned. His colors gave away his discomfort over the sudden disruption of politics as usual. Without his second sight, Alexander would have been totally unable to read the man; his face revealed nothing.

They reached the dining hall and Alexander stopped to face Crandall. "In fact, I'd like you to summon the petty nobles to a council meeting today so that Regent Alaric can introduce himself and explain to them the new political reality of Southport. That will be all." Alexander hated dealing with people like Crandall and he had far more important things on his mind than the concerns of courtiers.

Breakfast was lavish bordering on wasteful, but it was also delicious. The long banquet table was set with eggs, toasted bread, fluffy biscuits, sausages, bacon, sliced ham, potatoes fried with onions and peppers, six kinds of jam, butter, milk, hot tea, and three types of juice. The servants were attentive to the point of annoyance. Clearly, Landon liked to be pampered and waited on hand and foot.

Once they had finished eating, Alexander again tried to broach the subject of returning to Blackstone Keep.

"Isabel, I want to take you back to the Keep so the wizards can try to extract the poison."

She shook her head adamantly. "Absolutely not. The Sovereign Stone is too important. Look, we can make it to the Reishi Keep in a week, then sail to Northport and be back to Blackstone Keep within three weeks at the outside. You said you already sent a message to the wizards to start looking for a cure. What difference does it make if I'm there or not?"

"I don't know if it makes a difference, but I know I don't want to take the chance. What if we get delayed?"

She smiled softly but with determination. She'd made up her mind and Alexander could see in her green eyes that he wasn't going to change it. "If we get delayed, then I will spend my last days with the man that I love trying to save a world worth saving."

"Don't be so stubborn, Isabel," Kevin said. "Can't you see he's trying to save you? Please, just let him." He was of a similar mind. The world be damned— Isabel came first.

She shook her head slowly. "I've made up my mind. I'm going with Alexander and that's that."

Kevin sighed, "I know, but I had to try."

By afternoon they were sailing away from Southport aboard the Angellica. She was the flagship of the Southport navy, a big man-o-war with three masts and dozens of sails. She also had two banks of oars and a crew of rowers capable of making good speed even when the air was still. She was armed with catapults fore and aft as well as three heavy ballistae on each side.

The Angellica was built for war and had quarters for a platoon of marines in addition to a full crew complement. Alexander brought thirty Rangers selected by Kevin for their skill and experience. They were armed to the teeth with swords, spears, and composite bows. Alexander was confident that they were as well prepared as they could be for any enemy they happened to encounter.

Captain Targa commanded the ship with crisp and clear orders that were obeyed with speed and precision. He was clearly a man of experience, both with the ocean and with military matters. He was no-nonsense and plainspoken. Alexander decided he liked the man.

When Alexander boarded, Captain Targa was waiting for him at the top of the gangplank. He appraised Alexander openly before nodding permission to come aboard.

"Lord Alexander, you are the King of Ruatha, but I am master of this boat. While we're at sea I expect you and your people to obey my orders without question or hesitation. There are forces greater than the whim and will of political leaders in this world and one of those forces happens to be the ocean. It doesn't care if you're a King, it'll drown you just the same."

Alexander smiled broadly and nodded, offering the captain his hand. "I wouldn't have it any other way, Captain. I suspect we'll get along just fine."

He spent the first hour of the journey standing on the bow of the ship with Isabel and Chloe, talking quietly and enjoying the ocean air. Once they were well underway, a deckhand found them and invited them to the captain's mess.

As Alexander entered the room, he had to catch himself on the doorframe as the boat rolled over a wave. The captain smiled a little at that. The mess was a small room with a table just big enough to seat three on a side and one at either end. It was made of stout, rough-cut boards coated with several layers of lacquer, and the entire thing was bolted to the floor. The benches and chairs were bolted down as well.

The cupboards were closed and latched and the counters on either side of the room were bare and clean. Captain Targa stood when they entered and motioned for them to sit.

"We're underway and well out of port," Captain Targa said. "What's our destination?"

Alexander had deliberately withheld that information from the people in Southport. With the exception of Kevin, there was no one in the city he trusted and he didn't want to risk Commander P'Tal discovering his intentions, although he worried that Phane already knew where he was going. The Reishi Prince seemed to have access to information in a way that made Alexander wonder if he didn't have some means of clairvoyance as well.

He had played the message delivered to Landon by Kludge over and over in his mind, trying to find some reasonable explanation for why Phane had changed his orders to allow Alexander safe passage. The only thing that made sense was that Phane knew Alexander had the ability to retrieve the Sovereign Stone, and he was planning on taking it from him the moment it was back in the world of time and substance.

He fixed the captain with his golden eyes. "We're going to the Reishi Isle."

Captain Targa looked at him incredulously with his mouth agape. "No, we're not." he said firmly. "That's suicide and I won't risk my crew or this ship in those waters." He stood as if to leave, but Alexander grabbed him by the wrist and fixed him with his now glittering eyes.

"Sit down, Captain," Alexander said quietly. "You will take me to the Reishi Isle because the future depends on it."

Captain Targa's face contorted with anger but also with curiosity. He sat down without looking away from Alexander. "Anyone who's spent any time on the water knows that ships don't return from that island. It's guarded by those cursed wyvern riders and they don't bargain or ask questions. They just sink any ship that wanders into the shallows."

"Be that as it may, Captain, that's where we're going," Alexander said. "Tell me more about these wyvern riders."

Captain Targa took a deep breath and let it out with a huff. "Wyverns are like dragons, only smaller and without the fire. They fly out of one of the fortress islands that ring the Reishi Isle. Legend says those fortresses were called up out of the ocean and carved with magic to provide the Reishi Isle with a defensive line against any naval attack. For as long as men have been sailing, those wyverns and their riders have patrolled the skies around the Reishi Isle and attacked any ship foolish enough to get too close."

Alexander looked over at Isabel and shook his head. "It's never easy."

She smiled and put her hand on his across the table. "Captain, what do you know about the riders themselves?" she asked.

He shook his head. "Not much, I'm afraid. They don't make small talk. When they see a ship in the shallows, they attack. If you stay out in the deep ocean and hold your course around the island, they leave you alone."

"So they're not wanton killers. They have a purpose," Alexander mused.

Chloe buzzed into existence and came to rest standing in the middle of the table. Captain Targa's eyes went wide. Alexander had asked Chloe to remain out of sight but clearly she thought the captain could be trusted or she wouldn't have revealed herself.

"I know of the wyverns, My Love," she said. "Or at least I know of their origins. I cannot speak to their current purpose. They were bred by the Reishi to provide a defense against attack from the ocean or air. At the end of the Reishi War, there were thousands of them. They swarmed the skies and sank any craft that didn't have the permission of the Reishi Sovereign to be in his waters."

Alexander smiled at Chloe and the look she was getting from Captain Targa. "Captain, I'd like to introduce Chloe."

She curtsied formally and smiled at the look of awe and wonder on the captain's face.

"I've seen a great many things on the open ocean, but in all my years I never imagined I would see a fairy," Captain Targa said reverently. "I always thought that fairies were just a myth or the legend of a long-dead race of enchanted beings that had faded from the world."

"We are quite real," Chloe said as she flew up and tapped him on the nose.

He backed up, a little startled at how quickly she could move and at the fact that she was actually real, and then a smile grew across his face.

"Lady Chloe, it is a privilege and an honor to meet you. You are most welcome aboard the Angellica."

"Thank you, Captain. You have a beautiful vessel. I have inspected your defenses and it appears that you are very well armed," Chloe said.

"We are, but not against those wyverns. They attack from the sky with their spiked tails, and some of the riders wield magic." Captain Targa shook his head. "We might be able to defend against a patrol of two, but the moment we pose a real threat, they'll come back with a dozen or more and then we're sunk, literally."

"Is it safe to assume that the riders command the wyverns?" Isabel asked.

Captain Targa nodded. "Wyverns aren't terribly smart. Don't get me wrong, they're cunning and clever but they can't speak like a dragon. It's said that in the first moments after a wyvern hatches, it will bond to a rider for life. And they're protective and obedient."

Alexander and Isabel shared a look. "It would help to know why the riders guard the isle. If we knew their reasoning, maybe we could strike a bargain," Isabel said.

"That would require a conversation," Captain Targa said. "I've never heard of them stopping to chat. Either they're high overhead watching your course or they're attacking your boat."

"It sounds like we need to prepare for a battle then," Alexander said.

Captain Targa harrumphed. "Let's just say we get in past them and you get to shore. Then what? They aren't going to stop trying to kill you just because you made landfall. And what of my ship then? I can turn and run. Maybe I make it, but even if I do, you're stranded on the deadliest scrap of dirt in the world. If the stories of the wyverns aren't enough to keep ships away, then the myths and rumors of the things that haunt the Reishi Isle certainly are. That place is said to be home to unspeakable creatures, dark beasts that have no business in the world of the living."

Alexander and Isabel shared another look—this time they were thinking of the Nether Gate and wondering if it was somewhere on the Reishi Isle. In the back of Alexander's mind he knew time was running out. He needed to get to the Reishi Keep and then back to Blackstone Keep as quickly as possible, both to save Isabel and to put the Sovereign Stone in the Bloodvault where it would be permanently out of Phane's reach.

Then a thought struck him like a lightning bolt. There was a shade with Jataan P'Tal. If the commander of the Reishi Protectorate knew where Alexander was going, the shade would probably make the journey with him. If the Nether Gate was on the Reishi Isle, then the shade would be one very large step closer to unleashing a flood of darkness into the world.

The more he thought about it, the more certain he became that his fear was well founded. It stood to reason that Malachi Reishi would have put the Nether Gate somewhere on the Reishi Isle so he could protect it and control it. When he factored in the captain's account of dark beasts living on the Reishi Isle, it made even more sense, except the Gate was supposed to be closed. If it was closed, then how did creatures from the netherworld get there without being summoned? And if the Nether Gate was open, then why did Nicolai Atherton warn him about it so urgently? Alexander took a deep breath and imposed stillness on his mind. He had so many questions and too few answers.

What he did know for certain was that he had to make it to the Reishi Keep and then back to Blackstone Keep without being captured or killed. That was more than enough to worry about for the moment. The Nether Gate would have to wait. Even as he made his decision, he knew it might bring doom to the world. One threat at a time, he tried to reassure himself.

"Whatever the obstacles, whatever the cost, I have to get to the Reishi Keep," Alexander said.

Captain Targa shook his head in frustration and exasperation. "What's so important that you would risk so much?"

Alexander considered for a moment before he answered. He decided to be straightforward with the captain. He was asking the man to risk his ship, his crew, and his life. "Captain Targa, I'm going to retrieve the Sovereign Stone."

The captain whistled. "As I hear it, the Stone is outside the world of time and substance. Wouldn't we all be better off if it stayed where it is?"

"Probably, but Phane has already tried to get his hands on it twice, and I doubt he'll stop trying until he succeeds. If he gets the Stone, the Seven Isles will fall to him. I have to put it out of his reach for good."

"What makes you think he isn't just waiting for you to bring it out of the aether so he can take it? It could be you're playing right into his hands."

Alexander nodded. "That's a distinct possibility but it's a risk I have to take. If I leave it where it is, sooner or later Phane will find a way to get it." Alexander fixed the captain with a look of steady resolve. "One way or another, Captain, we're going to that island. What I need from you is passage there and back."

Captain Targa was silent for a long moment. He held Alexander's gaze without flinching before he nodded and a grim smile slowly spread across his face. "It would make for quite a story," he mused. "My catapults are useless against an attack from the air, but I have six ballistae that can swivel and fire nearly straight up. Might be enough to bring a wyvern down—if we can actually hit one, that is. Are your Rangers any good in a fight?" he asked with a little bit of mischief.

Isabel started to bristle before she saw the edge of his mouth turn up. "They'll stand their ground, whatever comes," she said proudly.

"Very well then, we have some planning to do," Captain Targa said. "Truth be told, I'm pretty confident we can run their defenses and get you onshore before they can muster their forces. I'm far more concerned with what happens after that."

"Once we're away on longboats, you should turn and run," Alexander said. "I suspect they'll let you go and focus on us. Once you're out of their sight, stop and wait. I'll send word when to head back in to pick us up."

Captain Targa frowned. "Not meaning any disrespect, but how do you expect to send word across several leagues of open ocean?"

Alexander smiled. "Either Chloe will come and tell you we're ready or a forest hawk named Slyder will bring you a message. Or I'll come to you in your sleep, so don't dismiss messages you receive in your dreams."

Captain Targa looked bewildered. "I won't pretend to understand how you might do such a thing, but I'll pay attention to my dreams and tell my men to watch out for a hawk."

"Slyder's perched on the yardarm at the moment," Isabel said. "I'll introduce you later this afternoon so you know what he looks like."

There was a knock at the door. A moment later, it opened and a grizzled man with weather-worn skin and a week's worth of graying stubble stuck his head in.

"Captain, rough seas ahead. Do we have a course?"

"Due west, steady as she goes." He gave his man a stern look to forestall any question or protest, but Alexander could see fear in the man's colors.

He nodded curtly. "Aye, aye, Captain, due west, steady as she goes," he said before closing the door.

"My crew is going to be afraid of the waters you're taking them into. Don't get me wrong, they'll follow their orders but they're going to talk. What can I tell them about our destination and purpose?"

"Nothing," Alexander said. "Phane has spies everywhere and ways of gathering information that I don't yet understand. The fewer people who know our course, the better chance we have of getting there in one piece. Fortunately, I have my own ways of gathering information, as well. I may be able to learn more about these wyvern riders. Hopefully, I can discover something that will give us an advantage."

"As you wish. For now I need to go take a look at the weather," Captain Targa said as he stood.

Alexander and Isabel followed him out of his mess and onto the foredeck of the big man-o-war. Anatoly was on the bow with Jack, looking out over the darkening ocean. Ominous black clouds clung to the horizon. Lightning flickered through the storm to the west. The deckhands were busy preparing for the coming turbulence. Isabel looked up and motioned to Slyder. He tipped off the yardarm and landed lightly on her forearm.

"Captain Targa, I'd like you to meet Slyder," Isabel said, holding her hawk up proudly.

"That's quite a well-trained bird you have there, Lady Isabel," he said admiringly.

She smiled. "Oh, he hasn't really been trained. He's my familiar."

He shook his head in wonder. "Today just keeps bringing me surprises." He chuckled, then turned his attention to the ocean, appraising the sky and the rolling water for a moment.

"It'll be two days before we're at risk of drawing the wyvern riders' attention. Once we cross into the shallows, it's a league or so to land. I can only take you about halfway there or I risk running aground. I have six longboats, each rated for a dozen men plus a commander and a rudder man. Three boats should get you and your platoon of Rangers onshore. I'd guess it'll take half an hour at most to make it from the ship to the beach, especially with the tide at your back. For now, I suggest you and your friends retire below decks or you're going to get wet. My crew will be in to check on you from time to time, but I'm going to be busy until we're through the worst of this storm."

"Thank you, Captain," Alexander said before heading to his cabin. The seas began to swell and the ship started pitching with the rolling water. Again, Alexander decided he preferred to be on land. His footing was better and he didn't have to worry about drowning.

CHAPTER 40

The rain battered against the ship and the wind tore at the sails. Alexander and Isabel held each other in their bunk during the night, trying to overcome feelings of total helplessness before the fury of the storm. He thought about the statement the captain had made when he stepped aboard. The truth of it was indisputable. He was just a man. The power that had been thrust upon him was nothing in the face of the raw and untamable power of the world around him.

The storm moved on to the south by midafternoon of the next day. Alexander was grateful to see the light grey clouds overhead instead of the black rain-laden thunderheads. The seas calmed as well, which was more important to Alexander. He'd tried to use his clairvoyance but with the rolling waves, he was unable to find the place of peace and detachment that led to the firmament.

Every time he got close, the boat would pitch and he'd have to catch himself to keep from falling over. He was anxious to learn what Commander P'Tal was doing. He feared they were both making the same voyage and he wasn't looking forward to facing the battle mage.

With the fury of the storm past, the captain raised more sail and the ship picked up speed. During the torrential rains and tearing winds, the ship had made little headway. Instead, the crew had been fighting to maintain a heading that kept the boat pointed into the swells to avoid being hit broadside by a wave and swamped or capsized.

Alexander found that he admired the captain. He was a skilled sailor who understood his boat and the ocean. During the storm he remained on deck, barking orders to his weary and rain-soaked crew. Once the worst of it was nothing more than a dark stain on the horizon, he began rotating his crew so they could sleep and recover some of their strength.

Alexander sat on his pack in his cabin and slowed his breathing while relaxing each muscle in his body with deliberate intent. Within a few minutes he was immersed in his meditative routine, facing and dismissing each stray thought that entered his mind until he arrived at the place of empty-mindedness that was his doorway to the firmament.

Then he was everywhere at once, floating on the ocean of limitless possibility. He listened to the music of creation for a moment before focusing his attention on his task. The fear and emotional turmoil was greater than he had ever heard before. People were becoming aware of the inevitability of war; their anxiety was reflected in the cacophony of thoughts, feeling, and events all taking place in the moment where the wave of the firmament crested into reality. The collective angst of the world only served to give greater urgency to Alexander's purpose.

He focused on Blackstone Keep, and his awareness formed above the mountainous fortress. The place was busy with wagon loads of supplies moving up the long road into the Keep. The garrison had grown and the patrols in the surrounding area were frequent and well organized. Off in the distance to the

north, Alexander could see a legion of his soldiers encamped on the open plain and
to the southwest he saw another large force positioned around the Reishi Gate.

Alexander moved into the Keep to Kelvin's workshop. The big mage was
busy at his furnace, shaping a breastplate made of dragon steel. He looked tired yet
driven to complete his work. Alexander went to the message board. What he saw
stirred up such a torrent of emotion that he nearly lost his focus.

The message said they thought they had a cure for Isabel's poison, but
they wouldn't know for sure until they tested it and then went on to say that
several wizards were hard at work looking for alternatives in the event that their
first plan failed.

Alexander drifted up through the Keep and into the sky, buoyed by the
good news, and floated high above the island of Ruatha looking down at the land
and people he was responsible for protecting. It was a daunting thought. The island
was huge and the population numbered in the tens of millions. So many people
counting on him.

He slipped back into the firmament and thought of Jataan P'Tal. His
awareness came into focus in the cabin of a ship rolling violently on a storm-
racked sea. Commander P'Tal was lying in his bunk, holding on to the headboard
to keep from being tossed to the floor as the ocean roiled around the Andalian
warship.

Alexander withdrew from P'Tal's cabin and took in the ship from above.
They were heading northwest through the same storm that had battered the
Angellica the night before.

Jataan P'Tal was headed to the Reishi Isle. Alexander pushed through the
ship and discovered that it was a Lancer transport vessel. The lower deck was
designed to transport the giant rhone steeds. It looked like six had died recently,
each one with broken legs—the rough seas were taking their toll on the enemy.
Alexander fleetingly hoped that the ocean would claim the ship and Jataan P'Tal
with it, but he knew better than to count on it.

He pulled away from the warship and quickly moved high in the sky over
the Seven Isles. He watched the world recede below him until he could see the
entire known world as if it were a map. It took him a moment to orient himself
because the actual shapes of the islands were slightly different than they were
depicted on the charts he'd seen all his life.

He found the Reishi Isle and drifted closer until he could make out the
shapes of two of the fortress islands that stood watch around the main island. He
went to the first to find the deserted husk of a fortress that hadn't been occupied
for many hundreds of years. The second was home to thousands of sea birds, but
no people or wyverns. The next was shrouded in clouds and took a while to find. It
too was empty except for some foul-looking creatures that Alexander had never
seen before and had no desire to ever meet in person.

The next island took even longer to find; it was cloaked by the edge of
the storm, with dark clouds reaching down to touch the top of a giant artificial
plateau. Alexander caught a glimpse of something big flying across the sky just
below the clouds. As he approached, he saw that the fortress island was
constructed much the same as the others. The place looked like it was riddled with
chambers and passageways cut through the stone. Sheer cliffs rose over a thousand
feet above the water, and there were countless openings where wyverns could

enter or exit. The flat top of the plateau was more than two miles across.

Alexander moved toward the structure and saw that it was indeed inhabited by people and wyverns all working together for their self-determined purpose. Pairs of wyverns carrying well-armed and armored riders on elaborate saddles came and went as if on patrol. He pushed in toward the cliff wall, but the moment he crossed the threshold of one of the entrance bays, he found his awareness suddenly scattered into the firmament.

It took a long time and a great effort to draw his awareness back into a whole again. It felt much like the time when Phane had scattered his awareness. He had to painstakingly gather the scraps of his essence before he could reunite with his body. His eyes came open with a start. Chloe was standing on the edge of the table, looking at him sternly.

"You know I don't like it when you do that. It's like you don't even exist anymore. It makes me afraid."

"I'm sorry, Chloe. I don't do it to worry you—sometimes I need to look in on our friends and enemies."

"What did you learn?" Isabel asked from their bunk.

Alexander smiled at her with a renewed sense of hope. "The wizards think they have a way to extract the poison."

She sat up with a look of relief. She had tried to hide her fear, but Alexander knew she was worrying about the poison almost constantly. The poison was a nagging source of anxiety for Alexander as well. The news that the wizards could help her took a huge weight off his soul.

"The bad news is, Commander P'Tal is headed for the Reishi Isle with a bunch of Andalian Lancers. I suspect Phane knows our plan and he's sent P'Tal to take the Stone from us once we have it. Worse, I tried to look inside the wyvern riders' fortress and my consciousness was scattered into the firmament. It took me a while to find my way back."

Both Chloe and Isabel looked alarmed at the danger he'd been in.

"My Love," Chloe said, "the firmament is a dangerous place, especially for one with so little experience with magic as you. Please don't send your mind there anymore."

"I agree with Chloe," Isabel said. "You can't risk getting lost and it sounds like you're vulnerable to forces beyond our understanding while you're there. Until you learn more, I think you should stop using your clairvoyance unless it's absolutely necessary."

Alexander thought about it for a few moments before nodding slowly. "There's definitely a lot I don't understand about the firmament, but I think the only way I'm going to learn more is with practice. Still, I'll stop using my clairvoyance if I don't have to. At least now we know that the wyvern riders' island is protected by magic, for whatever that's worth."

"Did you see any wyverns?" Isabel asked.

Alexander nodded. "They ride in patrols of two and they're well armed and armored. Even in the storm, they were still coming and going. The wyverns are similar to dragons except their hide is dark grey and looks leathery instead of scaled. They're about half the size of Tanis, but their tails are quite a bit longer and end in a bony spike. Their hind feet are taloned like a raptor's and look powerful. I doubt they'd have any trouble snatching up a horse and flying off with it."

"Maybe we should have a plan before we run into them," Isabel suggested.

They went up on deck and found the captain. He was standing at the wheel and looking off toward the horizon. The crew was working diligently at myriad tasks, from clearing the deck of standing water to adjusting the sails. A number of the Rangers were on deck as well—some at the railing waiting to be sick, although the ocean was much calmer and the skies were clearing.

"We should be within launch range by midmorning tomorrow," Captain Targa said when Alexander and Isabel approached. "The storm cost us some time but not much."

"Excellent," Alexander said. "I think we need to plan our approach and our defense so everyone is working together when the wyvern riders come."

"Agreed. Why don't we meet in my mess for dinner and discuss it then?" Captain Targa suggested.

Later that evening, Alexander and his friends sat around the little table with Captain Targa and Lieutenant Wyatt, the commander of the Ranger platoon. After dinner was eaten and the table was cleared of everything except a jug of rum, Alexander recounted his clairvoyant experience and described the wyverns in detail.

They spent several hours discussing the best way to meet the inevitable attack. Every capability was discussed and every defensive measure considered. Ultimately, it came down to ballistae and arrows. The wyverns were unlikely to actually land on the ship's deck, so blades and spears would do little good. At best, they might get a swipe at the underside of a wyvern or maybe a slash at its tail.

Alexander wanted to stop them short of actually doing any damage and drive them off with arrows. He knew the first attack would probably come from a patrol of two. It was the second attack that worried him. He wanted to be onshore before they came in strength. More importantly, he wanted the Angellica to be well outside their area of interest in hopes that they would leave the ship alone.

Alexander assigned the Rangers to the catapult platforms fore and aft and had Anatoly man one of the ballistae—he was familiar enough with the weapon to make good use of it. Alexander, Isabel, and Abigail would take the crow's nest with their bows. He knew that he and Isabel might not be able to take down one of the riders, but he was confident that Abigail would be able to cause real damage with her magical bow. If they could bring down the first two that attacked, they might be able to make landfall before reinforcements arrived.

With their plan set, Alexander made the rounds to talk with the crew and the Rangers. He wanted to thank them for their service and reassure them that they would be victorious and that their purpose was both right and necessary.

The Rangers were reserved but ready for the fight. They knew the stakes and had volunteered for this voyage. The crew was a little more hesitant, especially since Alexander wouldn't tell them why he was taking them into such dangerous waters. But they were all loyal to their captain, and since he was convinced of the need to approach the forbidden island, they would do what they could to keep their ship afloat.

Alexander slept well that night, holding Isabel in their cozy little bunk. The gentle rolling of the ocean actually served to calm and relax him for the first time since he'd been at sea. He woke to a clear day with calm seas and clean-smelling salt air. At breakfast, Captain Targa informed him they should start looking for the wyvern riders within the hour. Not half an hour later, Alexander was perched high up in the crow's nest with Isabel and Abigail. They had a barrel of arrows and the best view around, save for Slyder who orbited high overhead scanning the horizon for the enemy.

"Slyder can see the Reishi Isle," Isabel said. It was still a little too far off for Alexander to discern land from ocean. A few minutes later, Slyder screeched.

"Here they come," Isabel said, pointing off toward the southwest. "They're heading straight for us."

Alexander signaled down to the captain and the Rangers. The deck burst into a flurry of activity as everyone made ready to meet the coming attack. It seemed to take a long time for the wyverns to arrive. They made a pass high overhead. When the Angellica didn't change course, they turned as one and descended to a lower altitude before making another pass. Alexander held his right hand up and open, a sign of goodwill to the passing wyvern riders, a man and a woman. The woman looked down toward him with intensity and surprise. They coaxed their wyverns to gain altitude and wheeled for another pass. This time their intent was clear. They meant to attack.

They made a run straight for the crow's nest. It looked like they'd decided that Alexander was the target. He wondered why they had singled him out on a ship bristling with weaponry. A moment later, he heard the sharp twang of Abigail's bow as she let the first arrow fly. It sailed out over the water and hit the wyvern squarely in the chest. The beast roared but held its course.

Alexander counted the moments before the wyvern was in range. The ballistae fired, and a moment later he and Isabel released their arrows along with a second from Abigail. Then the platoon of Rangers sent up a volley. The wyvern shrieked in rage as the deadly hail of arrows peppered its chest and wings, but it didn't stop.

Quite suddenly, Alexander felt his awareness plunge into the firmament. He was not on the surface of the ocean of possibility but in the quiet endlessness beneath the wave of creation. He knew what was happening so he didn't resist the strange sensation. Instead, he watched the wave of potential that crested in the present moment as it sped up. He was seeing the future. The few times this had happened, the knowledge he gained had saved him.

He watched the wyvern fly just over the crow's nest and snap its bone-bladed tail with such force that it shattered the top of the mast, breaking off the crow's nest and casting them into the water—broken, bloodied, and unconscious. It was a terrifying display of power, but what came next was even worse. He saw the second wyvern hook its wing under the yardarm and drive the entire ship onto its side. Just as the wyvern started to free itself from the sails of the sinking ship, Alexander was back in his body and watching the enemy come toward him.

Everything slowed down. He dropped his bow and pulled Abigail away from the coming attack while stepping in front of Isabel and drawing the Thinblade. He watched the shadow of the wyvern pass overhead; its tail flexed and snapped down toward the crow's nest. Just a moment before it struck, Alexander lashed out with the Thinblade and cleanly severed the wyvern's tail. The bladed end was still coming at them with force and it crashed into the mast supporting the crow's nest but didn't have the energy to do more than send reverberations through the entire ship. The wyvern screamed in pain and rage but passed over their heads and out of arrow range in a moment.

Alexander leaned over the edge of the railing and extended his sword to strike the second wyvern across the shoulder. The rider had intended to use the wyvern's weight and momentum to catch the main mast and drive the boat over onto its side, but the creature was met by the Thinblade instead.

The entire wing of the beast came off in a clean line. The wyvern shrieked in panicked fear as it spiraled off the side of the ship and into the water where it struggled in vain to stay afloat before slipping beneath the waves, taking its rider into the depths with it. Its severed wing fell across the foredeck and was quickly cast overboard by the Rangers and the crew. The other wyvern cast a look of fear and anger down at them before beating its wings and gaining altitude as it banked and made straight for the fortress.

Alexander looked down at the captain, who returned the look with renewed respect. He gave Alexander a firm nod, then started barking orders at his crew. Moments later the sails were full of wind and the oars were pulling the Angellica toward the Reishi Isle.

CHAPTER 41

The ship raced directly into the shallows as far as the captain dared before he dropped his sails, turned the rudder hard to starboard, and ordered the oars withdrawn from the port side, while the longboats were virtually dropped into the water.

Alexander and his friends scrambled down rope nets and boarded the longboats with the Rangers. They turned toward the shore a mile or more away and started rowing. Alexander, Jack, and Isabel were in one boat with eleven Rangers. Anatoly, Lucky, and Abigail were in the next boat with another eleven Rangers. The remaining Rangers filled the last longboat commanded by Lieutenant Wyatt.

The Angellica raised her sails and put her oars into the water to complete her turn and race away from the Reishi Isle. They weren't a hundred feet from the ship when Isabel warned that more wyvern riders were coming.

She pointed off to the south. "Looks like a dozen."

Chloe spun into a ball of scintillating white light. Alexander could feel her worry and fear in his mind. He did his best to reassure her, but he knew as well as she did that they wouldn't stand a chance against twelve wyverns, especially if they got caught on the water.

"Make best speed to the shoreline," Alexander shouted over the sound of the surf in the distance. "The enemy is coming in force."

He could see the fear in everyone's colors but he also saw resolve. The Rangers rowed with rhythmic order, bringing the longboats closer to the beach in surges as they pulled against the water. Alexander watched the enemy appear on the horizon. He felt useless. Every oar was manned. Isabel guided the boat at the rudder. All he could do was wait for the enemy to arrive, hoping against hope that they would make it to land before the wyvern riders descended on them.

The wyverns grew on the horizon until Alexander counted twelve. Two broke off and headed for the Angellica which was now running at full speed away from the Reishi Isle. Alexander silently wished them best speed and hoped the enemy would spare them. He knew they wouldn't spare him. Ten wyvern riders lined up in a column and began gradually diving toward the row of longboats, no doubt to attack with their deadly bone-bladed tails.

Alexander's boat was the first in the row. They were still a hundred feet from the shore as he nocked an arrow and waited, watching the wyverns build frightening speed for their attack run. He knew the sturdy wooden longboats would be smashed to splinters in the first pass. An arrow streaked past him from behind; Abigail had made her first shot, and it was a good one. It hit the lead wyvern in the right eye and drove into its skull to the feathers.

It pitched forward and careened into the water not fifty feet from Alexander's boat. The sudden wave created by the impact capsized the boat and sent everyone aboard flying into the water. A moment later the next wyvern lashed out at the empty boat with its tail. The keel of the boat shattered under the force of the blow, leaving two broken sections and a field of splinters and kindling scattered across the water.

Alexander went under and found that they were in six feet of water. In the back of his mind, he told himself it could be worse. He pushed off the ocean floor, bursting through the surface just in time to see everyone in the second boat bail out in near panic a moment before a wyvern smashed it into driftwood with one well-placed lash of its tail. The water was full of Rangers and his friends, all struggling to reach the shore in armor and waterlogged clothes and boots.

The Rangers in the third boat had stopped rowing. The rowers on the port side were kneeling while those on the starboard side were standing. All were armed with composite bows and fired on Lieutenant Wyatt's command. The next wyvern in line banked sharply to avoid the barrage of arrows. Lieutenant Wyatt ordered his men into the water the moment the arrows were loose. They all made it clear and swam for shore as their boat was shattered into splinters by a wyvern's tail.

Alexander looked around frantically for Isabel and Abigail. He heard Slyder screech overhead in distress. Anatoly burst from the water and took a breath only to be pulled under again by the weight of his breastplate. A wave came in and pushed everyone close enough to shore so that once it passed, they could all stand on the shifting sands with their heads just above water. Alexander heard a scream and whirled to see a Ranger snatched up by the powerful claws of another wyvern. The beast savagely dug its talons into him and dropped his lifeless body back into the surf from a height of fifty feet.

A loud slapping splash drew Alexander's attention in the other direction. Another of the terrifying flying monsters cut a Ranger in half with a tail-strike.

Another wave washed them closer to shore. Now Alexander was in water to his waist. He looked around for his wife and sister and saw them thirty or forty feet away. Just before he could start moving in their direction, a Ranger called out in warning, pointing up and behind him. He refocused his attention on his all around sight as he whirled to face the threat, drawing the Thinblade in the process.

He spun just enough to avoid being crushed by the whip strike and slashed out with his sword, cleaving the last several feet of the wyvern's tail. The section that came free hit the water with such force that the shock wave knocked Alexander from his feet.

Another wyvern tried to snatch Anatoly up with its deadly talons, but the old man-at-arms saw it coming and was prepared. He ducked low into the surf while planting the butt of his axe in the sand and directing the long top spike up into the underside of the wyvern's foot. It screamed in pain and beat its wings with a powerful stroke to lift it away from Anatoly. Another wave washed them into shallow water just knee-deep. They ran through the surf toward the solid footing of the beach, scanning the sky for the enemy. Another Ranger fell to a tail-strike. Another was snatched up and mutilated before being dropped from dozens of feet in the air.

The first wyverns to strike were wheeling in the sky to make a second pass even as the last of the column passed overhead. Alexander angled toward Isabel and Abigail as he moved toward dry land.

He was looking straight at his wife when the unthinkable happened. A shadow fell over her as a wyvern reached out and grabbed her with its talons. She screamed as the beast beat its wings and gained thirty feet of altitude with one stroke. Alexander and Isabel locked eyes. In that moment they both silently acknowledged their love and commitment. She was in pain, but the wyvern had grabbed her tightly without tearing into her.

"Isabel!" he cried out.

She didn't respond. Alexander stood in shock and disbelief as the wyvern steadily gained altitude and distance with each stroke of its wings. He saw Abigail send an arrow after the beast. Then the surreal scene played itself out again as a wyvern caught Abigail off guard and snatched her up as well. She cried out in surprise. Alexander watched helplessly as the two people he loved most were taken and his world crumbled around him.

He stood still, numbly watching his family recede into the distance when Anatoly tackled him and sent him crashing into the surf as another wyvern's tail slashed through the shallow water and cut a deep gash in the seabed where Alexander had been standing. Anatoly jerked him up and shoved him toward the shore, then turned to face the next attack.

The tail came fast but Anatoly knew what to expect. He'd seen the wyverns' strike enough times to know where to be and where not to be when it came. He whirled with his axe and cleaved the tail of yet another wyvern cleanly off. The creature roared in pain and drove itself into the sky, fleeing the fight. There were five of the beasts left in the air when everyone finally made it to the solid footing of the beach.

Alexander fought through the panic and fear that filled every fiber of his being, brutally shoving his emotions aside. Another wyvern descended on a knot of Rangers. They responded with a volley of arrows and upraised spears. The rider cast a javelin down and killed a Ranger.

The next wyvern to make a pass at Alexander didn't come low enough for a tail-strike. Instead the rider launched a javelin at him forcefully. Alexander stepped aside and pointed the Thinblade up at the enemy.

He was standing on a sandy beach that extended fifty feet from the surf to a craggy cliff rising a hundred feet or more straight up from the sand. With his all around sight, Alexander saw a movement. He looked up just in time to see a rock coming toward him. A dozen or more ganglings on top of the cliff started hurling head-sized rocks down at the men and wyverns fighting on the beach.

The first wyvern to be hit by a rock fell into the surf with a shattered wing. The remaining wyverns withdrew to gain altitude. Alexander pointed up at the ganglings and shouted for everyone to get into the boulder field at the base of the cliff for cover. They raced forward as a hail of deadly stone rain crashed down around them. A few Rangers fell but most made it to the relative safety of the jumble of giant boulders.

Alexander kept a wary eye on the four remaining wyverns. One broke off and went to retrieve the rider of the fallen wyvern and then headed off along the coastline to the south. The three remaining gained enough altitude to make an attack run at the ganglings on top of the cliff. Alexander took advantage of the enemy's distraction and ordered his people to move through the rock field to the north away from the scene of battle.

They made their way through the boulders until they rounded a bend and saw a dark cave at the base of the hundred-foot wall of stone. Alexander knew that it might be inhabited, but he also knew that the wyverns would be back as soon as they'd driven off the ganglings. They needed to find cover, so he made for the opening quickly but cautiously. He breathed a sigh of relief when he held up his vial of night-wisp dust and revealed that the cave was not as deep as it looked but opened into a large round room filled with little tide pools. They took refuge in the safety of the darkness.

Once the rush of battle subsided, the panic and terror of unendurable loss washed over Alexander and he fell to his knees and vomited.

He simply couldn't accept that his wife and sister were gone. The only consolation he could find was that they were both taken alive—the wyverns had clearly demonstrated the ability to rend the life from a person with their talons. He sat on his knees and sobbed without restraint. Lucky came to his side and tried to console him.

Anatoly took Lieutenant Wyatt aside and asked for a head count. Of the thirty Rangers, twenty-one remained. Anatoly ordered him to send scouts to determine if the wyverns and the ganglings were still a threat and to see if any of their packs had washed ashore.

Alexander looked over when he heard a sob and saw Jack trying to keep from breaking down himself. When he saw Alexander looking at him, he shrugged and took a deep breath to steady his voice.

"I'm afraid I have a confession, Alexander. I've come to love Abigail. I regret that I didn't have the courage to face it until just now. She was taken alive, though, so I choose to believe she'll be all right and that I will see her again so I can tell her what's in my heart."

Alexander actually smiled even though he felt like dying. Jack had made a choice to have hope. Alexander resolved to do the same. He looked up at Lucky and saw tears running freely from his watery eyes. Chloe buzzed into existence and flew up to Alexander.

"I'm so sorry, My Love," she said and kissed him on the cheek. "I followed them for a ways—Isabel and Abigail were taken alive and it was clear that the wyvern riders didn't intend to kill them, at least not in the battle."

He sat up at the news and took a deep breath to steady himself. With an act of will, he pushed his fears aside again and focused his mind. "Thank you, Little One. Were they taking them to the fortress island?"

"That's the direction they were heading," Chloe said with an emphatic nod.

Alexander looked over at Jack and they shared a look of hope. "You're wise to hold on to the hope that you'll see her again. She's worth it."

"I know," Jack whispered.

Alexander resolved to believe his sister would return to him, but he was less certain about Isabel. She had only a few weeks before the poison did its damage. Without the aid of the wizards, she would die.

Alexander couldn't overcome the inescapable conclusion that she was lost to him and yet he simply couldn't make himself face that reality no matter how hard he tried. Everything in him rebelled against the thought of it. His guts squirmed and his hands trembled. The lump in his throat threatened to overwhelm him again, so he shoved his feelings aside and focused on simply standing up.

It took an effort almost greater than he could muster to stagger to his feet and look around at the cave. It was filled with a number of Rangers who were all checking their weapons, cleaning the sand out of what equipment they had retained during the fight, and generally preparing for the next battle.

Kevin had chosen these men well. Every one of them was here in this impossible situation because Alexander had brought them here. At the very least, he owed them a leader who wasn't doubled over crying. He wiped the tears from his face and took another deep breath to steady himself.

Two Rangers returned, carrying waterlogged packs and then went back out onto the beach to look for more. Within an hour they reported that they'd retrieved everything that had washed ashore. They also reported that the ganglings and the wyverns had traded shots for a while before the wyverns withdrew south down the coastline and there was no immediate threat that they could see. They spent the next several hours drying, sorting, and cleaning their gear and supplies. Some of the food was wasted but they still had enough for a week or so. Mostly, they just needed to dry everything out so it would be light enough to actually carry. Water-soaked packs were far too heavy to be worth the effort; they would simply exhaust everyone and slow them down.

Isabel's medallion of Glen Morillian had washed ashore in a tangle of broken longboat wood. When a Ranger brought it to him, Alexander struggled to keep his composure as he wrapped it in a piece of cloth and put in into his pouch.

Alexander thought to Chloe, "Little One, I have to go see if I can find Isabel and Abigail. I need to leave my body for a while. I know you don't like it, but I have to do this."

She thought back to him, "I know." He could hear the worry and resignation in her thoughts. "Be careful, My Love."

Alexander sat quietly for several minutes before he could find the peace of mind to even begin his meditation routine. Once he began, it took almost an hour before he found himself in the firmament. He braced himself for the worst before willing his awareness to coalesce near Isabel. It was like running into a wall. Just before he started to become aware of his surroundings, his awareness was scattered into the firmament.

He schooled his emotions and carefully brought himself back to a single point of awareness floating above his own body in the cave. At least he knew where to look for his wife and sister. He floated up through the stone of the cliff several hundred feet into the sky. He saw three dead ganglings at the scene of the battle and several dead Rangers washed up on shore.

He rose higher still, scanning the island for the location of the Reishi Keep. It took him a while to find it; the island was wild and heavily forested in many places. The Keep rose up from a point dead center in the middle of the island and was made of black granite similar to that of Blackstone Keep. No doubt this keep was a magical construction as well. It was surrounded by a swath of open prairie in all directions for at least a league.

When he moved closer, he saw that the Keep itself was smaller than Blackstone but still formidable, with scores of towers, battlements, bridges, and chambers. It was a beautiful structure clearly designed to create an impression of awe in all who looked at it.

When Alexander tried to move his awareness within the confines of the walls, he was once again scattered into the firmament. This time it took even longer to draw himself back together even though he was becoming more experienced at recovering from his essence being torn apart and set adrift on the ocean of possibility.

It was like putting a puzzle back together when the pieces had been hidden all around the world. Each little scrap of his identity was like a beacon. He always started from the place of the witness, where emotion didn't exist. From there he searched out each memory, personality trait, and scrap of character and gathered them back into himself until he felt whole again, and then he spread his intact awareness across the firmament to be sure he hadn't missed anything. When he was confident that he had every part of himself, he tried to move back into his body. What he found terrified him.

He was inhabited by a being without substance yet possessed of such malice and rage that Alexander found himself locked in a battle for his life within his own body.

The unclean nature of the demon was revolting and terrifying. It struggled to hang on, to retain control. Alexander bore down with all the rage and fear of his loss but that only seemed to feed the demon and marginalize his own ability to exert any control over his arms and legs.

Dimly he became aware that he was standing with the Thinblade drawn— two Rangers were dead at his feet. His revulsion at what his body had been used to do only served to strengthen the demon's hold over him.

He thought of Isabel and her ordeal with the demon. At the first thought of her, the demon's grip loosened. Alexander bore in with the greatest power he knew—the power of his love for Isabel. He let it shine like a star in the center of his being, and the demon evaporated with a shriek of anger.

He focused his vision and saw a dozen Rangers arrayed around him, all under Anatoly's command. Lucky was poised to throw a shatter vial at him.

Chloe spun up into a ball of light and pronounced, "He's back!"

Alexander lowered the Thinblade and looked at the two men dead at his feet. He felt sick. He'd been warned that this could happen, yet he hadn't listened. Part of him simply didn't believe it was possible but now he knew. His clairvoyance left him vulnerable and with the Thinblade in his possession, everyone nearby was in danger. He dropped his sword and slumped to his knees, looking at the two loyal Rangers who'd been slaughtered by his own hand. For the second time that day, he cried.

Chapter 42

"You were right, Chloe," he sobbed. "I'm so sorry," he said to the Rangers all looking hesitantly at him. Then he hung his head and cried in shame and anguish. He felt like some indispensable part of him was breaking under the strain of the horrors he'd caused. Chloe spun into a ball of light and he heard her in his mind.

"You didn't kill these men, My Love. The demon did. You drove it away with your love and now it has no power to hurt you again."

He clung to the connection he had with her and wept. She was an endless source of unconditional love which she gave freely and without restraint. Her love nourished his soul until he was capable of facing the men who had sworn him loyalty, men his negligence had betrayed. He stood slowly, with tears still streaming down his face.

Anatoly put a hand on his shoulder and looked him in the eye with a mixture of sadness and relief. "We all know it wasn't you who killed these men."

The Rangers all nodded agreement, but Alexander knew differently. He had allowed it to happen. His carelessness with power had caused unintended consequences of the most serious nature to other human beings. Two good and loyal men had paid with their lives for his negligence. It was a stain on his soul that he would live with forever. He vowed to learn from the experience and to never forget the men who lay dead before him.

Instead of confessing his sins to the men assembled around him, he nodded, not because he wanted to avoid blame but because they needed to see that their leader was still strong enough to lead them. The journey to the Keep would be treacherous and dangerous. The terrain was wild and the denizens of the Reishi Isle were unfriendly at best.

He knelt next to each dead man and took the clasps emblazoned with the Rangers' crest off their cloaks as he offered each a quiet apology and a prayer to the spirits of the light that they would guide and protect them on their journey home.

He knew he shouldn't take the time but he couldn't leave these men for the scavengers, so he ordered the Rangers to build a funeral pyre for all of the dead, both from the battle with the wyverns and the two dead by his hand. They set the blaze and said a brief word of respect for their fallen before heading north along the coastline in search of a way up the cliff and into the interior of the wild island.

The Rangers kept a close eye on the sky and the top of the cliff as they moved through the boulder field. It was slow going, but the large rocks provided some measure of cover and after the battle with the wyverns that was worth more than speed.

Everyone was in a somber mood. Alexander struggled to keep his emotional desolation at bay and focus his mind on the task before him, but his thoughts kept returning to his wife and sister. He could see that his friends were also struggling to deal with their emotions. Lucky and Anatoly had been every bit as much a part of Abigail's life as they had Alexander's, and Jack had come to love Abigail even though he had only recently admitted his feelings for her, even to himself. While Isabel had become the very center of Alexander's life, she had also been welcomed into the family by Alexander's friends and traveling companions.

The Rangers were also feeling the pain of losing so many of their own. These men had trained and served together. They were friends of those who had fallen and they felt the loss deeply. In spite of the emotional turmoil coursing through each and every one of Alexander's party, they remained vigilant and cautious. The island had already demonstrated that it was home to dangerous creatures.

Chloe was more nervous than usual. She was so far away from her home and now Alexander had brought her to the most untamed place in the Seven Isles. She informed him that the island was inhabited by many things from the dark which Alexander took as another piece of evidence that the Nether Gate was here somewhere. He still didn't know what he was going to do about the Gate, but he was sure that the shade traveling with Jataan P'Tal had plans for it and he was equally sure that he had to prevent it from succeeding. He just had no idea how he was going to do that.

They traveled less than a mile up the coastline before they saw a draw cut by a stream into the cliff face. The stream was swollen with rainwater from the storm that had passed through a few days before. It looked treacherous and steep, but it was the only path to the top of the cliffs that they'd seen so far and Alexander wanted to get off the beach and into the cover of the forest.

A pair of Rangers climbed slowly, with coils of rope slung over their shoulders and across their bodies, testing each foothold and trying multiple handholds as they moved cautiously up the draw. Once they reached the top, each tied off his rope to a sturdy tree and cast it down for the rest of the party.

It took longer than Alexander would have liked but they eventually made it safely to the top of the cliff. While they rested, Lieutenant Wyatt sent out scouts.

One returned after a few minutes, moving quickly and silently through the low, dense forest. "Ganglings, I counted seven," he reported in a hushed voice. "They're headed this way."

Lieutenant Wyatt quickly organized his men and sent scouts into the forest ahead of them. Within a few moments they were moving through the trees away from the cliff and the approaching ganglings. When they heard the long-armed giants reach the top of the draw, they stopped and took cover. They were only a hundred feet or so into the forest and they wanted to avoid a confrontation if possible. Chloe buzzed away toward the ganglings. A few moments later Alexander heard her in his mind.

"They're heading down to the beach, My Love. It looks like they're going to inspect the funeral pyre."

He sighed with relief. They held still for several minutes to make sure the ganglings were on the beach before they started moving again. The forest was thick with giant ferns and short gnarled trees. It was teeming with birds, insects, and small mammals. Following Alexander's directions, the Rangers moved cautiously, carefully choosing their trail to reduce both the noise they made and the evidence of their passage.

They traveled for several hours through the dense forest but didn't cover nearly as much ground as Alexander had hoped they would. The density of the foliage and the care they were taking to move silently and without a trace were slowing them down. When they heard the crashing behind them, they knew their efforts had been in vain.

It sounded like giants were rampaging through the forest off in the distance and the noise was getting closer. There were trees all around with thick dense trunks that split into large branches only eight or ten feet from the ground. Alexander scanned his surroundings looking for a place to hide, but he knew that the ganglings would probably find them no matter where they went.

"You already know that ganglings throw rocks as big as your head," Alexander said to the Rangers. "They also fight with their fists and are almost twice the size of a man. Spread out and use the trees for cover. Try to drive them off with arrows before they get close enough to trade blows."

They took positions in a broad crescent formation. The crashing grew louder and then seven of the giant grey-skinned creatures came into view. The Rangers loosed a volley of arrows, and the charging giants roared with anger at being suddenly peppered with pain. They stopped and bellowed in challenge to the Rangers, who held their ground, silently hiding behind the stout tree trunks. A moment later, half a dozen small boulders crashed through the forest. The Rangers rolled out from behind their cover and sent another volley of arrows. Again the ganglings roared in anger, but this time they charged.

Alexander set his bow next to a tree and stepped out to face the long-armed giants while drawing the Thinblade. Anatoly came up on his left with his war axe, and the Rangers divided their forces; half remained in position to fire arrows into the enemy while the rest took up short spears and stepped up to meet the charge. The ganglings stopped twenty feet away and roared again, but Alexander and his men held their ground without flinching. The ganglings looked confused. They weren't terribly smart and they were accustomed to most enemies fleeing before them. They seemed unsure of themselves and it was clear that at least a few of them were hurt from the arrows they'd taken.

Alexander pointed his sword at the lead gangling and started to advance toward the creature. It roared. Alexander responded with a battle cry and then charged. The lead gangling hesitated for only a moment before charging to meet the challenge. The rest held back, grunting and barking encouragement to the strongest among them.

It swung its oversized fist at Alexander in an arcing punch that would have taken his head off, but Alexander ducked under it and severed the creature's hand at the wrist. His sidestep under the punch put him on the right of the gangling and slightly behind it. His next stroke cut it in half at the waist. It crashed into a heap on the ground, mewling and gurgling. Alexander finished it by taking its head. When he looked at the rest of the ganglings, they retreated a step. Alexander took one step toward them, and they howled in unison before turning and fleeing into the forest.

Alexander's party made haste to get some distance from the location of the dead gangling. The noise made by the grey-skinned giants during the brief battle had no doubt alerted every predator for miles around to their position and

Alexander wanted to be as far away as possible when they showed up. They stopped moving for stealth and started moving for speed. It was noisy and left a trail that could be easily followed, but they made much better time.

Far in the distance they heard the shriek of something dying. Chloe spun into a ball of light. Alexander tried to reassure her. She was so tiny and fragile and the wilds of the Reishi Isle were filled with deadly creatures looking for prey.

"It'll be all right, Little One."

"I don't like this place, My Love."

"Me neither," he thought, "but we have to get the Stone, no matter the cost." A lump grew in his throat at that thought. He had already paid such a price that he wasn't sure his soul could bear it, yet he had to press on.

"Have faith, My Love. Isabel is strong. She will return to you," Chloe offered silently in his mind.

They pushed on until dark without encountering any more of the beasts that prowled the wilds. Camp was made quietly and without any light. Lieutenant Wyatt set a four-man guard rotation and they lay down for an uneasy night's sleep. The sounds of the forest were strange even to the Rangers who'd spent most of their lives in the vast tracts of the Great Forest of Ruatha.

This place was different. The trees grew differently, as if they were tortured by some unseen force of dark magic. The flora was different and strange. Even the colors of the life all around had a taint to them that put Alexander on edge, especially after dark when the light of the living colors emanating from the trees all around shone more brightly.

He slept fitfully, dreaming of Isabel and Abigail. He saw them taken from him over and over and felt the hopelessness of being helpless to save them. He woke several times and listened to the sounds of the alien forest, expecting to hear the growl or snarl of some predator stalking them. Late in the night, sometime near dawn as he lay awake looking up at the thick canopy, he heard Chloe in his mind.

"Darkness comes," she thought to him.

"Don't get near it, Little One," he thought to her as he rolled out of his bedroll. Just as he came to his feet, a howl shattered the night—it was like the sound of metal scraping on metal mixed with the squeal of a dying pig. It was a sound he'd heard before, and it was close.

The camp erupted into a flurry of activity as the Rangers rolled to their feet. Alexander removed his vial of night-wisp dust from its bone tube, and light flooded into the forest sending shadows in all directions. A moment later Jack held his vial high, and a pack of nether wolves responded with a howl that sent shivers of fear racing through all who heard the unnatural keening of the dark beasts. Alexander quickly scanned the woods and picked out the blackness of their dead auras.

"Five nether wolves," he called out. "Use blades to take their heads off. Stabbing them does nothing." He heard the ring of steel as the Rangers drew swords as one. But the nether wolves didn't come. For a long moment they stood in a loose circle facing the enemy in the forest all around before Lucky started chuckling.

"The night-wisp dust stores the light of the sun," he said with a sense of wonder. "Nether wolves don't much like sunlight, if I remember correctly."

Alexander made his decision quickly. He sheathed his sword and ordered everyone to break camp and make ready to move. He and Jack kept their light held high, and they started moving through the night. In the shadows beyond the light, they heard growling, snarling, and snapping as they moved carefully through the forest. It was slow going but they managed to cover some distance even while maintaining vigilance against the creatures in the shadows. Every once in a while, they caught a glimpse of hateful yellow eyes peering at them from the dark.

They pressed on for the next two hours through the black of the forest. It was tense and terrifying. They took great pains to keep everyone well within the confines of the light. Alexander didn't want to risk a wolf darting in and killing someone before the light could drive it off. When dawn started to show through the gaps in the forest, Alexander felt a great sense of relief. A moment before the sun broke over the horizon, the nether wolves howled in fury and frustration and then turned to inky black smoke as they fled the light of day.

When they stopped to eat a quick breakfast, Alexander and Anatoly tried to diffuse the fear and anxiety of the Rangers by telling the story of their first encounter with the nether wolves. Hearing how Alexander had killed two of the beasts in battle helped boost the Rangers' confidence.

"Do you think Phane summoned these nether wolves to hunt you?" Lieutenant Wyatt asked.

Alexander shook his head. "No, I think these nether wolves live here. I think they've been here on this island for a very long time."

"I would venture that they've been here since the Reishi War," Lucky said.

"How could they live for so long?" asked one of the Rangers.

"They're not alive," Lucky answered. "Nether wolves are creatures from the netherworld. They have no life and therefore cannot be killed in the way we think of it. Their physical forms can be destroyed but that merely sends their essence back to the darkness."

"How did they get here?" asked another Ranger.

Alexander sighed before answering. "I think they came through the Nether Gate, an ancient constructed magical gate created by Malachi Reishi that has the power to open a portal to the netherworld. I suspect the Nether Gate is somewhere on this island, and I'm hoping it's closed."

"Why would anyone want a gate to the netherworld?" asked another Ranger.

Alexander shrugged, "I have no idea, but I suspect Malachi Reishi thought he could use it to his advantage somehow."

"What if it's open?" asked a Ranger.

"I doubt that it is," Alexander answered. "Otherwise this island would be overrun with creatures from the netherworld. More than anything else, the beings that inhabit the netherworld want to return to the world of the living. They can only manifest in physical form here and they crave the power of action that we take for granted."

"I mean no disrespect, Lord Alexander," said another Ranger, "but how could you know that?"

Alexander stared off into the distance for a moment, remembering the limitless darkness of the netherworld before answering.

"Because I've been there," he whispered.

The camp fell silent. All eyes were on him with a mixture of fear and awe.

"There is no time or substance there, only darkness and unrealized potential. The beings that inhabit the netherworld can only wish and imagine what they want but they can never actually experience anything because there's no form or substance there. The pent-up frustration and anguish of being denied their desires for all time leaves them broken and twisted, but mostly it fills them with unmitigated hatred for those who live in the world of time and substance—we can have everything they can only imagine but are forever denied."

When they started moving again, there were quiet murmurings among the Rangers. They looked at Alexander with more deference and even a tinge of fear. He didn't want them to fear him, but he wasn't about to lie to them either. They deserved the truth, even if it was hard to hear.

CHAPTER 43

By midmorning they came to an open prairie of rolling hills covered with tall grass and sage brush. It stretched on for as far as they could see. They pushed on into the grass, traveling due west toward the center of the Reishi Isle and the Keep.

In some ways, Alexander was grateful for the open range; it made for easier and faster travel. But it also left them exposed. There was nowhere to hide. He suspected the wyvern riders hadn't given up and he worried about an attack from the sky.

A few hours into the rangeland, they crested a rise and saw a herd of giant buffalo. The animals stood eight feet tall at the shoulder and easily weighed two thousand pounds each. Alexander stopped for a moment to marvel at the size of the creatures. He remembered herding cattle back on Valentine ranch and imagined what his father could do with a herd of creatures like these.

The buffalo were a good distance off and didn't seem to be aggressive, although the males did have horns. It looked like they behaved very much like cattle. Alexander knew they could easily avoid any trouble with the herd if they gave them a wide berth and didn't do anything to provoke a stampede.

They adjusted their course and stayed in low places in the rolling range to keep from being seen, on the off chance that these creatures behaved differently than every other type of herd animal Alexander knew of. Once they were well past the herd, they found a place of relative high ground and took a look behind them.

That's when Alexander saw the gorledons. There were three of the unnatural creatures stalking around the edge of the herd. The buffalo were facing the giant predators and stamping and huffing at the threat. As much as Alexander wanted to watch the standoff to see if the buffalo could defend themselves against the gorledons, he also wanted to avoid being seen by them. Chances were good that the terrifying cross between a giant lizard and a gorilla would choose to hunt a small group of people rather than face an angry herd of buffalo.

They slipped away down the hill and Alexander quickly briefed his men about the gorledons. He told them about their soft underbellies and their bone-hard armor carapaces. He wanted them to know where to strike to do the most damage if they did have to fight the creatures.

They moved on, staying low to avoid being seen by anything that might want to eat them. The Reishi Isle was proving to be quite a bit more wild and dangerous than Alexander had imagined. He was wondering what else might be waiting, when a Ranger called out and pointed to the sky. Two wyverns flew over. His blood started to boil. The riders had taken his wife and sister. If they wanted a fight, he would be happy to oblige. He just hoped he could bring one of the riders down alive so he could get information about Isabel and Abigail.

The wyverns banked and lined up for an attack run.

"Fan out," Alexander commanded. "Attack the first one in line with everything you've got."

The Rangers nocked arrows. No one was within ten feet of another when the first wyvern made its pass. It didn't attack with claws or tail but instead flew just twenty feet overhead. The rider picked Alexander out of the crowd and pointed her hand at him as she spoke a few words. A beam of bright, white-hot light struck him directly in the middle of the chest, scorching a hole through his tunic. The force of the blast knocked him over on his back, but his armor protected him from the heat of the spell.

The Rangers fired at just the right moment and the wyvern screamed in pain as nearly a dozen arrows tore into its chest and wings.

The next wyvern rider launched a javelin at Alexander as he lay stunned and dazzled on the ground.

His all around sight saved him. He could see the attack coming even though his eyes were blinded. He rolled to the side a moment before the javelin buried deep into the ground next to him. His armor probably would have saved his life, but the javelin would have broken his ribs again and that was the last thing he wanted to endure at the moment.

The wyverns didn't make a second pass. It looked like the first one was struggling to gain altitude with a wing torn through by several arrows. Instead they moved off toward the southwest, no doubt to report Alexander's position and send reinforcements for another attack.

Anatoly offered Alexander his hand to help him up. He got to his feet and shook his head to clear away the stunned feeling. After a few moments of steadying himself by holding onto Anatoly's shoulder, he started to get his vision and his balance back.

"I'm starting to get really tired of those things," Anatoly growled.

Alexander nodded agreement. "I think maybe we need to pay them a visit. I'd like to see how well those riders would do on their own two feet against my sword."

"Might take some thought to figure out how to get to that island fortress without being seen," Anatoly mused.

"I think we should go take a look once we have the Stone," Alexander said. "Isabel doesn't have much time and I can't stand the idea of leaving her and Abigail to the whim of those wyvern riders."

Anatoly nodded, "Maybe a longboat at night could get us into that fortress. Getting out in one piece might be harder."

"Not if they're all dead by the time we leave," Alexander said with an undercurrent of menace in his voice as he watched the two wyverns recede into the distance. He turned to the Rangers and said, "We have to pick up the pace. I don't want to be caught out in the open when they come back in force."

The rest of the day, they ran to the west as quickly as they could. It was exhausting but they covered a great distance. The range was far from empty of danger but most of the creatures were either herd animals or natural predators that wanted little to do with the group of men moving through their territory. A pride of lions trailed them for a while until Lieutenant Wyatt put an arrow into one that got too close. They even came across a herd of wild horses—beautiful animals but far too untamed to be of any use.

Toward late afternoon Alexander was relieved to see a wood line off in the distance. Once they were several hundred feet inside the cover of the thick brush and trees, Alexander ordered a halt. Everyone was tired and hurting. Lucky had lost a little weight over the past month and gained stamina, but he certainly wasn't up to such a grueling pace. Everyone needed rest and food. It was early evening when they made camp. Dinner was served cold, but no one complained. They were all hungry and ate quickly. Once they'd eaten their fill, Alexander asked Chloe to stand guard and wake him if any threat came their way. They all went to sleep even though the sky was still light.

Alexander knew the nether wolves would howl at sundown. Everyone needed rest so they could move through the night. He knew it would be hard on them but he much preferred to stay ahead of the nether wolves rather than move in a tight cluster within the dubious protection of the night-wisp light.

He woke after four hours or so. Chloe was sitting cross-legged on his chest watching him sleep.

She smiled, "Did you rest well, My Love?"

Alexander was still tired and his muscles ached but the urgency he felt to get to the Reishi Keep overcame his physical discomfort. "Well enough. Thank you for watching over us, Little One. Was there any sign of the wyverns?"

"No. There were a few animals that wandered close to the camp but I scared them off."

Alexander frowned in surprise. She was all of three inches tall and weighed maybe an ounce. "How did you do that?"

She smiled proudly and buzzed into a ball of scintillating white light for a moment before returning to her normal form. "Animals don't like sudden bright light," she said. "It startles them and they run away."

Alexander nodded and sat up, smiling at her. She was beautiful and vibrant and full of life. In spite of her tiny size, she was larger than life in many ways. More than anything, he had learned the power of love without condition from her. She gave of herself freely and without limit, never thinking of what was in it for her or even entertaining the thought of love as currency in a bargain. She had sustained him since Isabel and Abigail were taken. Without her, he didn't know if he would have had the strength to go on.

In the distance, the peace of the early evening was shattered by the otherworldly howl of nether wolves. The few Rangers who were still sleeping sat bolt upright and immediately started packing up their bedrolls. It was clear that no one wanted to face the beasts again. In the gloom of the forest under a darkening sky, they set out. Alexander and Jack tied their vials of night-wisp dust to sticks so they could use them like magical torches casting light out as far as possible. They made reasonably good time for several hours through the dense underbrush. Every now and then they could hear large creatures off in the trees but nothing tried to confront them.

An hour or so before dawn, they heard the howl of the nether wolves tear through the night. The dark beasts were close and gaining on them. The men clustered together within the confines of the night-wisp light and continued to move through the forest but more slowly and cautiously.

A Ranger called out when he saw the first gleam of a nether wolf's faintly glowing yellow eyes in the darkness. They stopped and faced the beasts as they snarled and snapped in frustrated rage. For the rest of the night, they moved through the forest slowly in a huddled mass with the sounds of the nether wolves in the shadows. By the time dawn came, they were exhausted and the fear was so palpable that Alexander could almost smell it in the air. When the nether wolves went to ground to avoid the sunlight, everyone breathed a sigh of relief.

Alexander considered challenging the monsters. He knew he could kill one or two, but there were five, and he was pretty sure it would cost the lives of a few Rangers if they stood and fought. They were more of a nuisance than a hindrance to his ultimate goal, so he chose to simply avoid them. They moved on from the place where the dark auras of the nether wolves stained the forest floor and then made camp. The night and the previous day of running had taken its toll on everyone and they were badly in need of rest. After a cold breakfast, they slept until noon under the cover of the forest canopy. Lieutenant Wyatt assigned his Rangers to very brief stints at guard duty to allow everyone to get as much sleep as possible.

After a quick lunch, they moved out again. Alexander knew they had to be getting close to the Keep and he wanted to get there before nightfall. At least the Keep might afford some protection from the nether wolves and maybe even give them the opportunity to trap the creatures within it so they could avoid a fight altogether. Otherwise, they would be dealing with them all the way back to the coast.

After a couple of hours, they came to the edge of the forest and approached the wood line cautiously. The Keep was about a league away on top of a gently sloping hill. Grassland stretched away in all directions from the ominous-looking structure, providing a clear field of view for miles. The Keep itself was black and awe-inspiring with scores of towers, battlements, turrets, bridges, and buildings within.

Once, it housed tens of thousands of people, but now it was dark and foreboding. Scorch marks were etched into several towers and a few of the ancient spires were shattered, leaving nothing but ragged and broken edges reaching into the sky.

At its height, it would have been a magnificent thing to behold with gold leaf glinting from the conical roof caps atop many of the towers and brightly colored pinions flying in the wind over the enormous castle. While it had the look of a traditional keep, it was clearly not built or positioned to withstand any form of normal siege. There was no moat protecting the perimeter and there were no catapults or ballistae on the battlements, but then the Reishi Keep would have housed hundreds of wizards, so such mundane forms of weapons were unnecessary.

Even more than the Keep, the dozens of wyverns orbiting over it caught Alexander's eye. They were clearly aware of his destination and they meant to stop him. He wondered for a moment at their motives. For centuries they had guarded this island, ensuring that no ship made landfall. Now they were out in force to prevent him from reaching the Keep.

The thought that Isabel or Abigail had been tortured to extract his destination made him sick to his stomach. He ruthlessly pushed the unspeakable horror of those thoughts aside and focused on the dilemma before him.

In the light of day, they would never make it the three miles up the gently sloping hill to the Keep, yet if they waited for the cover of night, they would have the nether wolves to deal with. They could keep the nether wolves at bay with the night-wisp dust, but that would reveal their location to the wyvern riders. Alexander motioned for the Rangers to withdraw under the thick forest canopy so they could discuss their options.

Chapter 44

The big wyvern rider unbound Isabel's hands and shoved her roughly into a cell. She stumbled and fell to the cold floor as the door slammed shut behind her. When she removed her blindfold, she found she was locked in a small stone room just eight feet square.

One small window a foot in diameter looked out over the ocean. It was a hole cut through four feet of stone and barred with three stout steel rods. There was a pallet on the floor with a single blanket. There was also a bucket full of water and an empty bucket that looked unclean and smelled foul.

The door to the room was made of oak bound with heavy steel and had a small window with a cross grate. A metal plate in the middle looked like it could be opened from the outside to push food or water through to the prisoner within.

Isabel sat heavily on the pallet and put her head in her hands. The journey had been painful and frightening. The wyvern held her so tightly during the flight that she found it hard to breathe. A few times she felt like she was going to lose consciousness. The moment the wyvern had deposited her on the stone deck, she was seized by two big men wearing the same armor as the wyvern riders. They roughly bound her wrists behind her back and blindfolded her before half guiding, half dragging her to the cell she now found herself in.

During the terrifying journey, she had looked through Slyder's eyes to gain as much information as possible about her abductors. The big man who rode the wyvern wore formidable-looking heavy armor and carried an array of weapons on his elaborately constructed saddle. He moved with the beating of his wyvern's wings with practiced ease and didn't seem too concerned that his prisoner might be dropped by his mount at any moment.

She was both heartened and afraid when she saw that the wyvern riding just behind and to the left of her had Abigail clutched tightly in its talons with her bow pressed up to her chest. She didn't look like she was conscious during the flight and Isabel found herself worrying that her new sister was already dead. Unfortunately, Isabel had been brought in first and didn't have a chance to see Abigail land.

Now that she was back on solid ground and her heartbeat had slowed to a normal rhythm, she started to feel how bruised and battered she was. She carefully lay down and curled up in the blanket while she thought about Alexander, hoping that he'd survived the fight.

In the brief moments before she'd been snatched up, it looked like the wyverns were trying to kill Alexander and all of the other men while they had specifically targeted the two women to be captured. She didn't know what was coming, but she knew she would need information and all of her strength to meet it. Once she got as comfortable as she could on the little pallet, she relaxed her sore muscles while sending her mind to Slyder.

He was perched in a tree on top of the fortress island. To her surprise, the top of the island was beautiful and well cared for. It was covered with manicured gardens of all varieties. Artfully designed flower gardens, neatly laid-out vegetable gardens, and bountiful orchards covered the plateau. No part of the surface was wasted. There were no buildings except for a few gazebos here and there, and there was a railed deck around the entire outer edge. The gardens were being tended by a number of people wearing simple robes. They were repairing damage caused by the recent storm.

She had Slyder fly in a circle around the outside of the fortress island while she carefully looked at all of the openings cut into the stone. The entire plateau that jutted so abruptly from the sea was riddled with level after level of chambers. Some of the openings looked like big bays where wyverns came and went, while others looked like nothing more than windows for living quarters. There were a few balconies with comfortable chairs and small tables.

She saw a number of wyverns return after a while, looking battered and injured, hopefully from damage done by Alexander and his Rangers. Frequently she saw people within the windows, doorways, and large bays as Slyder floated around the place. Finally, she found a bank of tiny little windows that looked very much like the window to her cell.

Slyder carefully maneuvered in and made a pass by the ten windows, but he floated by too quickly for her to see inside any of them. Next, she had him land on the windowsill of each little window in turn. The first three cells were empty. She was in the fourth and Abigail was in the seventh, standing at the door and looking out into the hall. Isabel breathed a silent sigh of relief that she was alive. She had Slyder squawk gently, and Abigail whirled.

"Isabel, is that you?"

Slyder bobbed his head up and down. Abigail smiled past her bloody lip. It looked like she'd been treated more roughly than Isabel, but then she'd probably tried to get an arrow off the moment she was let loose. Isabel smiled to herself and hoped that her new sister had managed to kill at least one of the brutes who'd taken them before she was subdued.

"I'm so glad you're alive," Abigail said to Slyder. "Are you nearby?"

Again Isabel had Slyder bob his head up and down, then turn in her direction and peck the windowsill three times. Abigail frowned for a moment.

"You're three cells down?" she asked.

Slyder bobbed his head again.

"Are you injured?" Abigail asked.

This time Slyder moved his head from side to side.

"I'm so sorry they took you, Isabel, but I'm also glad for your company," Abigail said to the bird in the window. "Alexander will find us. I know he will."

Slyder's head bobbed up and down.

"Now that I know you're all right, I'm going to try to get some rest," Abigail said. "That wyvern just about squeezed the life out of me, and the men in the bay knocked me senseless when I killed one of them." She smiled with mischief. "It was worth it though. Let me know if you learn anything."

Slyder bobbed his head up and down and then came back to curl up on Isabel's windowsill and watch over her while she tried to rest. It was difficult for her to fall asleep—she was too worried about Alexander. The wyvern riders knew he was on the island and they were probably hunting him in force. He was also probably distraught at losing her and Abigail.

She wanted to send him a message letting him know they were alive, but she needed to keep Slyder close. He was her only source of information and that might make all the difference. She was also worried about her abductors' intent. So far they hadn't said anything about their reasons for attacking the ships that approached the Reishi Isle or why they'd taken her and Abigail but they were clearly serious, whatever their reasons. Then there was the poison that was trying to kill her. The wizards thought they had a solution, but it wouldn't do her any good unless she could get to them.

Once she finally drifted off, she slept fitfully despite her fatigue. Late in the day she woke when the bolt to her door was thrown open. A big man wearing a breastplate and armed with a short sword pulled the door open and eyed her intently as if she were the source of evil in the world.

"Stand up," he commanded.

She got to her feet, feeling greater pain in her bruised body now that her muscles were stiff and cold.

"Put your hands out," he said, holding a pair of shackles out in front of him.

Isabel pursed her lips and decided that now was not the time. She needed to know more before she made her move, and obedience might cause them to lower their guard in the future. She put her hands out and the big guard roughly slapped the shackles on her wrists and locked them in place. They were heavy and cold. This was the second time in the past month that she'd been locked in irons; she decided she didn't like it at all.

"Come with me. If you give me any trouble, I'll knock you out and drag you. Is that clear?"

Isabel nodded mutely. She felt indignation starting to build but she shoved it aside and focused her mind. They didn't blindfold her this time; she was grateful for that. When she exited her cell, she saw another big man in armor waiting in the hallway. He stood a fair distance from her like she might be able to stop his heart with a touch. It suddenly occurred to her that these men were afraid of her. She almost laughed.

She paid careful attention to the path they took as the big man led her by the shackles through the interior of the fortress. She counted turns and staircases but eventually realized that the place was so enormous that she would probably need a map to find her way around. He took her on a path that led higher through the stone labyrinth and finally to a large double door.

The second man pushed the doors open to a giant chamber, easily a hundred feet on a side and forty feet to the ceiling. Two rows of black stone pillars were spaced evenly a third of the way in from each side and supported giant stone beams that ran the length of the ceiling from front to back. Large crystal chandeliers hung from the ceiling, but the majority of the light came from the high arched windows on the far wall stretching from floor to ceiling and made from exquisitely crafted leaded crystal. Each of the five huge windows was nearly twenty feet wide. They stood side by side with sturdy-looking stone pillars between them. The glass was clear in all save for the center window which was stained in a beautiful depiction of a wyvern in flight.

Just in front of the windows, a raised bench that could seat thirty or more people ran the width of the hall. Directly in the center of the finely crafted, well-polished wooden bench was the glyph of the House of Reishi emblazoned in gold. The rest of the room was filled with row after row of benches, stopping at the last pillar where a small railing divided the room. On the other side of the railing were two tables with four chairs facing the raised bench. A single chair was set in the center of the open floor between the tables.

Sitting behind the raised bench were three women. Each looked middle-aged and each was beautiful in her own unique way. All had the unmistakable air of power and authority. But more than that, they each had a mysterious quality about them that seemed to charge the air in the room with energy. All three had blond hair, each of a little different shade, but the thing that struck Isabel the most was their eyes—they were filled with wisdom, purpose, and intelligence that belied their apparent age.

The men led her into the room and sat her down in the chair facing the three women, then moved a few paces behind her to stand guard. Aside from Isabel, her jailers, and the three women sitting in judgment, the room was empty.

She sat with her chin held high and schooled her expression. She reminded herself that she was the Queen of Ruatha, and as such represented much more than her own personal interests. She was an advocate for her King and for her people.

She didn't shrink from their scrutiny. Instead she returned it, sitting straight-backed and proud, facing the three women arrayed before her. In each she saw formidable strength and unshakable resolve. These three women believed in their purpose, whatever it was, and they would likely die in service to it. Isabel smiled inwardly—she'd found something they all had in common.

She didn't speak or protest but waited for them to make the first move while she took a measure of their character and mettle. It was a little like a staring contest between children for a minute or so before the one seated in the middle smiled ever so slightly.

"We have many questions for you," she said.

Her voice was strong yet beautiful and had the unmistakable quality of one who expected her commands to be obeyed without question. Isabel focused her piercing green eyes on the woman and waited, without so much as acknowledging her statement with a nod.

"I am called Magda. This is Cassandra," she motioned to her right, "and this is Gabriella," she said, motioning to her left. "You will address each of us as Mistress."

Still Isabel didn't acknowledge them with anything other then her inquisitive gaze.

"What is your name?" Magda asked pleasantly enough.

"I am Isabel Ruatha, Queen of the Island of Ruatha. You will address me as Your Majesty."

Isabel was angry and she was in a mood to be bold. She thought it might get her beaten, but it might also force them to reveal something of value. She didn't flinch or blink when she spoke her name, and her voice was strong and clear.

Magda arched her eyebrow and looked to her left and right with a bit of a smile.

"She's not the one we need to speak with," Gabriella said. "I say we dispose of her and call for the other."

"I have questions," Cassandra said.

"As do I," Magda said. Gabriella nodded her acquiescence, and Magda continued. "The line of Ruatha is no more. It ended two thousand years ago, so how is it that you claim that name?"

Isabel thought furiously. She didn't know who these people were or what their agenda was, so she didn't know how safe it was to reveal the truth to them, but then she didn't like the idea of being "disposed of" either, so she decided to give them some measure of the truth as she knew it.

"The House of Ruatha was destroyed, yes, but the line was preserved by Mage Cedric. For two millennia it has been hidden and protected. Now it has risen again to claim the throne and protect our people against the threat of Phane Reishi. My husband is Alexander Ruatha."

"Mage Cedric, you say, yet it was Mage Cedric who ended the Ruathan line and razed the capital city," Gabriella said. "Why would he preserve a line which he destroyed?"

"Because he knew that Phane would wake one day to threaten the Seven Isles, and he felt responsible for that. He preserved the line in order to provide our people with a champion capable of standing against Phane's ambitions," Isabel said, then shifted her focus to Magda. "Why have you abducted my sister and me?"

Again the three shared a look. "Sister? You are not of the same blood as the other," Magda said.

Isabel had no idea how they could know that. But more importantly, she didn't understand why it seemed so important to them.

"She is my husband's sister by blood and my sister by marriage," Isabel said.

At that the three women whispered back and forth for a few seconds before Magda resumed the questioning. "Why did you and your companions trespass on the Reishi Isle?"

They had finally come to the crux of the matter. Isabel knew she couldn't betray Alexander's purpose because doing so would betray his destination and put his life in jeopardy. She decided to stall.

"I've answered all of the questions that I intend to answer unless and until you answer mine. Why have we been abducted? Who are you? Do you serve Phane?"

Magda considered her for several moments before speaking again. "I will answer one of your questions. We do not serve Prince Phane Reishi," Magda said before she leaned forward slightly and fixed Isabel with her penetrating gaze. "Do you?"

Isabel was taken aback. She started to protest angrily but stopped herself short and gave Magda a hard look. "Phane Reishi is my mortal enemy," she said coolly.

Magda held her eyes for several more moments as if she was trying to discern her truthfulness. Finally she nodded slowly.

"I say we adjourn and verify her answers. Perhaps the other one will be more forthcoming," Cassandra said.

Magda thought about it for a moment before nodding her agreement and looking to Gabriella, who nodded as well.

"If what you say is true, then your life may be spared," Magda said calmly. "But," she held up her finger for emphasis, "if I discover that you are truly in league with Phane Reishi, you will answer all of my questions under torture and then you will die."

Isabel smiled defiantly. "I'm already dead, Magda. In four weeks' time, an assassin's poison will end my life. If I die here in your care, my husband will come for you, and when he does, you will all die." Isabel spoke in a matter-of-fact tone without anger or bluster as if she was telling them that rain was wet.

Magda was impassive. Cassandra frowned slightly, but Gabriella was indignant at the threat.

"How do you suppose your husband, one man, has the power to destroy the Reishi Coven?" She spat out the question, but her expression changed even as she clipped off the last word.

Isabel's smile widened. She had gotten one of her questions answered and even though she didn't understand the answer, she knew it was important from the way Magda and Cassandra were looking at Gabriella.

Her mind worked furiously. She had never heard of the Reishi Coven, but then she had never been away from the Great Forest before she met Alexander, let alone off the Isle of Ruatha. Both words carried great meaning. Witches organized in covens, so the three women peering down at her from the long wooden bench were probably very powerful witches.

The fact that they called themselves Reishi made no sense. The Reishi were dead, except for Phane, and they didn't seem to be on his side. If they were Reishi, how had they remained hidden from the world for all this time? How had Mage Cedric failed to discover them? And most importantly, what was their purpose? She needed to think.

Magda turned to the guards. "Return her to her cell and bring us the other one."

Isabel stood and faced them with her chin held high and her posture one of defiance. Without a word and before the guard could seize her shackles, she turned and started toward the door. They returned her to her cell along the same route. She made a point of scuffing the floor at each turn by dragging her toe; the guards didn't seem to notice. They removed the shackles once she was back in her cell. After locking the door, they moved off down the hall, and she heard another door being opened. They were taking Abigail to be questioned.

A minute or so later, Abigail was led past Isabel's door. Their eyes locked and they shared strength and resolve in that brief moment.

"Don't answer their questions," Isabel said.

Abigail smiled over her shoulder. "Not a chance."

Isabel waited for a long time, listening for movement in the hallway. When it finally came, it was a different guard and he had Abigail over his shoulder. She was unconscious.

Isabel called out to the guard, "What have you done to her?" But he didn't answer. He took Abigail to her cell, locked her in, and left without even acknowledging Isabel.

Chapter 45

Alexander stood with the Thinblade in hand. He had carefully positioned his men in the area where the nether wolves had gone to ground. Jack and Anatoly each had a vial of night-wisp dust and Alexander put them both exactly where he wanted them to stand with the light held high. The sun had set and the gloom of the forest settled into darkness. Alexander scanned the ground and saw the blackness of the nether wolves' colors, but they didn't rise and take physical form. His plan was working.

He told Anatoly to move the light a few feet away from him so it was no longer falling on the place where one of the nether wolves had hidden in the ground. For a long moment he waited, poised to strike before the inky black smoke rose up out of the thick brush covering the forest floor and coalesced into a beast of bone and fang.

The moment it became solid, it tried to lash out at Alexander with its enormous, fang-lined jaws, but Alexander was ready. He brought the Thinblade down across the back of the beast's neck and cleanly cleaved its head from its body. It toppled to the forest floor and the hateful yellow glow faded from its eyes.

One by one, Jack and Anatoly moved the light away from the spot on the ground where Alexander could see the dark aura of a nether wolf, and one by one, he took their heads. Only one managed to strike out at him. It became solid at a different angle than he expected and was able to spin around and attack. Its huge jaws snapped at his midsection but slipped off his dragon-steel chain shirt. A moment later the nether wolf fell.

"Good plan," Anatoly said.

"It'll make for a great song," Jack added. "Of course, I might have to embellish it just a little."

After an hour of travel with the aid of the night-wisp light, they doused their magical lanterns and moved the rest of the way through the dead-black forest. It was slow going and treacherous, but they made it to the wood line well before dawn. Alexander breathed a sigh of relief that the sky was cloudy enough to blot out the light of the moon.

They started toward the Keep moving slow and low. It was a painstaking three miles. Alexander kept track of the wyverns from the colors of their auras while he and his friends moved toward the Keep under the cover of darkness. There were dozens of the pseudo-dragons perched on towers and battlements all over the Keep, but they didn't seem to notice the platoon of Rangers creeping through the tall grass toward them.

They reached the broken gatehouse and silently crept inside the twenty-foot-wide and thirty-foot-high passageway that led into the courtyard. The outer gates were long ago torn from their hinges and the portcullis that once barred passage had rusted into nothing more than a stain on the floor. The inner gates were smashed and the courtyard had been open to the creatures that lived on the Reishi Isle for millennia. Once in the dark of the gatehouse, Alexander stopped cold in his tracks and his men froze with him. In the middle of the courtyard stood a wyvern guard in front of the Keep's main gate, which was also smashed and open.

Alexander knew that the moment he engaged the wyvern, the alarm would sound and they would be in a very dangerous fight. He much preferred to slip by unnoticed in the dark, but he doubted they would be able to accomplish such a thing. The alternative was either an outright attack or a diversion. The trouble was he had to be totally silent, so he couldn't discuss his plan with anyone. Alexander thought about it for a moment before he came up with an option.

"Can you draw them out, Little One," he thought to Chloe, "without getting hurt?"

"I can go outside the gates and make light," Chloe thought back to him.

"Good, but be careful. They have magic," Alexander thought to his familiar. "Let me know just before you do it."

She flitted off without a sound or so much as a flicker. Alexander had watched her over the past several weeks and it seemed that she could become completely invisible or glow brightly at will. He held his breath and waited.

"Now!" she thought to him.

At first, nothing happened, then one of the wyvern riders caught sight of the brightly glowing ball of light in the grass several hundred feet from the Keep. The rider coaxed his wyvern, and the beast let out a roar that sent the rest of the wyverns into the air—all except the one in the courtyard. It held its ground, but at least it was alone. Alexander whispered to the Ranger nearest him, "Arrows." The man whispered to the next man behind him and they began setting up a line of archers under the cover of the shadows, while the other wyverns searched out in the grass for intruders.

Chloe buzzed into the cover of the gatehouse and whispered in Alexander's mind, "How was that?"

He thought back to her, "Perfect, Little One."

A few moments later, a dozen archers were lined up shoulder to shoulder facing the dim silhouette of the lone wyvern standing guard. Just before they were set, a light flared high overhead. No doubt they were using magic to help them search. The glaring light was enough to give away their position. The wyvern roared and started forward when the line of Rangers fired a volley of arrows. The beast screamed in surprise and pain and launched into the air with one powerful stroke of its giant wings.

"Run!" Alexander shouted and everyone sprinted for the door of the Keep. It seemed like a very long way under the threat of a wyvern descending on them, but they made it through the door and into the Keep before the injured wyvern could drop back down to the courtyard.

They ran down the broad hallway that led from the courtyard into the giant entry hall and stopped to see the wyvern thrust its head inside, but it was too big to risk crawling in after them; in the confinement of the hallway, it would be far too vulnerable. It retreated and gave a terrible roar which was answered by dozens of other wyverns, but Alexander didn't care. He was in the Keep and that was all he needed for the moment. He would worry about getting out once he'd retrieved the Sovereign Stone.

As the darkness of the Keep closed in around them and they gained distance from the enemy, Alexander brought out his vial of night-wisp dust. The broad corridor leading from the courtyard ran for a hundred feet before it opened into a giant reception hall that was too big to see fully, given their limited light.

Jack held up his light as well and they tried to get some perspective on the room they'd just entered. In the shadows, it looked like it must be a hundred feet wide and easily twice as long. The ceiling fifty feet overhead was arched with rock ribs running from the floor up the walls to the apex of the arch in the center. Between the support ribs in the arched ceiling were broken windows that had once allowed natural light to fill the room.

Alexander scanned the giant reception hall looking for some indication of which way to go. The Keep was huge and would take forever to search room by room. The legend of the death of Malachi Reishi said he was directing the defense of the Keep from high atop the battlements when Nicolai Atherton, possessed by the shade, made his attack and pushed them both into the aether. Alexander had to find that place.

From overhead, through one of the broken-out windows, a javelin came hurtling down, just missing one of the Rangers and driving several inches into the stone floor. It was time to move.

"Run for the far end," Alexander commanded, and the platoon of Rangers surged forward into the darkness. They were fifty feet from the far wall when Alexander saw the telltale colors of three living auras. He'd seen colors like these before. They were twisted and tortured by magic, but radiated great power.

One by one, three gorledons leapt up on top of a pile of rubble that was pushed into one corner. They made the strange hunting call that was a cross between a growl and a scream. The Rangers stopped and drew weapons.

Alexander handed Lucky his night-wisp light and drew the Thinblade.

"Gorledons," Alexander announced. "Remember, they have armor on their backs and sides."

Jack and Lucky fell back and held the light high. The Rangers fanned out in two ranks. The rear group nocked arrows while the front rank drew swords. Alexander stepped up into the center of the first rank with Anatoly at his left. The gorledons were still shrouded in shadows and hadn't yet made their move to attack.

It was possible that they were confused by the fact that nobody ran. They were one of the most fearsome predators around and most of the creatures on the island, at least the living ones, probably avoided them. They growled again. When the Rangers held their line, the gorledons charged.

"Here they come," Alexander said calmly but loudly enough for everyone to hear. The Rangers with bows drew and took aim in the general direction of the enemy and waited a few moments until the three giant predators came into the light. On command, they targeted one of the creatures and loosed their arrows. Ten arrows found their mark high in the gorledon's chest, penetrating through to the bone carapace covering its back. It didn't even make a sound as it fell dead.

The other two came fast, both leaping high in the air to come down on top of their prey. Alexander moved quickly to intercept one. He knew it would try to pin him with one of its huge hind feet but he was ready. He also knew that once it was committed to a path through the air, it was almost impossible for it to change course.

At the last moment, he spun quickly to his left and brought the Thinblade around to slice the beast's leg off at the knee. Anatoly was ready and waiting for it to fall. It came down with a scream as it toppled over behind Alexander. Anatoly flipped his axe around and brought its eight-inch spike down into the gorledon's skull. It died quickly.

The final gorledon jumped over the first Rangers and landed squarely on top of one of the Rangers in the archer rank, pinning him to the ground with its giant clawed foot. The beast's bony armored back was facing the sword rank, and the archers couldn't get a clean shot. The only two farther back were Jack and Lucky, who were both unarmed except for the light they held.

The gorledon grabbed the injured Ranger by his arm, lifted its foot off his chest and whipped the doomed man in an arc over its head, impaling him on the row of spikes running down its spine. It roared in triumph, leapt over Jack, and sprinted off into the darkness.

Another man had fallen. The now all-too-familiar feeling of the weight of command settled on Alexander. Yet another life was gone by his order, another family torn asunder because he had sent their loved one into harm's way.

It made him think of Isabel and Abigail. The thought of losing them drove him dangerously close to madness. The crushing pain of such loss seemed too much for anyone to bear, yet there was another family that would suffer those terrible feelings.

For the thousandth time, Alexander silently wished that none of this had been thrust upon him. All he ever wanted was a little ranch and a herd of cattle. He just wanted to live his life. Most of all he didn't want to feel the crushing weight of responsibility and guilt for sending good people to their doom. He stood stone-still, looking off into the darkness where the gorledon had taken the latest victim of his unwanted duty as he struggled with his feelings. It was Chloe who brought him back from his dark thoughts.

"The suffering you feel from the death of a single man under your care is why it must be you to lead this struggle, My Love," she thought gently into his mind.

Alexander closed his eyes and silently offered her his thanks. He didn't feel any better about the death of the Ranger, but his resolve to succeed against Phane hardened. He took a deep breath and pushed his sorrow into the dark corners of his mind.

"We'll mourn him properly, but not today," he said to the Rangers.

They were already regrouping and assessing the situation. Lieutenant Wyatt was clearly saddened by the loss of another of his men but that didn't stop him from doing his job. Within moments of the battle's end, Wyatt had his Rangers ready to move.

They pressed into the interior of the Keep, moving slowly and carefully. Alexander relied on his all around sight to peer through doors before he gave the go-ahead to enter. He knew the Keep was probably inhabited by far more than gorledons. It had been open to the creatures living on the wild Reishi Isle for far too long. There was no telling what they might encounter.

They were also cautious to guard their rear; the wyvern riders were probably hunting them as well. While they didn't pose nearly the threat dismounted that they did riding their wyverns, they could still be a danger, especially if they managed to attack by surprise. Additionally, at least one of the wyvern riders had demonstrated skill with magic. If there was one, there were probably more.

The Keep was huge. There were myriad passages, halls, corridors, staircases, chambers, public areas, and private quarters. It had been abandoned for so long that the artwork and much of the furniture had rotted into piles of moldering dust. Yet, even in a state of such disrepair, the place had an air of grandeur. It presented a mixture of practical functionality with just enough ornamentation to create a sense of subtly understated authority.

They moved cautiously, looking for any sign that they were close to the inner chambers. But traveling through the Keep was confusing. They got turned around several times and found themselves entering rooms on the periphery.

They entered one of these rooms just before dawn. It was a large lounge with an open-air balcony jutting out the side of one of the central buildings. The windows were long ago smashed out and the furniture was little more than lumpy stains on the floor, but the balcony did offer a view of the front of the Keep and the main courtyard below.

Alexander carefully crept out onto the balcony and up to the stone railing. He peeked over just as one of the wyverns perched on the gatehouse gave a deafening roar. His first instinct was to retreat back into the room, but then he saw a number of wyverns come off the Keep from perches even higher than where he stood.

They were headed toward the forest. He looked out across the gently sloping range surrounding the Keep and saw a platoon of Andalian Lancers led by Jataan P'Tal headed toward the Reishi Keep. The wyvern riders were lining up for an attack run against them.

Anatoly came up beside him and looked out toward the impending battle. A smile slowly grew across his face. "Huh, I guess luck is breaking in our favor this time. I say we have breakfast while we watch our enemies kill each other."

Lucky and Jack both chuckled. The Rangers came up along the railing to watch as well. Lucky handed Alexander a hard biscuit and a piece of dried apple. He took it with a nod of thanks as he puzzled over his enemies. The Reishi Protectorate he understood. And the Andalians had made a deal with Phane. But the wyvern riders seemed intent on killing anyone who set foot on this island and were especially offended when intruders tried to enter the Keep, yet they didn't even live there. They could have cleared the island of most of the predatory creatures and tamed a large part of it if they wanted to claim it as their home, but they hadn't. Instead they left it wild and extremely dangerous while living on the fortress island and sinking any ship that got too close to the shoreline.

He didn't understand their motives and that worried him all the more because he was pretty sure that his wife and sister were their prisoners. He needed to know more about them, but the only way that was going to happen was to capture one of their riders and interrogate him. So far that had proven difficult. Maybe if they ventured into the Keep to search him out, he'd be able to turn the tables on them, but as long as they stayed on their wyverns, his chances of capturing one were slim to none.

The Andalian rhone mounts charged across the range toward the Keep with alarming speed. They were nearly twice as fast as a horse and moved with fearsome power. Watching them charge, Alexander knew that he'd made the right choice in surrendering on the southern shore of Ruatha.

He worried about the army he'd sent to southern Ruatha. They would be facing this enemy soon. The battle would be terrible. He just hoped that General Talia could come up with a way to fight them that didn't involve meeting them on an open field where they could bring the strength of the rhone and their force lances to bear.

The battle happened quickly. The Lancers had fanned out, so the wyverns could strike only one at a time. The first wyvern whipped its tail down at a Lancer. Even at this distance, the wyvern's deadliness was clear. The rhone and rider were both crushed into carnage in an instant by the powerful blow from the bone blade at the end of the wyvern's tail.

The next Lancer was more prepared for the attack. He brought his lance up and pointed it at the tail of the wyvern as it snapped down toward him. A moment before it struck, the Lancer released a burst of magical energy that caught the tail and forced it up and over the Lancer's head. Alexander knew from personal experience that the burst of force projected by a force lance was formidable. The wyvern roared in pain and rage.

The rider of the next wyvern to attack directed a blast of light and heat from her hand down toward another Lancer. He toppled off the back of his rhone, tumbled through the tall grass and never moved again.

The next wyvern rider in line hurled a javelin at Jataan P'Tal. He deftly caught the weapon, spun in his saddle, and launched the javelin back up at the soft underbelly of the wyvern. It struck home with such force that it penetrated through the wyvern's body, came out of its back, and flew thirty feet into the air trailing a streamer of blood. The wyvern screamed in pain and crashed to the ground, skidding to a halt. The rider was tied into his saddle or he would have tumbled off the dying beast into the tall grass.

The next wyvern targeted the giant, but he hurled a javelin so hard that the wyvern rolled to the right at the last moment to avoid the attack and missed its opportunity to strike.

The rhone thundered toward the Keep with such speed that the remaining wyvern riders were only able to launch attacks with javelins as the Andalians passed beneath them. Two more Lancers were killed in the barrage of javelins that rained down on them, but the rest reached the Keep before the wyverns could line up for another pass.

They rode through the gatehouse and into the courtyard. The first three charged the waiting wyvern with their force lances, each unleashing a magical blast of energy into the wyvern as it thrust itself into the air and whipped its tail beneath its body. It took the force lance blows, roaring in anger from the assault, then used its tail to tear one of the Lancers in half at the ribcage. The remaining Lancers charged into the Keep.

The wyverns regrouped and returned to their perches all over the high points of the Keep. It appeared that they intended to wait for the enemy to leave and then attack from the air rather than dismount and fight. Alexander watched two of the wyverns break off from the main force and head southeast. More would be coming.

Anatoly frowned. "That was fun to watch but not nearly as satisfying as I thought it would be."

Alexander nodded and motioned to the Rangers to follow him into the dilapidated lounge.

"Listen up," Alexander said. "The Andalian Lancers are dangerous when they're mounted, but when they're on foot, their lances are too big and unwieldy to use very effectively. On top of that, the men will be slowed down by their heavy armor, so I'm not too worried about facing them.

"The giant and the small man in black are something else. The one in black is Jataan P'Tal, General Commander of the Reishi Protectorate. He's a battle mage and he is beyond deadly. You all saw him catch that wyvern rider's javelin and kill the wyvern with it. I watched him kill six armed and armored soldiers in as many seconds with nothing but a knife. He's been hunting me for the past few months. I've managed to stay one step ahead of him until now. If we face him, use your bows to engage. If he gets close, he'll kill you. Hopefully, we'll be able to get the Sovereign Stone and get out of here without running into him at all."

Chapter 46

They went back inside the Keep, more wary now than ever, and took every staircase up that they found. The place was musty and smelled of death. Occasionally, they found the remains of someone long-dead. The Keep had been the site of a horrendous battle long ago. Forces of magic had been unleashed in that fight that hadn't been seen for millennia.

About midday, they came to a room with an observation deck on the north side of the Keep. Alexander carefully probed the room for threats with his all around sight before he cautiously ventured out onto the broad stone deck, looking for nearby wyverns. He didn't see any above him, but he did see a few perched below on the outer walls of the Keep.

Then something else caught his eye outside the walls of the Keep. He motioned for his friends to join him while the Rangers secured the room and prepared a hasty lunch. Not a mile from the outer walls of the Keep was a broad stone platform about thirty feet square, raised three feet off the ground on three sides and gently sloping down to meet the grass on the fourth. It was made of flat black stone with a single wall a foot thick rising from the edge opposite the slope. The wall was rounded at the top, twenty feet high and thirty feet across at the base. What drew Alexander's interest was the aura of pent-up power that radiated from the thing. There was magnificent magical energy contained within, yet it was somehow dormant and inaccessible.

Alexander pointed at it. "What is that?"

"That is the Reishi Gate," Lucky said. "There's one just like it on Ruatha a couple of leagues from Blackstone Keep. There's supposed to be a Gate on each of the Seven Isles. They were built by the First Reishi Sovereign so he could move soldiers quickly without the need for a navy. He used the power of these Gates to bring all of the Seven Isles under his dominion. Later, they were used more for trade than anything else, until the Reishi War when they were again used to move armies. They've been dormant since the Sovereign Stone was lost."

Alexander frowned. "What happens when the Sovereign Stone is retrieved from the aether?"

Lucky shrugged. "That's hard to say. Perhaps nothing, but they may become active again for anyone to use. Or they may become active only if the Sovereign Stone is bound to one with Reishi blood. There are many things about the ancient times that are a mystery."

Alexander stared at the Gate and weighed his options. He knew Phane planned to use the Gates to move soldiers from Karth to Ruatha. He also knew that Phane had sent Jataan P'Tal to take the Stone from him as soon as he retrieved it.

He had already risked so much and lost far more to come here. Now that he was so close, he wondered if retrieving the Sovereign Stone was the right thing to do. It had been safely outside of the world of time and substance for millennia. Bringing it back into this world could do more harm than good, yet he also knew that Phane would stop at nothing to get it. With the shades in the world, it was entirely possible that Phane could join forces with one of them or even bind one of them to his will and retrieve the Stone himself. The only place Alexander knew for certain that Phane couldn't reach the Stone was within the Bloodvault at Blackstone Keep.

His plan was born of desperation but it was the only sure way to give the future a chance. With the Stone, Phane would be unstoppable. Without it, he would be a formidable enemy but he wouldn't have the knowledge necessary to build an army of wizards. Alexander decided again that his plan was the only way to save the Seven Isles.

They moved back into the Keep. By now Alexander wasn't sure where he was or how he was going to get out once he found the Stone. He reminded himself to face one problem at a time. They came to a hallway that was thirty feet wide and had the stain of what was once a carpet running down the center. The ceiling was so high they couldn't see it with the light of the night-wisp dust. The hallway looked like it led somewhere important.

Two Rangers were scouting several dozen feet out in front. Alexander was scanning the way ahead when he saw the shimmer of magic across the hall not three steps in front of the Rangers.

"Stop!" he commanded. They both came to an abrupt halt and faced into the darkness with their short spears at the ready. Alexander approached carefully and inspected the field across the hallway with his second sight. It gave off a faint aura of magic. Just past the field was a set of giant double doors on the left wall of the hallway, which continued on into the darkness. Directly across from the double doors was another hallway that formed a tee with the hall they were standing in. It was equally as wide and the ceiling was shrouded in darkness.

"There's a magical field across the hallway just a couple of feet ahead," Alexander said. "Lucky, can you see it?"

Lucky shook his head. "Nor do I feel the tingle of magic that I do when I come to the warding shields within Blackstone Keep. I advise caution, Alexander. This is likely a trap and probably a deadly one if it has stood here for all these years." Lucky gestured to the giant set of double doors. "If I had to guess, I'd say the room beyond those doors is the throne room. There will undoubtedly be passages leading from there to the royal chambers."

Alexander motioned for everyone to back up a few paces. He stood ten feet from the magic aura, drew an arrow, and carefully tossed it. Three inches into the field, the plane glowed intensely, stopping the arrow in midflight. With a flash, the shaft burned in two and clattered to the floor. The faint aura of the trap remained.

"Huh," Alexander said, "doesn't look like we'll be going that way."

Then he saw lights coming from the other end of the hallway. His first instinct was to retreat, but then he reconsidered. He held his light higher and waited. The torchlight grew closer, but then it started to move more slowly toward them.

"What's your plan?" Anatoly asked with characteristic bluntness.

"If I'm the only one who can see that field, then maybe this is our best chance to kill the battle mage," Alexander said.

Anatoly nodded. "I like it," he said and then turned to Lieutenant Wyatt. "Prepare your men for a fight but do not attack until the order is given."

Wyatt quickly formed his Rangers into two groups left and right of Alexander and his companions. They waited until the enemy was only thirty feet away. Alexander was almost disappointed to see that it was Duke Truss with a dozen Andalian Lancers, only three of whom carried the long force lances that were so effective on horseback but were so heavy on foot. The rest were armed with swords. Jataan P'Tal was nowhere to be seen.

When Truss saw Alexander standing his ground and flanked by Rangers, he smiled a little and motioned for his men to stop. The three with the force lances pointed them at Alexander and his men.

Alexander idly wondered about the range of the force blast the lances projected.

"Rexius Truss, you're looking well with only one hand," he said with a taunting smile. "I'm tired of running. If you want a fight, then come and get one."

"Where's my whore?" Truss said. "Have you tired of her already?" He shook his head sadly. "Perhaps she was never worthy of my attentions."

Alexander stood his ground, his eyes glittering. He wanted to cut Truss into pieces, but he knew better than to move through the magical field. Instead he decided to taunt the petty little noble some more.

"She's quite well," Alexander said. "You know, she laughs about you and your, um stature, from time to time. She really doesn't like you. I can't say I blame her. In fact, I'm sure I'll get a hero's welcome when I tell her that I cut off your other hand." Alexander drew the Thinblade and smiled at Truss.

"Phane wanted us to spare you until you get the Stone for him like a good little lapdog, but I really never cared about any of that," Truss said with building rage. "Everything was perfect until you came to Glen Morillian and ruined it all. I was going to marry Isabel and become the deciding voice on the council. The whole valley would have bowed to my whim. Then you arrived and took my woman and my holdings—and my hand!" He shouted the last word with veins bulging from the sides of his head.

"Attack!" Truss commanded with such force that his voice broke.

The three Lancers released their energy blasts, and all of Alexander's men were knocked from their feet and sent sprawling to the floor. As Alexander sailed through the air, he thought to himself that at least now he knew that the range of the Andalian lance was greater than forty feet. He also knew that the magical field in front of him only stopped things of substance from passing while allowing magic through without hindrance.

A moment after Alexander and his men were hit by the magical blasts, five of the Lancers reached the magical field on the other side of the giant double doors. Alexander hadn't noticed the second field because it was obscured by the aura of the first. The fact that there was a second field only served to reinforce the importance of the room behind the double doors. All of these thoughts rushed through Alexander's mind as he lay flat on his back trying to regain his breath.

He looked up to see the five Andalian Lancers frozen in the plane of the field for a brief moment before it glowed brightly and sliced them neatly in half from the center of their heads down through the middle of their bodies. Parts fell away on both sides of the field, with the severed edges neatly cauterized by extreme heat.

Alexander shook off the fog in his head, got to his feet, and approached to within a few feet of the field on his side of the giant double doors. The three force lances were lying in pieces on the floor along with the remains of their owners.

Alexander smiled and waved the enemy to come forward. "Come on, the trap's spent, it can't hurt you now."

They didn't buy his ruse. Truss cursed him and ordered his men to retreat. They carefully withdrew down the hallway.

"I was really hoping to get Truss," Alexander said, shaking his head.

He went to the wall, put his hand against it, closed his eyes, and pushed through the stone with his all around sight. The room on the other side of the double doors was large, perhaps even vast.

He stepped back and carefully slid the Thinblade through the stone, then drew a doorway in the surface of the wall. He put his boot against the center of the outline and pushed. A section of wall a foot thick fell inward, crashing to the floor and sending chips of stone skittering off in all directions. The echo returned to him a moment later.

Alexander cautiously stepped through the impromptu door and surveyed the chamber within. It was well lit by a series of mostly broken-out windows high overhead in the arched ceiling. It resembled the entry hall in construction, over two hundred feet long and a hundred feet wide with stone support beams running up the walls, then arching over to meet their counterparts in the center of the high ceiling. The floor was made of white marble shot through with veins of blood red.

On the far end, a raised dais formed a half circle stretching from one corner to the next and reaching forty or fifty feet into the room. A single chair carved of white marble and gilded in gold occupied the center of the dais. Alexander stood in the Reishi throne room.

Anatoly entered next. The moment he set foot on the marble floor, the figure sitting in the throne stood. Alexander hadn't even noticed it at this distance, but when it stood, he knew exactly what it was. He had faced a creature like this in Blackstone Keep.

The sentinel was the size of a man and was made completely of black stone. It was armed with a shield and a spear with a sword at its belt. Alexander remembered the last time he had fought a sentinel. It had been all but immune to normal steel weapons. He hoped the Thinblade would prove effective against this magical guardian or they might have a real problem.

In the back of his mind, he wondered why it had only awakened when Anatoly entered the room. He'd been in the room for several moments before Anatoly. He'd cut a hole in the wall and pushed a section of stone onto the floor, and yet the guardian only woke when Anatoly set foot on the marble floor.

It started toward them. Alexander quickly scanned the room for any magical traps or auras but saw none. He moved in a few paces to give the Rangers room to enter.

"Stay clear of it," Alexander said. "I doubt your weapons will harm it." With that he drew the Thinblade and began to advance. The thing stopped midway across the room and faced Alexander but didn't challenge him. Alexander took another step forward but still the magical guardian did nothing.

Anatoly began to advance and the sentinel started moving toward him while ignoring Alexander. The animated statue strode past Alexander with its spear leveled at Anatoly.

"Stand down," Alexander commanded.

Anatoly stopped as did the sentinel.

"Anatoly, come toward me but give the sentinel a wide berth," Alexander said.

Anatoly nodded and carefully circled around the sentinel. It stood stone-still like it was nothing more than an ordinary statue. Alexander gave Anatoly a questioning look.

He shrugged.

"Turn around," Alexander commanded.

The sentinel obeyed.

"Return to the throne and sit down."

The sentinel marched to the throne and sat down.

"Lucky, why is that thing obeying me and why did it start advancing only after Anatoly stepped into the room?" Alexander asked.

Lucky shook his head slowly, looking perplexed. "I have no idea. Nothing about this makes any sense."

"I guess I'll take what I can get," Alexander said. "Lieutenant Wyatt, search the room for exits. There'll be at least one hidden door."

Wyatt nodded and started issuing orders to his men.

Alexander went to the throne with Anatoly and Lucky and faced the sentinel. He stood staring at the impassive magical guardian for several long moments.

"Will you obey my commands?" he asked.

The sentinel nodded once.

Alexander looked at Lucky, who shrugged.

Jack came up alongside them, keeping a wary eye on the sentinel. "Wyatt found two exits that look like they lead to servants' preparation areas, and there's one leading from the dais over in the corner, plus a secret door directly behind the throne."

"Good, send scouts through the door in the corner," Alexander said.

Jack left to relay the order while Alexander tried to understand the inexplicable behavior of the sentinel. It just made no sense.

Jack returned and reported: "It leads to a sitting room. There are three doors leading out."

"Anatoly, take everyone into that sitting room. I'll be along in a moment. Maybe we can put this thing to use."

Once the room was empty of his people, Alexander faced the sentinel. "Stand," he commanded, and it stood. "Do not allow anyone to pass from this room through those two doors, except me," Alexander said pointing at the door in the corner of the dais and the secret door directly behind the throne. "If anyone comes from those two doors, they are permitted to leave without challenge. Do you understand?"

The sentinel nodded. Alexander wasn't sure the magical guardian actually did understand. It was a little like having a conversation with a rock, but at least it nodded. He left the throne room and joined his friends in the sitting room. There was one door that was slightly larger than the other two and it was in perfect condition while the other two were warped, rotten, and brittle. He tried to open it and found that it was securely locked. One slash with the Thinblade cleaved the door down the middle. Half fell away clattering to the floor while the other half swung silently open on its triple hinges.

They cautiously moved down a narrow corridor that opened into a circular room at least a hundred feet across. The ceiling was ten feet high supported by a ring of columns. At one time it might have been a very plush bedchamber, but now any furniture that once filled the room was nothing but dust. Two sturdy doors led out of the room, each in perfect working order with no sign of age or decay.

There was also a spiral staircase leading both up and down. After a cursory search, Alexander decided to take the stairs up. If Malachi Reishi died while commanding the defense of his Keep, it stood to reason that he would have been somewhere high where he had a view of the surrounding area. Alexander was getting closer to his goal.

On the next level was a library, but the years had destroyed the contents. Bookcases were toppled or crumbled under the weight of the books that had once lined their shelves and the books themselves had turned to dust. Alexander wondered at the difference between this place and Blackstone Keep. There, the books and many of the rooms were intact, while here, most everything seemed to have suffered the ravages of time.

They moved up another level. It looked like it had once been a laboratory or a workroom for a wizard or an alchemist. It was in a shambles as well. The tables were broken and decayed to the point of crumbling. Most of the glassware was shattered on the floor and the shelves had fallen over, haphazardly scattering their contents. The place was a mess. Alexander quickly surveyed the debris littering the floor. Most items were broken, but a few were intact.

One in particular caught his eye. It glowed with such an intense aura of magic that for a moment all he could do was stare in disbelief. It was a heavy glass vial sealed with a glass stopper that was secured with silver wire. It contained a pure white powder, the color of sunlight on new-fallen snow. It was something that Alexander had only seen once before in powder form. He knew at a glance exactly what it was.

Wizard's Dust.

CHAPTER 47

He stepped through the debris, glass crunching under his boots, and reverently picked up the little vial of concentrated magic. He had no idea how much Wizard's Dust was a lot but he got his answer when Lucky gasped in delight and astonishment. Alexander had found a treasure beyond price. The heavy glass vial was an inch in diameter and four inches tall, and it was full to the top.

"Alexander, you hold in your hands enough Wizard's Dust to initiate a dozen new wizards," Lucky said. "That alone could tip the balance of this war in our favor."

Alexander gently handed the vial to Lucky, who took it with deliberate care, still staring at the priceless powder. He carefully set it on the floor and rummaged around in his bag until he found a small steel tube lined with soft leather. It was just big enough for the vial to slide inside. He packed the top with a small square of cloth and screwed the cap tightly into place, then handed the safely packed Wizard's Dust back to Alexander. Lucky produced a similarly packed vial of fairy dust along with a healing potion and healing salve.

"Take these and put them in your pouch," Lucky said. "I still have some of the fairy dust and plenty of healing salve, but that is my last healing potion. The Wizard's Dust and the fairy dust are priceless beyond measure, so it's only fitting that you carry them; you're far better equipped to protect them than I."

Alexander nodded. He knew he had to keep the magic powders safe until he could discuss the best uses for both with the wizards at Blackstone Keep.

When they reached the next level of the Reishi Keep, they found what looked like a storeroom for magical ingredients. Many of the shelves were broken and rotted through but there were still several intact containers. Lucky spent a few minutes looking for anything of use. He found several items that he seemed pleased with and slipped them into his bag.

The level above looked like another bedchamber or sitting room. A broken door led out to a balcony. Alexander cautiously looked out and saw a sky bridge leading to a tower a hundred feet away. It looked like they were in one of the three central towers that rose up out of the Keep and reached highest into the sky. Several levels up, a sky deck filled the space between all three towers. It formed a triangle and offered a view of the entire countryside around the Keep.

Alexander thought to Chloe, "Please check to see if the Sovereign Stone is in the aether on that platform. If I was directing a battle, I'd do it from there."

"I'll return in a moment, My Love," Chloe said in his mind, then buzzed into a ball of scintillating white light and vanished. Alexander held his breath while he waited for her to return.

A wyvern roared, drawing his attention. Far below, perched on the top of a flat tower, it was looking straight at him. Chloe reappeared a moment later in a ball of white light before taking her normal form.

"The Sovereign Stone is there," she said in Alexander's mind. "The bodies of Malachi Reishi and Nicolai Atherton are there as well, My Love."

"Thank you, Little One," Alexander said aloud with a smile. She buzzed into a ball of light at his praise.

The wyvern roared again, then launched itself into the sky and started beating its wings steadily to gain altitude.

Alexander returned to the room and led the way up to the next level. They entered a bare stone room with a magical gold-inlaid circle filling the center. There was only enough room to continue up the staircase against the outer wall without crossing into the circle.

The next room was similar, except there were two smaller circles only a few inches apart; both were inlaid in gold as well. These rooms looked like summoning chambers where Malachi Reishi had no doubt called forth servants from the netherworld to do his bidding.

The next several levels were libraries, workshops, and studies that had been ravaged by time. As they climbed, Alexander knew he was getting closer. The sky deck would be the next level or two above. His heart started racing. As soon as he retrieved the Sovereign Stone, it would be vulnerable. Phane and his minions would stop at nothing to get it from him. Yet he still had Isabel and Abigail to worry about. It would be a dangerous detour to go to the fortress island—but he knew he would.

He had to.

Alexander was the first to reach the next level of the tower. He froze in place the moment he entered the room. It was another summoning chamber. The magical circle stretched from wall to wall, leaving only the staircase on one side. On the other side of the room was a broken double door that opened onto the sky deck.

Chloe spun into a ball of light. "Darkness is near," she said in his mind.

Alexander didn't need her warning, although he did appreciate it. He was staring at a demon the likes of which he'd never seen and could not even have imagined. It was a black orb easily five feet in diameter. It had no eyes, ears, or nose—but it did have a mouth that seemed to split the orb in half and opened with row after row of razor-sharp teeth. Sprouting from the rest of the slick black orb were at least twenty tentacles that ended in heavy, club-like bulbs glistening with a thick, viscous-looking substance.

Even though it had no eyes, it started right toward him with surprising speed, running on four tentacles while the others flailed about looking for a victim. It closed the distance quickly and thrust three of its tentacles at Alexander. He tried to retreat down the staircase while drawing the Thinblade. The demon would have had him had it not been trapped within the circle; its tentacles stopped as if they'd smashed into a wall when they came to the edge of the magical barrier.

Its mouth came next as it thrust itself at Alexander with a fury that was terrifying. He saw the giant maw filled with teeth crash into the magical barrier and rebound from the impact. The creature roared with rage and frustration. The sound was like nothing Alexander had ever heard. It was deafening and terrible. Worse, the colors of the thing were so dark and hateful, they made Alexander's eyes hurt and his soul squirm. He slowly retreated down the stairs to the room below, while trying to school his breathing and calm his trembling.

"We have to find another way," Alexander said, still shaken from the encounter. "We'll go down to the sky bridge and cross to the other tower."

Everyone looked alarmed and a bit wary. They'd all heard the beast but none had seen it except Alexander. Anatoly asked the question that was on everyone's mind.

"What was that?"

Alexander shook his head slowly. "I don't know. It was a big black orb with a huge mouth and a bunch of dangerous-looking tentacles. Whatever it was, I'm just glad it's trapped inside a magic circle."

"How long can a circle like that hold a demon?" Jack asked.

"As long as the circle remains physically intact," Lucky said. "It may have been trapped in that chamber since the Reishi fell."

Jack whipped out his notebook and started writing furiously.

They descended to the level of the sky bridge and cautiously peered out the door. Alexander threw himself back when he saw the wyvern rider perched on the bridge raise her hand. His head just cleared the door frame when a blast of white-hot light stabbed past him and burned a hole three inches deep into the stone wall on the opposite side of the chamber.

He stayed well clear of the door and used his all around sight to look at his adversary. The wyvern was facing the doorway with its head pulled back like a cobra ready to strike. Its taloned hind feet gripped both railings, and its wings were poised to thrust it into the air.

A woman with blond hair and golden-brown eyes was mounted on the wyvern. She was pretty, except for the fact that she was trying to kill him. Her hair reminded him of Abigail's shade of silvery blond. She was holding her hand out toward the door, waiting for another opportunity to strike with her magical fire.

"We will never permit you to have the Sovereign Stone, Phane!" she shouted.

Alexander had to replay her statement in his mind to be sure he'd heard her correctly. Even after he was certain of what she had said, it made no sense. He gave Lucky a quizzical look, but only got a shrug of confusion back.

"I am Alexander Ruatha," he shouted. "Phane is my enemy."

There was a pause. Alexander watched her with his all around sight. She looked confused for a moment before certainty returned to her expression.

"You're a liar. The Ruathan line was destroyed in the Reishi War."

Another blast of light leapt from her hand. This time it wasn't concentrated in a beam, instead it was a flood of such intense brilliance that it would have dazzled Alexander if his eyes were open. He saw everything through his all around sight. The wash of brilliant, scintillating white light flooded through the door. His friends all covered their eyes, but a moment too late. They were temporarily blinded by the brightness of it.

A moment later, the wyvern launched itself into the air and in the same moment, thrust its tail underneath itself and through the doorway. Alexander saw it coming just in time and drew the Thinblade. The tail reached ten feet inside the room, but before it could thrash around and hurt anyone, Alexander came up with his blade and sliced it cleanly off.

The wyvern roared and beat its wings furiously before turning into a diving glide to get distance from the source of its sudden pain. Alexander stepped out onto the balcony and saw another wyvern coming. It looked like it was going to attack the bridge with its tail. He unslung his bow, smoothly nocked an arrow and sent it at the wyvern's head. The beast dove and went under the bridge, then banked hard to avoid crashing into the third tower.

Alexander and his companions raced across the bridge, trying to regain their full vision. They reached the other side and entered a room that used to be a study or a library; it was in such a dilapidated state that it was hard to tell what purpose it once served. Alexander wasted no time. He found the staircase leading up. The next few rooms were much the same.

They stopped briefly to let everyone rest their eyes in safety.

Alexander led the way up to the next level and then the next. He wasn't interested in looking for trinkets or treasures in the long-unused workrooms or laboratories. He had his eye on the prize.

In the back of his mind, the words of the wyvern rider nagged at him. She thought he was Phane. And she was trying to stop him from getting the Sovereign Stone. There was a scrap of hope in this new understanding. The wyvern riders saw Phane as their enemy. If he could convince them that he wasn't Phane, maybe they could form an alliance, and even more importantly, maybe they would release Isabel and Abigail.

But then, if they thought he was Phane, why had they taken his wife and sister? What would they want with them, if not information? The thought of either of them being tortured made him nauseous. He had to push that idea out of his mind and cling to the hope that they were alive and safe. When he reached the level of the sky deck, his focus returned to where he was and what he was doing.

They entered a room with a wrap-around balcony. A few windows looked out on the surrounding countryside. An open double door led to the sky deck and a door on the opposite side led to the balcony.

In its glory, the room would have been impressive. The view was magnificent. The sun was just slipping toward the horizon and wisps of clouds traced streamers across the distant sky ablaze with orange and red. The colors washed across the forests and rangeland of the Reishi Isle and painted the landscape with a thousand soft hues, ranging from deep purple to vibrant yellow to fiery red.

"Even in a place as dark and dangerous as this, the world still has the capacity for indescribable beauty," Chloe said aloud with a tone of deep reverence.

Alexander smiled at her ability to stop and appreciate beauty even here, but then a thunderous roar broke the serenity of the moment as a wyvern descended on the sky deck. Alexander spun and knew in an instant that the wyvern was making a fatal mistake. Stretched across the deck were three layers of smoke that seemed to hang in place in spite of the breeze. The layers floated one foot, three feet, and five feet above the deck, blanketing the entire area and shining with deadly magic.

As the wyvern landed, all three layers of magical energy glowed brightly, cutting the beast and its rider into pieces in an instant. The wyvern fell in chunks all over the sky deck without so much as a whimper. The rider was cut off at the knees. He hit the ground hard and screamed. When he tried to rise up, he passed through the lowest layer of magical energy, which lit up again, cutting him in half across the torso.

Everyone froze in place, shocked by the sudden carnage.

Alexander cautiously approached the doorway. He stopped short of the threshold and examined the magical fields that still shimmered with deadly power. He carefully held an arrow out into one of the layers but nothing happened. Perhaps it was triggered by living beings rather than inanimate objects.

His friends stood a step behind him.

"Lucky, can you see the trap?"

"No, just the effects of it."

"Can you see the location of the Sovereign Stone, Little One?" Alexander thought to Chloe.

"Yes, it's near the railing midway between this tower and the one with the darkness in it," she answered silently.

Alexander looked across the sky deck to the other tower and saw the tentacle demon pressed up to the edge of its magical prison, eager to get out so it could feed. He glanced to the third tower and saw the telltale colors of life within.

Jataan P'Tal stood watching him from the shadows. Alexander quickly withdrew behind the cover of a stone wall. There were over a dozen men with P'Tal. He had no doubt seen the effects of the trap and wouldn't try to cross the sky deck, but he was still far too close for comfort. Alexander knew all too well how quickly and accurately Commander P'Tal could throw a javelin.

"The Reishi Protectorate are in the other tower," Alexander said, pointing toward the enemy.

The Rangers took up positions around the room, at the windows and guarding both staircases.

"Chloe, can you pull the Sovereign Stone back into this world and bring it to me?" Alexander asked her out loud.

She shook her head. "The Stone is entangled with the bodies of Malachi Reishi and Nicolai Atherton. I can pull it into this world, but their corpses will come as well. And once it is free of the aether, I won't be strong enough to move something as big as the Sovereign Stone. It's easily three times my weight."

Alexander smiled at the simple logic of it. He hadn't given much thought to the way she must see the world. She was only three inches tall and weighed about an ounce. It only made sense that she wouldn't be strong enough to do what he asked.

"Lucky, do you have a roll of sturdy string?"

He nodded and started rummaging around in his bag for a moment before he produced a roll of lightweight but very strong string and handed it to Alexander.

He ran out a length of about sixty feet and handed the end to Chloe.

"Take this out to the place where the Stone is," Alexander said. "Once you bring it back into this world, tie the string to the Stone and I'll pull it to me. Chloe, be careful and stay low. The magic that killed that wyvern is floating about a foot off the deck."

She flew up, kissed him on the cheek, took the string and flew not an inch off the deck, stopping about fifty feet from the door. A moment later she spun into a ball of scintillating white light and vanished. Alexander held his breath.

A moment passed.

Then another.

He started to worry. He'd bonded with Chloe for this task, but he found his worry was for her safety. He loved her and couldn't stand the thought of losing her too.

She flared back into existence in a brilliant ball of light and settled to the ground with the corpses of two men locked in a bear hug. They were frozen solid and hadn't decayed a bit in two thousand years. Around the neck of the man wearing the polished armor was a heavy gold chain. As gravity pulled on them for the first time in millennia, the Sovereign Stone rolled out from between them and fell to the ground. Chloe tied the end of the string to the chain.

"I'm ready, My Love," she thought to Alexander.

"Well done, Little One. Remember to stay low," he thought back to her.

Gently, he pulled the string. There was a bit of resistance as the chain stuck to the frozen clothing of Malachi Reishi's corpse, but then it broke free and slipped from around his neck, clattering to the stone floor of the sky deck. Alexander carefully started dragging the Sovereign Stone.

Before he'd pulled it half the distance, the temperature fell quickly as two apparitions flickered into existence. They were silvery, translucent silhouettes of the men they had once been.

Malachi Reishi's face contorted in rage and hatred for a brief moment before the Sovereign Stone glowed bright red and his form was drawn into it in a whirling cone of magical energy.

Nicolai Atherton smiled and waved in gratitude to Alexander before he flickered out of sight. From very far away, Alexander heard him say, "Thank you," and then he was gone.

As he watched the two ghosts move on to their final resting places, Alexander heard one of the Rangers call out, "They're on the move."

He started pulling the Stone toward him more quickly. Chloe was out of danger and at his side when a Wyvern flew over and cast a javelin down at him. It missed, but not by much. He gave the Stone a yank and it skittered across the floor of the sky deck and into the tower room.

The chain was made of heavy gold links a quarter inch across. The Stone itself was a blood-red, teardrop-shaped gem the size of a walnut. It was polished smooth and fastened to the chain with a heavy gold clasp. Alexander held the stone up by the chain for all to see. There was a cheer from the Rangers. Lucky smiled with unabashed joy. Anatoly gave Alexander the lopsided grin that meant he was proud of him. Jack smiled with boyish joy even as the lines to a song began forming in his mind.

Alexander laid the Stone against the palm of his right hand as he held the chain with his left. It felt warm to the touch. It was exquisite in size, color, and craftsmanship—but mostly the aura of magic surrounding it was intense.

Then it pulsed with bright red light.

Alexander wasn't sure if it was the light of its aura until Lucky gasped. The intensity of the light grew until it seemed to be all-encompassing. It filled him up and surrounded him until there was nothing but blood red light.

Then he was standing in a chamber without walls or a ceiling. There was a round table with seven chairs. Each was occupied, save one. Each of the men seated around the table were looking at him with a mixture of curiosity and appraisal. Alexander scanned their faces and saw that each of them had one feature in common.

Their eyes.

They were golden brown with flecks of gold in the irises.
Then he saw Malachi Reishi, and his wonder turned to fear.

CHAPTER 48

Alexander slumped to his knees, holding the brightly glowing Stone. After a moment of intense brightness, it diminished to a gentle, blood-red glow the color of the sunset. Alexander's eyes were wide open, but they were vacant.

Chloe spun into a ball of light momentarily, then buzzed up to Alexander with a look of worry and fear. "My Love, where have you gone?" she asked plaintively.

Lucky knelt before him to examine his eyes. He looked closely, felt for breath and pulse, then shook his head in disbelief and confusion.

"I don't understand. The Sovereign Stone is supposed to be tied to the Reishi bloodline the same way the Thinblades are tied to the bloodlines of the Island Kings. How can this be happening?"

No one answered. They were all more confused by the strange turn of events than he was.

A sudden cry of pain from the scout in the staircase leading to the level below demanded everyone's attention.

A moment later, Jataan P'Tal was in the room.

He slipped past the spear of the Ranger guarding the top of the staircase and sliced deeply into the inside of his thigh. The man stumbled backward and fell with a strangled wail of pain. The General Commander moved with such precision and speed that the next Ranger who tried to strike him thrust into empty air. Jataan P'Tal rolled around him and deftly knocked him off balance so he fell into another Ranger who was bringing his bow up for a shot.

The giant came close behind followed by half a dozen Andalian Lancers. Jataan P'Tal scanned the room and saw Anatoly standing in front of Alexander and Lucky. Anatoly was holding his axe high in a ready guard and wore a mixture of grim determination and resignation.

Jataan P'Tal glided through the Rangers as if they were children standing before a trained soldier. He didn't attack but simply avoided their strikes and moved past them in jerky spurts of impossible speed. One moment he was walking like a man with a purpose, the next he moved with the speed of an arrow just released from a bow.

When he was within range, Anatoly attacked. Jataan P'Tal darted inside Anatoly's guard and rolled around him with the flow of the strike so the blade of the axe chased behind him as he moved. As he rolled around the big man-at-arm's left side, he thrust his knife just below the ribcage. It wasn't a kill strike, but it was debilitating. Anatoly followed the momentum of his swing around from right to left and toppled over, his grievous wound spilling blood onto the floor.

Behind them the battle raged. The giant wielded his war hammer with punishing effect and the Andalian Lancers wielded their swords and shields with well-trained precision. The Rangers divided into two groups, those in the center of the room engaging with spears and swords and those on the periphery firing arrows into the enemy.

As Lucky knelt in front of Alexander, Jataan P'Tal slipped past his right shoulder and raised his knife for a kill strike. Lucky looked up and saw the threat, but he wasn't even close to fast enough to stop the battle mage.

Jataan P'Tal began his thrust.

The knife moved toward Alexander's jugular—but halfway to its mark, it stopped. The expression on Jataan P'Tal's face flashed from surprise to confusion to realization and finally settled on hope.

Chloe buzzed up to within a foot of Jataan P'Tal and shook her finger in his face. "You will not harm My Love or I will send you away into the aether where you will be trapped as a ghost for all time."

He cocked his head and gave her a little smile before he turned to his men and commanded, "Stand down!"

The giant stopped in midswing and brought his hammer up onto his shoulder. The Andalian Lancers stopped their charge into the nearest group of Rangers and withdrew without breaking formation.

Lieutenant Wyatt called out, "Hold!"

His Rangers re-formed between the bulk of the enemy and Alexander. Wyatt pointed at Jataan P'Tal and the Rangers with bows all shifted to face him.

Alexander was still sitting on his knees with vacant eyes and the glowing Sovereign Stone clenched tightly in his hand. Chloe buzzed in a protective orbit around his head.

Lucky scrambled to Anatoly to treat his wound. He quickly dug into his bag, pulled out a jar of healing salve, scooped out the contents, and packed the thick ointment into the deep gash in his friend's side.

Anatoly grunted in pain but didn't protest or even try to move. Lucky's face went white. Anatoly was one of his oldest friends, and he knew him well enough to know that he would never accept healing without some complaint. Yet he just lay still, trying to conserve his energy.

Jataan took a position in front of Alexander and faced the soldiers arrayed before him. He looked over at Lucky. "The wound is not immediately fatal. With attention he will recover."

Lucky gave him a confused look before returning to his task.

Jack walked up to Jataan P'Tal with his hands out and open. "I'm Jack Colton, Master Bard of Ruatha—and I'm confused. For months you've hunted us, yet now, in your moment of triumph, you halt your attack. Why?"

Jataan smiled with a mixture of relief and purpose. "I am Reishi Protectorate. My highest duty is to protect the Reishi Sovereign, then to obey the commands of the Reishi Sovereign, and finally to preserve the Reishi line. The man behind me, whom I have hunted and come to view as a worthy adversary, is in the process of bonding with the Sovereign Stone." Jataan stepped aside and motioned to Alexander. "I give you Lord Reishi, the Seventh Sovereign of the Seven Isles."

In unison, Jack and the Andalian Lancers all said, "What?"

Before Jack could more clearly articulate his question, the Lancers started to advance toward Alexander.

The leader of the Andalians spoke as they moved in their tight formation with shields up and swords out. "The King of Andalia made a deal with Prince Phane," he said. "We came here to kill the pretender and bring Phane the Stone."

Jataan's smile faded and he nodded to the giant. The moment the Lancers started moving, Wyatt signaled for his men to be ready. When they broke into a fast charge toward Jataan, Jack, and Alexander, the giant swung his war hammer into the right flank of the formation. It hit the shield of the first man with such force that it crushed his arm and propelled him into the man behind him. Two Lancers clattered across the floor and came to a halt at the feet of three Rangers who drove their short spears into them before they could regain their feet. On command, Lieutenant Wyatt's archers fired into the now exposed flank of the Lancers and three more fell. Jataan slipped in with frightening speed and sliced the throat of the final man.

When he turned, Jack was standing in front of Alexander, looking at him with a curious expression. The Rangers were still on guard, watching Jataan P'Tal and the giant carefully.

"What about Phane?" Jack asked.

"Prince Phane is Reishi, but he is not the Reishi Sovereign," Jataan said. "The one bonded to the Stone is the Reishi Sovereign."

"So just like that, you serve the man you've been trying to kill," Jack stated with incredulity.

"My loyalty is and has always been to the Reishi," Jataan said. "It would seem that the Old Rebel Wizard outsmarted us all. Had the Protectorate known of a living heir to the Sovereign Stone, we would have reconstituted the Reishi line millennia ago."

"That's the thing," Jack said, still standing between Jataan and Alexander. "Alexander is Ruathan, not Reishi."

"The Sovereign Stone says otherwise," Jataan said.

A wyvern flew past the window of the tower room and roared. A Ranger posted at one of the other tower windows pointed off in the distance. "More wyvern riders are coming."

Jataan quickly assessed the situation and turned to Jack. "We should move one level down. Lord Reishi is too vulnerable here."

Jack frowned and looked to Lucky.

Lucky shrugged. "If he wanted to kill Alexander, he would have."

Jack nodded and said, "Lieutenant Wyatt, have your men secure the level below and carefully carry Anatoly and Alexander downstairs."

Wyatt nodded and directed his men to their tasks. Within minutes, they were one level down in a room with no windows. The only ways in were the staircases leading up and down.

Lucky took the healing potion from Alexander's pouch and started toward Anatoly, when Jataan stepped in front of him.

"What have you taken from Lord Reishi?"

"A healing potion; it's the last one we have and Anatoly needs it."

"It is more important to save it for Lord Reishi," Jataan said.

Jack stepped up, shaking his head. "If you truly do serve Alexander, then you should know he'll kill you himself if you let Anatoly die. It'll be hard enough for him to trust you as it is."

Jataan frowned and reluctantly stepped aside. "I'm not sure this is the right decision, but I will defer to your judgment. You know Lord Reishi better than I."

Lucky went to Anatoly and carefully made him swallow the potion before gently helping him lie down.

"He'll be unconscious until morning," Lucky said. "How long will Alexander be enthralled by the Stone?"

Jataan shrugged. "I don't know. We will wait for as long as it takes."

Lieutenant Wyatt cleared his throat and drew everyone's attention. Jack smiled at the simple technique he'd used himself so many times in the past.

"Commander P'Tal," Wyatt said, "how many men are in the other tower? Are they likely to attack? And do they have any wizards with them?"

"Seven men, six are Andalian Lancers, two with force lances. They are led by Vasili Nero. He is loyal to Elred Rake out of Headwater and is mostly an opportunistic thug. They have no wizards. It is highly likely that they are moving to rejoin forces with me and will attack once they realize that I no longer serve Phane." Jataan spoke like a soldier giving a report. "They will approach from the level below. I would prefer to engage them there."

"I agree," Lieutenant Wyatt said.

He picked out eight of his remaining fourteen men and sent them downstairs to ambush the enemy. Jataan nodded at the giant, and he trailed along behind them.

"My lieutenant, Boaberous Grudge, is a good man in a fight," Jataan said in explanation.

Not ten minutes later, the sounds of battle came from the floor below. It didn't last long before the Rangers and Grudge returned.

"Four Lancers dead, Nero and the other two ran away," Grudge reported to Jataan P'Tal. A Ranger nodded in confirmation to Lieutenant Wyatt.

Chapter 49

It had been several days since Isabel had been brought before the triumvirate of the Reishi Coven. Guards gave her food and water twice a day but otherwise they ignored her. She tried to engage them in conversation but they didn't respond. They averted their eyes when she asked them questions and remained mute when she railed at them or insulted them.

Every day she sent her mind to Slyder and scouted the fortress island looking for any information that might be useful. She stopped by Abigail's cell window at least once a day and tried to have what conversation they could given Slyder's limitations.

She learned that Abigail had killed the two guards who took her to the triumvirate. When she started advancing on the three witches with one of the dead guard's swords, Magda cast a spell and Abigail woke up in her cell with a splitting headache.

Three days after she arrived, Isabel saw at least two dozen wyverns leave the island heading northwest. She knew they were hunting Alexander, but she also knew that they hadn't found him yet or they wouldn't be sending reinforcements. She worried about him and wished again that she could send him a message. It would give him strength to know that she and Abigail were alive.

On the fifth day she was floating high over the fortress island in Slyder's mind when two wyverns returned from the northwest. Not an hour later, four dozen wyvern riders launched from the fortress island and flew off to the northwest in formation. The size of the force both worried her and made her proud. Alexander had probably bested the two dozen they sent before and now they were sending an airborne army against him.

Somewhere in the distance she heard a cell door open, so she drew her mind back from Slyder. There were four guards, two with spears at the ready. The one who entered tossed a set of shackles at her feet.

"Put them on," he commanded.

Isabel slipped her wrists into the iron rings and held them out for the guard to lock. He did so roughly, then dragged her by the chain from her cell. She watched the path they took and knew from the scuff marks on the floor that they were headed back to the chamber where she'd been questioned by the witches. Something had happened. She found herself thinking through every conceivable possibility, worrying about Alexander as she walked.

Abigail was already sitting in one of two chairs facing the triumvirate. Her hands were shackled behind her back and chained to the chair, and there were four men standing behind her with spears in hand.

Magda, Cassandra, and Gabriella were waiting. The guard directed Isabel to the empty seat but didn't chain her to the chair.

She and Abigail shared a look. Abigail's split lip was healing and her black eye had faded to yellow. She smiled.

"It's good to see you," she said.

"You too," Isabel replied.

Magda pointedly cleared her throat and directed her gaze at them. Both Abigail and Isabel lifted their chins and returned her stare.

"We have verified some of what you've told us," Magda said. "I paid a visit to Blackstone Keep and spoke with a Mage named Kelvin Gamaliel and a Ranger named Erik Alaric."

"Did Erik look well?" Isabel interrupted, eager for any news of her family.

Magda frowned, clearly irritated by the distraction. "Yes, he looked well. He claims you are betrothed to the new King of Ruatha, a cattle rancher born Alexander Valentine and marked by Mage Cedric's warning spell as a champion against Phane Reishi. He claimed that Mage Cedric hid the Ruathan bloodline and created the Rangers to protect and serve the House of Ruatha when it returned to claim the throne. He claimed that Alexander Ruatha has recovered the Ruathan Thinblade." She shifted her gaze to Abigail. "Mage Gamaliel also told me that you are Alexander Ruatha's sister by blood. Are these claims true?"

Isabel's mind raced. She was trying to decide if confirming what the witches already knew would put Alexander in greater danger. She still didn't know what their agenda was but she needed more information, so she decided to play along.

"Mostly," Isabel said. "Alexander and I were married since my brother last saw us. Otherwise the information you have is correct."

The three witches shared a look of serious concern. Isabel found herself wishing she could see people's colors the way Alexander could.

Magda looked at Abigail. "Can you explain why Reishi blood flows through your veins?"

Abigail was stunned speechless. She looked to Isabel for help, but she was just as confused. Abigail shook her head angrily.

"I was born Abigail Valentine and have only recently come to understand that my family descends from the House of Ruatha. I am not Reishi! The Reishi murdered my oldest brother. They are my enemy."

"Yet the blood of the Reishi flows within you," Cassandra said.

Abigail fixed Cassandra with a glare. "I'm not Reishi!"

Cassandra looked to the other witches, who both nodded. She took a deep breath as if marshaling her thoughts before she began. "The Reishi Coven was formed by Aliyeh Reishi, wife of Malachi Reishi, the last Reishi Sovereign. When she discovered that her husband had made bargains with the netherworld, she feared for the future of the Seven Isles. She stole the secret of Wizard's Dust and had seven copies made, which she distributed, one to each of the Seven Isles.

"Malachi Reishi became so enraged at the theft that he declared war on all non-Reishi magic. In many ways, Aliyeh Reishi started the Reishi War, although certainly not intentionally.

"Her husband never discovered her treachery and she remained at his side, all the while working to aid the rebels and bring the war to an end. She knew better than anyone the evil in her husband's heart.

"When Malachi Reishi was destroyed, she thought she had preserved the world until she learned that Phane had fled into the future by sealing himself away from the effects of time within his obelisk. He was her only remaining child, and she hated him; he had murdered her other children to ensure that he would be the only choice to succeed his father.

"She created this coven to prevent the Sovereign Stone from falling into Phane's hands. In order to aid us in that task, she imbued the maternal line of the original members of our coven with the ability to recognize those of the Reishi bloodline." Cassandra paused and fixed Abigail with her eyes. "You, and your brother, are Reishi."

Isabel was dumbstruck. She had read the history of the Reishi War and much of what she knew, or thought she knew, matched Cassandra's story. The part that made absolutely no sense was the idea that Alexander and Abigail were descendants of the Reishi. Her father was the Keeper of the Royal Bloodline; he was charged with protecting the secret of the Ruathan line. Even after Alexander arrived in Glen Morillian, her father never said anything about a connection to the Reishi.

If Isabel was dumbstruck, Abigail was indignant. "You lie!" she said flatly with defiance flashing in her pale blue eyes.

Magda shook her head gravely. "That is why we brought you here. When we saw both a man and a woman with Reishi blood approaching the Reishi Isle, we sent riders to retrieve the woman and kill the man because we assumed he must be Phane. Sky Knights who are not of the maternal line of the Reishi Coven cannot see the bloodline, so they took you both. It's vital that we learn the truth of you and your brother."

"The truth is simple," Abigail said, still angry, "Alexander and I lost our brother to the Reishi and since that day, Phane has been trying to murder us. He's sent beasts from the netherworld, soldiers, assassins, and wizards to try to kill us. Since that day, we've been struggling to survive and fight back. We never asked for any of this."

Magda's expression hardened a bit and Isabel knew they were coming to the heart of the matter. "What is Alexander's purpose on the Reishi Isle?"

Abigail and Isabel looked to each other only briefly before Isabel answered, "I will not betray him."

"Very well then, let me speculate," Magda said. "The Sovereign Stone is trapped in the aether within the Reishi Keep. Your husband entered the Keep this morning and not long after, a force of Andalian Lancers led by General Commander Jataan P'Tal of the Reishi Protectorate entered the Keep in spite of our best efforts to stop them."

Isabel and Abigail looked at each other with both elation at hearing that Alexander was still alive and fear for his safety.

"I suspect he intends to retrieve the Sovereign Stone," Magda continued, "although I'm unsure of his reason. If, as you say, he does not know he is Reishi, then what can he hope to accomplish by bringing the Stone out of the aether? How does he expect to accomplish such a difficult task? Does he not understand the danger to the world if Phane gets the Stone?"

Isabel's mind raced. Magda had guessed so much. If she was truly trying to keep the Sovereign Stone from Phane, then they had the same purpose. It was even possible that they might form an alliance. The Reishi Coven would be formidable allies against Phane.

But if they were actually agents of Phane, then they may be trying to determine if Alexander could actually retrieve the Stone so they could decide whether to let him proceed in hopes of stealing it from him the moment he succeeded. She decided that the truth was the best course. If they were truly on the same side, they might help Alexander, and if they were working with Phane, it would buy Alexander time if they believed that he could retrieve the Stone from the aether.

She looked to Abigail before she answered. Abigail nodded, clearly thinking along the same lines.

"Alexander is trying to prevent Phane from getting the Sovereign Stone," Isabel said. "Phane already made it to the Reishi Keep once in spite of your best efforts to stop him. He tried to use the powersink to get the Stone, but it didn't work, so he went to the Temple of Fire to use the powersink there, but the dragons chased him off.

"He won't stop until he gets the Stone and we can't allow that to happen. Alexander plans to secure it in the Bloodvault at Blackstone Keep where Mage Cedric left the Thinblade for him. The Bloodvault will only allow Alexander to enter and it can't be breached, even by magic as powerful as Phane's. The Stone will be safer there than anywhere. As for how . . . Alexander has bonded with a fairy named Chloe, and she will retrieve it from the aether for him."

The three witches were leaning forward with great interest. When she told them about Chloe, they all sat back with a gasp. Isabel hoped she hadn't revealed too much.

"That's not possible," Gabriella said, shaking her head. "The fairies have forsaken the outside world."

Isabel smiled fondly at the memory. "Alexander and I were married in the Valley of the Fairy Queen. Ilona herself bore witness to our vows."

Abigail nodded, smiling softly at the memory.

Magda composed herself with a visible effort. "Assuming what you say is true, you risk far too much. The Stone is safe where it is. Phane has already failed twice. He doesn't have the power to retrieve it or he wouldn't have needed a powersink."

Isabel's face went deadly serious as she slowly shook her head. "You're wrong. The shades are loose. As soon as Phane discovers this, he'll bind one of them to his service and he will have the Stone."

All three witches stared in shock, fear, and disbelief. "How can this be?" Cassandra whispered.

Isabel looked down for a moment. She still felt a stab of guilt for her part in the shades escaping from the netherworld. "Alexander accidentally freed them," she said when she looked back up at the three witches. "I was lost in the netherworld and he came in and saved me. The shades were waiting. They escaped when Alexander brought me back into the world of time and substance. I can tell you their names if you like."

"No!" all three said in unison. Isabel smiled slightly. She had their attention. Before they could regain their composure, she pressed on.

"We're fighting for the same thing. We both have more than enough enemies. Help us . . . please. Alexander can put the Stone beyond Phane's reach once and for all. Call off your wyvern riders and stop trying to kill my husband."

The three witches were impassive, although Isabel thought she saw a flicker of emotion in Magda's eyes, but she couldn't tell what it might represent.

"We must discuss what we've learned before we make any decisions," Magda said. The other two nodded agreement. "If you will promise not to kill any more of my people, I will provide you with more comfortable quarters."

Isabel and Abigail looked at each other and nodded slightly. "We will not harm any of your people for now," Isabel said, "but understand, I will die from poison in three weeks' time. If that happens, any chance we might have to form an alliance against Phane will die with me."

Magda smiled warmly. "Mage Gamaliel gave me something to help with that. He said it will draw the poison from your body. We are examining the item and will administer the remedy once we're confident that it will work."

Hope flooded into Isabel. She could see the relief in Abigail's eyes as well. When the guards removed the shackles, the sisters hugged each other and followed their guards to a much nicer suite of rooms with comfortable furniture, ample space, a bathtub, and a high balcony overlooking the ocean. Then they heard the guard bolt the door and the feeling of being in prison returned, even if it was far more comfortable and they had each other to talk to.

CHAPTER 50

Phane sat in his Wizard's Den with his feet up on the table and a bowl of nuts cradled in his arm. He was looking through his magical mirror at Jataan P'Tal fighting his way into the tower chamber where the pretender was.

He had to admit that he was impressed how his young adversary had managed to retrieve the Sovereign Stone from the aether when he himself had failed twice. Of course, in all fairness, the pretender did manage to enlist the aid of the fairies.

Phane knew he would never be welcomed into Ilona's valley. In fact, if he were to attempt to enter, the Fairy Queen would probably violate her highest law and send him bodily into the aether just like the shade had sent his father away. No matter. He was on the brink of victory.

Commander P'Tal quickly dispatched two of the pretender's Rangers as he made his way up the staircase and into the room. Phane adjusted the view through his mirror as he popped another nut into his mouth. He was going to enjoy this. P'Tal moved with impressive speed. Phane had never known a battle mage before. The man was formidable, especially in close quarters.

He watched P'Tal advance on the pretender's axe-wielding protector and chortled gleefully when he saw how easily the big man was bested. Phane dropped his feet to the floor and leaned in for a closer look as Jataan P'Tal slipped around the alchemist and raised his knife for the kill strike. The pretender was on his knees, holding something in his hand.

Phane's mouth fell open when he saw that the item in the pretender's hand was the Sovereign Stone . . . and it was glowing.

"That can't be," he said to the empty room.

Then Jataan P'Tal stopped his strike.

"No! No! No!" Phane spoke each word louder as he stood looking at the mirror in disbelief.

When he saw Commander P'Tal order his men to stand down, he tipped his head back and screamed in rage. He watched helplessly as Jataan P'Tal helped kill the Andalian Lancers, and he felt his rage build into something beyond murderous when he heard the General Commander of the Reishi Protectorate declare that the pretender was the Seventh Sovereign of the Seven Isles.

Phane sat back down heavily and stared at the scene of his greatest triumph as it morphed into defeat, and he felt hot fury well up within him, supplanting what little restraint he possessed. He stood quickly and stomped out of his Wizard's Den into the well-appointed sitting room of his chambers in the modest keep on the southern Isle of Tyr.

He opened the door and barked to the serving girl sitting outside his quarters, "Bring me travel food for a month and a barrel of water."

She didn't hesitate. The rumors of Prince Phane's temper and unseemly appetites were well known. She sprang to her feet, nodded, and ran off down the hall.

Phane slammed the door and paced back and forth in front of his Wizard's Den, muttering curses and oaths of vengeance to himself while he waited. He stopped in midstride.

"Kludge!" he bellowed. His familiar appeared in a cloud of inky black smoke a moment later, beating its wings furiously to hover just below Phane's eye level.

"Yes, Master. How can I serve you?" The little monster wrung its hands as it spoke with subservience and a hint of fear.

"Go to Karth and tell General Rada that the Gates are open. Tell him to invade Ruatha with all of his forces and to crush everything and everyone without mercy. Then go to Andalia and tell the Andalian King to prepare to move his Lancers through the Gate as soon as the army on Karth has moved through. Go now!" Phane barked the orders at his familiar, which only made it nod and wring its hands with even more subservience.

Kludge swirled into an inky cloud of darkness and vanished with a loud clap. Phane resumed his pacing until he heard a timid knock at the door.

"Enter!" he barked. The door opened and three young women filed in with two large bags of food and a barrel of water on a cart. None of them would meet his eyes. He regarded them for a moment and an idea started to form. He actually smiled, but without any humor at all.

"Put it in there," he commanded, pointing to his Wizard's Den.

The three young women stared in surprise when they saw the magical room. Everyone knew magic existed, but most people never saw any real magic, let alone something as wondrous as a Wizard's Den. They loaded the food and water into the little room while Phane watched. When they stepped out of the Wizard's Den, he waved his hand and the door vanished.

"Come with me," he commanded as he went to his summoning chamber. The three young women followed, sharing nervous looks with each other. He held the door for them and then closed it loudly behind them. Then he threw the bar and cast a simple binding spell to hold it shut.

The three serving girls looked around at the bare circular room with a mixture of wonder and fear. Phane started chanting and their wonder dissipated as their fear grew. Everyone had heard the whispered stories of Dora, Phane's first serving girl.

The air within the circle started to darken. Then it turned inky black and swirled into a great vortex that filled the magic circle to the ceiling. When the hateful yellow eyes started peering out of the darkness, one of the serving girls screamed.

Phane turned to them with murder in his eyes, roughly snatched the first girl's arm and tossed her into the blackness. The other two screamed hysterically, backing toward the door as their friend was torn apart. He reached out with his magic and grabbed them both. With a flick of his mind, he tossed them into the circle with the nine nether wolves he had summoned.

He turned to the swirling darkness and listened to the dying screams of the three women he'd just sacrificed to bind the beasts of the netherworld to his will.

"Go forth and kill everyone on this island except for me."

The nether wolves howled with lust and fury. Phane waved at the door;

the bolt slid open and the door swung wide. He stepped across the edge of the magical circle, breaking the hold on the nether wolves. The nine beasts crossed the threshold and bounded through the door, eager to begin their slaughter.

Phane whistled to himself as he walked through the halls of the keep, listening to the screams of panic and death that tore through the night. He entered the stables and found the stable master hiding under a staircase, trembling in fear.

"Prince Phane, what's happened? It sounds like the netherworld itself has come to destroy us all."

Phane smiled at the man. "It has," he said before strolling to his horse.

The animals were terrified from the sounds of death and fear, but Phane placed a hand on his horse's neck and spoke a few words. The animal settled immediately. He saddled his steed and rode out of the keep. People were running in every direction, some moving to engage the threat, others fleeing the sounds of death and dying.

Phane fixed his rage on his target. He would skin Jataan P'Tal alive and boil him in salt water. He'd killed people that way before. The Reishi Prince remembered how satisfying it was.

When he got to the top of the hill half a mile away, he dismounted and tied his horse to a fence post. He faced the keep, extended his hands and started casting a spell. A bubble formed between his outstretched hands and filled with the swirling orange-red glow of liquid fire. It started out two feet in diameter but he fed more power into it, and the surface of the bubble undulated and rippled as it grew. Still he fed it and it grew even more. When he released the bubble, it was twelve feet across. It streaked toward the nearest tower of the keep, glowing bright and angry, and burst explosively, sending a shower of liquid fire down on the people, buildings, and streets below. Within moments the entire place was ablaze. Sounds of panic, terror, and the howling of nether wolves filled the night.

Phane nodded in satisfaction at the carnage and destruction he'd inflicted on the Reishi Protectorate. He knew they would serve the bearer of the Sovereign Stone. With the pretender bonded to the Stone, everyone on this island was now his enemy. Phane mounted his horse and rode toward the Reishi Gate, whistling to himself.

CHAPTER 51

Lord Zuhl, King of the Isle of Zuhl, the northernmost of the Seven Isles, stood atop the stone tower he had built so many centuries ago. He remembered stacking one stone on top of another until the modest little twelve-foot-tall structure was complete. He built it as a monument to his goal, as a symbol of his life's work. He had come here often during the past seven hundred years to remind himself to be patiently persistent.

Kaja Zuhl smiled to himself. His long effort and consistent devotion to his singular purpose was bearing fruit.

When he inherited the House of Zuhl, it was little more than a minor territory on the southern coast of the island, but it was a proud house with a long and storied history. His family had ruled the Isle of Zuhl for two millennia, presiding over an age of peace and prosperity that had never been seen before or since. They had been loyal to the Reishi and to the Old Law—their loyalty had been repaid by betrayal, treachery, and murder.

When the secret of Wizard's Dust was stolen from the Reishi, a number of secret Wizards Guilds formed as a result. One of those guilds was located on the Isle of Zuhl.

The wizards it produced were sworn to the Old Law and did good works for the people. Then the Reishi declared open war on any non-Reishi magic. The House of Zuhl helped the wizards go into hiding and protected them against the penalty of death that had been decreed by the Reishi Sovereign. When Malachi Reishi discovered that they were harboring those he thought of as enemies, he declared war on the House of Zuhl.

At the beginning of the Reishi War, all seven of the Island Kings owned a Thinblade—each given to their line by the First Reishi Sovereign as a gift for their loyalty and as a badge of office, a symbol of the Reishi Sovereign's support of their right to rule.

What none of the Island Kings knew was that the Thinblades could be used against them.

The Swords of Kings were tied to the power of the Sovereign Stone, and the holder of the Stone could release the ancient magic that bound a Thinblade. The result was a catastrophic explosion of magical energy capable of killing anyone nearby.

When Malachi Reishi discovered that Zuhl was protecting non-Reishi wizards, he detonated the Zuhl Thinblade and killed most of the Zuhl bloodline in one moment of indiscriminate murder. Only a few survived, but the Reishi Sovereign wasn't satisfied with that. He wanted to eradicate the entire line of Zuhl for all time.

With beasts conjured from the dark realms of the netherworld, Malachi Reishi savagely attacked what remained of the House of Zuhl. He sent his inhuman minions to wantonly slaughter the people of the island, people who looked to the House of Zuhl to protect them. Seeing the indisputable evil of

Malachi Reishi's tactics, those of the line of Zuhl who survived the destruction of the Thinblade sided with the rebellion against the Reishi.

The Reishi War ravaged the Isle of Zuhl, leaving it broken and desolate for centuries. The scattered tribes who survived eked out a living hunting dangerous beasts that roamed the frozen wilds of the north and fishing the frigid waters in the south. It was a thousand years before the population of the island had recovered to the point where building cities even made sense. During those dark years, hundreds of petty nobles, more accurately described as warlords, staked out their territories and fought viciously to protect the scraps of mostly frozen and barren land they claimed.

The House of Zuhl had reestablished itself in the rich southern tip of the island when Kaja Zuhl inherited it just over seven hundred years ago. The relatively tiny territory was rich in gold, iron, and coal, and had a fishery that was teeming with all manner of sea life. Zuhl spent the first years of his life studying magic and history. The more he learned about the injustices done to his House, the more his hatred for the Reishi grew.

He thought back to the day he had learned about Prince Phane, the day the first seed of his plan was sowed. He remembered the journey to the Isle of Tyr. He posed as a possible recruit for the Reishi Protectorate, even though he secretly wanted to lash out at them. He remembered standing in front of the obelisk that contained the last heir to the Sovereign Stone. He could still hear the Commander of the Reishi Protectorate telling him that one day the Reishi Prince would emerge and claim the Sovereign Stone and with it reunite the Seven Isles under the House of Reishi.

Zuhl had other plans.

When he discovered that the Reishi Gates were tied to the magic of the Sovereign Stone, another piece of the puzzle snapped into place. The Isle of Zuhl had very little natural timber resources so he had no way of building ships to move his soldiers around the Seven Isles. If he was to establish his empire, he would need a navy. He knew just where to look for the timber, but he could never hope to get enough soldiers there by conventional means. The Reishi Gates were the only way and they wouldn't function until the Sovereign Stone was back in the world.

He returned to his home and studied magic. He knew what he wanted to accomplish, but he needed several more pieces of the puzzle before he would be able to pull it off. He turned to necromancy, both out of necessity and out of a sense of poetic justice. He would use the power discovered and wielded by the last Reishi Sovereign to end the Reishi line once and for all, while at the same time laying the groundwork for the rise of the House of Zuhl.

When he discovered how to use the dark forces of the netherworld to draw the life from another and use that vital energy to stop and even reverse the physical aging process, he knew his goal was within reach. For the past seven hundred years, on the eve of the winter solstice, he had sacrificed a virgin girl who was mature enough to become pregnant.

That was his favorite time of year. He shuddered every time he thought about the exquisite feeling of drawing the life energy from a vibrant young woman and using her vital force to infuse his body with longevity and youth. Even though he was over seven hundred years old, he looked like he was a man of twenty-seven.

Zuhl stood just over six feet tall and had pale white skin and ice-blue eyes. His hair was shock white, cropped close and squared off on top. His features were angular and his face had a drawn, almost gaunt look to it. He was thin and almost frail-looking, but that appearance belied a strength of will and a talent with dark magic that more than compensated for any physical shortcomings he may have had, perceived or otherwise.

He had a shrewd intellect and a practical, pragmatic way of approaching problems, always flexible about the means to his ends but totally driven to achieve those ends, no matter the cost.

He viewed other people as objects, tools to be used in the pursuit of his goals. Over the centuries, he had established himself as the most powerful and prominent of the warlords, but he had never moved to consolidate his power over the entire Isle of Zuhl. That would have been counterproductive.

Over the many years, enemies came and went, many of them dying of old age. Zuhl patiently waited. Century after century, he delivered a message to the people of the Isle of Zuhl. He used every means of telling the story that he could conceive of—from storytellers to the written word to songs.

The message was always the same. All of the suffering, poverty, hardship, and despair felt by the people of Zuhl was the result of the treachery and evil of the Reishi, and one day the Reishi would rise again to murder their children.

The natural harshness of the frigid Isle of Zuhl played to his advantage. It was an inhospitable place that made for hardy and tough people. Their lives were difficult by the simple nature of their environment. But that wasn't enough for Zuhl to realize his lifelong dream. For that he needed an army. Being a student of history, he knew that a standing army in a secure nation would become soft and complacent. When it came time to wage war, they would be unwilling and ineffective.

Zuhl wanted an army of hardened soldiers who had spent a lifetime fighting and killing. For centuries, while constantly projecting the message that the people's problems and suffering were the fault of the Reishi, he stirred up trouble between the warlords. He kept them at each other's throats. He made sure there were always border disputes and wars that flared and faltered, always planting the seeds of the next conflict. Through treachery and deceit, he ensured that the culture of the Isle of Zuhl revolved around war, killing, and death.

By the time the warning spell alerted the people of the Seven Isles that Phane had awakened, every able-bodied man on the entire Isle of Zuhl was a hardened killer, steeped in a culture of violence and warfare. And every single one of them had grown up from the cradle hearing the story that the Reishi were the ancient enemy who had blasted their home into a barren wasteland and that one day the Reishi would rise to do it again.

As predictable as sheep, the warlords who had been fighting and killing their neighbors for centuries all turned to Lord Zuhl and begged him to lead them against the Reishi. He was the natural choice. His family had led the struggle in the Reishi War and he was the most feared and powerful wizard on the entire island. Like a flood, they poured forth to kneel at his feet and swear loyalty to him, if only he would lead them against the ancient enemy who had risen to subjugate them once again. Even though he had planned for this very reaction, he found it almost disappointing that people could be so easily manipulated.

Lord Zuhl stood atop the tower that was his own personal monument to his hatred for the Reishi and smiled. He was dressed in a rich, flowing, white robe made from the pelts of baby snow seals. His robes were enchanted and glowed so brightly that looking directly at him was nearly impossible. He stood like a beacon in an ocean of soldiers all marching through the Reishi Gate. It was open before him and led to a green grassy field in the heart of the Isle of Fellenden. Like a lake behind a broken dam, his soldiers flooded into the heart of Zuhl's first objective.

Fellenden had a warmer and more productive climate with rich farmland and vast rangeland. Most importantly, Fellenden was the home of the Iron Oak forests. Trees of such hardness it was said that an Iron Oak shield was as good as one made of steel. It was another piece of the puzzle. He would use the Iron Oak to make a navy of such power and reach that Zuhl would rule the entire Seven Isles by dominating the seas that separated them. Phane would control the Gates, but Zuhl would control the oceans. He would be able to land troops where he needed without resistance.

He knew Phane would fight, and he relished the challenge. If the old stories were to be believed, the Reishi Prince was a formidable enemy, but Zuhl was patient. He had planned for this day for seven centuries. He had contingencies and capabilities that Phane could scarcely imagine. Even if Phane managed to survive the war that Zuhl intended to wage against him, he was at a distinct disadvantage.

Lord Zuhl literally had all the time in the world.

Chapter 52

Alexander wasn't sure what was happening or even where he was. The place had a surreal quality to it. He wasn't inside a building and he wasn't outside under the stars. The floor was smooth and black but not made of stone. The round table was solidly made with high-backed, comfortable chairs all around. A soft white light emanated from above, although he couldn't determine its source.

Malachi Reishi sat at the table with five other men. He stared at Alexander for a long moment before another of the men seated around the table stood and held out his hand toward the empty chair.

"Where am I?" Alexander asked, without moving. He was paying careful attention to his all around sight, but there was nothing behind him except darkness.

The man who offered him the empty chair remained standing.

"That's a little complicated," he said. "Your body is where you were when you first touched the Sovereign Stone. Your mind, on the other hand, is inside the Stone in the Reishi Council Chamber. Please sit. We'll answer all of your questions. My name is Balthazar Reishi. I was the First Reishi Sovereign."

Alexander blinked in surprise. The last thing he remembered was picking up the Sovereign Stone and now he was standing in a magical space looking at the previous six Reishi Sovereigns. It made no sense.

The Sovereign Stone was tied to the Reishi line.

"Before we begin, I must ask, is your body in a safe place? Are you in potential danger?"

Alexander was suddenly alarmed. He was surrounded by enemies on all sides and had no idea if his friends would be able to defend him. Then the bigger question slammed back into his mind.

How could he be inside the Sovereign Stone?

Malachi Reishi started laughing at Alexander's sudden look of fear. "I'm sure Phane lured you into retrieving the Stone for him, and any moment now, you'll become a permanent addition to our little council here. Then he will pay us all a visit."

"Silence, Malachi," said another of the men at the table before he turned his attention to Alexander. "I am Demetrius Reishi, the Fifth Sovereign. Malachi is my disappointment of a son. You may command him, or any of us for that matter, and we will be compelled to obey."

The magnitude of the situation began to sink in. His knees went a little weak and he took hold of the back of his chair to steady himself.

It made no sense.

The Sovereign Stone was only supposed to bond with those of Reishi blood. He was Ruathan, yet here he was standing in the Reishi Council Chamber with the men who had ruled the world during the rise and fall of the Reishi Empire.

Alexander looked over at Malachi and fixed him with a glare. "Do not speak unless I command you to do so." Malachi glared back but said nothing.

Alexander sat down at the table and surveyed the men arrayed before him.

Balthazar sat down as well. "Welcome to the Reishi Council. May I ask your name?" he said.

"I am Alexander Ruatha. How can this be? How can I be here?"

Balthazar sat back in his chair with an expression of surprise that quickly turned into understanding. He nodded and sat forward.

"One of the things I kept secret from the world was the origin of the Reishi family line. I was, in fact, born Balthazar Ruatha. My elder brother inherited our family estate, and I left to study in seclusion. It was there, in my secret laboratory, that I discovered the secret of Wizard's Dust. The truth is, the Reishi line and the Ruathan line are one in the same. When I created the Sovereign Stone, I bound it to my line. I never suspected that doing so would also bind it to my brother's line, although now that I think about it, it makes perfect sense."

Demetrius sat forward with a serious expression. "When last Malachi consulted with us, he was waging war on the Seven Isles. Time doesn't exist for us here so that was only yesterday. May I ask what has transpired and how you came to be in possession of the Sovereign Stone?"

Alexander realized that these giants of history who had ruled the world knew nothing of the current state of affairs. He wanted to explain in detail but he had more pressing concerns.

"I'll answer all of your questions, but first, how do I get out of here?"

"Simply walk away from the table, but you will not be able to do so for several hours," Balthazar said. "The bonding process takes some time and cannot be stopped once it has begun, hence my concern for the safety of your body."

Alexander closed his eyes. He might have just made a fatal mistake. Jataan P'Tal was close and Alexander wasn't sure if the Rangers and Anatoly could stop him if he attacked.

"The General Commander of the Reishi Protectorate is near and he's been trying to kill me for several months now by order of Phane Reishi," Alexander said.

"That shouldn't be a problem," Demetrius said. "The Reishi Protectorate exists to protect the bearer of the Sovereign Stone before all other things. Perhaps if you explained the state of the world, we would be better able to help you."

Alexander took a deep breath. As long as he was here, he figured he might as well tell them what he knew. They might have insight or understanding that could help him. He leaned forward and began his story.

He left nothing out. He told of how the Reishi Empire had fallen and how Phane had locked himself away in a magical obelisk to escape Mage Cedric and awaken in the future. He explained the preparations made by the Rebel Mage and how he had been marked as the one to stand against Phane. He told them everything he'd been through over the past several months, starting with the day his brother had been killed, how he had been visited by ghosts, how he had been hunted by creatures from the netherworld, and how he had found the Thinblade.

He told them everything he knew about the state of the other islands and that Phane had already taken command of Karth and Andalia. He told them about Chloe and his bonding and even told them that his wife and sister had been abducted. He spared no detail and dredged his mind for any scrap of information that might be of use. His story ended with him standing in a tower in the Reishi

Keep holding the Sovereign Stone with danger all around him.

He had no idea how they would react. For all he knew, they would side with Phane and try to destroy him or trap him within the Stone or any number of other possibilities.

The men around the table traded looks. They all deferred to Balthazar—all except Malachi who looked mad enough to spit but kept his mouth shut as ordered.

"It would seem that much has transpired since the last time we were convened," Balthazar said. "Allow me to be the first to apologize for the crimes committed against you by my distant progeny and in the Reishi name. I built the Reishi Empire because I saw how uncivilized humanity was and I wanted to change that. When I discovered the secret of Wizard's Dust, I knew it had the power to change the world and I wanted to ensure that it changed it for the better. That's why I drafted the Old Law and formally committed the House of Reishi as its protector and champion.

"My plan for the world worked for a time, until Malachi succumbed to his own self-importance and strayed from the path that I had laid out. He turned everything that we'd built to the purpose of tyranny. As is always the case, tyranny cannot be sustained. Unfortunately, it's the people of the world who are the ultimate victims of the limitless ambition of a tyrant."

Balthazar looked down at the table sadly. He took a deep breath and fixed Alexander with his glittering golden eyes and held him with a look of such intense passion and need that Alexander felt frozen in time. "May I ask your intention now that you are bound to the Stone?"

Alexander blinked. He hadn't thought that far ahead. Everything was happening so quickly and he'd only just begun to accept his new reality—but when he faced the question, the answer seemed so clear.

Balthazar was right.

There was terrible suffering in the world and the biggest source of that suffering was government, or more accurately, those who sought power over others. It seemed that petty thugs were the ones who gravitated to the seat of power like flies to dung.

Those who couldn't be trusted with anything were the ones who craved power over everything. He reviewed the leaders he'd met in the last few months. The only ones he had any faith in either didn't want the power they had or viewed their power as a means to protect people. In both cases, they were committed to the Old Law and genuinely believed in government by principle rather than government by ambition.

All the rest were petty, self-serving, narcissistic liars who wanted power for the sake of lording it over others.

Alexander thought about all the horrors that government had invented. War, tyranny, slavery, genocide, and the soft slavery of taxation were all creations of government, and they were all committed at the urging of self-important political figures who had something to gain by inflicting harm on others. For two thousand years, the Reishi had imposed limits on the power of the governments of the Seven Isles by demanding that they govern according to the Old Law. The more he thought about it, the more certain he became of his answer.

"I intend to conquer the world and bring it back under the just governance of the Old Law."

Balthazar sat back with a broad smile. "Outstanding. The willingness to risk yourself to protect the Old Law is the most important quality a Reishi Sovereign can possess. The Sovereign Stone confers upon its possessor a number of important powers. Unfortunately, the first, and perhaps most important, will be of little use to you.

"More than anything else, politics is about information. Knowing who owes whom, who is allied with whom, and where the bodies are buried is powerful. The Sovereign Stone gives each successive Sovereign access to the storehouse of knowledge contained within the minds and memories of all of the previous Sovereigns. Since the Stone has not been bonded to anyone for so long, I'm afraid that our political knowledge is well out-of-date.

"The second is the magical knowledge we possess. We can mentor you in your calling and assist you to overcome the challenges that all wizards encounter from time to time."

Alexander sat forward with sudden interest. "I don't know my calling. The Guild Mage is stumped as well."

"That's unusual," Demetrius interjected. "Occasionally, a wizard will have a rare calling but most often it has been seen before. You said you've only recently undergone the mana fast, which poses another important question. The Sovereign Stone will only bond with one who has undergone the mage's fast because it requires an unrestrained link to the firmament. Perhaps if you describe your experience with the firmament, it will shed some light on your calling, as well as the apparent contradiction your bond with the Stone seems to create."

Alexander started with his second sight and then described in detail all of his magical experiences one by one. He left nothing out, from the precognition that had only happened three times in his life to his two brief forays into the netherworld. He told them how the firmament felt and sounded, how he projected his awareness to the other side of the world, and what it felt like when it was scattered into the firmament by Phane, the fortress island, and the Reishi Keep. He described the process he used to reach the firmament and how his other talents didn't require him to connect to the firmament at all. They sat and listened patiently while he scrupulously recounted his entire life history of magic.

All of the men at the table looked from one to the other. By silent consensus, they settled on the man two seats to the right of Balthazar.

He leaned forward and fixed Alexander with his golden eyes.

"I am Constantine, the Third Reishi Sovereign. You are the rarest of all types of wizard. You are an adept."

Balthazar nodded, deep in thought. "It makes sense. No other calling would have the necessary magic to form the bond without first undergoing the mage's fast."

Alexander was excited. Finally someone knew something about his magic. "What's an adept?"

"An adept is a wizard who can't cast spells in the conventional sense," Constantine said. "Instead, an adept develops abilities that naturally draw on the power of the firmament. The more you use your magic, the more your natural abilities will manifest and develop. As for what those abilities will be, it is difficult to say.

"One thing is certain: The power of an adept, within the confines of his abilities, is greater than even that of the most accomplished arch mage. For example, you said you've used your clairvoyance to see and hear places on other islands thousand of miles away. I was an arch mage of considerable power and I knew how to cast a clairvoyance spell, but I could only look at a place within a hundred miles, and at that distance, I could only maintain the spell for a short time."

"I had a bad experience with my clairvoyance the other day," Alexander said. "When I tried to return, there was a dark spirit from the aether that had taken possession of my body and killed two of my men. Is there any way to protect myself when I'm using my clairvoyance so that never happens again?"

Constantine nodded. "That's always one of the dangers when projecting your consciousness away from your body. There are opportunistic spirits that will take advantage of your vulnerable position. The solution is to draw a magic circle around yourself when you project your mind. Any wizard can draw a circle that will protect them, provided they place the symbols correctly."

"Will you show me?"

Constantine smiled and waved his hand. On the table in front of him appeared a magic circle drawn in light. It was actually two circles, one within the other. Between the two circles were seven symbols. Each was arcane and complex.

Alexander studied the image closely and committed it to memory as best he could. He closed his eyes and saw the circle in his mind's eye, then checked the image again to be sure he had it right. If nothing else, he could always come back or even ask Lucky; he would probably be able to help him.

Alexander nodded and the image faded away.

"Practice sending your mind into the firmament every day," Constantine said. "Focus on a place and concentrate your awareness there. Look at the place for a moment and slip back into the firmament, then move on to another place. By exercising your abilities, you will expand them." He paused and thought for a moment.

"My brother was an adept, one of only two known to exist during the entire reign of the Reishi Empire. He studied his calling quite extensively and wrote a great deal about what he learned. His keep was in the high mountains on the southernmost island of Ithilian. I don't know if it's still there, but if it is, you may find much better information there than we have to offer."

Alexander nodded thoughtfully. He had many more questions but decided there would be plenty of time later. He nodded for Balthazar to continue.

"Next, you are the master of the Thinblades. You can cause any of them to be destroyed at will in a violent explosion of magical energy. I would caution you not to use this power lightly. The Thinblades are precious beyond measure, not only as weapons but as a means of establishing your authority over the Island Kings. As the Reishi Sovereign, the Thinblades cannot harm you."

"I'm not certain, but I think there are only two left, Ruatha's and Ithilian's."

Balthazar turned to Malachi. "How many Thinblades did you destroy?"

Malachi sat defiantly.

Alexander snapped, "Answer him."

"Four."

"Which ones?"

"Zuhl, Fellenden, Karth, and Andalia," Malachi said.

Alexander turned to Balthazar and nodded for him to continue.

"What a loss," Balthazar said, shaking his head sadly. "The Thinblades are priceless beyond measure. At any rate, there is more to the Stone that you must be aware of. After some time, it will allow you to access its Wizard's Den. This is a place beyond the world of time and substance, a sort of pocket world where only one room exists. It's an ideal place to store things of value, and it provides a place to sleep in complete safety if you happen to be traveling. No one can access it except you."

Alexander whistled. His mind was spinning with all the possibilities such a place had to offer. No more guard duty. Faster travel because they wouldn't have to carry their packs. The idea of having such a place at his disposal was beyond his wildest imaginings. He remembered Mage Cedric's Wizard's Den in the top room of the highest tower in Blackstone Keep and idly wondered at the contents that he had yet to fully investigate.

Balthazar continued and brought him back to the present. "You are the master of the Reishi Keep as well. There are many magical defenses and capabilities built into the walls and halls of the Keep and a number of secret areas that can only be accessed by the Sovereign."

"Mage Cedric left me the Keep Master's ring of Blackstone Keep. With it I can see anywhere within the Keep in my mind's eye."

"You have that ability with the Reishi Keep as well, in addition to many others. The final power the Sovereign Stone confers upon you is control of the Reishi Gates. With the Stone back in the world of time and substance, the Gates are once again active," Balthazar said.

"What?" Alexander was suddenly alarmed. He remembered Phane telling him his plans to use the Gates to move his army from Karth to Ruatha. If the Gates were active, soldiers could be pouring into the heart of Ruatha at this very moment.

"How do I shut them down?" Alexander asked urgently.

Balthazar looked a little alarmed at Alexander's sudden concern. "The main Gate is in the Reishi Keep and allows control of all the island Gates. From there you can shut the Gates down entirely so that only you may access them, limit access to holders of the Thinblades, or allow open access to anyone. Otherwise, you must go to each individual Gate to restrict access to it."

Alexander's mind was racing. He feared the worst. Phane would have known this was going to happen. He would have been ready.

Alexander could only hope that his father had taken adequate precautions to defend against invasion through the Gate. He knew from his last clairvoyant visit to Blackstone Keep that there was at least a legion dug in at the Gate. He only hoped that would be enough.

"Phane said he was going to use the Gate to move his army from Karth to Ruatha. I have soldiers at the Gate on Ruatha, but I'm not sure if I have enough."

"Where is your body right now?" Balthazar asked.

"I'm in one of the three tallest towers in the Reishi Keep at the level of the sky deck."

"When you face north on the sky deck, the master Gate is in the tower directly in front of you, five levels up," Balthazar said. "It's guarded by a shield, but it will yield to you."

The light emanating from above momentarily turned blood red, then returned to a soft white glow.

"The bonding is complete," Balthazar said. "Alexander Reishi, you are the Seventh Sovereign of the Seven Isles. Walk out of the circle of light and you will find yourself back in your body. If you wish to return, simply hold the Stone in your bare hand and think of this place and you will be here. Go to the master Gate quickly and restrict access to the Gates to you alone until you can determine if those who hold the other Thinblades are friend or enemy."

Alexander stood quickly. "Thank you," he said as he turned away from the table and walked into the darkness. He had so many more questions but they would have to wait. Right now he had more pressing concerns.

CHAPTER 53

Alexander opened his eyes. He was sitting with his back to a wall. There were Rangers all around the room. Anatoly and Lucky were nearby. Chloe was sitting cross-legged on his knee, looking up at him.

"You were gone again, My Love," she said in his mind. "I was worried."

"I was within the Sovereign Stone. It's bonded to me," he said to her without speaking. She looked at him with surprise and then buzzed up to look him in the eye.

"You do have the eyes of the Reishi, My Love," she said in his mind.

Then he saw Commander P'Tal standing not ten feet away with his back to him. Alexander quickly and quietly slipped the Sovereign Stone around his neck and under his armor before he got to his feet and drew the Thinblade. Chloe buzzed up into the air circling his head in a wide orbit.

"Turn around," Alexander growled to the man who had been hunting him.

Jataan P'Tal turned and stood before Alexander with his hands clasped behind his back. He appraised him for a moment before nodding once deferentially.

"I am General Commander Jataan P'Tal of the Reishi Protectorate and I am at your service, Lord Reishi. This is my lieutenant, Boaberous Grudge."

Alexander was at a loss for words. He stood pointing the Thinblade at his adversary and tried to come to terms with the situation. The Sovereigns told him that the Reishi Protectorate would serve him now that he was bound to the Stone, and Commander P'Tal's colors said he was speaking the truth, but Alexander had learned an abundance of caution, largely due to Jataan P'Tal's unwanted tutelage. Then Jataan went to a knee, and the giant who was his companion bowed as well.

"Stand up," Alexander snapped.

Both men stood without a word.

"You killed my brother," he said with an undercurrent of rage and menace.

"Regrettably, I gave the order to assassinate your brother," Jataan said. "He was a clear threat to my charge and I was bound by duty to eliminate any legitimate threats to the Reishi Sovereign and his line. I have since learned, to my horror and deep sorrow, that your brother was in fact Reishi. You have my sincere apology even though I recognize that my words are hollow and powerless. If you wish to take my life for my crime, I will submit to your will, although I believe such an action would ultimately prove self-destructive."

Alexander surveyed the situation. He saw Lucky sitting with Anatoly and was relieved to see the encouraging nod for the well-being of his old mentor. Rangers were arrayed around the room, and Jack stood off to the side watching the confrontation.

He looked to Jack. "How long have I been out and what's happened?"

"You slumped to your knees when you touched the Stone just over five hours ago. Not long after, Commander P'Tal attacked with a squad of Lancers. He drove through our defenses and bested Anatoly, injuring him severely. He was within striking range but when he saw that the Stone was bonding to you, he abruptly stood down and helped kill the Lancers when they threatened you. We moved you and Anatoly down one level in the tower because this level is more easily defended. A squad of Lancers led by Nero attacked; four were killed and the rest were driven off by a squad of Rangers assisted by Lieutenant Grudge. The wyvern riders have sent a large force of reinforcements, but so far they haven't attacked." Jack sounded almost like Anatoly giving a report.

"What of these two? Do you trust them?" Alexander asked, motioning to Jataan and Boaberous.

Jack shrugged. "From the moment they realized you were bonding to the Sovereign Stone, they've acted to protect and preserve you. After the past several months, I'm skeptical but hopeful. Alexander, how is it that the Stone bonded to you?"

"Apparently the Reishi line is an offshoot of the Ruathan line. I'll tell you the rest later." He turned to Lucky. "How bad is it?"

"He'll mend by morning well enough to travel, although it will be several days before he's fully recovered. I gave him the healing potion from your pouch."

"Good. Lieutenant Wyatt, report," Alexander said to the Ranger commander.

"I have fourteen Rangers, none are injured. We've successfully repelled the Lancer attack from below but didn't pursue the three that fled. I have a scout upstairs who reports that the wyvern riders are swarming around the Keep, but they've made no attempt to enter or attack."

Alexander turned back to Lucky. "Can Anatoly be moved without killing him?"

"Yes, but I'd rather not. Moving him now will delay his healing."

Alexander shook his head. "The Gates are open. Phane's army on Karth is probably pouring into Ruatha as we speak. I have to get to the Gate Room and I don't want to divide our forces. Lieutenant Wyatt, make a stretcher with spears and a blanket. I'm going upstairs to get my bearings."

Alexander started for the staircase. Jataan nodded to Boaberous who went ahead while he followed behind. Alexander stopped and faced Jataan.

"What are you doing?"

"We're protecting you, Lord Reishi."

Alexander studied his colors for a long moment but saw only sincerity. He turned without a word and went upstairs. Boaberous was crouched down next to the door leading out onto the sky deck, peering into the night. A Ranger scout was at the door leading onto the balcony. A wyvern streaked by outside as Alexander and Jataan made their way to the Ranger.

"Report," Alexander said.

"Lord Alexander . . ." the Ranger said but before he could continue, Jataan cut him off.

"He is now Lord Reishi. Please address him as such."

Alexander frowned and the Ranger blustered a bit, "I'm sorry, Lord Reishi, I meant no disrespect," he said with a look of confusion.

Alexander shook his head and put his hand on the man's shoulder. "Titles mean very little to me, so don't worry about it. For what it's worth, I'm just as confused by this turn of events as you are. What are the wyvern riders up to?"

"I count over fifty, now that their reinforcements have arrived. Most are perched on the towers and battlements, but a few continue to circle the Keep. They've made no move to attack, so I suspect they intend to wait for us to leave."

Alexander nodded and started to go out onto the balcony, but Jataan stopped him with a hand on his shoulder. "What do you intend to do, Lord Reishi?"

Alexander's anger flared and he didn't try to hide it. "I need to see the stars, so I can figure out which way north is."

Jataan nodded and slipped out onto the balcony. He looked up to the sky for a moment, then dodged to the side with frightening speed as a javelin dropped from above almost straight down on his position. It missed by only a few inches and buried six inches into the stone floor. Jataan returned to the cover of the room.

"North is that way," he said, pointing as if nothing had happened.

"Where'd that javelin come from?"

"There's a rider on top of this tower."

Alexander nodded. "We have to get to that tower," he said, pointing to the tower where Jataan and his men had been waiting when Alexander arrived the evening before. Boaberous stood and made a move toward the sky deck.

"Stop!" Alexander commanded.

The giant stopped dead in his tracks and looked at Alexander with confusion.

"The sky deck is trapped. If you set foot out there, you'll be cut in three. We need to find another way to get over there."

Boaberous looked at Alexander and then at the sky deck and the carnage of the dead wyvern and nodded slowly.

They returned to the level below and found that the Rangers had secured Anatoly to a makeshift stretcher, and two of their biggest men were ready to carry him. Alexander didn't want to risk any further injury to Anatoly but he knew that every passing moment meant more enemy soldiers on Ruathan soil.

They moved slowly and carefully. There was no telling if the wyvern riders had dismounted and were moving to attack. Boaberous led the way on an unspoken order from Jataan P'Tal. They descended several levels until they came to one with a bridge leading to the tower containing the master Gate. Perched on the bridge was a wyvern with a woman sitting on its back. Boaberous peeked around the corner and stopped those behind him with a hand signal. Alexander slipped up beside the giant and sent his all around sight through the wall to assess the situation.

The woman was watching the doorway intently as if she expected them to try to pass. Alexander decided he wanted to send a message to the wyvern riders. He held the Sovereign Stone inside the doorway for a moment, dangling it by its heavy gold chain so she could see it glowing softly, and then he put it back around his neck and under his armor.

"I am Alexander Reishi, Seventh Sovereign of the Seven Isles," he said loudly. "I command you to stand down and permit us to pass."

There was silence for several long moments before she answered. "You lie, Phane. You are the only male Reishi left in the Seven Isles. You may have recovered the Stone, but you will never make it off this island alive."

Alexander shook his head. He searched for some way to convince the wyvern riders that he was telling the truth but realized it was futile. They were going to believe what they wanted to believe—and they were blocking his path. He thought of the soldiers pouring into his homeland and his resolve hardened.

"We have to get past her. Lieutenant Wyatt, have your men nock arrows and be ready," Alexander commanded. "Once she's off the bridge, we'll have to move fast."

Alexander drew the Thinblade.

Jataan stepped up beside him. "What is your intention, Lord Reishi?"

"I'm going to drive her off the bridge or kill her."

Jataan shook his head. "Such risk is unnecessary. Do you wish her dead or injured?"

Alexander thought about it for a moment. If she was left alive, she could report what he'd said and the fact that he had the Sovereign Stone. That might serve as leverage when he went to get Isabel and Abigail.

"Alive, but out of the way," Alexander said.

Jataan nodded and held out his hand to Boaberous. The giant slipped a javelin out of his oversized quiver and handed it to Jataan without a word. Alexander's new protector stood with his back to the wall just beside the door, then rolled into the open space of the doorway and hurled the javelin with terrifying force, then rolled to the far side of the door behind the cover of the wall. The entire attack took less time than the blink of an eye.

The rider screamed, and the sound of a wyvern beating its wings was accompanied by the swirl of air and dust from the downdraft. Jataan nodded to Boaberous, who darted out onto the bridge and ran with surprising speed to the far side. A javelin from high above missed him as he reached the cover of the far tower.

They moved across in a tight group, scanning the sky. Rangers loosed arrows at anything that moved in an effort to put the wyvern riders on the defensive. Jataan stayed close to Alexander, scanning for danger. A wyvern came in for a tail-strike but veered off sharply when three Rangers sent arrows into its path. The wyverns nearby roared and were answered by others farther away. It was frightening to hear the predawn calm shattered by the fury of so many of the beasts.

They moved up through the tower as quickly as they could and reached the level of the sky deck just as the sky started to lighten. The tower room was similar to the other. It had a wrap-around balcony, several smashed-out windows and two doors, one leading to the sky deck and another leading to the balcony.

"The Gate Room is five levels up. Have you scouted the levels above?" Alexander asked Jataan.

"No, Lord Reishi. Prince Phane said the Sovereign Stone would be on the sky deck, so we waited here."

Out of the corner of his eye, Alexander saw a blast of magical energy like nothing he'd ever seen before; it came from below on the rangeland surrounding the Keep. It tore up through the tower where the demon was held in the magical circle, shattering part of the tower where the sky deck was attached. The entire Keep shuddered from the impact. A terrible cracking noise reverberated through the structure as the sky deck broke free of the other two towers and plummeted to the courtyard below.

Alexander raced to a window. A man mounted on a horse was on the Gate platform. The Gate went from an open portal to a solid wall as the man took aim at an approaching wyvern rider. Another terrible blast of inky black magic shot forth from his extended hand, streaking toward the wyvern as it tried to roll out of the way. The black magic hit like a stream of liquid, splattering on impact. Everywhere it touched, the wyvern simply transformed into a heavy black smoke that sank toward the ground. Within moments, the wyvern and rider were reduced to nothing but a jumble of parts amidst a swirl of dark and unnatural smoke.

"Phane," Jataan P'Tal said.

CHAPTER 54

Alexander felt a thrill of fear. How could he hope to stand against such terrifying power? Phane was clearly beyond him. Before he could pull his mind back from the brink of fear, a Ranger cried out, pointing to the far tower—the one with the demon trapped inside.

The magic circle had been broken. The beast with the mouth and dozens of tentacles pulled itself out through the doorway. The bulbous ends of its tentacles stuck to the stone where they made contact, leaving smoldering indentations.

With one powerful thrust, it propelled itself away from the tower and sailed through the air toward Alexander. It hit the side of the tower far below and started climbing up the stone wall.

Alexander could see Phane riding toward the Keep, fending off the attacks of the wyvern riders with dark magic that sent chills of terror up his spine. All the while, the tentacle demon climbed toward him. The situation had quickly gone from bad to worse.

"To the Gate Room," Alexander said, wheeling toward the staircase.

Boaberous took the lead with his big war hammer at the ready.

The next several levels were surprisingly intact, as if some ancient magic had preserved the contents against the effects of time. The first was a laboratory filled with all of the glassware, tools, and ingredients an alchemist might ever need. Alexander wished they could stop and explore, but there just wasn't time. The next room was a library and study filled with shelves of ancient and arcane volumes. Alexander shook his head in frustration as they moved through the room and up the next staircase. The next two rooms were more libraries filled with ancient tomes, all intact.

Alexander made a note to himself that, given a chance, he would return with some wizards to retrieve the knowledge stored there. They moved up the staircase to the Gate Room. Boaberous tried the door, but it was locked. He hit it with his shoulder, but it didn't budge.

Alexander slipped past the Rangers in the stairwell.

"Stand aside," he said.

When he placed his hand on the door, there was a faint shimmer in the colors of the ancient magical portal and it opened smoothly and silently. The room had no windows and only the staircases leading up and down for exits. On the far wall, opposite the staircases, was a large black slab of stone about thirty feet wide at the base and twenty feet tall at its arched top. Traced along the edge was a double line seven inches apart that marked the outline of the Gate. Between the two lines etched into the smooth black stone were countless ancient symbols, runes, and glyphs. In the center of the room was a pedestal facing the Gate.

Alexander motioned for everyone to enter the room, then closed the door and dropped the bar in place. He saw the shimmer of color across its surface and took that to mean that the room was once again sealed with a magical shield.

He went to the pedestal with Jack at his side and Jataan two steps behind and to his left. It was also made of black stone and stood three feet high. The surface was angled slightly so the edge closest to the Gate was higher than the edge nearest Alexander. Engraved in the surface was a map of the Seven Isles. A rectangle was etched into the stone just above the map. Below the map were two squares of equal size; the left bore the image of a sword and the right was struck through with an X.

The islands of Karth and Ruatha were glowing pale blue, while the islands of Zuhl and Fellenden were glowing pale yellow. Alexander stared at it for a moment, trying to process what he was seeing, then he touched the square with the X and all of the islands abruptly stopped glowing.

With a frown, he touched the outline of the Isle of Ruatha. The surface of the stone slab before him shimmered, and suddenly they were looking into the early dawn on the plains of Ruatha. There was a terrible battle taking place. Countless soldiers were marching away from the Gate as if they were part of a column that had just come through it.

One soldier noticed them and called out. Dozens of soldiers turned and looked back through the Ruathan gate at Alexander. As they started to mount a charge, Alexander touched the bar above the map and the Gate abruptly turned to stone again.

Ruatha was under siege. Alexander only hoped he'd stopped the flow of soldiers in time to give his father a fighting chance against the invaders. He had hoped he would be able to use the Reishi Gate to return home and escape the wyvern riders, Phane, and the tentacle demon, but that was clearly a bad idea with so many enemy soldiers surrounding the Ruathan Gate.

Next he touched the island of Fellenden. The outlines of the Reishi Isle and the island of Fellenden began to glow pale blue, and the Gate shimmered to reveal a different army stretched out on the rolling grasslands of Fellenden. There were thousands of big, hardy-looking men armed with an incredible array of gruesome-looking weapons.

"Zuhl," Jataan said. "Lord Zuhl is a mortal enemy of the Reishi. He blames the Reishi for all of the hardships his people endure. He is every bit as much your enemy as Phane."

One soldier with emblems of rank on his shoulders was standing off to the side of the Gate, watching to see if it would open again. When he saw Alexander, he called out to the other soldiers and charged through the Gate to attack. Before any of the other soldiers could follow him through, Alexander touched the bar above the map and the Gate returned to black stone. In the same moment, Jataan P'Tal threw a knife at the charging soldier. It struck him in the chest just left of center and buried to the crossbar. The man toppled forward and crashed to the ground.

"Darkness comes, My Love," Chloe said silently in his mind.

"It would seem our troubles are multiplying again," Jack observed.

As if to punctuate his remark, there was a thud on the door. Then another. Alexander looked back and saw a little piece of the magically protected door burn through and the tentacle of the demon start to push into the room through the hole. A moment later, a second hole started to form.

Alexander's mind raced. He didn't want to fight that demon. It had dozens of tentacles, each dripping with stone-eating acid, and he knew he could only cut off one or two before the thing would be on him.

He thought of Isabel and Abigail. More than anything, he wanted to go to the fortress island and free them—but he couldn't do that if he was dead. With a deep breath and an act of will, he touched the Isle of Ithilian on the map and the Gate opened again. This time the dawn revealed nothing but a wild grassy plain empty for miles beyond the magical portal.

"Everyone through the Gate, quickly," Alexander said as the tentacle demon reached inside the room through the first hole in the door and began thrashing about wildly in a blind effort to snare its prey. Alexander and Jataan were the last ones through the Gate just before the door gave way. The demon entered the Gate Room with alarming speed.

Once he was through the Gate, Alexander quickly found the map of the Seven Isles etched into the stone of this Gate. The only difference was the addition of an engraving of the glyph of the House of Reishi exactly the same size as the raised glyph on the butt of the Thinblade. He touched the rectangle above the map, and with a shimmer, the open Gate solidified into a slab of black stone. A single section of demon tentacle lay smoldering on the platform.

"Don't touch it," Lucky said to the two Rangers approaching it. "Use your spears to toss it into the grass."

They did as he said. When the points of their spears melted away before their eyes, they tossed them into the grass as well. Then they both looked behind the Gate and gasped.

"Trouble," the first Ranger said.

Alexander went to them and saw an army encamped not a hundred feet behind the Gate. It looked like they had been there for a long time. They had a fortified position surrounded by a berm lined with sharpened wooden stakes. There were wooden towers with catapults lining the edge facing the Gate and a trench filled with oil-soaked straw surrounding the entire thing. It was big enough to house a legion or more.

Alexander scanned the countryside looking for any tactical advantage but saw none. They were in a vast rangeland that stretched out in rolling fields for as far as the eye could see, and a column of cavalry was thundering from the encampment toward them. He looked at the map on the Gate and thought about trying another island but none made any sense. Karth and Zuhl had armies that were moving through the Gates just a few minutes ago. Andalia was probably poised to move through the Gate as well. Ruatha and Fellenden weren't good options. Phane was on the Reishi Isle. That left Tyr.

He turned to Jataan, "Would we be safe on Tyr?"

Jataan thought for a moment before shaking his head. "Phane was on Tyr when you secured the Sovereign Stone. He was no doubt watching and knows the Protectorate will no longer serve him, so I suspect he has set something dark loose on the Reishi Protectorate's island, which is where the Gate is located."

"Let's hope the stories about the House of Ithilian are true," Alexander said, walking out onto the center of the platform and facing away from the Gate. "Form up on me," he commanded. "Disappear, Little One," he thought to Chloe. "I don't want them to know you exist until it's safe."

Chloe buzzed into a ball of light and vanished. The Rangers arrayed themselves on either side of Alexander with Jataan on his left, Jack on his right, and Boaberous at his back. Lucky remained with Anatoly behind the formation. Alexander concealed the Sovereign Stone beneath his armor and covered his sword with his cloak. He thought about Isabel while he watched the company of heavy cavalry approach.

The horsemen rode with skill and discipline. They maintained formation and wheeled into position for a charge but stopped fifty feet short and held. Alexander appraised their colors. They were mostly honorable men. He began to feel a bit more optimistic. He had enemies enough. It would be a welcome change to find a friend.

Two men dismounted and approached on foot with open hands. Alexander watched them come. One was dressed in a breastplate emblazoned with the crest of the House of Ithilian. He was a fair-haired man in his middle twenties with strong facial features, a sturdy build, and grey eyes. The other was older and softer-looking, with long white hair and dark brown eyes. He was a wizard, but Alexander couldn't discern his calling, only that he was a mage. They stopped ten feet from him.

"I am Conner Ithilian, Commander of the Gate Legions of Ithilian and son of King Abel," the younger man said as he appraised Alexander and his companions. "Who are you? What is your purpose here and how is it that you have come through the Reishi Gate?"

Alexander took a moment to look at their colors more closely. The younger man wasn't afraid, but he was nervous. The wizard had clearly cast a few spells prior to their approach and he was looking at Alexander with a mixture of curiosity and apprehension.

"I am Alexander Reishi, Seventh Sovereign of the Seven Isles," he said as he withdrew the Stone from beneath his armor and let it fall against his chest. The blood-red, teardrop ruby glowed gently with the ancient power of the Reishi Sovereigns.

"I've come to offer Ithilian an alliance."

Here Ends Sovereign Stone
Sovereign of the Seven Isles: Book Two

www.SovereignOfTheSevenIsles.com

The Story Continues…

Mindbender
Sovereign of the Seven Isles: Book Three

Made in the USA
Middletown, DE
02 August 2020

14270755R00170